THE ?

Catriona King

ISBN: 978-1539044741

Copyright © 2016 by Catriona King
Photography: Dima Sobko
Artwork: Jonathan Temples:
creative@jonathantemples.co.uk
Editors: Andrew Angel and Maureen Vincent-Northam
Formatting: Rebecca Emin
All rights reserved.

Hamilton-Crean Publishing Ltd. 2016

For my mother.

About the Author

Catriona King is a medical doctor and trained as a police Forensic Medical Examiner in London, where she worked for some years. She has worked with the police on many occasions. She returned to live in Belfast in 2006.

She has written since childhood and has been published in many formats: non-fiction, journalistic and fiction.

'The Tribes' is a new Craig Crime novel, being released in September 2016.

The Craig Crime Series

A Limited Justice
The Grass Tattoo
The Visitor
The Waiting Room
The Broken Shore
The Slowest Cut
The Coercion Key
The Careless Word
The History Suite
The Sixth Estate
The Sect
The Keeper
The Talion Code

Acknowledgements

My thanks to Northern Ireland for providing the inspiration for my books.

My thanks also to: Andrew Angel and Maureen Vincent-Northam as my editors, Jonathan Temples for his cover design and Rebecca Emin for formatting this book.

I would like to thank all of the police officers that I have ever worked with for their professionalism, wit and compassion.

Catriona King
Belfast, September 2016

Discover the author's books at:
www.catrionakingbooks.com

To engage with the author about her books, email:
Catriona_books@yahoo.co.uk

The author can be found on Facebook and Twitter:
@CatrionaKing1

The Tribes

Chapter One

The River Lagan, Belfast. Wednesday 27th January 2016. 2 a.m.

One hand, gripping and slipping off the slime covered path. Scrambling for safety. The other one numb. Frozen. Finger pulps whitening, tips blueing in the cold of the urban waterway. The youth gazed up, drowsy from his struggle; his eyes beseeching, begging for reprieve. He already knew that it was futile; there was no sympathy in his attacker, much less for a man he considered an enemy.

The killer watched his victim coldly, no emotion there but curiosity at how long it would take for him to die. He viewed the process of dying inquisitively, like it was performance art. The long overture of resistance and struggle, then the frantic gaze backwards at the water as he fell, to the real commencement of the show in the winter river; the true beginning of his end.

The boy was fighting the cold now instead of him, grabbing and scrabbling for a hold on the tributary's sleek stone wall; until finally he nodded, defeated, acknowledging that his opponent would stamp on any further attempt at escape.

The watcher saw his victim's eyes droop and then close slowly, flickering until exhaustion stripped his hand from safety for the final time and he sank backwards, limp and exhausted, submerging slowly into the river's murk.

He waited for a while longer, as the ripples grew smaller and the bubbles shrank and moved away, and when his burning cigarette had reached its filter he launched it into the stream, a smouldering symbol of disrespect.

****

Docklands Coordinated Crime Unit, Pilot Street, Belfast. The Murder Squad. Thursday 28th January 2016. 12 p.m.

Marc Craig ripped up the card that he'd been writing and threw it into the bin, the graveyard of its five predecessors. He shook his head in disgust at his inability to write a simple 'missing you' without believing it was enough, and turned his chair to face the river, a howling wind-ripped mass of grey. It suited his mood and the month. January, glaring back at twenty-fifteen and staring disdainfully at the coming year. Aptly named for the two-faced Roman god.

Normally the Lagan cheered him, buoyed him if you were into bad sailing jokes. But today its gloomy aspect just magnified his own, focusing his mind on the very question he'd been trying for weeks to avoid. What happened if Katy never forgave him? What would he do if she *never* took him back? He wouldn't blame her; there weren't many women who could get past one of their partner's murder suspects almost killing them. It wasn't something that could be glossed over with chocolates.

He shook his dark head, unable to cope with a negative answer, and kept shaking until his neck hurt so much that he realised no amount of pain would wipe away his guilt. Because he *was* guilty, wasn't he? If he'd had a normal job like an academic or a doctor, one where his role with psychopaths was limited to theory or therapy instead of hunting them down and locking them up, Ronan Miskimmon would never have targeted Katy to slow him down.

Ronan Miskimmon and Eleanor Corneau, a brother and sister team of computer hackers, had hacked a series of operating systems before Christmas, causing several deaths. Katy had almost been one of them. So right now it was no comfort that someone had to catch the bad guys, or that he was bloody good at it; he'd almost got the woman that he loved killed.

Outside his office Craig's deputy, Liam Cullen, was perching on his P.A.'s desk, and for once Nicky Morris wasn't pushing him off or moaning about him untidying the place. Strangely she was finding Liam's bulky presence comforting today, although her tolerance was suddenly pushed to its limit by a loud crunch and a spray of apple juice across her computer screen. The D.C.I. started speaking with a mouth full of Granny Smith, completely missing the baby-wipe the secretary was rubbing ostentatiously across the glass.

"Of course, there're only two choices."

He paused for a nod or a yes but got neither. Nicky was at the kitchen-roll stage now, drying the wipe's residue with a loud tut.

Liam continued undeterred.

"Which are... morose and grumpy, or sad and driven."

The P.A. glanced up from her cleaning with a puzzled frown. "What are you talking about?"

The detective sighed dramatically. The sound said 'why does no-one ever listen nowadays?' He wouldn't have dared say the actual words.

"The boss. I said he'll either turn morose and grumpy or sad and driven." He turned his apple around to an unbitten portion and was just preparing to sink his teeth in again when Nicky grabbed it and chucked it into the bin. Liam's whine was instant.

"That was mine!"

She was devoid of sympathy. "Then keep it to yourself in future. Half of it ended up on my screen." She softened her theft with an encouraging smile. "Anyway, what do you mean, morose or sad?"

The smile had the desired mollifying effect so Liam obliged with an answer.

"When the boss shot old man Pitt he was hell to live with for months. Morose and grumpy and snarky as hell. He said he felt guilty, although God knows why; if he hadn't shot Pitt *he* would have shot me."

His expression said everyone knew that would have been a very bad thing and that in a choice between an octogenarian serial killer being shot and him there was no contest. Nicky's raised eyebrow said there'd never been a poll. He continued.

13

"OK, so now he feels guilty again, this time about Katy, so my guess is it'll be morose and grumpy on repeat."

The P.A. shook her head immediately. "It won't. He's sad. Barely said a word to me for weeks. Driven...? I'm not sure about that bit."

They got the answer to the driven part a second later, when Craig's office door burst open and he raced past them onto the main office floor.

"Gather round, everyone."

Five everyones peered up from their desks, with expressions that ranged from shocked and wary to curious and pleased. They'd barely seen their boss since Christmas Eve. Craig was in his office by the time they arrived each morning, and was still cloistered in there when they left at the end of the day. Anything he'd wished communicated had been delivered by Liam, his noisier and far less erudite mouthpiece. It had worked well enough because they hadn't had a new case, so part of the 'everyones'' curiosity was why the sudden change now? As far as anyone knew Katy still wasn't seeing him and no-one had been murdered in Belfast for weeks, so why Craig was suddenly re-appearing now was anybody's guess.

They were about to find out. When the group had gathered the sad and driven superintendent scanned the row of faces and then began to speak.

"OK. We have a rare respite from murder and mayhem in Belfast at the moment, so I intend to use the free time to tidy up loose ends."

He turned towards the team's inspector, Annette Eakin, to find her shifting about in her seat, attempting to find the single elusive comfortable position in the hard-backed chair. Even more elusive given that she was six months pregnant and her abdomen was growing at an alarming rate.

"Annette, I want all the court summaries for outstanding cases completed by the end of next week. You're in charge of that."

Before she could argue or sulk he swung round in search of Andy Angel, the most sugar addicted and lethargic, yet skinniest chief inspector on the force. Craig's mind was still on the fact that it was time to find Annette a more comfortable seat and he glanced at Nicky in silent request as he passed.

Craig found his junior D.C.I. slumped so far down in his chair that he was eye level with the top of his desk. He barked "ANDY" so loudly it jolted the D.C.I. upright, making him bang his knee and swear not so quietly beneath his breath.

Andy rubbed his leg hard and nodded in reply, wondering sulkily why Craig always seemed to think that he was deaf. He wasn't deaf; he just thought deep thoughts, mostly about chocolate if the content of his desk drawers meant anything. When Craig was certain he had everybody's attention he continued with his speech.

"Right. I want you to look at any cases going to court in the next three months and check them for outstanding reports from forensics, victim statements, etcetera. Same deadline. End of next week." He turned to find another victim and then changed his mind, turning back to stare pointedly at a heap of folders beside Andy's desk. "Unless you're deliberately building a model of the Eiffel Tower with those files, Andy, get them off the bloody floor!"

As Craig turned again, this time in search of Ash Rahman, the team's temporary analyst until their permanent team member Davy Walsh returned from France the next day, Liam glanced at Nicky meaningfully. The boss was definitely sad; the dullness of his normally lively eyes was as eloquent as if he was weeping openly. But he was obviously driven as well which, preferable as it was to him being morose and grumpy and pissing them all off, meant that he'd be finding extra work for everyone in the coming weeks. Liam fancied that like a hole in the head and was just trying to think of a way out of the jobs inevitably heading his way when they were rescued by the appearance of someone who knew Craig better than anyone but his mum.

Doctor John Winter entered the squad-room

quietly, the same way he did everything. The Director of Pathology was a gentle man as well as a gentleman, and carried himself with the self-effacing modesty of the truly intelligent. He'd known Craig since school and they each possessed tendencies that the other lacked. Where Craig was passionate, physical and with a tendency to be dark, Winter was cerebral, rational and almost too calm. If anyone could stop the detective spiralling into obsession, something that his driven moods had a tendency to become, it was John, so Liam and Nicky exchanged a look of relief as the pathologist took a seat behind their boss and tapped him gently on the back.

Craig spun round as if he was under attack, only for his face to break into the first smile that they'd seen that week.

"John! What are you doing here?"

"I wanted to discuss something with you, if you have time?" He glanced at his watch. "Lunch?"

Craig went to object but Liam jumped in before he could.

"I can finish up here, boss. I know what needs doing."

Craig went to object again but it was half-hearted this time. "Don't forget-"

"The Public Prosecution Reports. I know." He waved Craig out briskly, before he handed someone a vacuum and told them to clear the floor. "Off you go to The James, lads. We'll join you there in half-an-hour."

He was surprised when Craig didn't refuse and even more surprised by the almost meek way he followed the pathologist off the floor. That was when Liam knew things were really serious. They'd seen the boss sad and moody and they'd seen him obsessed, but if Katy didn't reconcile with him he was pretty sure that they didn't want to see what came next.

****

The James Bar. Pilot Street.

The James Bar had been the squad's watering hole for years and with the blindness that came from familiarity Craig never noticed when anything changed. It was no different that day as he slumped in a dark-wood booth with his hands wrapped around a coffee mug, so it was up to John to express surprise at the expensive upgrade wrought on the bar by its new landlord.

"Joe Higginson's really improved this place, hasn't he?"

He waved a thin hand at the shining brass maritime fittings and then at the stained glass panels set randomly around the space. Craig gazed around him dully, taking in the indicated alterations without emotion or surprise. He turned back to his coffee almost immediately, making his friend emit a loud tut. It made the detective raise an eyebrow and John took it as a good sign; it was the most emotion Craig had shown in weeks. He decided to take his life in his hands and mention the 'K' word.

"Natalie saw Katy last night."

Natalie was his wife of eighteen months and a surgeon at the same local hospital where Katy was a physician.

Craig inhaled sharply, the mention of her name like a blow. After a long pause he croaked out a response. "She's back at work? But she's not well enough."

John was tempted to say 'did I say it was at work?' but decided that sarcasm didn't fit the topic, never mind that he'd be taking his life in his hands. Craig might be his best friend but he was quick with his fists at the best of times and especially unpredictable right now. He softened his voice.

"She visited Katy at her mum's. She's staying there while she has rehab on her wrist because it's closer to the physios."

Amongst Katy's injuries during her accident, although accident definitely didn't describe it accurately, given that Ronan Miskimmon had computer hacked her car straight into a high stone wall, had been a broken wrist. It had healed but left her with some nerve damage that her consultant hoped would be improved by physiotherapy.

Craig nodded, trying to ignore the burning pain in his heart. He would have been tempted to dismiss it as indigestion if he hadn't been there constantly for over a month. As John waited expectantly for some comment, Craig wondered what he wanted him to say. 'Oh, that's good' or 'Her mum's house is closer so that makes sense.'

He was thinking neither. What he *was* thinking was far less altruistic and he would have been ashamed to hear it hit the air. He was thinking thank God that Katy wasn't out socialising yet, in case she met another man. As he blushed from shame John watched his friend carefully and decided that the Katy topic was too dangerous to pursue any further that day.

He shifted tack to one that wasn't.

"I wanted to see you because I have a case that -"

He was cut off by Craig lurching towards him, as if the case was something that he could physically grab from his hand.

"I need every detail."

They were back on solid if ghoulish ground. A dead person and a less than straightforward explanation as to how they'd got dead. Happy days.

John topped up their coffees and sat back, adopting his puzzled scientist face.

"I had a body brought in this morning. Colin McAllister, a dairy farmer near Armagh who was working at his slurry pit around seven a.m. and collapsed."

Slurry pits were a common fixture on farms; places where farmers gathered organic matter and animal waste, often to convert it into fertiliser. The problem was that decomposing waste produced deadly gases, presenting farm workers with a lethal threat.

Craig's expression changed from wide-eyed excitement to 'been there done that' apathy in the

18

space of a breath. He slumped back, his tone changing to bored.

"So he succumbed to the slurry fumes. It happens all the time."

But John's "Welll..." said not to be so quick. "*Maybe*... except he was wearing a top of the range slurry suit."

Craig sat forward again. "Had it been breached?"

The pathologist's shrug was equivocal.

The detective was growing more interested. "You think it was sabotage?"

John removed his glasses and wiped them on his sleeve before answering. When he finally did there was reluctance in his words.

"I really... I don't know. And I'm loath to raise the possibility of murder until I'm sure." He shook his head. "The local hospital said they haven't been able to contact his wife... and apparently they have a six-year-old son."

Craig made a face, picturing the widow and child trying to run the farm alone. "Is Des examining the suit?"

He knew that Des Marsham, Northern Ireland's Head of Forensics, would find anything that there was to find.

John nodded. "Started an hour ago. That's partly what I wanted to talk to you about. Would you mind nipping down to the lab?"

Mind? Anything that stopped him thinking about Katy right now was like manna from above. If it hadn't been considered unseemly to celebrate a death he would have been jumping up and down. Instead he nodded and stood up, handing twenty pounds to a nearby waiter before pushing open the bar's street door. John gulped down his coffee and followed hastily, exiting just as the rest of the squad were coming in. Liam stopped the pathologist mid-flight.

"Where's the boss racing off to? Have we got a case?"

John's twisted smile said maybe, and his wave goodbye said I'll let you know when we have. It was enough for now. Liam wasn't a man to go looking for work until it landed on his desk. He nodded the others into Craig's newly vacated booth and took their orders. Thirty minutes later, after Andy had embarrassed himself by making cow eyes at Rhonda, the squad's new constable whom he'd dated and been dumped by weeks before, and it was clear that the hard wooden benches weren't helping Annette to relax, they got ready to leave. Just then Liam's mobile rang.

As the theme from The Musketeers, the new ringtone Ash had downloaded for him, filled the bar, Liam turned his back to avoid his subordinates' inevitable smiles. A few seconds nodding and 'un-huh'ing later he cut the call and beckoned Annette to follow him outside.

"A body's been found at the Lagan Weir."

"We should call the chief."

Liam gawped at her. "Are you nuts? That was the happiest I've seen him look for weeks. Let him have fun with the Doc for a few hours. We can go check it out."

She didn't argue, secretly pleased that she was getting the chance of real work. The men on the team had started protecting her as soon as she'd said that she was pregnant: not calling her late at night, which although she could do without it was an integral part of the job, and dancing around her like she was made of glass, so this was definite progress. Liam's automatic summoning of her to a murder scene was proof positive that her china doll treatment was over, or so she thought.

She seized on the opportunity gratefully. "Great. Shall I call the C.S.I.s?"

"Check first. They might already be there."

As he nodded her to a bench in Barrow Square and walked off saying "Wait here a minute. I'll go and get the car" Annette's eyes narrowed to a squint and her feminist antennae began to twitch again. She decided against objecting, reckoning he could have made the suggestion to any of the team and not wanting to overreact, but her radar was well and truly on.

Five minutes later they were on their way to the scene and the others were on their way back to the ranch to push more paper. From no murder cases for weeks they now had a possible two. They didn't know it yet but it was the start of something far bigger than both.

Chapter Two

The Pathology Lab. Saintfield Road Science Park. 2 p.m.

Craig peered at the small tear in the slurry suit, wondering if it could have allowed in sufficient fumes to kill a man. His answer was as ambivalent as John's earlier one had been.

The tear was irregular, with random threads that protruded from each edge; its partial thickness revealing only the faintest view of his finger as he held it up to the light. The hole could have been the product of normal wear and tear, but why would anyone handling such dangerous material not have had it repaired immediately? It was something they would be looking into.

He peered at the tear again, trying to picture someone creating the breach with a knife. It wasn't outside the bounds of possibility. A tiny nick followed by some judicious shredding and only a forensic expert could rule deliberate intent in or out.

Craig held the suit at arm's length, picturing exactly where the hole would have sat on its wearer when he was alive. Left sleeve, just above the elbow at the back; not a place that normally got worn, and a place that a farmer in a hurry might have missed. It *could* have been sabotage.

As the detective perused the garment John was perusing him. He'd been right to involve Craig; even if it turned out that the death was from natural causes it was the liveliest that he'd seen him for a month. He broke the silence with a question.

"What do you think - accident or incident?"

Craig shook his head. "Hard to say." Something occurred to him. "Did he have anything else on him that could have torn it? In his clothes under the suit."

"Like what?"

"Knife. Keys. Anything?"

John frowned. "Now you mention it. No."

Craig set the suit to one side. "The breach is in an unlikely position for wear and tear, but on the other hand it's not obvious that it was made by a knife." He perched on a nearby stool. "What does Des think?"

John rolled his eyes. "That the Matterhorn's bloody high."

"What?"

The pathologist sighed. "He's taken up mountain climbing. Personally I think it's just an excuse to grow his beard even longer. He looks like Grizzly Adams at the moment. It's a wonder that he can find his mouth to eat."

Craig raised an eyebrow. "Fascinating, but I meant what does he think about the hole?"

"Oh, that. He's refusing to commit until the electron microscopy results are back. He muttered something about air as well and then wandered off." He turned towards the door. "Come and see the body." Only when uttered by a pathologist could such words not sound bizarre.

Craig squinted as he tried to decide if looking at a man who'd been gassed to death was going to add anything to his day. Eventually he shrugged; all evidence was good evidence or at least that's what his tutor at The Met had always said. He slid off his stool and meandered into the dissection room, where a quick flourish of a sheet later and they were staring down at a very dead man.

Death was death of course, but, and he already knew that this was nonsense; some bodies definitely looked deader than others. Time contributed; the long dead making the newly deceased look positively vibrant, but it wasn't only the length of time dead but the mode of death that played a part. Until that moment Craig would have said that drowning deaths were the deadest dead people that he'd ever seen, but the man on the slab in front of them looked even worse than that. His face looked furious, as if he'd felt cheated of life. It fitted with someone totally shocked by the suddenness of their demise.

John's voice broke through his thoughts.

"Slurry can release methane, carbon dioxide, ammonia and hydrogen sulphide. The symptoms vary accordingly to the concentrations of each. Some of the gases are odourless or destroy the sense of smell, so the person doesn't notice the threat and just falls down dead, or, with the hydrogen sulphide, they can suffer discomfort, disorientation, collapse and then death. Most people die within a couple of breaths."

Craig shook his head and walked away. When they were settled back in John's office holding a brew, the pathologist spoke again.

"For a man who died non-violently; he looks as if he fought very hard."

Craig nodded. "I thought he looked angry. Is that common with gassing deaths?"

A pall came over John's face. Craig had seen him look like it once before, in the summer of eighty-eight when they were still at university. John had spent his holiday working with a charity in Halabja in Southern Kurdistan, where, as part of the Iran-Iraq war, Kurds had been gassed by Saddam Hussein.

The detective waited for a moment before prompting his friend with a cough.

John nodded. "I saw something similar in eighty-eight. People who'd witnessed the chemical attack said some victims dropped in their tracks with the expressions still fixed on their faces; others took much longer to die. You don't want to know how."

Craig moved the discussion along. "So McAllister definitely died of gassing then?"

"Yes."

"So no ambiguity as to cause of death, only as to how the gas got in."

John frowned. "I don't know much about slurry but I assume the gas entered through that hole. The only decision is whether it was made deliberately."

Craig wasn't convinced. "You think? The hole wasn't full thickness and if only a little gas got in McAllister might have had time to escape. We'll need permeability tests as well as microscopy."

John's voice was firm. "He was definitely gassed."

The detective raised a hand in peace. "All I'm saying is that neither of us is sure how the gas got to him, and we'll only know when Des has finished testing the suit." He stood up. "Meanwhile, you and I are taking a trip to that farm."

****

The Lagan Weir, Belfast. 3 p.m.

Liam watched the water gushing over the weir for so long that finally Annette gave his arm a nudge.

"Wake up. I'd like to get out of here this side of Easter. It's freezing."

The D.C.I. ignored her, his mind on other things than the temperature. He was picturing all of the possible ways the dead youth could have ended up there. He could have jumped in, fallen in or been pushed in, of course; that was how bodies normally ended up in the drink. Either right beside the local wonder of engineering or nearby, then the river's current would have forced him swiftly onto the manmade barrier. Maybe.

He lifted his eyes and stared past his shivering companion, beyond the Queen Elizabeth Bridge and towards the Waterfront Hall. Or...the lad could have entered the water much further upstream and been carried there more slowly, meandering towards the weir over an unknown length of time. As he thought it Liam shrugged. Dead was dead. He didn't need to work out where the youth had met his end right away; forensics would tell them where he'd been and the computer geeks would work out when.

He made a note to attend the post-mortem then turned to Annette as if she'd just made her comment the second before.

"Aye, it is cold. 'Course I'll be feeling it worse than you, given that you've a wee radiator on board."

Annette suddenly wasn't so sure that she liked being treated as one of the boys, thinking that she might prefer being cossetted like before. Of course, if she could make up her mind it would help, but before she could Liam had crossed to the covered body and pulled back its sheet, completely oblivious to the gawping of passers-by. Annette stepped in front of him, hissing urgently.

"For God's sake cover him up. People are looking."

Before she'd finished, adding sadly "he's just a kid" Liam had entered another trance. He stared hard at the young man's swollen face, as if enough scrutiny would make him wake and tell them how and why he had died. The D.C.I.'s gaze lingered for another moment and then travelled past the youth's sodden clothing to his badly frayed hands. Bruised, cut, and by the shape of them, fractured.

Liam donned a glove and turned over one misshapen appendage and then the other, scrutinising their skinned palms. The injuries spoke of a fight not long before he had passed. The detective shook his head immediately. No, not a fight; the cuts weren't on the man's knuckles, they were further back. Someone had stamped hard on their victim's hands.

He sprang to his feet, bemoaning the fact that Andy wasn't there to see him do it. The scrawny D.C.I. had made one too many jokes about his paunch before Christmas, so Liam's New Year's resolution had been to get fit and his eight a.m. visits to the gym were starting to pay off. He'd soon be slating the unfeasibly skinny Toblerone addict for not going there himself.

He signalled the mortuary attendants to remove the body and turned to look for Annette. He found her clutching a coffee supplied by a kindly C.S.I.

"Definitely murder. My guess is he was chucked in further up river and someone stamped on his hands to make sure he didn't get out again. It would fit with the bruises, plus some of his fingers are broken and his palms are skinned, like he was trying to grab onto the bank."

She sniffed sceptically.

"Speculation."

Liam didn't take offence. He'd been blessed with an ultra-thick skin at birth. "Informed conjecture, I think you'll find, Inspector. Anyway, we'll see when the Docs get at him."

She set down her mug and took out a five pound note. "I'll bet you a fiver that you're off the mark."

He was tempted, but there was something in his DNA that wouldn't let him take money from a woman several months along.

"Keep your money. We'll wait and see."

Annette's eyes narrowed, her feminist radar pinging again. "You'll take bets on my due date with the chief but not with me on this? Or is it *because* I'm pregnant? Eh? You chauvi-"

But Liam was already walking to the car, thinking of other things. A rumbling in his only slightly shrunken stomach told him it was time for afternoon tea.

****

The C.C.U. 4 p.m.

By the time Craig arrived back at Docklands, courtesy of a trip to the farm that had been aborted halfway by a call informing him the farmer's widow was actually somewhere in Belfast, people were piled up outside his office like planes circling over Heathrow. Two of them were Ash, sporting green hair instead of his normal blue or purple, as a patriotic nod to the New Year, and Jake McLean, the squad's detective sergeant, previously confined to a wheelchair, courtesy of his attempted murder by his partner Aaron Foster, but now getting around on crutches following intensive physio.

The third man was one that Craig didn't know and didn't like the look of; he had a lean and hungry look that would have made Julius Caesar suspicious, and it was having much the same effect on him. He tutted at his quick prejudice; the man couldn't help how he looked, and besides, if he were being honest, he would admit that his dislike of the visitor was based more on the instantly recognisable Public Prosecution files

27

beneath his arm than anything related to his physique.

He walked past the three men into his office, collecting Nicky on the way and nodding her to shut the door. Once inside he gave her a baleful look.

"Why do they all want to see me?"

She smiled kindly at him, like a mother whose child had been hurt and wanted to make it better. It was an expression she'd worn for most of the previous month, alternating it with loud shushes at anyone who made noise while he was in his office and copious unsolicited espressos. Craig was half expecting her to sing him a lullaby but instead she took a seat.

"Ash wants to talk to you about Ronan Miskimmon's computers, Jake wants to know if he can get out on the street more, and the-" She stopped abruptly, noticing that Craig was still on his feet. She waited till he'd sat down before restarting. "The other man is from the Public Prosecution Service. His name is Martin Grant."

His sigh was heavy and automatic; she'd confirmed his guess and P.P.S. emissaries were seldom the bearers of good news.

"He's here about the Miskimmon and Corneau case?"

She nodded and then swallowed hard. "And Aaron Foster."

Foster had been Jake's live-in partner for ten years, and so consumed with jealousy that rather than allow Jake to end their relationship he'd decided to kill him, something he'd almost succeeded in doing the October before.

Craig's eyes widened. "How do you know?"

He doubted the P.P.S. visitor would have given up his tightly held secrets to a P.A. Nicky's conspiratorial smile confirmed that he was right.

"My friend Ruby works in the P.P.S.' office and she told me."

He gawped at her. "And I'm just hearing that you have a spy in the P.P.S. *now*? After how many years of us working together?"

She shot him a sceptical look.

28

"You know fine well that if I'd told you before you would have taken liberties. You'd have been asking me to find out all sorts of things and that would've landed Ruby in a mess."

She was right. It was a wise secretary who knew her own boss.

Craig thought for a moment and then made his choice.

"OK, tell Jake yes to his request to get out there again, and I'll happily speak to him later if he still wishes. Tell Ash he can have half-an-hour later this afternoon, and diary it, please. And you'd better send the lean and hungry one in."

Her look was quizzical but her action decisive. She opened the door and beckoned Martin Grant in; leaving to make coffee so strong that it would assuage Craig's caffeine pangs for the whole hour she knew the meeting would take. As it happened the discussion didn't take that long, but what it lacked in length it made up for in noise.

Martin Grant shook Craig's offered hand with a grip that was both weak and strong; it was a strange combination. His palm pressed hard against Craig's while his fingers wiggled limply in the air, making the detective wonder if it was the sign of some secret club. He gave the matter all of five seconds consideration and then nodded the lawyer to a seat.

"You wanted to see me about two of our cases, Mr Grant."

The reply was a nod and an inscrutable "Hmm."

Craig carried on, hoping fervently that the conversation wasn't going to be hints and signs throughout.

"Good. The Miskimmon and Corneau and Aaron Foster cases, I believe."

"Hmm."

The hmming was annoying Craig already and if the solicitor 'hmmed' one more time his politeness was likely to slip. To prevent the coming assault the detective sat back in his chair and bit his lip. If he didn't ask anything then he couldn't be hmmed at, and

Grant would be forced to speak. It worked. The solicitor set the files he was still holding on the desk and opened the one on top. He started to recite without glancing at the page, making Craig wonder why he'd bothered to open the file at all.

"Aaron Foster, date of birth first of June-"

Craig raised a hand, halting him. "Let's take the details and charges as read."

It threw Grant momentarily but to his credit he gathered himself quickly and moved on, turning over the page and leaning in to peer at the next. His second soliloquy obviously required an aide memoire.

"Mr Foster's solicitor has changed his plea to..."

Craig's heart sank twice. Once at the inevitability of what Grant was going to say next and then again at the idea of telling Jake.

"Not guilty by reason of insanity." Temporary of course.

And there it was. The phrase that had wriggled criminals out of taking responsibility for their crimes and into the warm hugs of group therapy and soft cells for sixty years. Valid in some cases perhaps, but not half as many as the number of cons who used it. Craig heard his next words as if they were being said by someone else.

"You've done a deal."

Grant was looking more like Cassius with every word and something about Craig's tone must have conveyed it, because the lawyer rushed to caveat his words.

"The Director insisted...taxpayers' money...five years in a psychiatric unit...save months of court time..."

All Craig heard after five years was 'blah, blah, blah'. White noise generated by the angry rush of blood inside his head. He knew it was nothing to the anger that Jake would feel. He leaned forward, his voice rising but still controlled.

"So Sergeant McLean won't get his day in court."

Grant leaned back as Craig's voice grew louder.

"He won't get to confront Foster and make him

30

admit how he deliberately planned to end his life."

Nicky heard the words outside.

Grant retreated even further as Craig stood up and leaned forward on the desk.

"You're going to do something for me, Mr Grant."

Any further retreat was barred by the chair's high back, so the solicitor nodded hurriedly, already determined to give the obviously unhinged superintendent in front of him whatever it was he asked. Nicky moved her chair closer to the door to listen, just as Ash stood up at his desk and mouthed "what's going on?" She shook her head and kept eavesdropping, picturing Craig squeezing out his next words through gritted teeth.

"You're going to explain all of this personally to Sergeant McLean, aren't you, Mr Grant."

The civil servant nodded frantically. "I am. I am. I can do that. Definitely. Not a problem. Not a problem. Whatever you wish."

For a moment Craig didn't move. He just stood, fists grinding against the desk's veneer, jaw set and leaning so far forward that he was barely six inches from the hapless lawyer's face. Suddenly he realised how he must look. He drew himself upright abruptly and strode to the door, opening it so quickly that Nicky slid off her chair. He helped her up with no comment but "two more coffees, please", before going back inside.

It was the pause he'd needed to admit that the Director of Public Prosecution's decision had absolutely nothing to do with the man in front of him.

Nicky entered with a full percolator, new cups and her best biscuits for good measure, something that made Craig shoot her a wry look; good manners said that guests should be offered coffee, but there was no need to indulge the bringer of bad news with chocolate carbs. She backed out, smiling a warning at her boss. Craig ignored the silent lecture and retook his seat, sliding a fresh drink towards his guest.

When they had sipped in silence for a moment and Grant had confirmed that his physique was nothing to do with dieting by eating two chocolate digestives in a row, Craig nodded towards the second file.

"Miskimmon and Corneau."

It was the solicitor's turn to look angry. He set down his cup and tapped a finger repeatedly on the desk.

"I want to know what you're doing about this case."

Craig raised an eyebrow, pleasantly surprised. Grant hadn't come to say that the P.P.S. didn't have enough to prosecute the siblings; his words implied that they just needed something more. The Public Prosecution Service applied two tests to a case to decide whether to prosecute or not: One; was there enough evidence to provide a 'realistic prospect of conviction'. Although of course there was no guarantee of that when the barristers got to their feet in court. And two; was it in the public interest to prosecute? On number two, there could be no doubt that the answer was yes. Ronan Miskimmon and Eleanor Corneau were dangerous and everyone would be safer without them on the streets, so Grant's words *had* to refer to test number one. They needed more evidence to convince the D.P.P. to proceed.

"What more do you need?"

Grant squinted, searching for some sarcasm in the words. When he found none he became enthused.

"I need something that puts Miskimmon near that plane." He was referring to a private jet that Miskimmon had sabotaged, killing an MLA and his staff. "Or some concrete proof of his hacking, even at just one of the incidences here, then we can make a case for all of the rest."

Craig sat back and closed his eyes, reluctant to commit on either. Andy had been viewing the CCTV tapes from the airport for two weeks, but he still had another week's worth of footage to go, and Des and the tech division were finding the computers they'd seized from Miskimmon's home in Moygashel absolutely impossible to crack. The computer genius had set programmes to wipe all content as soon as they turned

32

the laptops on.

After a moment's thought Craig opened his eyes and got ready to obfuscate. Ash was working on the hacking and would tie it to Miskimmon given time, and Andy was a super-recogniser; someone with enhanced facial recognition and other cognitive abilities that gave them an uncanny ability to recognise faces from even the poorest angle, so there was no doubt that if Ronan Miskimmon was anywhere on the airport tapes he would spot him eventually, regardless of any disguise.

"We can get you both. We just need more time."

Grant shook his head. "The Venezuelans are pushing for a prosecution on the visa fraud." Miskimmon had cleverly committed the lesser crime of visa fraud when setting up their escape to Venezuela, preferring the few years possible sentence for that to a life sentence in the UK for murder. "And if we convict on that they've openly said they want them to serve their time in a Venezuelan jail."

Craig felt surprise, pleasure and hope all at once. Surprise that a foreign government was actually following through on their initial anger; in his experience very few actually did. Pleasure at the thought of Ronan Miskimmon serving time in a prison system far less benevolent than their own, although he wasn't so sure that his sister deserved quite the same fate. And hope, because Martin Grant had just given him a last resort idea if they failed to gather enough evidence. The threat of the overseas penal system might be enough to get Eleanor Corneau to turn.

Grant was still speaking. "Plus, the Director is kicking off about them still being on remand. He wants the case finalised and a court date set-"

Craig suddenly saw the man opposite for what he had always been; a potential ally. He knew that he let his personal prejudices blind him at times, and studying law at university had made lawyers one of his favourite bêtes noires. Perhaps it was because he was too similar to them, and their proximity made him see something in himself that he disliked. Cold logic topped the list.

He lifted the still hot percolator and topped up the solicitor's cup. Grant stared at the drink, knowing that so much caffeine would keep him up half the night but not fancying telling Craig that he'd had enough. He sipped dutifully as Craig asked the all-important question.

"How long do we have?"

Grant looked glum. "Seven days maximum, then it's the visa fraud and nothing else."

Seven days; it would take Andy that long to view the rest of the tapes. Craig took a punt.

"We can do it in ten."

Grant's eyebrows shot up and he leaned toward intently. "You're bluffing."

Damn. Not only lean and hungry looking but sharp as well. But Craig was sharp too.

"Prove it." He knew the lawyer couldn't so he pressed on. "Tell the D.P.P. we'll have your evidence, providing we get ten days."

Whether Grant believed him or not he would never know because he was literally saved by an old fashioned bell. Grant's ring tone. After a few moments muttering and nodding the lawyer rose to his feet.

"OK, I'll get you ten days." Craig was about to say 'great' when Grant added a caveat. "Providing that *you* tell Sergeant McLean about Aaron Foster's sentence."

He had him over a barrel and he knew it. As Craig nodded him out, dreading his next conversation, he remembered again why he'd disliked Grant on sight.

Chapter Three

5 p.m.

Liam was leaving The James just as Craig was heading in. It resulted in a rapid U-turn and another cup of tea while Craig added an espresso to the barrel of coffee he'd just drunk. He was grateful for the company and Liam's presence would deter any of the team joining him at his table if they decided to pop out for afternoon tea, certain as they were that senior officers spent their coffee breaks discussing things of major import. It also gave him some breathing space - he wasn't ready for questions, from Jake in particular. After five minutes of Liam's slurping, Craig was finally ready to speak.

"Anything to report?"

His tone said he expected a "no" in return.

Liam gulped down the mouthful of tea he'd just taken and nodded his head. "We've got a case."

Craig was just wondering how he'd found out about the slurry death when he realised Liam was talking about another death. His eyes widened as his deputy carried on.

"A lad washed up against the Lagan Weir earlier. Definitely drowned, but his hands say it was murder. They'd been stamped on. A lot."

Craig pushed away his drink. "You're saying he was forced in."

"Yup. So the question is when and where."

Craig was put out that he hadn't been informed immediately and it made him picky. "That's two questions. Third and fourth; who is he and who killed him?"

Liam shrugged. "Not a clue. That's as far as we've got. He's at the morgue, so I'm heading down there now."

Craig shook his head, marvelling at how quickly their workload had gone from no cases to two. Now he wouldn't have time to breathe, never mind think about Katy. Even better, he had a legitimate excuse for

35

deferring telling Jake what the P.P.S. had agreed.

Liam was puzzled. "Why are you shaking your head?"

"John has a possible case for us too, so I'll come with you to the lab, but it will have to wait for an hour. We have a team to brief."

****

McMorrow's Bar. Oxford Street, Belfast. 5 p.m.

The saloon bar's glass and mahogany door swung open, just as it had done to admit frock coated gentlemen generations before; inviting revellers to a hostelry in permanent dusk, regardless of the time of day. It wasn't a cold dusk, being broken by the gleam of brass fittings, and because it was winter, the orange-red of an open fire. Here and there blue lights flickered incongruously, as some early evening patrons stroked and tapped at their mobile phones. Without them it could have been nineteen hundred and sixteen instead of one hundred years further on. But it *was* twenty-sixteen and the traditional setting had been chosen because it echoed Michael Hanratty's old-fashioned view of the world.

Michael 'Micky' Hanratty was a man of tradition. Traditions like 'listen to your enemies, but only once' and 'raising a hand in anger is likely to get it cut off'. He was a man who kept a low profile; everything about him quiet and restrained. His suits were bespoke and dark; ditto his shoes, socks and ties. Refined, restrained and high quality, fit to be worn by a City of London banker or a Manhattan CEO, except that Micky was neither but richer than both, and the secret to nobody ever questioning where his money came from was looking less like a criminal than anyone you would ever meet.

Hanratty wasn't an old man but he liked the old ways; he put a fresh rose in his lapel every morning and he wouldn't deal in girls, drugs or guns. It made him feel like he had a moral code and that was

36

important to him. He was a family man was Micky: two daughters under ten and a wife, Gráinne that he adored. None of them knew about his shadier ventures, living the life of the gentleman horse breeder's family on his spread near Navan. He intended to keep it that way, and anyone who threatened different would find themselves being dealt a rough hand.

He scanned the bar, admiring its antique furnishings but not the town that it was in. He didn't like Belfast, didn't like any big city if the truth was told, but if he'd had to state a preference for any conurbation then it would have been for the Dub. He'd been born in Dublin, the Liberties, long before it had become trendy. He knew everyone there, from the knackers in the street to the politicians preening themselves in the Dáil. He preferred the knackers; they were by far the more honest men.

He only knew a handful of the Belfast equivalents but he knew they were men who'd cut your throat and steal your drink before you'd hit the floor. Men like that were useful to keep an eye on things while he was at home, and it was things in the north that were proving problematic that were the reason for his visit that day.

McMorrow's was his branch office when he was in town and its landlord Billy Ross acted as his P.A., arranging his meetings and serving alcohol to his clients, plus topping up his own twelve year old Jameson without him having to say the word. It was the perfect arrangement; no company registered at Companies House in Parnell Street, no tax paid and no address for the Gardaí to raid, but a comfortable location to hold his meetings and a landlord who knew which side his bread was buttered on.

He and Billy had an understanding; he'd bought the bar to launder some Euros and Billy could run it as he wished so long as he kept an ear out for anything going down. Which was why he was sitting there now when he should've been taking his daughters to ballet class. Billy's ears had been burning red hot for weeks so he'd decided the time was right to come north and see what was going on.

Ross was just topping his boss' whisky when the bar door swung open again. The barman withdrew to a respectful distance when he saw who had just walked in.

Tommy Hill stood in the saloon bar's entrance, glaring into its corners as his eyes adjusted to the dusty gloom. Most of the phone-strokers stroked on in blissful ignorance, but the few that recognised him finished their drinks hurriedly and then left by the bar's side door. Tommy might have been old but he was still a legend in Belfast and the thing that made him legendary was his ability to kill without a blink. His Loyalist exploits during The Troubles had earned him a twenty-year stretch for shooting four Catholics, although early release under the Good Friday Agreement had meant that he'd served only ten. Now he lived in the rural idyll of Templepatrick, near Antrim, to be close to Ella, his young grand-daughter; a supposedly changed man, except that no-one believed a word.

When the bar was almost empty and his eyes had adjusted to the dark Tommy glanced at Ross and followed his finger to where it pointed near the back of the bar. The street fighter approached Michael Hanratty's high-backed booth cautiously, taking up position behind it, just out of sight of its occupant. It was a stand-off; Tommy not prepared to step forward into what might be a bullet - there were still plenty of Catholics who hated him for what he'd done; and Hanratty who couldn't be arsed to coax an old lag to sit down and join him, especially an old lag who'd been firmly on the other side.

It was Ross who eventually broke the stalemate, bringing over two fresh glasses and a bottle of Jameson's and setting them on the table as he made the introductions.

"Mr Hanratty, this is Tommy Hill. Tommy, this is Mr Michael Hanratty. I think that you two should talk."

And so it was that the staunchly Loyalist Tommy

and the ideological Republican Micky Hanratty shared a whisky on a winter afternoon, while less than a mile away the Murder Squad was unaware what was about to be unleashed on their patch.

****

The C.C.U. 5.30 p.m.

Craig stared at his team through eyes that were only slightly less dull than that morning but he noticed several things. Almost everyone was there: Jake, Annette, Andy, Liam and Ash. Even their jet-haired, pale-skinned Snow White lookalike Rhonda, fresh back from her course on voice projection, was watching him eagerly. He was pleased that she'd agreed to attend the course and hoped that it had worked; weeks of trying to hear what she was saying in her naturally abnormally quiet voice had almost worn him out.

The two people missing were Davy, who was still in Paris, and Sergeant Reggie Boyd who was on annual leave. Craig wondered how much longer he could legitimately hold on to the experienced sergeant, given that he'd only been brought in to cover Jake's sick leave and he was back now, and they were getting a new inspector that week in preparation for Annette's maternity leave. But he was keeping Reggie until someone from HR turned up and pointed out that he was overstaffed, or until the sergeant decided he wanted to return to his nine-to-five existence on the Demesne, one of Belfast's worst sink estates.

Amongst the other things Craig noticed was that Nicky had been baking again, as evidenced by the crumbs around everyone's mouths. What had started as a cake baking competition between her and Rhonda was in danger of making them all obese. He decided to have a word with her and then he thought again; it would be more fun to make Liam, the biggest cake eater of them all, be the one to tell Nicky that she shouldn't bring any more pastries in.

When he'd finished his sweep he nodded Liam to

start. He was too tired. It wasn't insomnia and it wasn't malnourishment, and to admit to his fatigue would be to support his mother's view that his feelings about Katy were wreaking a physical toll.

Liam stood up and started to boom.

"Well now, you bunch of miscreants."

As a team building tactic it was a novel one.

"We had no cases at nine o'clock this morning and now it looks like we've got two-"

Annette cut in, making him sigh. He remembered the good old days when she'd raised her hand when she'd wanted to talk.

"Two? What's the second one?"

"Might be the first one, depending on your point of view."

Craig overcame his lethargy and stood up, waving Liam back to his seat.

"Right. The first case has come from Doctor Winter, and we're not even sure yet if it actually is a case but it's beginning to look that way." He reached behind him for his coffee and took a sip before carrying on. "There was a farm death near Armagh early this morning. A dairy farmer, Colin McAllister, was working in his slurry pit and he was overcome by the fumes."

Liam raised a forefinger uncharacteristically. Craig was wondering why he was being so polite when he saw him point his other one first at Annette and then at the one that he'd just raised. Annette's response was to blow a raspberry at the lesson in etiquette. Craig couldn't be bothered commenting. Life was too short to get between those two.

"You wanted to say something, Liam?"

"Didn't he have an air supply, boss?"

"What?"

"You can't work safely with slurry without an air supply."

Craig nodded him to continue, retaking his seat. Liam had grown up on a farm whereas what he and John knew about farming could be written on the back of a stamp.

Liam scanned the group. "OK, who knows what slurry is?"

To Craig's surprise the very urban Ash raised his hand. "Collections of decomposing waste, usually found on farms."

"And the dangers of working with it are...?"

"Succumbing to the effects of gas. It can kill in seconds so you need to have an air supply."

The D.C.I. gawped at him. "How the heck do you know all that?"

Ash shrugged. "My head's full of random facts. Mostly from Wikipedia."

Liam was put out. He was the farming expert and now he'd been upstaged by a computer geek. Rhonda opened her mouth but he shut it again with a glance. All he needed was for her to know even more about farming and he might as well retire.

"Aye, well." He gestured at Ash. "Kermit's right."

Ash straightened up indignantly. "Kermit? I thought my nickname was Smurf!"

"Your hair's green now. And anyway, I thought you didn't like nicknames."

Ash's mouth closed silently in defeat, giving Liam his second wind.

"But I bet you've never seen a slurry body, have you?" He gave them all a 'so there' look. "Well, I have and they're not pretty, I can tell you."

Craig interjected. "Good, then you can have a look at the one at the morgue." He made a rewind motion with his hand. "Go back a little. What was that about a separate air supply? So you're saying that a slurry suit alone wouldn't have been enough protection? Does that mean having a hole in it wouldn't have killed him?"

Liam scoffed. "It wouldn't have helped, but a suit's no good without an air supply. It's the fumes that kill them."

"What about a face mask?"

"Not a blind bit of use unless it's attached to a tank of air. Did your man have that?"

"Not that John mentioned."

41

There were still a lot of questions to be asked. As Craig thought of some of them he signalled Liam to move onto their second case.

"OK, so Annette and I went to a scene a few hours ago. A body washed up against the Lagan Weir. Young male; late teens early twenties. Drowned."

Craig shook his head. "Apparently drowned."

Liam rolled his eyes. "Drowned subject to P.M. So that means what?"

He scanned the faces of his class. Jake answered first.

"Accident, suicide or was pushed."

"Very good. Exactly right. So what else do we need to know?"

He turned to Annette but she shook her head. They'd already had this discussion, time to give one of the others a chance. Rhonda seized the gap and with a heave of her shoulders she added.

"Where did he enter the water and how long was he in it?"

There was silence while Liam grinned first at her and then at Craig, while the others gawped, openly surprised. Not only could they hear the statuesque brunette's voice clearly for the first time but some of them had obviously just realised she hailed from another continent. Jake pointed a finger at her in shock.

"You're from Australia! When did that happen?"

Ash looked puzzled. "I thought you were from Ballymena."

Annette chipped in. "No, she won a cake competition in Ballymena."

It brought a sceptical sniff from Nicky.

Rhonda looked shocked. "I've always been from Australia!"

Liam interrupted, laughing. "What he means is no-one could hear you before so no-one could tell where you were from -"

Craig cut in. "Nice and all as this international entente is, could we please move it along?"

Liam obliged. "OK, so we have a man in the Lagan,

possibly drowned, and we need to know when he went into the river and where. So Ash, liaise with the Docs and get all the algae, time of death and current stuff, then plot our man's journey. We need to know when and where he went in and what exactly killed him."

He spotted Andy eying the remainder of his muffin and grabbed it to take a bite, continuing through a mouthful of sponge. Craig allowed the ensuing "Phff...tho..." to continue for five seconds before cutting him off.

"What Liam's trying to say is that leaves us with questions: was this suicide, an accident, or was this man murdered? There are signs that point to the latter being the case. We'll go into more detail following the post-mortem, but until then, Andy, when you've stopped giving Liam the evil eye over that muffin, I want you to get an I.D. on our victim and find everything about him there is to know. Jake; you, Rhonda and Ash check out all the CCTV available anywhere along the Lagan for the past..." He glanced at Liam for an approximate time of the victim's submersion but his mouth was still occupied so Annette obliged instead.

"He looked as if he'd been in the water around one or two days, sir." She glanced at Liam for confirmation and was answered by a nod.

"OK, good. Jake, let's check the last seventy-two hours of Lagan CCTV just to be safe, and don't forget any shops, garages, traffic cams and residences overlooking the river as well. Someone might have seen or heard something. If you need to you can contact Joe Rice and he'll get some uniforms to do door-to-door. Can anyone think of anything else?"

"Bar staff." It had come from Andy. "There are pubs along the river so the bar staff or bouncers might have noticed something going on."

"Good. OK, Andy, you and Annette take that. Also boat clubs. There are rowing clubs along the river, so let's see if anyone was out rowing on any of those nights."

Liam finally found his voice and he used it to

insult the baker. "Here, Nicky. That muffin was a bit chewy. Not up to your usual mark."

She jumped up at her desk. "Don't you dare insult my baking! Of course it tasted chewy. You're supposed to wash it down with tea, not inhale it!"

But she hadn't missed Rhonda's smirk. The Bun War that had settled down just before Christmas looked as if it was about to restart.

Craig sighed and shook his head. "Liam, if you can't say anything nice don't say anything in future." He sounded like his dad. He rose from his chair before anyone else could speak. "Right, that's it for now. You've all got plenty to do. We might brief again later so remember you're all on call."

He jerked a thumb at Liam and headed for the lift, waiting until they were inside before letting rip. "Honestly, you have all the tact of a JCB. The whole cake contest thing had just quietened down and now you go and start it again!"

It took him another minute of ranting to notice that Liam was smiling and only a second more to realise that this was exactly what the D.C.I. had planned all along. Liam had seen his looming office cake ban and had stopped him in his tracks by pitting Nicky and Rhonda against each other again. Craig leaned back against the wall and laughed, accepting that he'd been expertly outplayed.

Chapter Four

The Pathology Lab

John Winter lifted the man's right hand in his own and held the magnifying glass in his left, six inches from its cold, swollen flesh. After a moment's consideration he turned the hand over to peer at its palm. The Lagan's fish residents and animal visitors had begun feasting on the appendage, but there was still no disguising the abrasions covering it. They spoke of their victim's palm scraping frantically against a hard surface sometime before he had met his death.

The pathologist's gaze travelled along the fingers to the raw, ripped flesh at their tips; signs of gripping and the possibility of particulates that might lead them to where the youth had entered the water first. He stared for a moment longer before deciding that only a microscope could tell him more and he was just turning to find one when Craig and Liam clattered noisily into the room. John's "shush" was automatic, borne from respect but more for his own comfort than that of the man lying on his slab.

He continued his examination assiduously, Craig standing beside him in silence, seeing everything that the scientist saw. Liam meanwhile was slumped against a bench along one wall, tired out by a week of sleepless nights with his young children and a looming weekend that looked like it was promising even more. He yawned loudly just as John began to speak, drawing a reproving glance from Craig. The pathologist continued undeterred.

"Right. The dorsums of both hands are bruised; one to two days old approximately, which means the bruises were made on-"

"Tuesday or Wednesday."

Craig smiled. "Good news. Liam can count."

John ignored the interruption as if it hadn't occurred. "The bruising is almost certainly from someone stamping on them, in fact there's a faint shoe print on his right hand that Des will be photographing once I've finished here. The bruising on the left is less than that on the right, which suggests what?"

This time Craig answered. "That he was right-handed."

John's "correct" clashed with Liam's "How do you work that out?"

The pathologist set down his glass and pulled up a stool, waving the others to two more.

"Marc said he was right-handed because the bruising on his right hand is worse, which tells us that hand was stamped on more, meaning it was probably the one he used most to hang onto the bank, most likely because it was stronger. The dominant hand is stronger, therefore he was right-handed. OK?"

Liam thought for a moment and then gave a pragmatic nod. John picked up his thread.

"Both hands suffered fractures, mainly of the metacarpals, the long bones of the palms."

Craig nodded. "Which fits with them being stamped upon."

"Most likely, but the types of fractures will confirm it. Both palms show abrasions all over, plus there are tear abrasions on the finger pulps."

Liam sniffed. "So basically he was scrabbling to hang onto the bank and some bastard was trying to force him in."

John gave a small smile. "Said like a true poet. I'll get you to write Natalie's Valentine card."

Craig was staring at their victim's bloated face. He'd seen drowning victims before of course, and they were never pretty. Days of submersion in water had a bad enough effect; imagine your whole body like one huge macerated finger pulp from too long in the bath. But the feasting of fish and encasement in vegetation made drownings a particularly horrific sight. He would take a shooting any day; at least if it wasn't in the face the victim's family could view the body without throwing up.

But it wasn't just the man's appearance that was bothering him and after a minute he asked a question.

"*Did* he drown, John?"

Liam snorted rudely but John slowly shook his head.

"Yes. Well, no and yes. Before I tell you what I mean, why did you ask?"

Craig gestured at the man's trunk and legs, still hidden under the sheet. "He looks strongly built, so unless he couldn't swim at all..."

John nodded. "Well spotted." He smiled as Liam's scepticism morphed into surprise. "First the abrasions were starting to heal, meaning he was still alive for some hours after he fought his assailant, and I found something that makes me think he was sedated before he entered the water." He slid off his stool and returned to the dissection table, lifting the hair behind the man's right ear and then standing back for them to see.

"Can you see it?"

Liam shook his head, but Craig kept staring and then gave a faint nod.

"A red spot?"

John retook his seat. "It's an injection site. I've put a rush on the tox-screen but my guess is he was injected with something and then thrown in. He was still awake enough to try to climb out, until he tired of fighting his captor. He succumbed to the combination of drugs and fatigue at some point and drowned, but I'm not sure how quickly. It's very possible that without the drugs he would have survived." He gave a grudging smirk. "It was clever. If it hadn't been for the injuries to the backs of his hands we might never have thought this was anything more than a drowning."

Craig smiled. "Except that you spotted the injection site."

"I have to be honest. I probably wouldn't have done if I hadn't, like you, questioned how such a sturdily built young man had drowned. It made me look much harder-"

Liam had had enough back slapping for one day.

"OK, you're both geniuses." He ignored Craig's arched eyebrow. "So we're saying he was injected and

47

shoved in, then the guy who did it stopped him climbing out. Bit careless to stamp on his hands, wasn't it? Seeing as it's the only thing that told us it was murder."

John shrugged. "Not really. I mean, what are the odds you'll trace him through a shoe print? And it was always likely to come out he was sedated from his tox-screen, and if nothing was found in his stomach contents we'd have gone looking for an injection site."

Liam wasn't giving up. "But you still might've assumed he'd injected himself."

John's eyes widened. "Behind his ear? I don't think so."

Craig had been watching the ping-pong dialogue thinking of something else. He added it now.

"OK, so whoever did this knew it would come out as murder eventually, but even if they'd thought about the footprint they'd have reckoned the odds on it being enough for us to trace them were low."

Liam nodded. "They'd have been right."

"Even allowing for all that I don't think they would have cared." He hesitated before he said his next words. "To me this feels like a hit."

John's eyes widened in excitement. This was why he loved working with the Murder Squad. The pure pathology part of his job was intellectually stimulating, especially when he visited sites abroad or attended international meetings with his peers. But for sheer adventure none of it touched the murders that came to Craig.

Liam was thinking something else entirely and if it had hit the air it would have sounded like "oh shit". They'd already had their fill of hitmen in Belfast with Stevan Mitic, a Serbian sniper still on the run for several murders. They needed another one like him like a hole in the head.

Craig saw his reaction and dealt with it first. "OK, let me caveat that. I don't mean a hired hit man. This wasn't a contract; it feels too personal."

The D.C.I. wasn't appeased. "OK, so it's not a Mitic, but that's even worse."

John glanced from one detective to another looking puzzled. "Why is it worse? Surely not having someone roaming the streets with a sniper rifle is good news."

Craig shook his head. "Not necessarily. In a way Liam's right. A contract killer only does things for payment and at as big a distance as they can, hence Mitic using a rifle. But this guy did it up close so that means the killing was personal, either him or to someone that he's linked with."

Liam continued the thought. "And the fact that he was able to get our John Doe to the river means they probably knew each other, and... " He gestured at the body. "He trusted his killer." He winced. "This says rivalry to me, boss."

John wasn't going to be left out of the scenario building. His eyes gleamed as he spoke. "Funny you should say that."

"What?"

John waved him away. "I'll tell you in a minute. But how about this for a scenario... he injected his victim, put him the boot of his car and then drove him to the river and dumped him."

Craig decided to humour him; it was a way of rehearsing the arguments he would be having with himself later that night.

"OK, so how would that work? The victim's a big man and young, so he would have to have been heavily sedated for the other man to get him in the boot. So why would he have allowed his assailant close enough to inject him? And he obviously woke up again when they reached the river, enough to fight, so how did his killer get him into the drink?"

John scrambled for an answer and found one, hurling it back triumphantly. "He fought because the cold water woke him up."

Liam supported him, switching sides for a moment. "Or there were two attackers. They shoved him into the boot un-sedated, then took him out, walked him to the river, injected him there and then threw him in."

49

Craig thought about it for a moment. "So he was awake in the car boot?"

"Yes."

"Fine, then there'll be fibres or something else to say so."

Liam searched for a way to cover his ass just in case there weren't. "Not if they were washed away by the water."

Craig snorted. "If *you* were in a boot on your way to be killed wouldn't you be scratching hard at anything nearby trying to find a way out? The fibres will be wedged under his nails." He turned back to John. "Did you find any, John? Or any signs of restraint, tape, anything to say he'd been held awake anywhere before death?"

John made a face. "Possibly. But-"

"It's early days. Agreed." Craig hopped off his stool. "OK, all of these scenarios are possible and it's our job to work out which one fits." He turned for the door but both of the others waved him back. John got in first.

"I've got something else to show you." He enlisted their help in sitting their victim up. On the man's back were two small symbols. Craig lifted a magnifying class to look then raked his dark hair, puzzled.

"What are you thinking, John?"

"It's a small castle and the word 'Rock', but you already know that. If you mean what's their relevance..." He shrugged. "Search me. That's your bit. But they might help us with his I.D."

"Does he have others?"

"No. That's why these seem curious. What do you think, Liam? Could they be gang tattoos? It might fit with the hit theory."

Liam frowned. "They're nothing I've seen before, but nothing would surprise me about gangs. Some of the idiots would stamp their tribe on their forehead if they thought that it looked good. Anyway, the boss still hasn't explained why this feels like a hit."

Craig gave a twisted smile. "Drugged, pushed into a river with his hands stamped on, probably in the dead of night. It would be a hit in any book I read."

****

McMorrow's Bar. 5.30 p.m.

Tommy had been playing with his whisky tumbler for half-an-hour, turning it this way and that and now and again running his finger around the rim, to generate a high-pitched whine that he knew would get on the Republican's nerves. Micky Hanratty watched him with gritted teeth, feigning uncharacteristic tolerance. He really wanted to clock the wee bastard one on the jaw and would have done so the second time Tommy had played his tune, if it hadn't been that he really needed him for a job.

Finally the Dubliner had had enough and he reached for the whisky and re-filled Tommy's glass. At least it would change the song.

"Time to talk turkey, Mr Hill."

Tommy stopped rubbing and shot him a sceptical look. "And wat the fuck wud we huv to talk about? When I'm wan of God's own people and yeer lousy Fenian scum."

Hanratty felt his bile rise and with it his contempt for the man across the booth. Maybe what he'd heard was wrong and Tommy Hill wasn't the route to the Loyalists in Belfast. Maybe there was someone better and he should just have the wee scrote given a kicking and be done with Belfast's stench. Billy Ross read his mind and appeared beside the two men, his eyes seeking permission to sit down.

Micky Hanratty liked Ross, even though he was on the opposite side he had never played him false, so with a barely perceptible nod he signalled the barman to take a seat. Ross lost no time in shifting close to Tommy and hissing in his ear.

"Unless you're *very* fucking stupid, you'll do business with this man. He's got money to burn and he's trying to give it to you."

Tommy turned so sharply his nose was barely

51

inches from Ross' own. "Give me money? Fenian money? I'd rather die than work with the likes af him."

Ross' follow up was instant. "Not even if it meant hammering some Belfast Taigs? Thumping the other side, Tommy. Remember how that felt?"

The shine in the ex-paramilitary's eyes was immediate. It was followed by a shadow twice as dark.

"It's a trick and yer in on it, Ross. Yer betraying yer own fer Republican scum." Tommy made to stand and with his next movement Billy Ross took his life in his hands. He grabbed Hill's arm and dragged him back into his seat, ending the contact on the retired criminal's murderous glare.

"I'm not betraying anyone, Tommy. Mr Hanratty's religion isn't part of the game here and he doesn't give a flyin' fuck about anyone else's. This is business, pure and simple. Someone's killing his men up here and he knows there'll be more to come. This is war and he needs someone with Belfast street smarts to find out who's startin' it and help him sort them out."

He sat back and took a deep breath. He'd either just made a smart move or his dumbest ever; whether he was still alive tomorrow would tell. Tommy didn't move for a whole minute and even then he only shifted his eyes. They swivelled from one man to another and then back to his drink, fixing there for another minute before he spoke in a cold, dry croak.

"Yer tellin' me wan Fenian gang's killin' anuther?"

Ross nodded. "Looks like it."

Hill's face contorted into a sneer. "And why wud I give a shite about that? The more Taigs that kill each other the more food there is fer us."

Micky Hanratty retrieved his façade of tolerance from the murderous rage threatening to engulf it.

"I'll tell you why, Mr Hill. Because this bunch hate Loyalists, *really* hate you." He had no idea whether the interlopers hated them or not; he didn't know who they were, or whether they were even Catholics for that matter, as Ross had implied, but it served his purpose to have Tommy fired up, whatever motivated him.

"They're dealing drugs and trafficking girls to

work in brothels, neither of which I can abide. They're also encroaching on my other businesses, but the bit that really affects the north is that they're using the funds they steal from me to build dissident Republicanism here and bring in guns."

He prayed for forgiveness for the lie and promised himself he would halt things if it looked like people would get killed.

Tommy snorted scornfully. "And yer nat?"

"No, I'm not. Any money I make goes into my farm, horses and other property that I own near home; the rest is put away for my kids." Hanratty took a deep swig of his whisky and got ready to tell one of the biggest lies of his life. "I don't give a damn about a united Ireland, Tommy. As far as I'm concerned if the north wants to stay with the British then they're welcome to it. All I want is to stop these scumbags killing my men and wrecking my business interests up here."

Tommy's interest was piqued. "Why can't ye do it yerself?"

Hanratty shrugged. "I *could* bring men up from Dublin, but that would take them away from other business I have. Besides, they don't know the north like you and your men do, so there would be wasted time and mistakes and we need to move fast."

He sat back, expert enough in body language to sense a slight thaw. The last thing he wanted to do was blow it now by seeming too keen. It paid off. After another minute of thinking and sipping Tommy asked the question that Hanratty had been waiting an hour to hear.

"What wud ye want from me?"

The Dubliner smiled inwardly but his face remained poker straight. "Information. You have contacts all over Belfast. Get them to keep their ears to the ground. Anything they hear feed back to me immediately and my men can do the rest. Unless..." He paused, spotting the glint of battle in Tommy's eye. "Unless you want to do it yourself, of course?"

Hill's mouth turned dry from excitement.

Whacking dissidents who would never see them coming; it was the stuff of his dreams. He pulled himself up abruptly, remembering the granddaughter that he loved. He had to keep his nose clean for Ella's sake, so there was no way he could be linked with trouble in any way. Still, he knew plenty of men who would do it without a second's hesitation. His next question was asked in a matter-of-fact tone.

"So I get paid just fer passing ye information and linking ye up with men who'll dee yer dirty work?"

"You will. But as a matter of interest... why won't you be doing it yourself?"

Tommy bared his teeth in a snarl. "That's my business, nat yeers." He drained his glass and signalled for a refill and as Ross obliged the Loyalist asked the most important question of all.

"How much?"

Micky Hanratty's reply was a slip of paper drawn from his pocket on which he'd already written a sum. He slid it across the table and watched Tommy's face blanch as he read.

He dragged his eyes up from the note, astounded. "Fer killin' how many?"

Hanratty's hands flew up immediately. "Now hang on. Who said anything about killing? Work them over by all means, but..." His voice tailed off as the realisation of what Tommy really was hit him. When he restarted it was in a robust voice. "Let's be very clear..." He took a swig of whisky for courage. "...that money's *just* for information. For each man persuaded to back off it will be that again, until I'm satisfied that the problem has gone." He stared straight into Hill's eyes. "But no killing, Tommy. Understood?"

Billy Ross risked a smile. "Do you see now why I wanted you to stay, Tommy?"

If he'd been expecting gratitude he was wrong. Tommy's disappointment about the ban on capital punishment made his temper flare. He leapt up and shoved his face close to the barman's.

"Yeer still working for a Taig, Ross, and I won't forget ye grabbed my arm."

But it was bluff. Tommy had just found a way to bolster his non-existent pension and he'd no intention of spending his remaining years inside. Billy Ross was safe for now.

As he turned for the door the old lag added the words that Micky Hanratty wanted to hear.

"Monday. Back here."

Then he was gone, leaving the horse-breeder satisfied that he would get his information and planning that once he did Tommy Hill would pay for calling him names.

****

St Mary's Orthopaedic Hospital. Balmoral Avenue, Belfast.

Katy Stevens winced as the lithely built physiotherapist moved her left wrist expertly into place. Not so much because it hurt but because she thought that what was coming next would; electrical stimulation to help her wrist work normally again. Stimulation; it sounded like an intellectual workout, an interesting episode after which she should feel refreshed. And perhaps it would be if the neurons in question were located in her brain and she was at a pub quiz, but not when they lay inside her wrist. Her mind drifted back to her accident, except that it hadn't been an accident of course. More a collision between her and a stone wall, engineered by Marc's latest psychopath.

Marc. As the physio adjusted the electrodes she allowed herself to think about him for the first time that day. It brought mixed emotions. Love of course, that was always there, strong and unwavering since their very first date. She would die for him and very nearly had, so why wasn't she still with him and why was she punishing him for something that clearly wasn't his fault?

She defended herself against her own accusation immediately. She *wasn't* punishing him, well, not deliberately anyway. As a defence it failed. She loved

55

him and felt guilty about hurting him, so why couldn't she just answer his calls, tell him that she still loved him desperately and then everything could be as it had been before? A cheerful voice cut through her thoughts. English, no, not English, a New Zealander, she could hear the distinctive accent on the therapist's first word.

"Er you ready?"

She wasn't but there was no backing out unless she wanted to wear a wrist brace all her life. She gritted her teeth and waited for the buzz that heralded the anticipated pain. As a completely painless tingling ran through her arm and hand, she felt like a complete wimp. It wasn't sore at all. As usual her fear of something was far worse than the reality.

She'd never been good with strange things. It had taken her three cancelled appointments just to get there, each time backing out the day before. Only her mother's insistence on her staying at her house nearby, and her pursed lips and smiles of encouragement had finally got her there that day.

As the tingling continued Katy closed her eyes and tried to think of something new. It didn't work; she was soon back facing her own cowardice and realising that it wasn't just over the accident, but over far too many things in life.

She'd always been on the shy side, especially with strangers; only really relaxed and chatty when someone was already a friend. It had been the same when she was little; hiding behind her mother's skirt when visitors called and crying for the whole of her first week at primary school. Medicine had helped bring her out of herself, having to chat to hundreds of strangers each week has a way of doing that, and by the time she'd reached consultant level the hiding child and tearful schoolgirl appeared to have been relegated to the past. Except that they hadn't really. Only while she was wearing her white coat. The rest of the time that little girl was bubbling just beneath the surface, waiting to reappear when something scared her, which seemed to happen every day now.

She'd reappeared in every romance she'd ever had as well, making her love life a disaster. She'd been so terrified of rejection by a man she'd really liked that she'd run away and sought refuge in her books. Until Marc that was, and then she'd only stopped running because he'd very firmly made the moves.

She bit her lip as a sting signalled the stimulation's increase. After a moment she got used to it and returned to her thoughts again. She shook her head at the conversation inside her head, prompting an "Er you OK?" from the therapist.

"Fine, Josh. I was just thinking of something."

Trying not to think of it if would have been nearer the truth. And that truth was that she wasn't just shy, she was timid; far too many things in life frightened her. The dark, high winds, spiders, aggressive people, and most of all, making a mistake in a patient's care. The list was endless. Yet she knew that she would take a bullet to protect someone that she loved and she protested at the injustices in the world, joining Marc's sister Lucia on her many marches. It was a confusing mix, but then wasn't everyone? Perhaps that was why she loved Marc so much; he was fearless and let nothing get in his way, while she was so busy apologising for breathing that it was a wonder that she ever got anything done. The voice broke through again.

"Last level, Keydy. Brace yerself."

She did and again it wasn't as bad as she'd feared so she settled down for the final stretch, returning to her thoughts.

The media didn't help of course; substituting the oppression of one female stereotype for another at random intervals and making any woman who didn't fit them feel that they were wrong. Today's fearless, kick-ass, warrior princess model was as big a tyranny as the nineteen-fifties' perfect, passive housewife had been, both guaranteed to make any woman who didn't fit the mould feel inadequate. She blushed as she realised she was naturally closer to the second than the first in many ways, but the truth was that she *was* scared of a lot of things in life, and that was really why she had pushed the man she loved away.

She didn't blame Marc for what some murderer had done to her, his life was spent putting such people in prison, but the fact was that if one killer had targeted her to get at him then another could do the same in the future and they might actually kill her the next time, or even worse kill him, and she could never bear that.

As the session ended and she said thank you, she realised that she had a decision to make. Life with Marc and all those risks and fears, or life alone, living in a safe but loveless world.

****

The Lab. 6 p.m.

Five floors up from John Winter's domain Doctor Des Marsham was busy working in his. It was a much noisier floor, with the sound of machines whirring, and pinging when their results were ready, combined with chattering white-suited figures wandering around in a sterile clean room. It reminded Liam of a dream scene in the movies, the ones where someone has been abducted by aliens and is about to lose their bits.

Amidst the slightly surreal scene and sound track stood the far less other-worldly Des. The two detectives laughed when they saw him; since they'd last seen him, just before Christmas, his beard hadn't only grown down but out. What had been firmly confined to his chin before had now joined with mutton chop side-burns. With their mix of red and grey and the extra pounds that he'd put on over the festive season, the scientist looked like Santa Claus crossed with a portly Henry the Eighth. Liam couldn't allow it to pass.

"Does Annie know she's for the axe then?"

Des' wife Annie was tolerant to the nth degree, except on the subject of his beard which she very vocally loathed.

Des raised his eyes from the fuming cabinet he'd been peering into. "What?"

"Divorced, beheaded, died. Divorced, beheaded, survived. The six wives of Henry the Eighth, your doppelganger. As far as I remember the first Anne lost her head."

As Des got the joke and objected noisily Craig and John found chairs and sat down. The forensic expert stroked his beard possessively.

"You'd better be comparing me to him because of my beard and nothing else."

Liam said nothing, just stared at Des' paunch and then down at his greatly diminished own. Before the scientist could object again Craig outlined the reasons that they were there.

"You've got two of our cases, Des, so we'd just like a quick catch up." He waited until the others were seated before continuing. "Number one; the slurry death. Was the hole in the suit made deliberately, and could it have caused his death?"

Des turned his chair so that his back was to Liam and answered in three words. "No and no."

Craig leaned forward. "The hole was wear and tear? But wouldn't it have allowed gas in anyway?"

"It was definitely wear and tear, and even if it had allowed gas to access it shouldn't have made a blind bit of difference. He had an air tank."

Liam had been right. Craig was puzzled.

"But he definitely died from the fumes. John said so. And if he had air-"

Des shook his head. "I didn't say he had *air*, I said he had an air tank. But he would have had air if its valve hadn't been wrecked."

Craig's eyes widened. "Wrecked how? Are you suggesting-"

Des shrugged. "I'm not suggesting anything, I'm telling you."

It was unusually brusque for Des and Craig knew Liam's wisecracks had got to him. He'd deal with him later.

The Head of Forensics continued. "Your farmer was wearing all the right gear and the air tank was three quarters full, so he should have been fine. But

59

something had blocked the valve so that instead of air travelling from the tank to his mouth his expired oxygen wasn't being replaced."

Liam cut in. "But wouldn't his mask have stopped the slurry fumes getting in? Surely without air the worst that would have happened is he'd have passed out?"

Des addressed his answer to Craig. "He'd have needed a perfect seal and it had been cut, letting poisonous slurry gas in. It was all over for your man in seconds."

Craig stood up. "Can you show us?"

Des led the way next door. There was no arguing with the facts; the tank's valve was blocked and the seal had been cut away.

"Deliberate?"

"Definitely. The valve's been filled with rubber cement and you can see what they did to the seal. Someone wanted your farmer dead."

Craig gestured at the apparatus. "Can you get anything off it?"

Des' face was deadpan but he didn't say no. It was a good sign. "I'll let you know."

Craig crossed his fingers and moved on. "Thanks. OK. The drowning. Anything on that?"

"The body was printed and swabbed and I've sent the prints over to Ash for I.D."

"I didn't mean his I.D. particularly, although that's great. I really meant any fibres or hairs. We know it was murder so anything that might have belonged to his assailant would be great."

"I was just getting to that. If you'd give me a second."

Craig shot Liam a look that said he was going to pay big time for putting the scientist in such a huff.

"There were traces of fibres beneath the victim's nails, and no, I don't know what they are yet but they could be carpet."

"Car boot carpet?"

"Possibly. There was also a trace substance on one wrist. Some sort of adhesive. You're lucky there's still that much after days in the water."

Craig nodded his thanks and turned to leave. Des'
next words caught him by surprise.

"Don't you want to know what I found in his
pocket?"

Craig stopped in his tracks, thinking it was too
good to be true. "His name?"

It elicited Des' first laugh of their visit. "Now, that
would be too easy." He reached behind him and lifted a
clear plastic bag, holding it up in front of Craig. Inside
was a pale yellow sheet of paper covered with lines of
numbers and words.

"It's still drying out. When it has I'll get a copy to
Ash and you can try to make sense of it."

"Great." He stared at Liam who was still peering at
the sheet. "I think Liam has something to say to you
before we go." He gave the D.C.I.'s arm a shove. "Don't
you, Liam."

Liam gave his boss a jaundiced look, then he
composed his face in a mask of fake contrition and
turned to face the forensic lead.

"I'd like to say sorry, Des. You don't look like
Henry the Eighth at all." No-one noticed him edging
towards the exit as he spoke but his next words told
them why he had. "More like Santa with a bad dye job."
Then he was out the door and down the stairs, leaving
Craig with nothing he could do but roll his eyes.

****

The C.C.U. 6.50 p.m.

It was almost seven when they arrived back at
Docklands, but any hope that Craig might have had of
Jake having left for the day died as soon as they
stepped onto the tenth floor. Nicky had taken his late
briefing comment literally and asked everyone to stay
on. Hope was revived again as a plan developed in
Craig's head: do a quick update, give them all tons of
work and then slip into his office for an 'urgent'
discussion that only he and Liam were privy to. When

he didn't reappear after ten minutes both Jake and Ash would leave and he could defer their meetings for another day. He was halfway through updating them on the farm death when Rhonda innocently derailed it all.

She raised a finger politely; just as Craig had said that he and Liam were travelling to Armagh the next morning, and in the spirit of rewarding her efforts on the voice course, he paused and nodded her on to speak.

"Nicky said someone from the P.P.S. was here earlier, sir. Was that to do with the Foster case?"

Her speech was audible now but her volume control still needed fine tuning, with the beginnings and ends of phrases loud and the words in between still low. Craig wished fervently that 'Foster' had been buried in the middle.

At the mention of his ex-lover's name Jake jerked upright in his seat and Craig knew that there was no way now to avoid the truth. But if he couldn't avoid it he could finesse it, so he answered equivocally, trying to downplay Martin Grant's sojourn.

"That wasn't the main reason."

Strictly speaking it wasn't a lie. Of their thirty minute conversation Aaron Foster had only taken up ten.

"We were discussing the Miskimmon case."

She opened her mouth to speak again but he moved on quickly, pointedly avoiding Jake's gaze.

"OK, so Des believes that the air source for Colin McAllister's slurry suit was sabotaged deliberately-"

Anything that involved a gadget or widget excited Ash so he cut in.

"How'd they do it? Was it a fake valve, a dud filter or an empty tank?"

Craig smiled at his need for detail. "None of those. The valve should have been working but someone had filled it with rubber cement. It just didn't open. Plus they cut the seal on his mask."

The analyst's eyes widened. "That's like something from a mob movie."

He wasn't wrong and it sat uncomfortably with Craig's feeling that both deaths that day could have been hits. He nodded and carried on.

"Ash has just echoed my feelings about our killings. Both cases were deliberate, seemingly planned and organised, so that begs the question; what had either man done for someone to want them dead? Let's focus on our dairy farmer first. Colin McAllister." He sat back, adding. "Ideas, anyone?"

They ranged from the ridiculous, "the cows were getting their own back", to Andy's very possible in the Wild West but unlikely in Armagh "he was a cattle rustler", via the more feasible but yet to be proved "maybe cows weren't the only things he was farming" from Liam, and "so maybe he was growing cannabis?" from Jake.

Craig turned to his sergeant, furrowing his brow. "Follow that thought through for me, Jake."

Jake was surprised. He'd thrown the comment out there just to contribute, without actually considering that it would ever be taken seriously. He scrambled for something to say, growing more confident as his words emerged.

"OK, let's say our man wasn't the simple dairy farmer he portrayed and maybe even his family thought he was, but he had a side line that wasn't so legal." He paused, thinking, before starting again. "How about if his farm was losing money... we've all seen the protests from dairy farmers lately, about how much they're losing on the low prices they're getting for milk. So...McAllister was losing money and needed an income from something else to stop him going down."

Liam raised a finger to interrupt and Jake nodded him on, grateful for the respite. He'd been running on fumes.

"As you know, my family have farms."

There was a muttered "farm boy" from Ash.

Liam gave a regal sniff. "Rude and all as he is, Kermit's right. I *am* a farm boy, and proud of it." He paused, staring pointedly at the analyst's green hair before carrying on. "My brothers and uncles mostly have dairy farms and they've all been getting hammered by the low milk prices so they've turned some of their fields to crops this year to help make up the loss, and rented out barn space to local artists. So what if McAllister decided to use his barns to grow weed, or maybe even to make something worse? Crystal Meth maybe? He wouldn't be the first."

Ash chuckled. "Breaking Bad comes to Armagh. How will the local elders cope?"

The image of vicars passing out from shame made everyone smile.

Craig nodded tentatively.

"OK... so let's say McAllister *was* up to something hooky, whatever it was, and someone took exception to it and bumped him off. Who are we looking at?"

Annette chipped in. "A rival drug dealer? Someone who didn't like competition for their customers."

"OK. Or?"

Andy had been doodling quietly on his notepad and although Craig was too far away to see what he'd written he could hazard a guess; the doodles would be declaring his love for Rhonda in nauseatingly saccharin terms. Ever since their pre-Christmas night of passion, which the no-nonsense Ozzie had dismissed as 'only sex', the D.C.I. had been nursing a determination to change her mind. So everyone was surprised when the lethargic Lothario suddenly joined the debate.

"Maybe some local worthy or vigilante decided to show their disgust."

Liam nodded at the suggestion.

"You're saying that some anti-drugs boyos took McAllister out."

"Why not? There're plenty of groups in city estates who take the law into their own hands: anti-paedophile groups, anti-drugs groups. So why not in the country?"

Why not indeed? Craig wasn't convinced but he couldn't find a good reason to dismiss the idea.

"OK, good. So we know that McAllister was murdered and it may have been because of something he was up to. Maybe drugs and killed by a rival dealer or a vigilante, or maybe not. What else could have got him killed?"

The next suggestion came in a female voice. "Maybe his wife killed him because he was annoying her."

Craig turned to find Nicky smiling.

"You may joke, Nicky, but it's not that far-fetched. Four percent of men are killed by their partners, although 'because he was annoying her' might be a *bit* of a weak excuse."

She snorted. "You've never been married, sir. I'm just surprised more people don't do it."

He didn't argue the point. "OK, so maybe a domestic murder. McAllister's wife or someone on the farm on her behalf; they would have had easy access to the air tank. Maybe the motive was an affair, jealousy-"

He was stopped in his tracks by Annette's widening eyes and a warning glance at Jake. He rushed to cover his faux pas.

"But whatever the motive: rival, vigilante or domestic, the evidence we're looking for lies with that farm and its staff. Liam and I will take a first look tomorrow and get uniforms down if we need them-"

Liam shook his head, interrupting. "They'll have hidden anything there is to see by tomorrow, boss."

Craig sighed, knowing that they were looking at a late night. "You're right. We need to get down there now. OK, Liam and I will take the farm tonight. Annette, you lead on the interviews in the morning. Jake and Rhonda can help you out. Bring in the wife first thing and make sure she I.D.s the body. Talk to the farm manager, anyone else regular-"

Annette chipped in. "Labourers, visiting suppliers. It's quite a list, sir. We'll need more help."

"Get some uniforms from Stranmillis and ask Jack if he can help out as well. Use his interview rooms at High Street."

Jack Harris was the desk sergeant at High Street Station, their first port of call for interview rooms and locking up anybody who needed locked up.

She nodded. "OK. The wife's at her sister's in Belfast, apparently."

"Good."

Craig paused for a moment to let anyone else who wanted to pitch in do so, but no-one said a word, no doubt subdued by the thought of the work lying ahead.

"Right, that leads us onto our second case. Liam."

Liam gulped a mouthful of tea and spluttered as it went down the wrong way. After a series of coughs and an unnecessarily enthusiastic slap on the back from Andy which earned him a glare, the D.C.I. carried on.

"OK, as you know, a body was found against the Lagan Weir. Floater."

Annette made a face at the word but he ignored her.

"Young guy, probably in the water between one and two days. Long story short, he had injuries on his hands that said he'd been helped into the water and prevented getting out. There was an injection mark on his neck so we're waiting for the tox-screen and Des is checking out his prints and anything else forensic he can find. Ash, he'll be contacting you about all that. He had adhesive on one wrist and fibres under his nails, so that would fit with being bound in a car boot and transported to the water. Whether it was by one man or two is anyone's guess. That's all to come, but we do know he's dead and he definitely didn't get dead by himself."

He paused for questions. Rhonda's hand was first up. Craig smiled.

"You don't need to put your hand up, Rhonda. It's not school, no matter how bossy Liam is."

Liam gave him a mock offended look and waved her on.

"Where do you think he entered the river, sir?"

"Forensics are doing their thing with algae analysis and..." He turned to Ash. "Des will be onto you about river currents and what not, so we should know in the next day or so."

"He's already sent me some stuff."

Rhonda asked another question. "So he wasn't

shot or stabbed?"

"Nope. He was still alive when he entered the water and we're pretty sure he tried to get out and they stopped him. His hands had been stamped on so hard they broke the bones."

Nicky gasped, a lone normal reaction in a sea of emotionally numbed psyches.

Craig nodded. "Whoever did this isn't a nice man." He looked around. "Any more questions? No? OK then. Andy, I want you to head this case up for tomorrow and report anything to Liam and me."

Andy gawped at him. "On my own?"

Liam didn't miss the opening. "Will you be lonely, diddums?"

The words were said in a babyish voice and with a glance at Rhonda that earned him a hard dig on the arm. That and the backslap were the most energetic Andy had been all day.

"What was that dig for?"

"Like you don't know."

Craig intervened before they embarrassed themselves even further.

"In response to your question, Andy; no, you won't be alone. Enlist some uniforms to help you and don't forget that we have a new inspector starting tomorrow, seconded from Intelligence. Kyle Spence. He can help you on the drowning case."

Craig had been to university with Spence and they'd even shared digs at one point, until Spence's untidiness and smoking had finally made him call it a day. He liked the inspector, but knew that his reluctance to leave his secretive and sedentary life in Police Intelligence would make him a challenge to motivate.

He saw Jake leaning forward to ask when they could meet and stood up, deciding to deal with both his and Ash's meetings at once.

"Jake, Ash, I'm sorry we didn't get to meet today. We'll do it tomorrow. Nicky, find some time in my diary, please. Once you've seen how things are progressing with the investigations." He turned towards the exit. "Annette, check if McAllister's wife has I.D.ed his body yet and then phone it through to Liam." He cast a final look around before nodding. "You all know what you're doing tomorrow and Liam and I will be contactable on our phones." He started walking. "Liam, you and I have a farm to visit."

It was Liam's cue to thump Andy on the back before making a swift escape to the lift.

****

McAllisters' Farm. County Armagh. 8.30 p.m.

Although it was dark when the detectives arrived at the dairy farm they could still tell that it was sprawling. Four hundred acres of prime countryside, with cows, crops and healthy looking fallow fields as far as the eye could see. As they drove up the long driveway off the Darkley Road, an enormous brick and flint farmhouse with an orchard on one side came into view. On the other side of the house was a small playground, with two swings, a carousel and a long slide. It all pointed to a prosperous young family that seemed to have little need for extra income, although, as Liam had pointed out in a cynical tone.

"Maybe the playground was built on the proceeds of Daddy's secret crop."

Craig didn't respond, instead pulling his Audi to a halt in front of the double fronted house and climbing out to scan the fields and outhouses in the dusk, his eyes searching for incongruous lights. Liam caught on instantly.

"You're looking for signs of weed growing."

The conditions needed for cannabis to flourish included a constant source of light to mimic the sun. But there was nothing to be seen.

Craig shrugged. "Just because we can't see anything doesn't mean it's not there. He could be growing it miles from the house." He turned to face the building. "Where did Annette say the wife was?"

"Staying with her sister for a few days."

Just then a slim but muscular man of around thirty strode towards them, his direction of travel saying that he'd been at the back of the house. He extended a thick, tanned arm, exposed by his rolled-up shirt sleeve even though it was barely two degrees.

"Mitchell Purvis. I'm the farm manager. Your secretary called to say you were coming down."

As Craig shook hands he noted the strength of Purvis' grip. It spoke of health and energy, and the capacity to do a serious amount of damage. Interestingly the manager's cheerful demeanour didn't seem forced, although he did seem slightly too cheerful for someone whose boss had just died.

"Thank you for meeting us, Mr Purvis. Has there been any contact from Mrs McAllister at all?"

Purvis shook his dark blond head, his tanned face unperturbed. "Mara's often away for a few days without contact. She was a city girl before she married so sometimes she needs time away from the farm."

Liam waved a hand at the playground. "Did she take the kids with her?"

The farmer nodded. "Kid. Ben's six. She always takes him, to see the museums and such like. She wants him to experience the finer side of life." He grinned. "Doesn't want him growing up wearing wellies."

Craig was staring at the house and frowning. "So Mrs McAllister and her son go away for days and never check in at all? Wouldn't she have called her husband?"

"Aye. On his mobile. But if she didn't catch him she wouldn't worry, unless she didn't hear for a fair few days. It's a busy farm."

He wasn't appeased. "We heard she might be staying with her sister. Have you any idea of her address?"

Purvis shook his head vigorously. "She won't be with her sister. She'll be in some fancy hotel or another, that's what she usually does."

It seemed strange behaviour for someone newly bereaved.

Purvis continued. "They've been gone since Monday. I don't know which hotel. I've been trying to find her to tell her about Col-"

Craig gawped at him. "She doesn't know that he's dead?"

"Not unless someone else told her."

Craig signalled Liam to check while he asked another question. "Where is Mr McAllister's phone now?"

Purvis turned towards the house, removing a key from his pocket.

"You have access to the house?"

The McAllisters must have been a relaxed couple. He wouldn't fancy someone being able to enter his home whenever they liked.

"Only part of it." Purvis unlocked the wide front door. "When you get inside you'll see what I mean."

As the door swung in, admitting them to a large black and white tiled hallway, Craig was surprised to see there were no stairs to the upper floor. Instead the manager turned right towards a door that opened into a large kitchen/dining room, with a cosy corner of settees and a television that boasted a sixty inch screen.

Liam hung up his phone and shook his head. Mara McAllister didn't know that her husband was dead, unless she had killed him that was.

The D.C.I. thumped down onto the plump settee, explaining to Craig where they were.

"This part of the house will be for the farm staff. They'll come in here for meals and relaxation." He gestured at the screen. "I bet it's lively enough here whenever there's a match."

Purvis shook his head. "Horse racing more like. We're not much for the football up this way."

As Craig scanned the room, still trying to work out the house's geography, Purvis opened a drawer and extracted an old mobile phone. He handed it to Craig and then filled the kettle.

"Coffee all right?"

It was Liam who answered. "Grand. As long as

there's something with it to stop it being too wet."

A home-baked cake was removed from the fridge along with a jug of milk and they were soon seated around a long dining table with their drinks. Craig interrupted Liam's chomping with an observation.

"OK, so the family have the rest of the house, which I'm assuming they access through another door."

Purvis nodded and wiped some crumbs from his mouth. "It's at the orchard side. I don't have keys."

"Where would Mr McAllister have left his keys when he changed into the slurry suit? Only the suit and the clothes he wore underneath were found."

Purvis' eyes widened. "I'd never thought about it, but they must be in the changing stall." He waved towards the door. "It's near the milking parlour."

"OK, we'll look in a minute." Craig sipped his coffee. "OK, so...if the phone you've just given me is Mr McAllister's mobile, why didn't he have it on him?"

Purvis laughed; it obviously wasn't the first time someone had asked the question.

"Col wouldn't carry the flipping thing. He hated technology. It drove Mara mad; she's the complete opposite. She was always moaning that she couldn't get hold of him when he was out on the land."

Craig's eyes narrowed. Not at the words but at the way Purvis' eyes lit up when he mentioned Mara McAllister; he hadn't noticed it before. And he was still far too cheerful, considering they'd just had a nasty death.

"OK, so is that why she doesn't worry if she can't get hold of him when she's away?"

"Aye. She used to panic when she couldn't at first, but now she just knows that it's Col."

Except this time it hadn't just been because of Colin McAllister's dislike of technology. Craig switched on the small mobile as Liam reached for another slice of cake and then thought better of it; Danni liked his newly flattish stomach so he was trying to be good.

As the phone beeped on 'Old Macdonald's Farm' blared across the room. Purvis gestured at the old fashioned handset.

"That'll be Ben's doing. Six years old and he's better with technology than his dad."

Craig didn't comment; he was too busy reading the screen. Three answerphone messages and a host of texts. As he worked his way through them Liam asked for more detail on the farm.

"So how many acres all told?"

"Four-fifty. Half dairy grazing and the rest crops."

Liam whistled. His knowledge of land values told him the McAllisters weren't short of a bob or two.

"What did the wife do before she married?"

Purvis raised an eyebrow at the assumption that Mara McAllister would have given up work. "She still does it. In fact I'm surprised that you boys don't recognise her name."

Craig glanced up from his scrolling, curious.

Purvis smiled proudly. "She's a criminal QC. Works with Cullons in town."

The detectives' hearts sank. Their wariness of lawyers wasn't as strong as it had once been; Judge Standish and Katy's friend Nicola O'Hara were to thank for that, but they'd still rather one wasn't involved in their cases and definitely not as a victim's spouse. Craig made a mental note to cover their asses on everything, then he deliberately made a double-edged comment and watched carefully for Purvis' response.

"You admire Mrs McAllister a lot, don't you?"

The farm manager had the good grace to blush. He recovered quickly.

"I think she's a very clever woman."

And the rest. Craig underlined 'affair' as a possible motive and tapped on the phone in his hand, setting it to speakerphone as the voice messages played. The first two were business: queries about the delivery of a new bull and some animal feed. The third was more interesting. A man's voice saying "call me" before cutting out.

"Any idea whose voice that is, Mr Purvis?"

Purvis' face looked genuinely blank. He gestured

Craig to play it again, the second time shedding no more light.

"Not a clue. But he doesn't sound happy, does he?"

Craig didn't reply, instead turning to the texts. They were dated the twenty-second to that day, and again seemed mostly to do with work. He turned the phone towards Purvis and motioned him to explain.

"First text's from the saddle makers in Keady, just letting Col know the new saddle for Ben's pony was ready-"

Liam cut in. "I didn't see any ponies."

"Aye, well, you wouldn't from here. They're in the back field miles away. Mara's horse as well. She's a great rider." He turned back to the phone quickly, in case they made anything of the comment.

"The next two texts are from the travel agents. Mara and Ben are off to Italy in two weeks, ski-ing." As the final message appeared he frowned, reading it completely and then scrolling back to read it again. Craig sensed something wasn't right.

"Who is it from, Mr Purvis?"

Purvis kept shaking his head. "It can't be. She wouldn't do it."

Liam lifted the phone and read aloud.

"'If you don't meet me. Robsons will be in touch. I've tried.' It was sent yesterday at nine a.m."

Craig was insistent. "Tell me whose mobile number that is, Mr Purvis. I can ring them, so there's no point in you lying."

Purvis' eyes were wide. "It's Mara's. But this can't be right."

"What can't? Who are Robsons?"

He was about to find out himself when Purvis finally replied.

"They're solicitors in Armagh."

"So what? Mrs McAllister is a lawyer. You said so."

Purvis' expression lay somewhere between shock and a smile. When he answered he sounded surprised. "They're divorce solicitors. It's the only work that they do."

Liam was surprised as well. Not that the

73

McAllisters might have been considering divorce, but that there was enough divorce work in County Armagh to keep a firm employed full time. The countryside had got a lot friskier since he'd been a boy.

Craig seized his chance. "Afraid that you'll be named, Mr Purvis?" Before Purvis could answer or Liam could express his shock, he hadn't noticed Purvis' earlier blush, occupied as he'd been with the cake, Craig added. "After all, you and Mrs Purvis *were* having an affair, weren't you?"

What followed was a whole love story played out in the expressions on the farm manager's face. Thirty seconds was all it took for Mitchell Purvis to portray his love, attraction and subsequent rejection. The next stage would be grief because Purvis knew that whatever had made Mara McAllister decide to leave her husband it hadn't been him. If the text and her absence weren't just a convenient alibi for murder that was, and that was something they would soon find out.

Craig raised a hand to stop him answering. "Don't bother, Mr Purvis. It's clear that whatever happened between you and Mrs McAllister was over at her behest. But that mightn't have stopped you hoping that if her husband was out of the way you could have stood a second chance. That's motive and it makes you a suspect in her husband's murder." He stood up. "You're coming back to Belfast with us."

He would summon the local uniforms to seal off the farm and house, in preparation for the next day's search, and once they were back in Belfast he would phone Mara McAllister's mobile. If she really had no idea that her husband was dead he needed to see her before she found out from John or Annette, and if she did know then he needed to watch her face when she realised they knew of her affair and suspected her of being involved in his death.

****

High Street Station, Belfast. 11 p.m.

While Liam booked Mitchell Purvis in for his overnight stay at High Street, Craig was in the station's staff room speaking to their murder victim's wife. All he asked the QC was where she was staying, informing her he needed to see her that night but not outlining why. As they spoke he listened carefully to Mara McAllister's tone of voice and recorded every word that she said. It was for his information and not the courts, she hadn't been cautioned, but he could get Liam's opinion on the conversation, so that by the time they entered the luxurious surroundings of Belfast's five star Merchant Hotel they would be on the same page.

Liam nodded sagely as he listened to the recording, waiting until Craig had knocked it off before he spoke.

"She didn't even ask why we wanted to see her."

Craig slumped back in his chair, raking his dark hair. "OK. So why not? If a police officer contacted me at nearly midnight, I would think the worst."

"You'd think someone was dead."

"Yep."

"And I'm assuming you told her you were a detective?"

"I said I was a detective from Belfast, but I didn't mention the Murder Squad. I didn't want to tip her off."

Liam continued. "OK, but the late hour still likely means bad news. And if someone *is* dead a detective coming has to mean it's a suspicious death, otherwise uniform would've called. She'd know all that being a QC."

"Yes again. Unless..." Craig frowned. Something didn't feel right. Mara McAllister had sounded neither anxious nor guilty. "Maybe she thinks we're working on a case she's involved in. She *is* a criminal lawyer."

Liam thought for a moment and then shook his head. "Nope. You specifically said we were from Belfast and she works in Armagh. She can't think it's one of hers."

It was a good point. Craig was about to make another suggestion when Liam shook his head again.

"And we couldn't be anything to do with her divorce. That's a civil matter, again in Armagh."

He was right on both counts. So why hadn't she been surprised to hear from them. There was only one way to find out. Ten minutes later they were in The Merchant Hotel's reception, waiting for the widow to appear. When she did Craig sighed inwardly at the sight of an older, suited man by her side. She'd brought a lawyer. Mara McAllister nodded the detectives through to the back room of the cocktail bar, specially opened at the manager's request.

"We won't be disturbed in here, gentlemen." She took a seat, nodding at the man by her side. "This is Johnny Corbett, my family's solicitor."

Craig was busy taking in everything about her so Liam asked the question that he knew his boss would ask. "When you say your family, Mrs McAllister, do you mean the McAllister family solicitor?"

She shook her head. "I mean *my* family; the Kennedys. Before my marriage I was Mara Kennedy."

Kennedy. The name made Liam sit bolt upright. The Kennedys were the wealthiest family in Northern Ireland. If he'd thought Colin McAllister was rich with his big farm, the Kennedys knocked his wealth into the ha'penny place. Craig wasn't impressed by her money but he would admit, although only to himself, to being impressed by what he saw.

Mara Kennedy had the sleek sensuality of a cat paired with an ice-blonde beauty he'd seen more frequently in Scandinavia. With her obvious intelligence it made for a potent mix. It explained why Mitchell Purvis was under her spell, although from where he was sitting the farm manager wouldn't have stood a hope in hell.

But this wasn't a speed-dating event and his heart belonged to someone else so, as Liam appeared to have been struck dumb suddenly, Craig decided that it was time for him to speak.

"May I ask you something, Mrs McAllister?"

She turned and smiled at him, a slow, playful smile that threatened to disconcert him again. He didn't let it. "It depends what it is, Mr...?"

"Superintendent Craig." It made her glance at her solicitor askance and confused Craig even more. He forged on anyway. "Where is your son? We understood that you'd brought him to town for a few days."

She frowned slightly, wrinkling her perfectly smooth brow. "He's upstairs with my sister. Why?"

"Just wondering." Craig stopped abruptly, his intended next question disappearing and a different one forming in his place. "Why do you think we're here, Mrs McAllister?"

He was playing a hunch. Her reaction to his rank had said she hadn't thought their visit was due to something serious enough to warrant a senior officer, but the presence of her companion said it *was* something that she'd thought might implicate her. If she'd murdered her husband she would have anticipated both points instead of just one. After a confused glance at Corbett she began speaking hesitantly.

"Because of Colin's..." She stopped, only restarting on her lawyer's supportive nod. "Colin's business dealings."

Liam had recovered from his awe and he slipped in a question. "You mean the farm?"

It resulted in more confusion and a whispered aside with her brief. Eventually she answered with "Not the farm. No."

Liam nodded and sat back. It was a gesture that told Craig to 'have at it' in the shorthand that they'd developed over the years.

"What other business is your husband involved in, Mrs McAllister?"

"Kennedy. Please. We're divorcing."

He didn't pretend surprise, instead expanding the original question. "And is that business the reason for your divorce, or is that because of your affair with Mitchell Purvis?"

She looked shocked and angry all at once. Behind

the emotions he glimpsed vulnerability and immediately steeled himself against it; female vulnerability had tripped him up too many times through the years.

"How did you-?"

At least she wasn't going to deny it. When her next move was to shake her head Craig thought that he might have been wrong.

"Mitchell was a mistake."

Ouch. But not a denial.

"And your husband's business?"

The shake changed to a nod. "That's why I'm divorcing him."

"Please elaborate."

She gripped the edge of her chair, her cool façade melting. "I don't know the details, but I'm sure Colin is involved in something illegal."

Interesting.

"What makes you think that?"

"I found money in our kitchen, money that has nothing to do with the farm. Wads of cash. At least fifty thousand. I stopped counting after that."

"When did you find it?"

"A week ago." Tears filled her pale green eyes, making her resemble a cat even more. She shook her head desperately, as if it would make everything go away. "At first I thought he just hadn't banked it. Colin's terrible with money, and anything technical. Then I realised there was no way the farm was making all that money legitimately."

They were entering dangerous territory where Mara Kennedy could incriminate herself. He needed to caution her, so he did. She nodded as if she'd expected as much, but it didn't stop her talking.

"As soon as I realised I consulted Johnny."

"Did you confront Mr McAllister?"

Her headshake was instant. "Johnny said not to. I planned to go back and do it. I just wanted to get Ben out of there first."

Liam decided to take the heat out of the situation. He leaned forward, asking a question to which he already knew the answer. "What age is your boy? I've a five and three-year-old myself."

She gave a watery smile. "Six. He adores Colin. And the farm."

Craig took Liam's hint, realising that he'd been pressing too hard. He sat back, feeling bad that she might not know that her husband was dead. But only *might*, because he'd seen great liars before. When he restarted his voice was softer.

"What exactly did Mr Corbett advise you to do, Ms Kennedy?"

"Remove Ben as soon as it was feasible."

"Which was when?"

"Monday. Once we were settled Johnny said to speak to the police. I'm just surprised that you came so quickly."

Craig sat forward urgently. "Are you saying that you contacted the police?"

It would be easily checked.

She nodded. "This afternoon. I spoke to an Inspector Dawson in the Fraud Unit."

Liam almost burst out laughing, stopping himself just in time. Dozy Dawson. She'd have been waiting all year for him to come. Craig knew that it was time to break the news. He leaned further forward, closing the distance between them.

"I'm sorry, Ms Kennedy, but we're not from the Fraud Unit."

It was the solicitor who spoke first. "Well, who are you then?"

Craig kept his eyes firmly on the widow. "We're from the Belfast Murder Squad. We're here investigating a man's death."

The scream came immediately, so immediately that it drowned out Craig's final word. He watched as Mara Kennedy's eyes grew red and then wild and then as she rose and grabbed for the brass handle of the door. He wasn't sure what to do; let her go and follow her, or stop her before she did. As they had no evidence to charge her he opted for the former and the three men raced through the hotel reception after her,

79

watching as she eventually came to a halt at the lift. She pressed repeatedly on its buttons until she saw them approach, then she covered her ears like a small child, sobbing as she shouted out her words.

"Please don't tell me. Please, please. Someone's killed him. Someone's killed Colin, haven't they? That's why you're here, isn't it...*that's* why you're here."

She didn't leave space for any of them to answer, not even her elderly solicitor, bringing up the rear. As the lift doors opened Craig stepped forward blocking her way and took her hands gently in his own.

"Come back and talk to us, Ms Kennedy. Please. You can't go to see your son like this; you'll frighten him."

He coaxed her back towards the cocktail bar, ignoring the curious looks of diners and drinkers as the group processed. When she was firmly back in her seat Craig started again, much more gently this time.

"A man, whom we believe to be your husband, was killed-" She ripped her hands from his and turned to the solicitor like a small child.

"Make him stop, Johnny. Make him stop."

Johnny Corbett cradled her head against his chest and nodded Craig to go on.

"He was working in the slurry pit at the farm and unfortunately-"

She sat bolt upright, shaking her head frantically. "NO! No... Colin never took risks. He wouldn't have. He was careful."

Craig continued slowly. "We have reason to believe his air supply was tampered with."

The solicitor whispered the word before Craig said it. "Murder. You said you were from the murder squad."

The detective continued as if he hadn't spoken. "We need a positive identification-"

It was too much for her and she started to scream again, this time at length, until Craig finally had to admit defeat. The solicitor helped her to her feet and nodded at the two men.

"Tomorrow morning all right? I need to call her

brother. He's a doctor."

"Fine." Craig handed over his card. "Call me in the morning."

The policemen watched as the broken woman and her old family friend left and then they ordered a very stiff drink.

Chapter Five

The Merchant Hotel, Belfast. Friday, 29th January. 8 a.m.

By the time Annette arrived to take Mara McAllister to view her husband's body, Liam had already taken the widow to complete the brutal duty and returned her to her hotel room. The inspector went to call Craig, confused, only to suddenly notice an unread text. 'Contact me before you go to collect Mrs McAllister'. Too flipping late, sir.

She was just about to call him and complain about his tardy transfer of information when she checked the message's time. Twelve-thirty the night before! She'd slept right through its delivery and failed to even spot it that morning when she'd unplugged her phone! Mike was right; she *was* very sleepy these days.

Mike was Mike Augustus, a pathologist who worked with John Winter. He'd been Annette's partner since she'd divorced Pete, her husband of twenty years, for abuse.

She'd hardly slept at all from the fifth month of pregnancy with her first two children, now teenagers, and she wondered if her current tiredness said something about the new addition to her brood. She shrugged, deciding that it probably had more to do with her age than her embryo's sleeping habits, but resolved to get a check-up anyway. Maybe it meant the baby would sleep through the night when they were born. She dismissed the idea instantly, for the fantasy that it was bound to be.

As she dialled Craig's number and waited for him to pick up Annette pictured the first night at home with her new son or daughter, genuinely excited. Mike would be a great dad. Pete had never been that bothered with the kids, going to the pub after work instead of coming home to see them or help put them to bed. Even on holidays he'd left all of that to her. She'd never really commented at the time; it had been the nineties, when feminism had still been the territory of high flying New York journalists and radicals like Germaine Greer. How mainstream men helping with their babies seemed now, although there was still a way to go.

She was just trying to remember if Pete had ever changed a nappy when Craig finally picked up. He sounded as if he was underwater.

"You sent me a text, sir."

"WHAT?"

She raised her voice to match his, drawing disapproving looks from an elderly couple walking by. The Merchant wasn't the sort of place where people shouted, so she took the conversation out into Waring Street.

"YOU SENT ME A-."

Just then the water sounds ceased, leaving her shouting at a man who could hear perfectly well. As she stopped Craig stepped out of the shower, thankful that his phone was waterproof. Katy had bought it for him after he'd dropped the other one in the bath too many times; down to his annoying habit of taking it everywhere he went.

He dried himself with one hand until he reached the bedroom, then he put the phone onto speaker and carried on.

"Thanks for getting back to me, Annette. Don't bother going to collect Mrs McAllister for the I.D. Her solicitor called us after midnight, saying she wanted to get it over with, so we said that Liam or I would take her early today."

She rolled her eyes. It would have been nice if Liam had mentioned it, although she would probably have missed his call as well.

"I'm already here, sir."

She managed to keep the edge she felt out of her voice. That would be saved for Liam. Craig raked back his wet hair and started to dress.

"Sorry. When we saw her last night she was distraught, so we'd planned to leave the I.D. for you, then her solicitor called."

He'd thought it odd when Liam had phoned him at five a.m. and offered to do the viewing, putting it down initially to him being concerned about his sleep deprived 'Katy' state of mind. Until he'd heard the noise in the background and the desperation in Liam's voice, and then he'd understood. Liam's house at five a.m. sounded like a playground at recess. Two young children obviously didn't make for much sleep, so going to work probably seemed like a holiday.

As he buttoned his shirt Craig added. "Still, it's not a wasted journey. You can escort her to High Street and we'll meet you there. Her farm manager Mitchell Purvis is there already."

Annette was curious. "Do you suspect him or her?"

"One of them, neither or both. At this point I just want to rule them in or out. She seemed genuinely shocked at her husband's death but she could just be a good liar." He wrapped his tie expertly around itself until he was satisfied with the knot, then he grabbed his suit jacket, still talking.

"You and Jake make a start with the manager and Rhonda can observe; she needs the experience. Liam and I will take the wife." He grabbed his keys and made for the door, grabbing his phone on the way. "Just a heads up, Annette. Purvis has a major crush on the wife and something definitely happened there. We're not sure how she felt about him but we're pretty sure she ended it, so whether she used his continued feelings to manipulate him into killing the husband only time will tell."

He raced down the stairs and jumped into the car, turning over its aging engine and slipping the phone into its handset as he talked. The Audi coughed its way to life, objecting to the cold morning and probably the time of day; even cars deserved a weekend lie-in. He'd looked at a few new cars in magazines and even driven past a few showrooms in the preceding weeks, but he couldn't bring himself to stop and look. Until Katy came back - he stopped himself mid-thought, always honest, but he was still reluctant to change 'until' for 'if', even in his own mind. *Until* she came back he wasn't changing anything but his clothes; it seemed too much like tempting fate.

He continued talking as if his thoughts hadn't deviated at all.

"The shock when we told her the husband was dead could have been an act, but it was a good one. So let's go into this morning's interviews with an open mind." He glanced quickly at his watch as he drove through the apartment development's gates. "OK, it's eight-thirty now. I need to drop into the office first, so you get Mrs McAllister down to High Street and then get started with Purvis. We'll see you there around ten."

He'd clicked off before Annette managed to answer, so she re-entered the hotel's reception and placed a call through to the new widow's room.

****

Craig's quick exit from his apartment had stemmed from several things but none of them were his eagerness to get to the office; Jake would be there until Annette summoned him to High Street. He still had to tell him what the P.P.S. had said and he planned to defer the inevitable for as long as possible.

Rather his exit had been swift because he'd felt like he was being chased; he'd felt that way since Katy had turned away from him five weeks before. Where once his apartment had been at worst a neutral space and at best a comforting place to switch off and listen to his old LPs, since he'd met Katy it had started to feel like a home. She hadn't tried to tamper with its décor, such as it was, which in Liam's very vocal opinion was aging student grunge, but she had added little touches: a picture here, a house plant there, not enough to desecrate his man cave but enough to say that a woman was sometimes in residence.

The bathroom was the hardest place to be; her shampoo and hairbrush were still by the bath, with fine strands of blonde hair in situ. He knew that he should remove them but he couldn't bear to, saying as it would

85

that she was never returning. And he couldn't face that possibility yet, he couldn't even entertain the thought. All of his energies were focused on winning her back, which was why he was stopping on the Stranmillis Road now, in exactly the same place that he'd stopped three times each week for the past month.

He climbed out of the car and entered the small florists, writing the same card he'd written before and ordering the same bouquet of her favourite flowers, camellias and white roses, altering the address so that this time they were sent to her mother's house. The florist smiled sympathetically as he scribbled the words, 'I love you. Marc', then paid and climbed into the car again, driving off down University Road and through town to the C.C.U.

When Craig entered the squad-room he was surprised to see most of the team there, although it wasn't yet nine o'clock. Nicky answered his question before it reached the air.

"They all saw the news."

Craig's heart sank. He normally watched the eight o'clock news before he left home, but nowadays his mind was always somewhere else.

He covered his whispered question with the noise of pouring a coffee.

"What news?"

She didn't look surprised, more sympathetic. His face showed the fatigue of another night's broken sleep.

"Two shootings in Belfast this morning. One west and one south."

He didn't show his shock.

"Dead?"

"No. Kneecappings. They're at St Mary's now. And D.C.I. Hamill asked if you could give him a call."

Where Craig ran Murder and Aidan Hughes ran Vice, Geoff Hamill presided over Gang Crime for the province. There was nothing that the diminutive detective didn't know about clans, tribes and gatherings in the north, from old school secret societies and lodges to the more malevolent gangs, both home

86

grown and imported, that peppered his patch.

Craig made quickly for his office and turned on his P.C., checking the internal bulletins and the TV news. As he sipped his coffee he read. 'Five-forty-five a.m. Male, twenty-seven, shot in the knee near Broadway in west Belfast.' 'Five-forty-five a.m. Male, thirty-two, identical injury at the bottom of the Ormeau Road.' The attacks were too similar and too time coordinated not to be linked. He thought for a moment then called Liam in, waving him to a seat.

"Thoughts?"

Liam eyed Craig's coffee. "I'm hungry." He reached behind him, pulling open the door. "Any chance of a tea and some biscuits, Nicky?"

The reply was swift. "Any chance of me meeting Brad Pitt?"

Liam smiled, undeterred. "Two sugars should do it. Thanks." He shut the door again with every belief that he would get his request. Craig smiled at his nerve and then repeated his question.

"Thoughts?" He added, for clarity. "On the shootings."

Liam puffed up his cheeks before slowly exhaling. The action said 'nasty business' and 'Belfast scrotes' clearer than any words could. Finally he spoke.

"Someone's sending a warning to someone. Or they were telling the victims to behave. Or... option three, they were looking for information."

Craig tapped his cup rhythmically. "I like one and three best, or a combination of both."

The door opened and Nicky entered with a steaming mug of tea and a plate of digestives, placing the latter in front of Craig. "Because you won't have had any breakfast. Again." She turned to Liam with the mug held ominously above his head. "What's the magic word?"

He thought for a moment, toying with making a joke. The glint in her eyes said not to, so "Please" emerged in a meek voice and the P.A. set down the cup. When she didn't leave Craig nodded Liam to finish his task and "Thank you, Nicky" was added in an equally subservient tone. She exited the room to the sound of him adding "You're a goddess, Nicky. Did anyone ever tell you that?"

Craig rolled his eyes. "Did anyone ever tell you that you never know when to shut-up?"

Liam grabbed a couple of biscuits. "My mother, father, teachers-"

Craig halted him with a raised hand and Liam decided to change tack.

"OK. So why only one and three?"

The reply was logical. "Because no-one's going to waste bullets telling two idiots to behave; they would have just beaten them up. A bullet sends a message. Several, in fact. To wit: we have guns; we can afford to waste ammunition so we obviously have plenty of it; we can organise two attacks in different parts of town at the same time so we're efficient and have several men; and you're too insignificant for us to dirty our hands killing you. Whoever did this thinks they're important. Especially as they probably dragged the men from their beds to do it."

"Talkative bullets and no mistake."

Craig continued. "So someone was sending a message and/or looking for information. The information could be anything, although it will be about the men's boss-"

"Or bosses."

Craig nodded. "True. So what was the message?"

Liam took a gulp of tea. "Everything you just said."

Craig shook his head. "No, that was just the surface bluster. We're important, don't mess with us, or stop messing with us more likely. The real message is about what's behind this."

Liam shrugged. "The two of them are still alive so it's not our case."

"I still want you to see if they'll talk. Send Joe Rice down to St Mary's." He changed tack. "So why does Geoff Hamill want to speak to me?"

"Pass. Why don't you ask him?"

Craig parked the subject and turned back to their two murders.

88

"OK, we've got Purvis and Mara Kennedy at High Street. She was pretty quick to ditch McAllister's name, wasn't she?" He suddenly remembered his manners. "Thanks for doing the I.D. this morning, by the way."

Liam gave a gracious wave. "Had to. She couldn't wait and you looked like crap last night."

Craig went to object but the D.C.I cut him off.

"You looked like you hadn't seen your bed for a week." He leaned forward, peering at Craig's tanned but heavily shadowed face. "It only looks like six days now."

"Ha bloody ha. So the fact that your kids were playing cops and robbers at five a.m. had absolutely nothing to do with it?"

The only answer was a martyred look so he carried on.

"OK, Annette's at High Street now with Jake. I told her to make a start on Purvis."

Liam rubbed his hands. "Saving the lovely widow for us, are we?"

Craig arched an eyebrow. That had been his intention but seeing Liam's enthusiasm changed his mind. "No. I'm letting Annette see what she can get from Purvis before you and I take over. Then she can have a crack at Mara Kennedy while we do him. Meanwhile, are the uniforms at the farm?"

"Yep. Been there for an hour. I used the local lads; it made more sense."

"As long as none of them are friendly with the McAllisters and try to cover things up."

Liam's startled expression said that the thought hadn't occurred to him. He made a grab for the phone but Craig waved him down. "It's pretty unlikely, but just in case I asked Joe to send one of his down to supervise."

He glanced at the clock behind Liam's head. "OK, I need to speak to Andy and Ash now and then nip down to see Geoff. You calm everyone outside down and then get off to High Street. See how Annette's getting on, and while you're there make some calls to your snouts, will you. I want to know more about these shootings and you've got your ear pretty close to the ground."

Liam gave a smug smile. "Any closer and it would get ripped off."

****

Garvan's Bookmakers. East Belfast. 9.10 a.m.

Tommy Hill slung his feet onto the penknife scarred desk, the product of many bored hours, lost bets and bad moods. He glared at the younger man opposite; it was early in the day for both of them and the aging Loyalist was in a foul mood.

"Ye stupid prick, McCrae! Ye said yer men cud make them talk. Ye said they wus spineless bastards who wud sell their mothers to miss the pain."

Rory McCrae gabbled frantically at his old boss. He might be head of the UKUF now, with all its scams and rackets, but for sheer homicidal capability he knew that Tommy was the man to fear. Sod the fact he was a pensioner and mightn't be as quick on the trigger as he once was, and screw the idea that decamping to Templepatrick meant that he'd laid down his arms. Maybe inside his head he had, for the hour a day that he pushed Ella on the swings, but the urge to kill didn't weaken like a man's body did and Tommy's legend had still rallied men eager to put a bullet in someone.

"Honest ta Gawd, Tommy, I thought they wud. 'Specially when my boys shot them. We'd heard they wus running fer the man-"

Hill cut across him venomously. "An' who's this fuckin' man they're all running fer? Eh? Does anywan huv his name? Dus he even fuckin' exist?" He dropped his feet to the floor with a thud. "Is it fuckin' Houdini tryin' to take over the west and south?"

McCrae leaned forward eagerly, forgetting he was taking his life in his hands as he did.

"There *is* a man, Tommy. Everywan knows it. A month, that's all it tuk him to start takin' over everythin' up west. Gamblin', counterfeits, smugglin', petrol stretchin', numbers; he's givin' the long-term gang up there hell. Nye he's movin' in girls and drugs. That's breakin' new ground. That's how we knowed he'd really arrived; that saft bunch up there wun't touch girls and blow. Bunch af pricks."

Tommy wondered how Hanratty would feel about being called a prick. He brushed past it and concentrated on the matter in hand, slamming his fist hard against the desk and barely missing his erstwhile disciple's head.

"He's nat the bloody invisible man! Sumwun knows who's takin' over an' I need to find out who."

As spittle gathered in the corners of Hill's mouth McCrae leaned well back. He'd seen the signs before; Tommy was about to blow. He wasn't wrong. Suddenly Hill jumped to his feet with the energy of a man twenty years younger, pounding his fist harder on the scarred desk with each word.

"I. Want. His. Fuckin'. Name." He moved towards the door, opening it with a kick, then he turned back for the final word. "I dun't care how ye get it, McCrae, but I want that bastard's name by tomara, or ye'll be the next wan with a bullet in yer fuckin' leg."

****

The C.C.U.

Craig poured two fresh coffees and topped up his own, then he retook his seat and stared at the men opposite. He stared for so long that they began to worry that they'd done something wrong, or rather Andy did. Ash had realised pretty quickly that Craig wasn't staring at them but through them, at something far more interesting inside his own head.

The detective suddenly remembered that they were there and realised that they were waiting for him to speak.

"OK. Miskimmon and Corneau."

He stopped again and wrinkled his forehead, considering whether to give them the P.P.S.' view of the world or start from the point that they just needed to do more to make their case. He plumped for the former and after a couple of minutes talking he ended with. "Ten days. That's all we have before we have to hand them to the Venezuelans for trial." He fixed his gaze on Andy.

"I need something that puts Miskimmon near that plane."

And then on Ash. "And proof that he planted the code. If you can find it in even one of the incidences that should be enough, then we can make a case for the rest."

Both men answered at once. Craig let them compete for a moment and then pointed a finger at Ash.

"Shoot."

The analyst blew a puff of air up at his green quiff, making it bounce up and down on his forehead as he thought. When he eventually spoke it was slow and considered.

"Miskimmon has firewalls on all his laptops and phones, so tight that the Computer Fraud Unit, Des and me, none of us can break them from the outside."

Craig wasn't persuaded. "What about GCHQ? They must have encountered this sort of thing before."

GCHQ is the Government Communications Headquarters, a British intelligence and security organisation operating under the direction of the Joint Intelligence Committee alongside MI5, MI6 and Defence Intelligence.

Ash nodded. "They have. Definitely. But I don't know if even they've successfully extracted information in a case like this."

Craig frowned. As he did so Andy frowned as well, so hard that his pale forehead funnelled outwards and his head looked like it was going to explode. Ash stared at him in alarm and shook his arm to break the spell, making the D.C.I. put his frown into words.

"What if..." He paused and then restarted with renewed vigour. "What if we look at it from the other end?"

Ash urged him on. "As in?"

The normally laidback detective warmed to his theme. "As in, we look at all the systems Miskimmon hacked. Check how he got in. See if he left something we can use."

Ash shook his head. "I found the hacks first and I would have-" He stopped abruptly and Craig lurched forward, spotting a doubt.

"You weren't looking for anything else then, were you? You were too busy looking for what the hack did."

Ash gave a hesitant "No...but-"

Craig cut him off, careful to avoid implying that he'd missed something. Ash's work in spotting first the pattern and then the detail of Ronan Miskimmon's killing spree had proved his genius, not just to him but to people much higher up the chain. He wasn't going to detract from that but he did need the analyst to take things one step beyond.

"OK. Let's think for a minute. Ash, you said Miskimmon had trialled the hack elsewhere in the world before he narrowed his focus to Northern Ireland. Yes?"

"Yes, but-"

Craig raised a hand, halting him. "Hear me out and then you can shoot me down. OK, so you said the first incidences affected things like media and weather drones. Sporadic incidents in random locations, where no-one seemed to have spotted the hack but you. Yes?"

He was answered by a sharp nod.

"But there're two things there. Point one, how do you *know* that no-one else noticed anything? Have you checked? Have you engaged with hackers or analysts in other countries to ask them?"

Ash's head was shaking furiously but his expression said that he was excited. "No. No, and they might not even have realised the significance because the incidents there stopped and concentrated here. I could put a call out and then..."

Craig tuned out for a moment as Ash descended into geek speak. When he tuned back in he nodded supportively and then cut the analyst off.

"OK, good. So that's a whole new avenue opening

up. But putting a call out won't do it. Get GCHQ to get onto the FBI, CIA, Homeland Security etcetera, and their equivalents in any country the early incidents occurred in. They'll have been monitoring the hackers in their own backyards for years and should be able to help speed things up."

Ash's eyes widened as he realised that GCHQ had probably been monitoring him since he'd been a teenager.

Craig rose and opened the door. "Nicky."

She'd been reading a magazine but she set it down immediately, his tone saying something important was up.

"When is Davy back?"

"He's back in Belfast today and back at work Monday." She screwed up her face, thinking. "Well, technically tomorrow if we're on call, I suppose."

A muttered "good, good" and Craig went back into his room.

"OK. Ash, you and Davy need to work on this together, as well as the two murders we've got. Sorry."

Ash stared up at him apologetically. "Sorry, chief. No can do. I'm leaving on Monday. I was only Davy's locum cover. Remember?"

"You can't leave!"

Ash gawped. "It's not my fault! I don't have a job here anymore."

"Says who?"

A look of confusion flashed across the analyst's face, and as it did so Craig did some rapid accounting in his head. With Annette going off on maternity leave in a few months, Kyle would just be her cost neutral replacement and he could fudge their few months overlap as a training course. Reggie would be leaving them as soon as Jake was back on his feet, although if he could find some spare cash he'd be fighting that. But at maximum staffing that meant he'd have two sergeants, one inspector, one constable, Rhonda, and two D.C.I.s: Liam and Andy. It wasn't a lot with the number of murders they caught. With a bit of jiggery-pokery he could afford another analyst, and if Ash

94

wasn't kept busy full time he could help support the other murder teams. They all worked for him anyway, so he knew exactly where he could shave their budgets to suit.

When he spoke again he was on surer ground.

"Have you got a new job to go to, Ash?"

Ash hemmed and hawed before admitting all that he'd got lined up was a bit of tutoring at Queen's and one week's work at a tech company in town.

Craig retook his seat. "Do you *want* to leave?"

The analyst considered playing hard to get but his smile gave him away.

Craig nodded decisively. "Well, OK then. You can stay with us full time. If you're not busy on my cases I'll allocate you some work from the other teams." He thought of the clincher. "And if you still have free time, I'll see if we can arrange for you and Davy to spend some time at GCHQ. I know they would jump at seconding both of you for a couple of weeks."

He sat back with a satisfied smile, expecting a 'thanks, chief' at the very least. Instead he got an uncertain look and then Ash slowly shook his head.

Craig lurched forward in his chair. "You don't want to stay!"

Ash tried for a mollifying look. "I didn't say that."

"You shook your head." He turned to a bemused looking Andy for support. "Didn't he shake his head?"

Andy nodded and then added a caveat. "Maybe he didn't shake his head to say no. Maybe it was just disbelief."

The look he gave Ash said that he'd better hurry up and agree. The computer whiz did. Partly.

"Thanks for your generous offer, chief, and I'd like to stay, of course. It's just-"

Craig finally understood. "Ah...you want to know if Davy will be your boss."

Ash nodded. "Yes. Will he? It's just that we graduated at the same time, and-"

"You're equally skilled, no-one's arguing about that. But yes, Davy will be your boss. He's worked here for quite a while and he's higher up the pay scale, plus he's far more familiar with our work."

The analyst went to say something else but he stopped him.

"Of course, I'm your boss overall, so in terms of assessments etcetera you'll report to me, and I have the final say on everything. But yes, day to day, Davy *will* be able to allocate you work." He watched Ash's face carefully as he continued. "But let's face it, you've seen us work and it's a team effort. And Davy's about as bossy as -" He'd been about to say "my mum" but the image of the formidable Mirella ordering them about as kids made it a bad analogy, so he substituted "Annette" instead. "And neither of them is hard to work with. Actually, I think Davy will be pleased that you're staying. It can't have been easy for him having no-one to speak computereeze to all these years."

Even he could hear that he was gabbling now. "Also, remember that he's studying part-time for his PhD and won't be here some days, and I'm sure we can find time for you both to pursue your specialist interests."

Which, given Davy's excitement about working with outside agencies was likely to include Interpol and the FBI, and he knew Ash would want to work with GCHQ. He decided to shut up; it was unseemly for the boss to beg. He filled the gap until Ash answered by making his next point on the case.

"OK, point two. As well as other hackers possibly noticing something, Andy is quite right. What about traces at the other end? I can't believe that when Miskimmon planted that code on the machines' computers that he didn't leave any trail from his side. Ash?"

He was still thinking about his new job so Andy gave his arm a shove, adding. "The other end of Miskimmon's hacks, Kermit."

The analyst considered the question for a moment. "I couldn't find anything that led back to him. He'd bounced off the internet all over the world and that just led me to Ukraine. But his earlier efforts...I guess he might still have been perfecting his procedure back then." He glanced at Craig. "If he got careless or made a mistake then we might be lucky with a reverse trace, but I can't promise anything."

Craig would take what he could get. "Good. Let's pursue those avenues then, please." He moved to the window, staring out at the Lagan, and carried on speaking without looking at the men.

"OK, Ash. I know you have a lot to think about. Just give me your decision about the job by close of business today, please." They rose to leave and Craig shook his head. "Not you, Andy. We still need to talk about the CCTV."

As Ash was about to leave he turned back. "I forgot to mention, chief. That paper Des found in the drowned man's pocket."

"Yes."

"The writing was gambling odds and riders. Cheltenham tomorrow."

Craig nodded him out and gestured Andy to top up their coffees as he thought.

"Where are you with the CCTV?"

Andy sat down with a thud. It didn't bode well for his answer. "I'm down to the last few days' footage at City Airport."

Something about his tone made Craig hopeful. "Consecutive days?"

A shake of Andy's head said that he'd been right. "Two days in the week before the explosion and the immediate twenty-four hours before the bomb. Miskimmon's nowhere else on the footage, but, as you know, he was an engineering student at Queen's so I had a hunch. I got onto the engineering department and checked when he was definitely signed in for practicals and lectures."

Craig's eyes widened. "They make them sign in for lectures?"

Andy grinned so widely his pale lips completely disappeared. "Yes, God bless them. I remembered 'cos one of my friends at Uni did engineering-"

Craig interrupted. "What did you study?"

"French and Greek literature."

97

He suddenly viewed the D.C.I. in a new light, with his laziness looking more like a renaissance poet's malaise.

"Anyway, I knew the engineers were strict about attendance, so I persuaded them to give me their lecture rosters and then I noted the days that Miskimmon wasn't there."

"Wouldn't it have been easier to check the dates he was allocated to do work experience at the airport?"

"If he had been. He was a first year and they don't do work experience. So I guessed that he'd taken the slot at City Airport belonging to a final year student and signed in using their name. Long story short, I found the culprit. Danny Myers. He said that Miskimmon had been eager to get some practical experience and he'd been even more eager to stay in bed with his girlfriend, so it had suited them both."

Craig smiled. Andy had made D.C.I. at thirty-seven and he hadn't gone the fast track route, so he'd always known that despite the detective's sugar addiction and lackadaisical attitude, there had to be something going on beneath his spiked up hair.

"So?"

"So, I checked the name Danny Myers, and it had been signed in at the airport quite a lot. I pulled the CCTV for the days he'd signed in but so far Miskimmon's not on any of it. Keep your fingers crossed that he got careless on one of the last three days."

He would. Craig thought about their final chances of pinning the crime on Ronan Miskimmon: three days CCTV in the hands of a super- recogniser, a reverse trace on the systems he'd hacked, and the possibility of a hacker in some other country having spotted Miskimmon's actions before Ash. It felt thin and theoretical, all of it. They needed something to get their teeth into closer to home.

He changed the subject.

"The drowning case. What have you got so far?"

Andy opened his mouth to say 'give me a break. I haven't had time' then he changed his mind, shutting it again. When he did speak it was Grade A obfuscation.

"Well, there's the forensics –algae, nail scrapings, to see what happened when he went in. Then Ash will look at currents to give us an idea of time-"

"And John can give you some idea of time of death and exact cause: drugs, drowning or trauma in the water. The usual. OK, what else?"

Andy cheered up, remembering something. "We had a hit on the victim's I.D. Just before you came in. Matias Rey. Address in west Belfast."

"You heard what Ash just said about the race-course."

The D.C.I. nodded. "Our dead man must have been into betting."

"He had something to do with gambling at least. OK, west Belfast."

"Yes. I was going to take Kyle with me."

Craig glanced at the door as if he expected Kyle Spence to be standing there. "Has he arrived? Nobody told me."

"No, but I was going to take him when he did."

Craig glanced at the clock. Where *was* Spence? If this was Roy Barrett in Intelligence playing games then he'd be playing the drums on his head.

He stood up decisively.

"I'll get Nicky to chase up Inspector Spence; he may be in Human Resources signing forms. Meanwhile, you get on with the CCTV. When the two of you head to west Belfast, take some uniforms with you; we're not the most popular sight in that neck of the woods. Call at the lab on your way back and check the forensics, please. You'll probably have one of Rey's relatives with you, so you can make his I.D. as well." He yanked open the door. "Then back here and on the CCTV again for the rest of the afternoon. We need to place Miskimmon at that airport. Kyle can work with Ash on other things for a few hours." He waved the D.C.I. out briskly. "Nicky, I'm off to see Geoff Hamill now. Then I'll be at High Street with Liam. Chase Inspector Spence, please, and tell him to get his ass up here ASAP."

10. 30 a.m.

While Craig was running down five flights of stairs to see Geoff Hamill, Liam was busy extracting information from every snout he'd ever had, and thirty odd years as a cop in Belfast meant that he had quite a few. None of them went by the names their parents had gifted them, as if nicknames were de rigeur in the underworld, their legal names only reappearing when they landed in a cell.

Dodgy, Fixer and Crunch were just three of his sources and every one of them was as thick as a plank. The mechanicals in a Midsummer Night's Dream reimaged through a dark lens, and without one iota of their charm.

The conversations so far had yielded slim pickings. A possible sighting of someone being tipped into a car boot on Tuesday evening, and a 'maybe I heered a shot on the Ormeau road last night', all disappearing like the morning mist once Liam had mentioned there was no cash to be had. But at least none of his snouts had run or hung up on him, not until his last one, Roller Brant, so called because he had a stomach like a barrel and the local sport after a night at the boozer was to roll him down the nearest available hill.

Roller was usually an affable sort. Not normally given to violence, unless you called mouthing off at the bouncers when they barred him from his favourite pub violent, or thought shouting 'Fuck you. Stand still till I clock you one' while wildly flailing his arms in the air, constituted a threat, but his response to Liam's 'who's behind today's attacks?' had resulted in the detective receiving a punch in the face and Roller barrelling away at a heck of a pace.

A few long strides and Liam had caught up, counting to ten through gritted teeth to stop him returning the punch in kind. Instead he grabbed his unlikely assailant by his protruding ears and threw him over the bonnet of his Ford, then he counted to ten again, out loud this time. When he thought he could finally trust himself not to do serious damage he asked "what the hell did you punch me for?" and slipped the cuffs around Brant's blancmange-like wrists.

"Ye asked me what yuh shudn't huv."

The answer cheered Liam up; it meant that Brant knew something. What cheered him up far less was the sight of the good linen hankie Danni had given him that morning covered in his bright red blood. He shoved his prisoner in the back seat less than gently and recited his rights through a blocked nose. By the time they'd reached High Street and Roller was sitting in a cell, the D.C.I. had partially recovered his good humour, courtesy of the leftovers of Jack Harris's birthday curry and a slice of additive laden cake. He was just heading back for a second slice when Annette, Jake and Rhonda entered the room. Annette's eyes widened.

"What happened to your face?"

Her expression was halfway between concerned and amused.

"A snout that needed persuading."

She shrugged. "In a cell now, I presume?"

Jake's question was nearer the point. "Still in one piece?" He wouldn't have fancied his own chances against Liam.

Liam smiled ominously. "For now." He waved a hand at Jack's cake with largesse. "Have some cake."

Harris was not amused. "Don't you bother your backsides! I'm taking it home." He shot Liam a caustic look. "I only gave *you* some 'cos I felt sorry for you."

Annette said what Jake had been thinking. "Thanks anyway, Jack, but cake at this time of the morning... I don't fancy diabetes just yet."

They poured some drinks instead and took a seat. Liam nodded towards the door.

"You've been in with Purvis, then?"

Jake answered for the two of them. His expression said everything before his words emerged. "It was nothing but 'Mitchell Purvis, farm manager' for a solid hour. He must have been in the army."

A glance at Annette confirmed that it was true. Liam shrugged.

"The boss says you're to make a start on the merry widow and he and I'll have another go at Purvis once he arrives."

Annette shook her head decisively and tapped her watch. "We're having a go at no-one else until I've had a cooked breakfast." She stared down at her abdomen. "This baby needs fuel, and its mother definitely does."

Liam cheered up. "Sounds excellent. I'll join you. It's a bit late for breakfast, but food is food."

She squinted at him menacingly. "I missed breakfast at the proper time because you didn't bother to tell me that you'd already done McAllister's I.D."

Jack gawped at Liam.

"You can't possibly still be hungry! You've just eaten half my curry and two slices of cake."

Annette shook her head dramatically. *"How* long have you known him?"

Jack was answered by "my sore nose made me hungry" as Liam headed for the nearest café.

****

Geoff Hamill answered the door of his fifth floor office cautiously, opening it just a sliver at first and gazing down the corridor, before throwing it wide with a sigh of relief. Craig nodded, understanding perfectly. The six-feet-six Liam tormented the shorter Hamill of his lack of height every time they met.

"Liam's at High Street."

Hamill covered his behaviour skilfully. "Just being security conscious. You can never be too careful working in Gangs."

Inside Headquarters? But Craig let it pass. He deserved a break.

The D.C.I. waved Craig to a seat.

"Nicky said you wanted to see me, Geoff."

"Just to give you a heads up, really." Hamill reached into his drawer and pulled out a file, setting it on the desk with his hand resting on top.

"You heard about the shootings this morning?"

Craig shrugged. "Low level, so we reckoned they were probably to send a message, or get information on someone higher up."

Hamill nodded. "You reckoned right. Mind you, they were well organised and coordinated. There'll be no witnesses of course; the local communities are too scared. We asked the victims who did it but neither of them will say a word."

"More scared of the shooters than of us." Craig checked his facts. "West and south, so both victims were Catholics?"

"Actually no. The westie was a Prod." The slang wasn't written anywhere in the force's handbook but it conveyed exactly what he meant. "From the Shankill. But they were both up to their necks in something."

"Which is?"

"Encroaching on another tribe's turf."

Craig raised an eyebrow. "Which tribe?"

"They're called The Rock."

He wondered if it linked with their victim's tattoo but didn't interrupt to ask.

"The name's supposed to indicate they're hard men. They're based up in Poleglass."

"And what does this Rock gang specialise in?"

"The Rock. And they don't like the word gang."

"Sensitive hoodlums."

"Very." Hamill opened the file and began reading. "Counterfeit DVDs, tobacco smuggling, petrol stretching, credit card fraud, numbers rackets, gambling. The list goes on. Oh, and the odd bit of protection and payback beatings."

"Busy boys. Any killings?"

He hadn't heard of the gang so it was unlikely. He heard about every murder in Belfast, unless the victims were buried extra deep.

Hamill shook his head. "No murder. It's their policy. No drugs or girls either."

Craig gave a hollow laugh. "My God. Villains with principles. What next?" He paused for a moment, staring at the D.C.I. curiously. "So you're saying The

Rock didn't do this morning's shootings?"

"Definitely not. Their boss is Matias Rey. Second generation Spanish. They have very strict rules."

He'd just named their drowning victim. Craig decided to withhold the information for now and asked another question. "So why call me in? No-one was killed today, and you say shooting's not The Rock's style anyway."

Hamill missed the word 'today'.

"It's not but something is definitely up. We think The Rock has a serious rival for their turf, but we can't get a handle on them. If a gang war does break out then there'll be plenty of work for everyone, including you, so I just wanted to give you a heads up." He rested back in his chair and stared Craig coolly in the eye, adding. "That's if you haven't already heard something, of course."

Perhaps he hadn't missed 'today' then.

It was time for Craig to show his hand. "We might have something for you. A body was pulled out of the Lagan yesterday; he'd been in there about two days. We're still waiting for all the details from John but foul play was definitely involved."

Hamill leaned forward eagerly. "Any I.D.?"

"Just ten minutes ago, from his prints, but the body hasn't been formally I.D.ed. yet. Andy's bringing in a relative-"

Hamill cut in. "But you think it's..."

"We think it's Matias Rey. That's what the prints say anyway. He had racing odds on him which would fit with the gang's gambling links."

Hamill slumped back, the blood draining from his face. "Shit! This is the start of it." He shut his eyes for a moment and Craig knew he was picturing blood on the streets of Belfast. When the D.C.I. reopened his eyes he spoke in a monotone.

"Belfast has been pretty lucky so far. We've escaped a lot of the gang warfare that the rest of the UK, and to an even worse extent, Europe and the States suffers, probably because gangs are too shit scared to cross our paramilitaries-"

"Our home grown gangs."

Hamill shrugged, conceding the point. "Yes, but not in the same way. The paramilitaries hated each other on the basis of ideology and religion, and yes, OK, since the Good Friday Agreement some of them *have* turned to crime, but they're still not the 'shoot them dead in the streets gang-bangers' that you'd find elsewhere." He waved a hand in the air, indicating the rest of the world. "London had Operation Trident to try to control theirs, and look at the Dublin gangsters at the moment, for God's sake. They're killing each other every other day and it stopped being about money a generation ago."

"OK, so..."

"So, The Rock have been pretty easy to handle and I'd like to keep it that way. Like I said: no killings, no drugs and no girls, and anyone who crossed that line got dealt with by their own. Now we're hearing rumbles that there *are* drugs and girls coming onto the south and west streets, and I'm not talking about hash. We're talking Crack Cocaine and Crystal Meth, stuff that makes people kill to fund their habit."

Craig frowned. "OK, so who's moving in on their patch?"

Hamill's face was blank. "If I knew that I'd be a Superintendent. We haven't a sodding clue. We're hearing nothing, not from our undercover drugs people and not from our snouts. Now you're telling me Rey's dead-"

"We don't know it's Rey for sure, yet."

Hamill dragged a hand down his face. "Well, we'd better pray to God it isn't because he was one of their top brass. The Major."

Craig was shocked. "But he was only a kid."

"It makes no difference. It's legacy. His father, Xavier, was The Major before him and the ranks are handed down like you or I might give our kids the deposit for a house. Xavier retired two years ago and Matias was jumped-in as the boss in a big ceremony. Twenty-one gun salute and all." He laughed dryly. "They even had the cheek to send an invitation here."

He shook his head. "If Matias *is* dead, Xavier will come out of retirement. And for one reason only. To kill whoever did his son."

"I thought you said they didn't kill."

Hamill raised an eyebrow. "This is his kid, Marc."

Craig thought for a moment. "OK, so if Matias was The Major, what's the rest of the structure?"

Hamill turned to the back page of the file and pointed to a chart. It read foot-soldiers, corporals, sergeants and lieutenants in increasing rank. There were five such trees and they all fed up to two captains, one each for west and south Belfast, then one major, and at the pinnacle the general.

Craig shook his head. Criminals playing at soldiers; God help them all. He tapped the page.

"Who's the general?"

"No-one knows. They work through an honour code and need to know. The lieutenants will only know the captains' names, the captains the major's."

"Which means the major must know who the general is."

Hamill shook his head. "Nope. We've tried asking but that seems to be where the information ends. The most we can find out it that the major receives his orders in coded drops."

"Computers?" Not more encryption.

"No. Old school. Radio and print. They pass the information on through classified adverts. It's real spy tradecraft and it's worked well for years."

Very clever. If no-one knows who the boss is but they all get paid, there's no chance or incentive for anyone to inform on him to the police.

Craig still wasn't convinced. "You must have some idea who he is."

Hamill shrugged. "We intercepted a transmission last year where one of the words was knacker."

"That's a Dublin word."

The Belfast equivalent was spide, and both words meant wee hard man. Scammers, dippers and hallions, the lowest branches on the criminal tree who didn't mind whether they stole the eye out of your head or

106

punched your teeth down your throat, just as long as they got paid.

"That's all we've got." He closed the file. "When will Rey's death be confirmed?"

"Andy's heading to see the family this morning."

Hamill spotted an opportunity. "Would you mind if one of my team went with him?"

"Fine." He saw a way to get information. "Providing you keep me in the loop on who you think is trying to muscle in on The Rock's patch."

Hamill slid the file across the desk.

"Take it. It's your copy. But you'll probably know more than us very soon."

****

The C.C.U. 11.15 a.m.

As Craig headed for High Street and two interviews, possibly expanded to three, courtesy of Roller Brant's fist connecting with Liam's face, Andy was stuck staring at a computer screen, waiting for Geoff Hamill's tagalong to turn up. The four uniforms parked out on Pilot Street weren't happy either. They'd been geared up to visit the Reys five minutes after Craig had said. Now they'd missed their breaks and were in danger of getting numb backsides while they waited for some flash git of a detective to swell their ranks.

Andy was just about to phone Hamill's office and give him an earful, a privilege only available to those of equal rank, when the click-clacking of heels made him sit up and take notice, signalling as it usually did the arrival of a member of the fairer sex. He dropped the phone and stood up hopefully at his desk. There, standing beside Nicky's desk in quiet conversation, was a sight that made the D.C.I.'s heart sink. A man in his early twenties wearing the shiniest shoes he'd ever seen this side of patent, and Andy knew that if he examined their soles they'd have metal Blakeys.

Nicky beckoned the disappointed officer across.

"D.C.I. Angel, this is D.C. Freeman. Sid. He's been

107

sent up from Gangs."

As the youth turned, Andy registered his pristine suit and the rucksack strapped to his back, like a teenager going to school. A manicured hand shot out and grabbed his, pumping it up and down enthusiastically.

"Constable Freeman, sir. Very pleased to be here."

Andy assessed the younger man quickly. Brown hair slicked back from his forehead, with something that shone suspiciously like oil. Over groomed eyebrows in a shiny face that was slightly chubby but not corpulent; as if his puppy fat still hadn't gone rather than that he ate five burgers for lunch. He looked like a stereotypical millennial just as he probably looked like a typical forty-year-old divorcee. Each stage of life had its style.

He retrieved his hand and nodded towards the door, adopting a brusque tone that he thought appropriate to his rank.

"Better go. Uniforms waiting." He turned grandly towards Nicky. "Nicky, we're heading to Poleglass. With some uniforms. Hopefully just transporting a family member. To the mortuary for an I.D. Then back here for a chat, but..."

Before Nicky could ask why he was using such short sentences they were gone. Andy striding manfully ahead, with his rucksack wearing apprentice scurrying behind. She smiled to herself knowingly. She hadn't missed the D.C.I.'s quickly hidden disappointment and judgemental assessment of the youth. Her smile changed to a grin as she pictured the interaction when Liam and Sid Freeman met.

****

Lift conversations, even between acquaintances, are awkward, characterised by a sudden desire to inspect the walls or ceiling, or an excited renewed acquaintance with one's shoes. But Andy relished such times as five extra minutes in which he didn't have to waste physical energy, propping himself against the wall and allowing his mind to go blank. Sadly Sid Freeman was no respecter of such etiquette and continued talking as if they were still on office ground.

"How are we going to handle this, sir? If the Reys know about Matias' death before we get there, we would be driving into a street war."

It made Andy jerk upright and he resigned himself to at least two hours of looking alert, if not because of Freeman's expectations of rank then because it might prevent him getting his head blown off.

As they disembarked the lift in reception another man in a suit was walking onto the tenth floor. Everything about him said cop, cop who wasn't happy to be there, and Nicky knew who he was right away. She gave Kyle Spence a half smile; full smiles were reserved for people who knew how lucky they were to be working with Craig and were suitably grateful for the chance. Behind the smile she sharpened her tongue, although not too sharp; Craig and the reluctant recruit had personal history.

She remained seated and considered Spence, so Ash immediately stopped what he was doing and sat back to watch the show. Nicky not rising wasn't a good sign. She always rose to greet guests, even if it was only a half ascent. Even he would have warranted the change in posture, if she hadn't first met him in the kitchen with Davy that was. He was just wondering why she'd taken against the visitor when his attention was diverted by beep from his screen, the signal for his FaceTime meeting with the FBI. He slipped on his earphones and tried to look intelligent, but the agent on the other end couldn't disguise her shock at his green hair.

Nicky was still staring at Kyle Spence, trying to work out why, despite his reluctance to be there and his mouth downturned in a scowl, she didn't instantly dislike him one hundred percent. It was a puzzle to her, but only for a moment, because if Nicky was one thing she was honest to a fault, to herself if not always to others. The reason she couldn't throw the full weight of her hostility at him was because Spence was an attractive man. A bit too pale and a bit too thin perhaps, but tall with good bone structure; definitely easy on the eye.

There, she'd admitted it; she was sufficiently shallow to be swayed by a handsome face. She decided a renewed effort to be hostile was called for and barked out her next words.

"You're late, Inspector. I had to chase you this morning..." Adding ominously. "...at the superintendent's request."

If she'd hoped to scare him she'd failed. Spence merely yawned and stared in distaste around the open plan floor.

"Where do I sit?"

His voice was soft and rounded and that annoyed the P.A. as well. A rude person should have an ugly voice; it was the natural order of things. She pointed towards a cubicle without looking.

"D.I. Eakin is the officer you'll be taking over from, so I've put you beside her. She's not here at the moment."

The intelligence officer shrugged and ambled over to the allocated space, sitting down in the cubicle and immediately trying to hide. His height and the low walls defeated the attempt. Five minutes later Nicky marched across and dropped two files on his desk from a three foot height.

"Two new cases we're working on." She walked away again, muttering. "You can get tea, coffee and biscuits from the machine."

It was a step too far for Ash so he decided to fraternise with the enemy. Ignoring Nicky's scowls he ambled over to the cubicle, reaching out his hand with a grin.

"Ash Rahman, analyst. Welcome to the team." He beckoned Spence to follow him to the kitchen. "This is where you can make a decent cuppa." Then, dropping his voice. "Ignore Nicky; she's just in a mood today. She's normally really nice." Although he knew that his perceived treachery would earn him the sharp end of her tongue for weeks.

As he updated their new member on the cases and staff in the squad, Nicky's evil eye was deflected as yet another man entered the floor, looking tanned and healthy despite the time of year.

"Davy! You're back."

She leapt up and hugged him hard, much to the ex-Emo's surprise.

"You saw me a few w...weeks ago."

"So I'm not allowed to be happy that you're here?" She stopped chiding and stared at him curiously. "Why are you tanned? It's winter in France as well, isn't it? And when did you grow a beard?"

It had only been stubble the last time she'd seen him and now he had a full hipster growth. He was changing, although she was strangely comforted by his occasional stutter on 's' and 'w' still being there.

He dropped his things on the floor beside his desk, acknowledging the fresh flowers she'd placed there with a smile. "Maggie came over last w...week and we w...went ski-ing." Maggie Clarke, the news editor of the Belfast Chronicle, was his fiancée of one month. "I'm only tanned on my face and hands." As his scarf came off and exposed a pale neck she saw that he was right. "Anyway, that's enough about me. W...What's been happening here?" He scanned the room as he spoke. "Where is everyone?"

"Annette, Liam and the chief are at High Street, with Rhonda and Jake-"

"I forgot Jake was back at work. That's great."

She continued as if he hadn't spoken. "Andy's off with one of D.C.I. Hamill's team, doing a victim I.D., and there's gossip there, I can tell you." She paused for a moment, wondering who she'd forgotten. "Oh, yes, and Reggie's on holiday-"

"Don't forget us, Nicky."

Davy turned at the sound of Ash's voice, grinning when he saw his friend. His grin fixed when he saw someone he didn't recognise following behind. Nicky's froze as well when she saw the decidedly non-machine coffee in Kyle Spence's hand, especially as it was sloshing on the carpet as he walked.

"Hey, Ash. I like the green hair. W...What's up?"

Ash nodded regally at the compliment. "Cheers, mate." He indicated his companion. "This is Inspector Kyle Spence. He'll be covering for Annette when she goes on maternity leave."

Davy's grin changed to eagerness. "You're from Intelligence, aren't you?"

Nicky knew instantly that she was defeated. When you put computer geeks together with a spook, there was only one place for the conversation to go. She went back to her desk and started typing furiously, venting her annoyance on her keyboard and trying to shut out the computer acronyms as best she could.

****

Poleglass. West Belfast.

Andy Angel was nervous, so nervous that the hairs were standing up on his arms. On the back of his neck was one thing, but when it reached his arms he really knew his adrenaline was on the rush. He gazed at the passing streets curiously, as their names changed from English only to English and Irish, and they entered an area where the kerbstones were painted green, white and gold. He wasn't bigoted; he felt exactly the same way when he entered an area bedecked with Union Flags and Loyalist symbols. People in both places hated the cops, mainly because they stopped them doing what they wanted to do, but today there was an added edge because the man they were visiting was the boss of a criminal gang.

But whatever Andy's hairs were doing and no matter how scared he felt, no-one in the car but him would ever have known what was running through his mind. He wouldn't show his nervousness to other men and he definitely wouldn't show it to the youngster by his side; so he pushed his chest out and asked the driver a question, in a voice that was as macho as he ever got.

"How far?"

Two words were all he could manage without a quiver.

"Just round this corner, sir. Two of us will come in with you and two wait outside, if that suits?"

"Fine."

As the car pulled up, Andy scanned the street at length before jumping out, followed by his acolyte. They'd barely turned towards the designated house when its front door opened and a broad chested man of around sixty appeared, with folded arms and biceps like two tubs of lard.

He scrutinised them for a moment before deciding on Andy as the boss; his macho façade obviously doing the trick. The man turned on his heels, barking "C'mon then if yer comin'" then the front door slammed behind them and the four police officers found themselves in a small, warm room.

The man turned to face Andy, and the detective suddenly noticed redness and swelling around his eyes.

"Ye've come to tell me my boy's dead."

There was no point in denying it.

"We've come to speak to Mr Xavier Rey-"

The pensioner nodded tiredly and slumped into a chair.

"That's me."

Andy felt genuinely sorry for the father who obviously already knew his son was dead and dropped his voice respectfully. There was little point asking how Rey had acquired the information. They were unlikely to get the truth.

"I'm sorry to say that we've found the body of a young man, Mr Rey." The gang boss flinched. "And I'd like you to come to the mortuary with us. Is that possible?"

It was a stupid question as well as ungrammatical. Of course it was possible; all it would take was a trip in a car. What he'd really meant to say was, is that OK? But even Andy was sensitive enough to know that OK wasn't a term to be used at a time like this.

Rey's answer was to stand up again and walk into an adjoining room. They heard him murmur something and a woman cry out, then he reappeared wearing a Crombie and walked straight past them to the car. A silent crowd had gathered around it: boys on bikes, women with folded arms and infants in tow, older teens and twenty something men, with close-cut hair and menacing looks that said on any other day and if they'd been here for anything else the policemen would have been fair game.

The only thing that stopped them being heckled as they left was a glance from the man in their back seat. Xavier Rey might have retired from The Rock but his power and control in his fiefdom was still very real.

As Andy wedged himself between the kingpin and Sid Freeman and they watched the street names change from Irish to English again, the hairs on his arms lay down again and a sense of foreboding replaced his fear.

****

Café Vaudeville. Arthur Street, Belfast. 11.45 a.m.

Craig stared openly at his deputy's bloodied nose. Liam's nose was hardly a thing of beauty at the best of times, given that it had been broken repeatedly since his youth, courtesy of playing rugby and Gaelic football for years and from being swung at by half of the perps in Belfast. But at least it was normally just prominent and misshapen, now he looked like Rudolph the Reindeer as well.

"Who did you say did it?"

Liam sniffed hard and then flinched at the pain. "Roller Brant. Short, round, big ears. You won't know him."

Craig winced in sympathy. "Get it checked out by a doctor. Anyway, this Brant. I take it he's a snout?" He gestured at Liam's face. "With a bad temper by the looks of it."

"He is, yeh. I had to restrain him at a riot in eighty-nine and he's been informing for me ever since."

114

For 'restrain him' read 'punched him and nicked him'. Liam's thirty years of policing in Belfast were useful in terms of experience and contacts, but Craig didn't want to delve too far into their darker parts. The D.C.I. was still talking.

"His temper's normally fine. I just asked the wrong question."

"Which was?"

"Who was behind today's attacks. He took it amiss for some reason. Silence must be contagious this week; the kneecapped pair wouldn't say a word either."

Craig thought for a moment. Brant's reaction said that he was scared of the attacks' mastermind; more than he was of a six-feet-six cop.

"You'll find out why, of course."

It wasn't a question. Liam nodded.

"First order of play, after we deal with Purvis and Kennedy. By the way, Annette and Jake batted zero with Purvis. Name, rank and serial number."

Craig rose to pay the bill. "Let's go with Kennedy first then. Purvis can stew until they've finished searching the farm."

As he walked past Annette he noticed she was picking out chips from her late breakfast and dipping them in sugar, before biting into them with excessive glee. Craving foods of dubious nutritional benefit, or to give its medical name, Pica. The next joy of pregnancy. Like a gentleman he decided not to draw attention to it but Liam had no such qualms.

"Danni used to put ketchup on her ice-cream. She ate bowls of the disgusting stuff." He shuddered.

As Annette set down her chip, blushing, Craig shot his deputy an irritated look.

Liam looked bewildered.

"What? What did I do?"

He was answered by silence. The others were already halfway out the door.

****

The C.C.U. 12.30 p.m.

"Have you had lunch yet, Davy?"

Davy smiled at Nicky's maternal concern. "I ate on the plane, thanks. S...Some rice thing."

She tutted and reached into her desk drawer, withdrawing a plastic box of brownies. "The light brown ones have hazelnuts in them. Eat as many as you like."

He didn't need to be told twice and after lifting a handful he wandered over to Ash's desk. "What are you w...working on?"

Ash puffed out his cheeks and shook his head. "The Miskimmon case. The chief's been given ten days by the P.P.S to find more evidence; otherwise they're only going to charge them on the visa fraud." He shrugged. "He can't stop it. The Venezuelans are breathing down our necks."

Davy pulled up a chair. "So you're trying s...something new?"

Ash nodded excitedly. "Two somethings, actually. I'm linking up with the hackers in other countries where there were incidents, courtesy of their homeland securities, and I'm searching for anything that might trace Miskimmon's hacks in the systems he breached here."

As Davy gave an admiring whistle Ash realised just how glad he was to have him back. The others smiled politely when he spoke computer, but it was the polite smile of a foreigner in a country where he only had enough of the lingo to order a cup of tea. Davy instantly understood what he was getting at and how hard it would be to achieve.

"Cool." The analyst hesitated. "If you'd like any-"

Ash cut in before he could finish. "Help? Yes. Anything you can think of." Suddenly he slumped back in his chair, his eagerness changing to a scowl as he waved at the two files in his in-tray. "Meanwhile we've got two new murders to solve."

Nicky had been watching the interaction maternally; it reminded her of when her fourteen-year-old son Jonny was at nursery, building his bricks with another boy, frowns of concentration on both their little faces. The analysts looked just the same to her; one green-haired and skinny, the other filling out into a handsome man, but both still just kids in many ways, even if the chronological difference wouldn't actually allow her to be their mum.

Davy was blissfully unaware of her scrutiny, so while Ash shot the P.A. an amused glance he lifted one of the files. After reading for a moment he set it down, shaking his head.

"No way are you leaving next week! There's no chance I can do both of these and the Miskimmon s...stuff on my own." He added a caveat. "Not in the chief's usual timescale anyway." He gave his friend a sly glance. "I don't suppose..."

Ash sucked air in through his teeth like he was preparing to give a builder's estimate. Davy nodded.

"I take it the boss already knows he needs you to s...stay."

The green head bobbed up and down.

"And he's already asked."

Another bob. Which meant that Craig saw the need for two analysts and had the cash to support it.

"But you don't w...want to report to me."

This time Ash raised a forefinger, in the universal signal for 'you've got it in one'. To soften the blow he added. "It's not you, mate, it's just..."

It was Davy's turn to nod. "We went to Uni together and you know just as much as I do."

It wasn't strictly true. Ash knew just as much about computers, but in terms of police work Davy had years of experience and it showed.

The senior analyst thought for a moment, choosing his next words carefully in the knowledge that if he didn't he could wave his friend goodbye. Nicky waited to hear what he said; hoping that some way could be found to keep them both on board. She really liked Ash, but she loved Davy for his shyness and gentle ways, and for pure skill he still had the edge. Plus, Ash was the more worldly-wise of the two so if anyone was going to get cast out into the big bad world, he had to be the one to go.

Thankfully Davy wasn't as innocent as the boy that had first joined the team and the solution he produced was sharper than Nicky could have imagined.

"OK. How's this? Yes, if you stay I'll nominally be your boss, w...which means if the pressure is on and I have to allocate something urgently to you then I will-"

Ash pushed back his chair in a show of displeasure, but Davy ignored it and forged on.

"But, the majority of the time you'll have your w...work and I'll have mine. We'll s...split things evenly, but as much as possible what each of us works on will play to his s...special interests."

Ash leaned forward slightly and Nicky smiled, knowing that Davy had hooked him. All he had to do now was reel him in.

"For instance. I want to keep up my links with the European crime agencies: Europol, Interpol, MI5, MI6 and CEOP, and now and again the FBI and CIA if it fits with my PhD. You could develop your links with GCHQ, the NCA, and other American agencies: Homeland S...Security, the NSA, FBI and CIA, and focus more on terrorism and cybercrime if you liked. Both of us can look for s...secondments to them, to increase our skills, and maybe to other branches of the force as well."

As he sat back and folded his arms Nicky knew the line in the sand was about to be drawn.

"But there can't be any compromise on murder cases. They have to be dealt with before our interests get a look in. Agreed?"

If Ash had still thought he was being persuaded, Davy's tone said he'd given as much ground as he could or would. But whether Davy's suggestions had seemed eminently reasonable or whether it was just his delivery, Ash's thin hand grabbed his and pumped his arm up and down. He added generously.

"You should be the one to tell the chief. But you can keep the NCA; that Agent Somerville woman scares the life out of me. Then get out of here until tomorrow. You're still on holiday..." He turned back to his screen. "And I've got work to do."

Nicky couldn't have been prouder than if Jonny had built Everest with his bricks.

****

The Mortuary. 12.30 p.m.

Xavier Rey had been staring at his son's swollen face for twenty long minutes and Andy wasn't quite sure what to do: hope that John would end the viewing by drawing the sheet over Matias' face; wait until the grieving father turned away of his own accord; or give a quiet cough and hope that it would be sufficient to break the gangster's trance. John wasn't making any such move, something the detective would have expected if he'd known him well. John Winter understood death in all its shades and forms; he also understood grief. He had lost both parents and his favourite aunt, and as an only child he'd had to carry all of the emotions and practicalities alone.

He knew what it was like to wish he could have had one last sight of a loved one, one last conversation, however trivial. 'Would you like some more tea? Would you like a lift into town?' Anything at all, just as long as that person was still there. At Uni he'd been the one in ethics class who'd best understood families' reluctance to turn off life support, even the warm body and touchable hand of their loved one, however unanimated, better than never seeing them again. And that was what death meant to him; placing someone you loved beyond reach for every single day of your life. Even with a religious faith of reunion it would seem final and desolate, and bad enough in itself without also knowing that some stranger had violently taken their life. So he stood and he waited, and he would wait for as long as Xavier Rey needed to say goodbye to his son.

Meanwhile Andy was beginning to panic about what he should do. The clock said they'd been there for

119

almost thirty minutes, far longer than any I.D. he had ever led. People normally glanced and nodded and then walked away, confirming that the dead person was who they'd suspected, and then they all went for the customary cup of tea. Or else they cried and touched the body; on one particularly painful occasion a mother had combed her dead daughter's hair and sung to her. He'd understood of course, and thanked God it wasn't his own son dead, but even then it had only taken ten minutes before they'd left the cold viewing room.

That was the other thing; he hated mortuaries. Loathed them from the bottom of his heart. They were cold and sterile and full of dead people, and if he'd wanted to spend his days like that he would have chosen a different job.

A slight movement to his left jerked him out of his thoughts, but it was only John shifting his foot. Xavier Rey still stood where he'd been standing for half-an-hour. His black eyes staring unblinkingly at his young son's face; his square jaw, softened by the years, set so hard that it looked as if it might crack. He hadn't uttered a word since they'd entered, just fixed his gaze where it remained now.

Andy was just screwing up his courage to try a gentle touch on Rey's arm when the father turned suddenly, catching the detective off guard. Before he could recover Rey was out in the hall and striding towards the exit and the car. The D.C.I. hurried after him to find Rey already in the backseat beside Sid Freeman and the uniformed driver pointedly checking his watch. He covered his embarrassment by snapping.

"Docklands. And make it quick."

They drove in silence towards a conversation that Andy knew would be just as hard.

****

High Street Station.

Mara Kennedy looked every bit as beautiful as she had

done the night before, although her eyes showed the fatigue of a night spent crying and her cheeks the grey smudged pallor of a mind that couldn't rest.

Craig watched her through the viewing room glass, squashing his natural sympathy for a widowed mother with his logic and cynicism, both of which said that most murders were committed by someone that the victim knew. She'd had access to the slurry suit and its air tank and she'd had an affair with the farm's manager. Beautiful she might be but there was nothing innocent about the woman on the other side of the glass.

As his gaze fixed forward Liam's flicked back and forth between Craig and his prey. Mara Kennedy had better be innocent and able to prove it or he wouldn't fancy being in her shoes.

Craig lifted the internal phone.

"Come in, Jack, and bring Rhonda with you. She needs to watch the interview."

Interrogation was more like it when he was in this mood, but Liam decided not to say so; he didn't need the grief.

Five minutes later the names and addresses had all been read and Craig put his hands in his pockets and sat back, leaving the only soundtrack in the room the whine from the tape recorder and Liam mouth breathing to avoid the pain in his nose. Johnny Corbett gazed at the policemen in turn before settling his gaze upon Craig.

"You said you wanted to question my client, so we're here."

Craig's only reply was a nod that made Corbett tut in irritation.

"If you're going to play damn silly games, we're leaving."

He made to stand up but a slim hand on his arm halted his ascent. Mara Kennedy's tone was cool.

"Superintendent Craig is waiting to see what I'll say first, Johnny."

Not just cool but bright.

"He wants me to fill his silence with babbling,

until I incriminate myself in some way and then he'll jump in." She smiled at Craig, peeling back her full lips and showing perfectly straight white teeth; the product of thousands of pounds of orthodontics he didn't doubt.

Craig smiled back. Either she was clever and innocent of her husband's murder, or guilty and too clever to give them a clue. He straightened up, still smiling.

"When did you last see your husband, Mrs McAllister?"

Liam smiled at the married name and knew Mara Kennedy wasn't going to get everything her way.

Johnny Corbett sat back, shaking his head in despair. Liam quite liked the old buffer; he seemed to genuinely have his client's welfare at heart but his shake had said Kennedy was like a runaway stallion; too highly bred and highly strung to be controlled.

She kept staring at Craig, her smile slowly melting away.

"I last saw him on Monday, but I was supposed to see him again on Thursday evening, at dinner."

The day that McAllister had died.

"At whose behest?"

"Mine. I wanted to talk to him."

"In a restaurant?"

"Yes. I didn't want to have the conversation at home. Too comfortable."

"Which conversation was that?"

She laughed sharply. "The one where I asked him where the hell all the money had come from, and if I didn't get a satisfactory answer the one where I would have been telling him that I wanted a divorce."

Craig leaned forward. "I thought you said you'd left soon after you'd found the money. For your son's sake."

She looked momentarily confused. "I...yes, I did...I did tell you that. But I didn't. Not completely. I found the money on the Friday and brought Ben to Belfast on the Monday, but then I asked Colin to meet me that Thursday evening to talk."

Craig sat back, not for comfort but to keep her off kilter. As he changed position he threw in another question.

"Which restaurant?"

"Moriarty's In Armagh."

"Who booked it?"

"I did. I told Colin where we'd meet."

It would be easy to confirm.

"You said you were supposed to see him on Thursday evening, but he was already dead by then."

"I didn't know that. I just thought he'd stood me up because he was angry at me." She stared down at her hands.

Craig stayed on point. "What time did you leave the restaurant?"

"Around ten o'clock. I came back to Belfast not long before you called at the hotel. You can check."

Nice of you to tell us our job.

He leaned forward again, sharply this time so that she was forced to retreat.

"Convenient theatrics for the day he died."

"I didn't kill him." Her voice rose. "I DIDN'T DO IT!"

Liam intervened. "That tape picks up everything. You've no need to shout."

Kennedy didn't acknowledge him, her eyes not moving from Craig's face.

"What was his answer?"

She looked confused, her earlier cool completely gone. Meanwhile, Rhonda was sitting so far forward in the viewing room her nose was touching the glass.

"This is better than TV."

Jack smiled kindly. He'd seen it too many times before to get worked up.

Craig was still waiting for his answer. He repeated the question. "What was your husband's answer?"

Kennedy frowned. "To what?"

"To the question of where he got the money from."

She shook her head. "I told you. He didn't turn up at the restaurant."

"But you'd asked him before then, hadn't you?"

He was playing a hunch. She stared him out for a moment before answering.

"On the phone. He denied knowing anything about it at first, so I said I wanted to ask him face to face. I knew I could make him tell me the truth then. Then he said someone must have just left the money there; one of the farm workers." She scoffed superiorly. "As if any of them had fifty grand."

Craig frowned, thinking for a moment. He nodded Liam on while he did.

"How often did your husband work at the slurry pit?"

Kennedy sat back, looking glad of the change in tack.

"Not very often. Maybe once a month. Mitchell normally does it."

Craig's frown deepened. Had someone intended Purvis to be the one to die? But Liam hadn't finished.

"Did they timetable it? Whoever would be working on the pit that month?"

Kennedy nodded and Craig noticed flashes of grey in her blonde hair. It added something. Beauty was always more beautiful when it wasn't perfect.

"Yes. They write everything on the wall calendar. Exactly where they're scheduled to work each day."

"In the room where the farmhands have their meals?"

"Yes."

His heart sank. Anyone could have seen when the slurry pit would next be worked at, *and* who was scheduled to do it. Seeing that Craig was still thinking the D.C.I. carried on.

"Mr Purvis is around five-feet-ten. What height was your husband?"

Craig's ears perked up.

"Six-three."

Liam nodded that it was the truth. The height difference blew the theory that someone could have made a mistake and killed the wrong man.

He stopped the tape and beckoned Craig out of the room.

"Slurry suits are sized, boss. There's no way a six-three man would wear the same suit as one five-ten. They couldn't have been aiming for Purvis and got McAllister by mistake; their suits would've been different sizes."

Craig's frown didn't shift. "Are the air tanks detachable? Maybe they sabotaged the tank aiming for Purvis but attached it to the wrong suit by mistake."

Liam didn't look convinced. "The tanks *are* detachable, but if they'd sabotaged the tank too early, what would've happened if someone else had decided to use it on a random visit to the pit? They'd have been killed and police would've started hunting for their killer, leaving the real target, McAllister, still doing whatever someone didn't want him to do."

"OK, but that doesn't mean that isn't exactly what happened. They could have been aiming for Purvis, sabotaged the tank and then McAllister picked it up." He suddenly realised something. "Or they could have sabotaged all of the tanks!" He pulled out his phone. "I need to call Armagh."

Five minutes later they had their answer. None of the other air tanks had been meddled with, so whoever had sabotaged the tank had been specific. They would have had to have sabotaged the tank and left it where only the next man scheduled for the slurry pit would have picked it up. Craig shook his head.

"We need to ask a different question."

He pushed open the door and restarted the tape.

"Did your husband just use any air tank that was lying around when he worked on the slurry?"

Mara Kennedy immediately shook her head. "No. he always used the same tank. He said it had the best connection with his suit."

"But how could he tell one tank from another? He might just have lifted the tank that felt most full."

She shook her head again. "Colin checked them all regularly to make sure they were full. He was meticulous about it, in case one of the farmhands had to go in, but he only ever used *his* tank. He'd marked it with his initials specially."

125

Craig made for the door again, leaving Liam to pause the tape. He entered the viewing room and made another call, this time to the lab.

"Des? Can you describe the air tank from the slurry suit to me?"

Des frowned. What did he mean? A tank was a tank. Craig was obviously losing it so he adopted the sing song voice he used with his kids.

"It's grey metal, probably steel but I haven't checked. Cylindrical with a-"

Craig barked down the line. "I know what a bloody tank looks like! Is there anything written on it?"

Des huffed back. "Made in Australia. So what?"

Craig thought for a second. "Look at the base."

"Why?"

"Just do it."

Even he knew that his manners were getting worse.

Des muttered to himself. "Bloody tank. What does he expect to see? A map of Australia on its ass..." He turned the tank upside down with a clang and Craig heard a faint gasp, followed by "Oh hell."

"Oh hell what? What are you oh-helling about?"

"There are letters on the bottom. Someone's painted them on. C.G.P Mc.A. How the heck did I miss that? I mean..."

He was left 'I meaning' to thin air because Craig was already back in the room. He hit the tape again.

"How did your husband mark his name on his air tank?"

Kennedy smirked and crossed her arms. "Believe me now?"

"How?" His tone said don't push it.

"CGPMCA, separated by dots."

"Give me them one by one."

"C dot, G, dot, P, dot, Mc, dot, A, full stop. It stands for Colin, George, Paul, McAllister. His mother liked the Beatles. He marked all his equipment with it, and before you ask, he *would* have checked he'd attached the right tank before he'd put on his suit. He was meticulous about that sort of thing."

126

It only proved that whoever their killer was they'd got the man that they'd been aiming for, but it still didn't rule Kennedy out.

"I'm pausing this interview, Mrs McAllister." Before she could object he turned to the solicitor. "We'll be re-interviewing your client, Mr Corbett, but in the interim she will remain here. Please make arrangements for the care of the child."

They didn't hang around to listen to the uproar, sending Jack in to deal with it and joining the others in the small staff room. Annette looked up as they entered.

"Any joy with her?"

Liam answered as he put on the kettle. "Some, but she's not out of the woods yet. At least we know they weren't trying to kill Purvis. They definitely got their man."

Jake chipped in. "Which means Purvis could still be our killer."

The D.C.I. answered with his head in the fridge. "Yep. But so could any of the farmhands."

Craig nodded. "We need to find the motive for killing McAllister, otherwise we'll just be interviewing at random." He glanced at his watch. "Annette, you're welcome to have another go at either of them, but I think you'll be wasting your time. I'd let them both stew until we have something more. Liam and I are going back to the office now to see what Ash has found."

Liam stood up quickly. "But I didn't get my tea."

Craig's answer floated back down the corridor. "Nicky has brownies in her drawer." It had the desired Pied Piper effect.

Chapter Six

The C.C.U. Relatives' Room.

Sid Freeman glanced first at Xavier Rey and then at Andy, before deciding that the floor was a safer bet to look at than either man. Rey because his face appeared to be set in such a permanent scowl that the constable wondered if he'd been born that way. Perhaps he'd taken one look at the world with all its dirt and chaos and decided to go back where he'd come from, only to find the option gone and seventy years of blood, sweat and tears lying ahead.

Andy wasn't scowling, but he wasn't looking happy either; his face moulded into a mask of perplexed macho-ness, that, even though he didn't know him, Freeman didn't think fitted him very well.

After five minutes of silence and the beige carpet burning a hole in his retinae, Sid Freeman made a decision, or rather his impatient nature made it for him; he'd never been very good at waiting for things. He rose to his feet and lifted the teapot, pouring out three cups and pushing two pointedly at the mute men, praying that politeness would force at least one of them to acknowledge his good deed.

To his surprise it was Rey who spoke first. OK, it was a curt "thanks", but at least he'd said something. Andy's response was to shoot the D.C. a grateful glance, and a nod that said 'go on'.

"I'm very sorry for your loss, Mr Rey."

The young constable leaned towards him as he said it, his arm reaching out in a virtual hug. Virtual it might have been but its effect was astonishingly real. Xavier Rey's stiff lips contorted, tugging first down and then sideways so that Freeman initially thought he was going to speak, and Andy thought he was going to punch the huggy youth. Then the gang boss' lips pursed so tight that both cops suddenly realised what he was trying to do. Stop himself crying. A lifelong crier himself Sid Freeman recognised the signs. Xavier

Rey was teetering between dry eyes and tears and it wouldn't take much to start the flood.

The young detective couldn't help what he did next, rationalising that if it was a child or a woman in front of him he wouldn't have hesitated to touch their hand in comfort, so why should a grown man need comfort any less.

Andy watched astounded as Freeman placed an arm around the godfather's shoulder. He kept watching as Rey's dam finally burst and fiercely held-in tears started to stream down his cheeks. When they had finally subsided the constable spoke in a quiet voice.

"Please let us help you, Mr Rey. Let us help you by finding the people who did this to your son."

****

A field in County Armagh.

The young woman gazed at her handiwork, assessing its effect before exiting the dark green car. She noticed a stain on her skirt and shuddered; that was the problem with arteries, especially the arteries of overweight old men; high blood pressure sent the spray everywhere. There was no point trying to clean it off; forensic labs could dig DNA out of the smallest blood drop these days. She would just have to burn it, and her top, and they'd cost her thirty quid at the market just the week before. She was bloody well adding the expense to her bill, plus fifty for almost having to have sex with the dirty old man before she'd seen him off. The boss would never know he'd already paid her, and she deserved way more than fifty for what the kinky git had tried to make her do.

She slammed the car door behind her and slipped off her wig and shoes, burying her toes in the wet grass as she walked. The man had wondered why they'd had to drive so far, so she'd said that the countryside always put her in the mood. The reality was far simpler; at the end of the field lay the border with the

Irish Republic, and a short stroll would take her into a different land. When she reached the low fence at the end the girl turned and waved sarcastically at her dead punter, then she stepped across and waited patiently for her lift.

****

The C.C.U.

Craig and Liam emerged from the lift at the same time as Andy was walking up the stairs. It was such uncharacteristic athleticism on his part that Liam couldn't allow it to pass.

"Don't tell me. You got out at the ninth and walked up to impress us."

Andy merely raised an eyebrow. "Aye, that's right. The same way that you broke your own nose."

Before Liam could retaliate Craig waved Andy through the squad's doors.

"You were in the relatives' room with Rey?"

The D.C.I. nodded.

"Positive I.D.?"

Another nod. Craig glanced around.

"So where's Geoff Hamill's officer?"

"Sid Freeman. He's still down there, holding Rey's hand." He made an appreciative noise. "He got more out of him with a hug that I'd have got all day."

Liam halted abruptly. "Hug? That's not in the interview handbook."

Craig tutted. "The man's just lost his son, Liam." He turned back to Andy. "He's safe enough there, isn't he?"

"Wouldn't have left him otherwise. I sensed Rey would say more without the boss man in the room. Macho stuff."

Craig shot Liam a warning glance; any cracks about Andy's masculinity could wait for another day. He strode across the floor to Ash, ending the exchange. On his way he noticed a pile of folders on Davy's desk.

"Davy won't be happy if his desk is untidy when he

gets back."

Nicky answered brightly. "He's back already and he put them there himself."

Craig turned towards her with a smile. "He's back? Where is he?"

"I sent him home. He was tired and dirty from the flight. He'll be in tomorrow."

Fair enough. He grabbed a chair and sat down.

"What have you got for me, Ash?" He turned, looking for Liam, only to find him by Nicky's desk, basking in her sympathy for his sore nose. "Liam, call Joe for an update, and when you've finished that get onto the lab. I want a definitive cause of death for Matias Rey; they must have his tox-screen back by now. We need to know if he drowned normally, was killed by a blow as he went into the river, or was drugged so heavily that he drowned. Hurry up."

He turned back to Ash, but not so quickly that he didn't catch Liam shaking his fist.

"Right, Ash. I need Rey's point of entry into the river, and the path he travelled. Plus anything else you've got."

Ash didn't move, not even to tap a key. As Craig leaned forward to urge him on, the analyst said "Yes."

Craig was perplexed. "Yes? Yes what?"

"Yes, Davy and I had a chat and I'd like to stay. If the offer's still open."

Craig grinned. "That's brilliant. I'm presuming you've divided the work in a way that'll keep you both happy."

Ash gave him a 'too right' look. "I'm going nowhere near Agent Somerville again. That was part of the deal."

Craig laughed. "OK, I'll get the details some other time. Nice to have you on the team." He gestured at the analyst's computer. "So, have you got what I need?"

So that was it. No fanfare and no cake; they had a new permanent member of the team and now he had to earn his crust. Ash lifted his smart-pad and tapped up a map. It showed the Lagan from its source at Slieve Croob in County Down to Belfast Lough where it

131

entered the Irish Sea. Every tributary was marked in red, every weir, lock and bridge in green.

"OK, so according to the different algae found in Matias Rey's throat and lungs, he entered the river here." He tapped on the screen and a gold star appeared at Shaw's Bridge. "He was still breathing when he reached here." Another tap and another star appeared at the near end of Lagan Meadows. "The algae's different in the higher part of his respiratory tract."

"Meaning it entered later."

"Correct. We think that's where he died. The algae downstream from there is different again, but there's no sign of it in his throat or lungs, so Des and John think he took his last breath somewhere around here."

Craig frowned at the screen, puzzled. The distance between Rey's entry point and where he'd died was less than two miles. He'd been young and fit, and in inland water even the weakest swimmer shouldn't have drowned. Ash read his mind.

"Yep, that's what I thought. A couple of miles in an inland river wouldn't seem enough to have killed him. I'm not that strong a swimmer and even I would have been OK. I checked the currents for Tuesday night and Wednesday and they weren't strong, so he's unlikely to have been pulled under for any time. And OK, the water was cold, but it wasn't freezing, so while hypothermia could've been a factor in his death, it couldn't have been the cause. So..." He moved to his P.C. and began to scroll. Before he could speak again Craig threw in a question.

"He *could* swim, couldn't he? Someone *has* checked."

Ash nodded, still scrolling. "Doctor Winter asked his father at the viewing. He was a strong swimmer."

"So...that means... either there was some obstacle in the river that caused his death that wasn't on the map, or he had to have been physically compromised in some way. Probably drugs."

"Or both." Ash nodded towards Andy. "Andy asked some uniforms to check the route and they found a heap of scrap metal dumped in the river..." He turned back to his pad and pointed just beyond the second star. "Just here. So it's possible Rey got caught on it, struggled to free himself and drowned. It rained heavily on Wednesday night so the current must have washed the body free, down to the Lagan Weir. It could explain why it took almost two days for him to be found. I checked and Rey's jeans had rips in them that were too big to have been made by stones-"

Craig signalled him to stop. "OK, so he enters here." He pointed to the first star and then moved his finger along. "And we know that here is where he acquired the last algae he breathed in, just a few feet before the scrap metal he got caught on. So was that it? He got stuck and drowned naturally?"

He was answered by a flurry of green. "No. It definitely wasn't natural; he could have freed himself if he hadn't been so compromised by drugs. Doctor Marsham has just phoned. They found enough Ketamine and Valium in Rey's system to render him completely incapable."

Craig nodded. Rey's attackers would never have taken the chance he'd survive to I.D. them.

"Good work, Ash."

Liam was at his desk, still talking on the phone. He cut the call just as Craig approached.

"Rey's C.O.D. was drug induced drowning. Ketamine and Valium. Enough to stop a truck."

"I know."

Liam wasn't deflated. "Aye, but what you don't know is that they've found something at the farm. Joe wants us down there."

Craig glanced at his watch. Two o'clock and it would take them until four to get to Armagh and back. He didn't fancy a late briefing so he strode across to Nicky.

"Nick, I want a briefing in one hour, please, and can you see if Sergeant Karl Rimmins from Drugs and D.C.I. Hamill from Gangs can join us. If Karl needs persuading tell him that it involves Ketamine."

As he turned towards the door she called after

him. "Where will you be until then?"

"Here. I'm just nipping down to get a sandwich."

Liam reached the stairs before he did. "Me too."

****

Katy typed in her credit card details and then hovered the mouse above the 'purchase' button, wondering if she was insane but deciding to go ahead anyway. She clicked twice and then shut down the screen. She was a grown woman and it was time to stop being scared. Life is dangerous; get over it, girl. She was more likely to get killed crossing the road than-.

She halted mid-thought, wondering if it was actually true about crossing roads and other accidents. Scientist that she was, she clicked on an actuarial site to check. Actually, it *was* true about the likelihood of accidents, but she was even more likely to die of the Flu! And they were both infinitely more likely than getting killed by one of Marc's psychopaths. It made up her mind.

If she could do even two of the things that she'd just paid for without running away in fright, then she would officially be brave. What that meant for her future, only time would tell.

****

Craig was sitting with his feet up on his desk and a chicken sandwich halfway out of his mouth when the handle of his office door began rattling; interrupting the five minutes quiet he'd allowed himself to think about life. He kept on eating, knowing that his intruder would enter a second later, whether he wanted them to or not. It would be either Nicky or Liam; no-one else would dare bother him when he was trying to take a break.

When no-one entered and the rattling continued he set his sandwich down and sighed.

"Come in before you pull the handle off."

It was Nicky, the rattling her way of warning him

of bad news. Her glum expression underlined it so effectively that he dropped his feet to the floor with a thud.

"Who's dead?"

"A man in a field in Armagh."

What was it with Armagh this week?

"I take it, it wasn't natural causes."

It was the P.A.'s turn to sigh. "Not unless he cut his throat shaving."

Everybody's a comedian.

He beckoned her in and consigned the sandwich to the bin. "OK, so tell me why a murder in Armagh is our problem? You don't think two deaths is enough for one week?"

"The officer in charge recognised the victim and he'd heard about our investigation and thought that it might be connected."

He sat back. "Who *is* the victim?"

"A Belfast bookie called Calum Fox. He owns..."

Craig had already tuned out. He already knew exactly what Calum Fox owned, the Fox chain of betting shops was well known across the north. The gambling link took his mind immediately to Matias Rey.

"Did he say Fox was linked with gangs?"

She shook her head, puzzled. "Gangs? In Armagh?" It was said as if the countryside was immune to such things. "No, he just said Fox was a well-known businessman and he wondered if there might be a link with our farmer's death, seeing as it happened just down the road."

Craig gave a sceptical 'huh'. "You mean he wanted to get a potentially high profile case off his patch." He thought for a moment. "OK, move the briefing to five, please, and apologise to everyone; I know it's late for a Friday but we are on all weekend. Tell Liam we're leaving for Armagh in ten minutes, please."

When the door had closed he cleared murder from his mind and turned to thinking about Katy. He had a hunch it was the last chance he would get all weekend.

****

Dundalk. The Republic of Ireland.

"So it's done, then?"

The girl zipped up her jeans and walked past the youth towards the house's back garden. As he repeated the question more firmly, she swung round, spitting out a reply in a heavy accent.

"You bloody know it done, Dermot. Your dog on phone to you as soon as I get in his car." She held up her soiled clothes. "I burn my clothes now because of it. You owe me cost of those as well."

As she dropped the bloodied outfit on the bonfire, the man relaxed down in his chair. He waved her back in, coaxing her onto his knee as they watched the evidence go up in smoke.

"Ach, I'm sarry, mo grá. Ye know I'd never have asked ye if it hadn't been important."

The girl wriggled in a show of displeasure. "Important to who? And what they want bookie killing f-"

She didn't finish the word, her throat suddenly constricted by the young man's strong hand. The message was clear; keep your mouth shut or I'll shut it for you. When fear had widened her eyes enough to please him Dermot Faloon relaxed his grip and trailed the hand down to her breasts instead, cupping one firmly in his hand. It was a different message to his first, but every bit as clear.

Chapter Seven

Armagh. 3 p.m.

"McAllister was on the take so the odds are Fox was."

Craig shrugged and then indicated off the Portadown Road, pulling into the city's main police station.

"We don't know they're linked yet."

Liam sniffed and climbed out of the car. "If they weren't dumping bodies at beauty spots, I'd say leave them to it. Scrotes killing scrotes is the way of the world."

"I'll pretend I didn't hear that." Craig locked the car and headed for the building. "Anyway, they *are* defacing beauty spots and all these killings are bad for the tourist trade." He pulled open the heavy steel front door. "What I don't like are the links with the Republic."

Liam frowned. "What links? The deaths were both in the north."

"A few miles from the border. And Geoff said something about The Rock; they intercepted a call that referred to knackers."

Liam's eyes widened. "You're linking the Armagh deaths with Matias Rey's?"

Craig walked to the desk, not answering, and pulled out his warrant card. "Sergeant O'Donnell, please. Say Superintendent Craig and D.C.I. Cullen from the Belfast Murder Squad are here to see him."

The W.P.C. behind the desk looked startled by his words, then she peered at his badge and looked even more shocked when she saw that it was true, knocking a pile of paper over in her grab for the phone. She turned her back to them and cupped her hand around the receiver. It made Liam comment in a loud voice.

"See the effect we have on women."

Craig snorted. "I think you'll find the word murder did the trick."

The woman turned back, her eyes still wide, and

pointed them shakily to a bench. "The sergeant's just popped out. They're phoning him now."

As Craig sat down he thought idly that words like 'popped' and 'nipped', however descriptive, probably didn't carry the authoritative ring that the force hoped to convey. When he'd trained they'd said things like 'he's on an enquiry', even if that enquiry was only how much the chips cost in the local café, or else they'd said 'he's liaising'; it had sounded good and covered a multitude of sins. He was just about to ask Liam what he'd said as a P.C. when a grey-haired Sergeant Frederick O'Donnell popped back in. He followed the flurry of handshaking with a buzzed entry through to a small briefing room. Its white boarded wall was covered with scenes that could have been from a slasher movie and Craig wandered across to take a closer look.

"Calum Fox, I presume?"

"Aye." O'Donnell ran his fingers under his collar like he was spiking a temperature. "I don't mind telling you we don't see much of this sort of thing. Thanks be to God."

Liam's reply was caustic. "We see far too much of it, and now you want to give us another one."

Craig shot him a warning look and took a seat. "We're happy to help in any way we can, Sergeant. Tell us what you know so far."

O'Donnell perched on the desk, pointedly avoiding Liam's eyes, and Craig made up his mind that another diplomacy lecture lay in his D.C.I.'s future. If rural forces were deterred calling on them for help, there'd be a lot of future murders in the country written off as accidental deaths.

O'Donnell was still feeling his own collar, in a way that said doing up his top button had probably only been for their benefit. Craig pictured him fastening it between the front desk phone call and the moment he'd popped back through the station's door, so in a show of consideration he loosened his own tie, relaxing the tone until O'Donnell felt confident enough to speak.

"Aye, well. We got a call from a local farmer around two o'clock, complaining that someone had parked a car in his field-"

Liam cut in. "I take it he'd only seen it from a distance."

"You're right there. I was just about to get Traffic to take a look when he phoned back ten minutes later to say it contained a corpse." He shook his head at the memory. "The accent's strong around here at the best of times but it was hard to get a word of sense off him. Anyhow, I went to take a look." He gestured at the board. "And found yer man."

Craig nodded. "You've obviously sealed off the scene and called forensics." He hoped. "Is that who took the photos?"

"Aye. They've a good lad who does all of that. They're down there now, doing the usual."

"And the body?"

"Gone to the local morgue. The pathologist started the P.M. ten minutes ago."

He made a note to get John to check out the results.

O'Donnell looked embarrassed suddenly and the detectives immediately knew there'd been something at the scene he hadn't photographed. Before Liam could put his foot in it Craig interjected.

"What aren't you telling us, Sergeant? There was something at the scene that isn't on that board, wasn't there?"

O'Donnell had turned bright red.

"OK, let me guess. Your victim was found in a compromising position. Yes?"

Liam guffawed. "You mean his -"

Craig cut him off. "Thank you, Liam. The sergeant can answer for himself."

O'Donnell searched for the words. "He's...he was married."

Craig smiled kindly. The practice of infidelity was universal; Armagh's dedicated divorce firm was probably testament to that, but O'Donnell's concern for Calum Fox's family and reputation still did him credit. Liam's laughter renewed.

"The dirty dog."

"I'll tell Danni you said that admiringly, shall I?"

The D.C.I.'s eyes widened. "Here now, there's no-"

Craig decided to save O'Donnell further blushes. "Mr Fox's clothing was in disarray from the waist down. Is that what you're saying?"

O'Donnell nodded.

"And was there a condom in the vicinity?"

The sergeant shook his head.

"OK. So either they didn't use one and his companion's DNA will be on Mr Fox, or they did and he or she took it with them-"

"A man!"

The thought that Calum Fox might have been bisexual obviously hadn't occurred to him. Craig went on as if the sergeant hadn't spoken.

"Which suggests that our killer was forensically aware." He shrugged. It made sense. Fox had been murdered in a remote location which said that it had been planned. His companion could be miles away by now with no way of finding them.

He felt a faint surge of hope.

"The farm is right on the border."

"Aye, the end of that field lies on the line." O'Donnell relaxed back in his seat, back on more comfortable ground.

"Did the farmer have perimeter cameras, by any chance?"

The sergeant looked surprised by the question but had the sense not to bluff. "I don't honestly know, sir. Do you mind if I make a quick call?"

Craig nodded him out then turned to Liam with a glint in his eye. "You're a rude bugger."

The Crossgar man feigned innocence. "Moi? What did I do?"

"Basically told the man he was dumping the case on us."

Liam shrugged. "Well he is, isn't he?"

Craig was taken aback. He'd expected some embarrassment at least, then he remembered how long he'd known Liam and wondered why he had. "Well, yes, OK. But better that we have it, if it's linked with McAllister, than they make a hash of things."

"So I wasn't rude, I was right. Admit it."

"Like hell. Anyway..." Craig gestured at the board. "Fox was obviously looking for some afternoon delight and chose the wrong girl. Or she chose him."

"So you do think it was a woman."

"It's more likely."

Liam sniffed judgmentally. "Serves him right getting killed, the dirty old bugger. He was seventy if he was a day."

"And seventy year olds aren't supposed to have sex?"

"Not with women that young, they aren't!"

"We don't know how young she was."

Liam snorted rudely. "Well she wasn't his age, that's for sure. A seventy-year-old woman would have more sense. Anyway, I don't like big age gaps. They're seedy."

Craig didn't disagree. He braced himself for what he knew was coming next.

"Mind you...it gives a whole new meaning to 'dying for a shag'."

Craig shook his head despairingly just as O'Donnell re-entered the room.

"We're in luck, sir. There are cameras at some parts of the perimeter, although not directly pointing at that field. We might get something."

"None on the nearby roads, I suppose."

"I don't know. I'll have to ask the Gardaí about that. It's their turf."

Craig stood up. It would have to do for now. "OK, I'll need everything you've got on Fox's family and then I'll need to see the scene."

Liam's ears pricked up at 'I'll'.

"D.C.I. Cullen will be watching the post-mortem. Could someone please take him down?"

That would teach him not to be rude on someone else's patch.

High Street Station. Viewing Room One.

Annette pulled her hair back from her face, surprised when it didn't end at her neck as it had before. Instead it was hitting her shoulders, a gift of her pregnancy hormones. She hadn't noticed, preoccupied as she'd been with buying the paraphernalia that a new baby requires. She was just making a mental note to visit the hairdressers when Jake nudged her and pointed through the glass.

"Look."

She looked but saw nothing different. Mitchell Purvis was still staring down at the table, stony-faced, with his brief entrenched by his side. He was one of Jonny Corbett's colleagues which said that Mara Kennedy was probably footing the bill. Caring employer or an ex-lover with something to hide? Either way the tableau looked no different to when they'd interviewed Purvis four hours before. Annette shook her head and glanced at Jake, who was leaning against the viewing room wall with his crutches propped up by his side.

"What? I can't see anything different to last time."

The sergeant leaned forward, almost pressing his nose against the glass.

"I can. The lawyer's getting pissed off. He rolled his eyes a moment ago. I saw it."

If he had then that meant there was tension between him and his client. It could mean that he wanted Purvis to speak, which made him sort-of on their side. She nodded for Jake to lead the way into the interview room, thinking of ways to use the mood change to their advantage.

When the naming and cautioning was done Annette smiled at the solicitor pleasantly.

"You're from Mr Corbett's firm, I understand."

The suited man hesitated, as if he thought the question was some sort of trick. Assessment over, he nodded.

"I am."

"May I ask you then...is Ms Kennedy paying for your time?"

Purvis lurched forward.

"I object."

Whether he was objecting on the grounds of privacy or macho-ness she wasn't quite sure. Annette turned her smile on him.

"To what, Mr Purvis? I merely wondered who was footing the bill."

He straightened up and threw out his chest. "I can pay my own way." Macho-ness it was then. She gave him a mollifying nod.

"I don't doubt it, but the fact is that your brief works for Ms Kennedy's family firm, which makes it likely that she appointed him to protect you. Now why would that be?"

The farm manager glanced at the solicitor and this time *she* saw the lawyer roll his eyes. It was a clear sign of exasperation and for the first time in hours that Mitchell Purvis had seemed uncertain of his ground. He thought for a moment and then gave them the most neutral answer he could find.

"She cares what happens to me."

Jake signalled to cut in.

"But what could possibly happen to you, Mr Purvis? If you didn't have anything to do with Mr McAllister's death then the evidence will exonerate you. In fact it's my understanding that we're viewing that more likely by the hour." He had no idea if they were or weren't; Des' examination of the slurry suit not yet being complete, but it was a vague enough statement not to land them in the shit and it might just make Purvis relax.

Purvis became more animated immediately.

"So you've found out who killed Colin? Who was it? And why? He never did anyone any harm that I knew."

Annette jumped in. "You liked him."

She was waiting for the brief to stop him answering. His lack of objection confirmed that he'd

143

wanted his client to speak.

"We went to school together. Best mates for twenty-five years." He looked sad suddenly. "When my own family's farm went under Colin offered every hand a job and took me on as his manager."

She followed up quickly. "And you thanked him by having an affair with his wife."

Purvis' sadness changed to guilt and then to anger. "You don't need to remind me it was a shitty thing to do. I know it. But..." He dropped his eyes and she knew what he was looking at wasn't the desk. He was seeing Mara Kennedy and remembering every stolen moment.

Her voice softened.

"You loved her."

He nodded so firmly that she knew he still did, but she didn't embarrass him by making him say it. They already knew that Mara had ended the relationship.

She moved her hand forward on the desk.

"I need to ask you, Mr Purvis, did the two of you ever plan a future together?"

His head shot up immediately and they could see his eyes reddening with tears.

"I used to dream about it...the two of us living somewhere with Ben." His jaw set and he shook his head sharply. "Mara didn't want it. She said she couldn't divorce Colin; he would never recover. That was when she ended it with me."

Annette held her tone and her position. "When exactly did the relationship end?"

He tapped his forehead hard. "In here, never. But we stopped meeting up in June last year."

Seven months before. If it was true then it was unlikely Colin McAllister's death had anything to do with the affair. She saw Jake signalling to ask something and sat back, nodding him on.

"Mr Purvis, when did you find out that Mrs McAllister was consulting a lawyer about divorce?"

"When your superintendent checked her texts yesterday."

The farm manager's face was sad and Annette

144

could read the thoughts running through his mind. Why hadn't Mara told him that things were rocky with Colin? And then the acknowledgement; the fact that she hadn't meant that they would never be together again. Then, even worse, the question; had she deliberately sabotaged her husband's slurry suit and left the farm on the Monday to give herself an alibi for his death?

As Annette watched the expressions flit across Purvis' face she became surer that he hadn't killed his friend. His reason for murder would have been his love for Mara, and that affair had ended months before. Even if hope had still burned that she might reconsider he would have had less reason to kill McAllister now than he'd had the June before.

Jake asked another question. "Do you know of any reason why Mrs McAllister might have wanted to leave her husband?"

The shake of Purvis' head was instant and his answer came in the voice of a broken man. "I've no idea. The business was doing fine and Mara loved Colin, even when we were together I always knew that."

The D.S. didn't sugar coat his next question. "So why have an affair with you?"

Ouch. The solicitor moved forward to object but Purvis waved him back.

"It's a fair question. The oldest reason in the world. Sex. Colin was always busy and Mara got bored on the farm. It started as sex pure and simple, but it turned into love." He shook his head at the reality of it. "At least I thought it had. Seems like it was only me in love now, doesn't it."

There was no kind answer, so Annette called a halt to the interview and Jack Harris took Mitchell Purvis back to his cell. Jake stared up at the ceiling, thinking.

"Do we let him go?"

Annette shook her head. "No. We don't know yet that the wife didn't do it, or Purvis, or both. He could still have been her accomplice, no matter how innocent he's just come across." She tapped the table with her pen. "I don't like the timing of her starting divorce proceedings with his death. It's too damn close for comfort."

She pushed back her chair and rose, getting ready to leave. "Let's see what else the chief has found out and make a decision then."

****

County Armagh.

Craig peered into the dark saloon's boot, taking in a toolbox and gardening gloves. As he closed it with a slam Liam walked round to the car's passenger side and noticed a baby seat in the back. He'd managed to convince Craig it would be more use if they viewed the scene and body together. He'd also promised to watch his mouth, although neither of them had believed that.

"I thought you said Fox was seventy. Who owned the kid?"

Fred O'Donnell had his notebook open, expecting the question. "His grandson, Cillian. Aged two. Fox looked after him twice a week. Don't worry, he was at home with his mum today. We checked."

Craig nodded and then walked round to the driver's side. The bloodied door was lying open and more blood streaked the grass at his feet; a product of the emergency services pulling Fox out for a futile attempt at resuscitation. Blood had flooded the rest of the car as well; the windscreen looked like a Jackson Pollock from arterial spray. Craig stared at the carnage as he asked his next question.

"Did you find the weapon?"

O'Donnell shook his head. "No. Sorry. But it'll have been a razor blade or sharp knife. The edges were very clean."

Liam nodded vaguely as he wandered towards the bottom of the field. "The P.M. will tell." He stopped a few feet in front of the low fence and beckoned them to take a look. "There's more blood here, boss." He hunkered down and was joined by Craig. Small spots of blood were visible on some of the longer blades of grass.

Craig sprang to his feet again. "Get the C.S.I.s back here please, Sergeant. There's a blood trail leading from the car..." He walked as he talked until he'd covered the full length of the fence, then he returned to Liam. "...it's only on this part of the fence, and the size and shape of the blood droplets says they probably fell from something. Possibly-"

Liam finished his sentence. "The blade."

The detectives stared at the blood, then Liam utilised the common travel area and stepped over the wooden barrier into the Republic, to stare at it from the other side. "There's more blood here, boss." He yelled past him to O'Donnell. "You need to tell the Gardaí to get their lads here as well. They'll need to follow the trail as far as they can on this side." He squinted down the rough track, shielding his eyes from the afternoon winter sun. "Mind you, my guess is she'd have been picked up here, so there probably won't be much more to find."

Craig leaned over the fence, his gaze fixing on a smudge halfway down. "Is that what I think it is?"

Liam bent down for a look and then straightened up again with a laugh. "It is! It's a print. Our girl forgot she had blood on her hands."

"I wouldn't get your hopes up. The chances of her having a record are slim to none. They won't have used anyone well known to do this."

O'Donnell had joined them so Craig continued.

"Your C.S.I.'s and the Gardaí need to do some very joined-up work, Sergeant, otherwise we'll be waiting all year to get the information across."

He turned on his heel with Liam following and they drove the ten minutes it took to get to the Armagh Labs. When they arrived in the car park John Winter was waiting for them. Craig smiled, guessing that he'd wanted to be in on the excitement and it was an excuse for an afternoon out of town.

Liam didn't let the visit pass.

"To what do we owe this honour, Doc? Don't you

trust the people you've trained?"

John blustered indignantly. "I trust them wholeheartedly. I just happened to be down here on a quality control check."

None of them believed it but Craig nodded the excuse through, moving quickly into the building before Liam could offend the pathologist again.

"It's an interesting case, John. It looks like Fox was with a prostitute and she cut his throat."

"Do you pay extra for that?"

It was as politically incorrect as anything that Liam might have said and made Craig roll his eyes.

"We need you to confirm cause of death and tell us about the weapon."

John nodded eagerly. "I can do that." His curiosity about the circumstances of death began to show. "Was she a Mata Hari type then?"

Craig shrugged. "We don't know anything about her. We're only speculating that Fox was with a prostitute because he was found in his car in the middle of a field with his equipment on display. It could have been his girlfriend, for all we know."

Liam shot him a knowing look. "In my experience they prefer dinner and a comfy bed."

"Says the great lover."

Liam's retort was aborted by John opening the dissection room door; he drew the line at discussing his love life in front of a corpse. John nodded hello to the pathologist, who was discarding his gown in a bin.

"How are you, Jamie? Long time no see."

The young pathologist slipped his mask beneath his chin, revealing a respectful smile. "I'm well, Doctor Winter. It's good to see you again."

Craig smiled. It was funny to hear John being addressed in such awed tones. He always forgot he was the lead pathologist in the country instead of just his friend and regular coffee supply.

John moved to stand beside the body, gesturing Liam and Craig across.

"Doctor James Bale, this is Superintendent Craig and D.C.I. Cullen from the Murder Squad in Belfast.

148

They've been asked to look at this case by Sergeant O'Donnell, so what can you tell us about Mr Fox's demise?"

The pathologist uncovered Calum Fox's face, revealing the throat laceration that had undoubtedly caused his death.

"Mr Calum Fox, seventy-one years old. Dead between two and three hours. General health: clinically obese with signs of being a smoker, so, as expected, his arteries and heart showed the commensurate wear and tear. He had a small cancer in his prostate which probably wouldn't have killed him for ten years or so, and other than that he was in good health."

Liam's tone was dry. "Apart from the hole in his neck."

Bale smiled nervously. "I was just coming to that. Mr Fox's cause of death was from complete bifurcation of his left carotid artery and partial severance of his right. He bled profusely from both arteries."

John nodded. "It would have killed him in minutes." He nodded for the face to be recovered and waved a hand down Fox's concealed body. "Our understanding is that he had engaged in coitus before death."

The pathologist nodded a tad too eagerly, earning him a chastising glance from his boss. He took a deep breath and continued reporting in a suitably sombre voice. "It appears that the deceased had sexual intercourse soon before death-"

Liam cut in. "How do you know it was soon?"

"Do you really want the details?" He turned back to John. "I've sent the samples to our labs. If a condom was used it seems the other party took it with them."

They were unlikely to get the woman's DNA. Bale was still speaking.

"I believe the C.S.I.s found a long blonde hair at the scene, so that might yield something."

John nodded, satisfied, and turned to leave. "Thank you, Jamie. I hope I'll see you at my lecture on Blood Tranfusions next month?"

The resultant nodding must have given James

Bale a sore neck. As John led the way to the lift Craig couldn't resist a quip.

"You were like a proud father back there, John. Practicing?"

The only answer he got was an enigmatic smile.

****

County Louth. Republic of Ireland

Inspector Magnus O'Shea was staring out of his office window when the call came. The view wasn't up to much, just a row of shops and the local dole office, but he was well placed by the border to keep an eye on things.

All his life he'd slaved at a desk or out on the street, risking his life for a pension less than half of what he was worth, and a spit in the ocean compared to the money made by the people he'd locked up. His wife had put up with a lot from the job; never knowing when he'd left in the morning if she would see him again that night. Mary had deserved better and soon she would get it; only eleven more months before he could take his pension and call it a day, then it would just be them and the kids and grandkids and whatever comfort he could provide.

He wouldn't miss the force at all, but he'd never have believed it if someone had said that when he was a young Jack-the-lad, first in uniform and then in a suit. He couldn't wait to join the Gardaí like his Da had; to carry a badge and nick the bad men like he'd seen in the movies. And for the best part of his time in the job he'd loved it, but the hours had been long and eventually his mind, body and goodwill to all had worn out. Now he marked the days till he left on the desk calendar Mary had bought him, and the rest of the time he did paperwork and watched the world.

That was why the call had made him smile; some boss up high had obviously decided to make him work. Armagh had had a murder and they thought the killer might hail from the Republic, so he'd been appointed

150

Gardaí liaison and was heading for his car and a trip up north. His border location had always made it likely to happen one day.

Ah well, he'd keep his ears open, make a show of the work and get home in time for tea, not like some eager young buck who'd go digging around and disturbing things he'd no business to, to make his mark. No, that wouldn't do at all.

****

McAllisters' Farm. County Armagh.

Liam's mouth dropped open and stayed open. Normally Craig would have told him to shut it, in case a passing fly thought it had found a new home, but not this time, because his own mouth was lying open just as wide.

Sergeant Joe Rice stood with his arms folded across his paunch and a grin on his rugby ball shaped face. The ex-Garda always worried when he called the Murder detectives down to see something, in case what he'd thought exciting barely warranted a jaded glance, so it was with more than a little satisfaction that he waited for their mouths to close.

Craig's closed first and he turned towards the Cork man, one eye still half on the thing that Rice had found.

"How the hell..."

He waved a hand in lieu of finishing his question. It gave the sergeant the permission he'd been waiting for to expound.

"Ah, now, you see. I took a trip down to check the lads were working, so, and that's when I noticed the cows-"

As Craig smiled at Rice's habit of saying 'so' at the end of every phrase, Liam interrupted him, repeating his last two words. "The cows."

"Aye, the cows, so. You see, my uncle Declan had a dairy farm, so, and when we visited as kids he taught us how to tell the weather by the cows."

It was a new one on Craig, but then he was a city boy. As Rice continued, Liam began to nod.

"You see, cows will stand in the middle of the field when the weather's going to stay fine, and huddle under the hedge when it's going to rain, so. Even when there's not a cloud in the sky they know hours in advance of the rain. Probably smell something in the air."

Liam's nods increased. "It's true. Another one that's true is red sky at night, shepherd's delight. Red sky in the morning, shepherd's warning-"

Craig waved him down. "Thank you, Liam, we all know that one. It's in the bible. Carry on, Joe."

Liam sniffed huffily as the sergeant continued.

"But you see, the cows didn't do it, so. Huddle, I mean. Not even when it started pouring around eleven o'clock."

Liam tried a quip for attention. He wasn't used to someone being more expert on the countryside than him. "Maybe they'd lost their sense of smell."

Craig cut him down to size. "All of them? Unlikely. So, what happened then, Joe?"

Rice didn't dare look at Liam, but he tightened his folded arms excitedly, signalling that he was about to ramp the tension up.

"I moved them to another field, just to check, so. But they were fine there, huddled under the hedge immediately." He gave a knowing nod. "That's how I knew it was the hedge itself, so we started digging along it and..." He gestured at the ground. "...well, you can see for yourselves what we found."

They could indeed and it had been the cause of their slack jaws. There, along the full length of the hedge in the field furthest from the McAllisters' farmhouse, extending to at least one hundred metres wide, and who knew how deep once the diggers Joe had called in had completed their job, was one of the biggest and deepest metal tanks that either detective had ever seen, and it was three quarters full of an oily liquid.

Craig smiled to himself. As clues went cows were a

new one on him but they'd certainly earned their keep.

"Have you had it tested?"

The rugby ball grin returned. "I have, so. It's red diesel with the dye removed."

Low-price dyed fuel, usually red diesel, so called because of the government imposed dye, was only approved for use in agricultural vehicles and equipment. Fuel laundering removed the dye so it could be sold on illegally to unsuspecting car owners at the much higher price of undyed fuel. It was a lucrative business.

Craig beckoned Joe to accompany them in the car back to the farmhouse and twenty minutes later they were seated in the workers' kitchen, their hands clasped around warming drinks. Winter in the city was bad enough but there was nowhere to hide from the elements in the countryside. Craig asked the sergeant a question to which he already knew the answer.

"What are you expecting to find when the excavation's complete?"

The reply was immediate.

"A pipe leading across the border to a tank on the other side, so. That field's bordered on the other side by County Monaghan."

Liam was nodding eagerly, all sign of his earlier chagrin gone. "It's like that IRA setup–"

"Alleged setup."

"OK, but it's like that all over again."

He was referring to an episode where a pipe had linked two tanks across the border, so that when the police on one side got suspicious the fuel could be shunted to the other side. Another country with a different police force, guaranteed to slow any investigation down.

As Liam recounted the story Craig's mind turned to the next steps.

"OK, we need this to be perfect. Send samples of the oil to the labs in Belfast, Joe. I'll tell Doctor Marsham to expect them by tonight. Also, get the tech guys down here with ground penetrating radar. I want an exact plan of the layout, including the pipe. The

Gardaí will have to pick it up over the border, so that we can get a plan of the other side."

He turned to find Liam with his hand wedged in a biscuit jar but ignored it; he had other things on his mind.

"Liam, find out who the Gardaí liaison is for the Fox murder and link him up with Joe as well. He needs to get his guys working on the other end of the pipe." He paused for a moment and then turned back to Rice. "Joe, we'll need the other fields along the border scanned too, but that's not urgent today. You've already given us plenty to go on. Well done."

Liam echoed his words, through the impediment of a half-chewed piece of cake. Craig rose to leave and then remembered something.

"Have your men managed to access the McAllisters' upstairs living quarters yet, Joe?"

Rice nodded, his mouth now similarly full of cake. He gulped it down and answered.

"Yesterday, sir, but so far there's nothing incriminating there, so. We'll keep searching though."

Craig had already reached the farmhouse's front door but they heard his "Good" echoing back. It was followed by. "Get a shift on, Liam. We've forty miles to go and rush hour's about to start."

****

The C.C.U. 5 p.m.

It was dead on five o'clock when the two detectives reached the office and the team had already gathered, with three additions: Kyle Spence, who seemed less than impressed at where he found himself; Geoff Hamill, and Sergeant Karl Rimmins from the Drugs Squad, looking even gaunter and edgier than when he'd last attended a briefing months before. Rimmins was already known to most of them, but out of politeness Craig asked people to introduce themselves. Nicky saw it for the ploy that it was; he'd wanted the time to grab a decent coffee and evict Andy from the

154

seat nearest the front of the room.

Missions accomplished he nodded Liam to pull over the white board and began bringing everyone up to date.

"OK, our two cases. Matias Rey, twenty, drowned in the Lagan with accompanying injuries that say he was forced in. His tox screen showed..." He turned to find Ash. His head was down but its luminous green colour made him impossible to miss. "Ash?"

Without looking up the analyst said. "Ketamine and Valium, Diazepam. It's a tranquilliser and the amount of Ketamine was enough to put him in the K-Hole."

The K-Hole was the state of dissociation, delirium and often catatonia experienced after high doses of Ketamine.

Craig turned to Karl, expecting to find his hawk-like gaze on Ash's face; the narcotics officer was on constant alert after his years on undercover Ops. But Rimmins wasn't looking at the analyst, instead his dark gaze was locked on Snow White lookalike Rhonda, seated halfway across the room, and she was returning it with an intensity that boded badly for the state of Andy's heart. Craig rolled his eyes; it would be a pairing made in Goth-Heaven but he had enough to think about without dealing with another romance. He barked "Karl" sharply.

If it hadn't occurred to Craig that he might be just the tiniest bit jealous of a budding romance, Liam's chastising glance reminded him that he probably was. He ignored it and softened his tone only slightly.

"Karl, how much Ketamine would it take to get in the K-Hole? For say, a sixty-five kilo man."

Rimmins shut his eyes, calculating. When he opened them again Rhonda had looked away.

"Around one-twenty-five milligrams injected, or up to two-fifty snorted or swallowed."

Craig nodded. "OK. Our first victim, Matias Rey, was injected and thrown into the river. His early attempts to climb out were prevented by stamping on his hands and he eventually drowned. Ash has the site of entry..."

"Shaw's Bridge. He travelled down the river until he caught on a some metal around Lagan Meadows and probably stayed there for about a day before being washed down to the Weir."

Craig turned to find Andy. He was murmuring to a youth who he thought was called Sid something; he really should pay more attention when people were giving their names. He worked for Geoff Hamill, he knew that much.

"OK, D.C.I. Hamill will tell us about the Rey family in a minute, but Andy, you took the father to do the I.D. and then interviewed him. What did he give you?"

Andy straightened up in a way that said he was trying to impress someone and Craig was damn sure that it wasn't him. He flicked open his notebook and started to read aloud.

"Xavier Rey, aged sixty-two, father of Matias Rey, the river victim. He identified the body of his son and then we brought him here to the relatives' room for a chat-"

Liam interrupted. "We?"

He knew damn fine who 'we' were but he wanted to throw Andy off his stride.

Andy gestured to the man by his side. "Constable Sid Freeman from D.C.I. Hamill's team joined me for the interview."

Craig stepped in. "D.C. Freeman was able to get some information out of Mr Rey, so let's hand over to him."

Freeman jerked upright in his chair, nodding first at Craig and then at his boss. He recited from memory.

"Mr Rey was very upset and D.C.I. Angel sensed that he wouldn't speak when he was in the room so he left the two of us alone."

Geoff Hamill shot Andy an angry look and he rushed to defend himself.

"I assessed Mr Rey as safe."

Hamill's eyes widened. "Are you insane, man? Xavier Rey would rip the head off a grown man if he accidentally spilled his pint-"

156

He was interrupted by a high tenor.

"I was perfectly safe, sir. The man was grief stricken and he wouldn't have said anything with the boss in the room." Freeman straightened his ever present rucksack briskly. "Now, if you don't mind I'd like to continue."

Craig wanted to give him a round of applause for putting his boss in his place.

"Mr Rey told me that Matias had gone out on Tuesday night to meet some friends." He retrieved his notebook from his pocket. "Ryan Phelan and Niall Henderson. The three of them had known each other since school-"

Liam snorted rudely. "Borstal was it?"

"Church school actually. They were choir boys."

Liam wasn't the only one who laughed. "So the church is a recruiting ground for gangs now. I give up."

Geoff Hamill wasn't laughing; instead he was scribbling some notes. Craig urged Freeman on.

"They were going to The Pit on May Street. When Matias didn't return home the next morning, Mr Rey phoned the club and they said the boys had left before twelve."

Craig nodded. "That may have been when Matias was abducted. Ash, see if there's any CCTV on that stretch of road. Jake, check if there were any patrols there that night."

Freeman continued. "When he realised Matias had disappeared, Mr Rey set some of his men looking-"

Craig cut in. "Is that how he described them? Some of his men?"

"Yes, sir."

"Did you ask him why he had men?"

"I did. He said he ran a cab business and they worked for him."

"Loyal employees to help him out like that."

Freeman smiled. "That's what I said. He didn't answer."

Craig turned to Hamill. "Any thoughts, Geoff?"

"Maybe at the end." He caught Liam smiling and glanced away quickly, girding his loins for the first short man joke.

Freeman continued.

"Mr Rey said he'd searched for almost two days and was just about to call the police when you arrived, sir."

The fact that the 'sir' was addressed to Andy made everyone smile. His laid back chocolate munching seldom commanded such respect.

Liam couldn't let the words pass. "Just about to call the police, my ass! Would you let your kid go missing for two days without calling us?"

Annette roused herself enough to speak. Thank goodness it was almost going home time; she was struggling to stay awake.

"To be fair... he was hardly a kid, Liam."

Liam was undeterred. "If it was your Jordan wouldn't you have reported it? There's only a year difference in their ages."

She nodded, conceding the point. "So what did the father do during those days?"

Geoff Hamill answered. "Probably had his hoods beating the crap out of everyone they met, looking for information. If you search hard enough you'll find a trail of split lips from Poleglass to town."

Craig turned back to the constable "Anything else?"

"No, sir, but if I could suggest I act as liaison officer with the family? I might get more information as time goes on."

"Let me think about it. OK, Geoff, could you bring them up to speed on the Reys, please."

As Hamill filled them in on The Rock and his suspicion of a gang war, Craig topped up his coffee from Nicky's percolator. She whispered quietly to him.

"Did you get any lunch?"

He screwed up his face, trying to remember and then nodding. The chicken sandwich seemed like a long time ago.

"Well, you still look hungry." She slid open her drawer to reveal a plate of coffee flavoured muffins he hadn't seen before. "Have one. You said you liked them last time."

He smiled gratefully and helped himself, then she noticed Liam craning his neck to see and slammed the drawer shut.

Hamill was summing up so Craig stepped back in.

"OK, good. As D.C.I. Hamill said, the potential rivals for Rey's gang are beginning to deal in girls and drugs, something that The Rock never did. That's why we've asked Sergeant Rimmins from the Drugs Squad to come along. Karl?"

Karl Rimmins uncrossed his long legs and unfolded his muscled arms, leaning forward to sit with his hands clasped between his knees. The posture seemed to enthral Rhonda more than was reasonable and Annette tapped her arm to remind her of where she was. It was no use; as Karl opened his mouth to speak and Rhonda opened hers in awe, Annette gave up the fight and rested back in her chair.

"OK, there's a lot of new stuff on the streets at the moment: Heroin, Crack and Crystal Meth mostly. Especially over the past four weeks. We managed to get hold of some to test it, and the quality's purer than we've ever seen before."

"Purer?"

The question came from Kyle Spence, who was looking interested for the first time that day. Rimmins nodded and Liam noticed suddenly that his mirror shine hair didn't move. He must be using some sort of gel; they had gunk for everything nowadays.

"That's what dealers do in the early days. They hook the punters by flooding the streets with high quality product and then a few months later they dilute it with all sorts of stuff. It makes it weaker but by that stage the punters are hooked so they just think they need more of it to get high. Sell more of what costs you less. The perfect business model."

Craig asked a question. "Have you seen any cut down yet?"

"Not yet, but when they do start it'll be cut with baking soda, talc; I've even seen rat poison used before."

Hamill signalled to cut in. "Any idea who's selling?"

The Narc's expression was equivocal.

Liam nodded. "In other words, yes, you have an idea, but no, you're not prepared to name them yet."

"Correct. We're pretty sure it's a new gang, but all we've managed so far is one name. Abaz Goga."

Hamill's eyes widened. "That's not a Dublin name."

Karl frowned. "Who said anything about Dublin? We think he's Albanian."

Craig elaborated. "Geoff's team picked up on the word knacker."

Liam nodded. "Knacker's definitely a Dublin word." He turned to Karl. "Could your man be second generation? Foreign parents but born down south?"

Rimmins shook his head. "Not from what our snout said, he implied that his English was poor. But I'll ask again."

Rhonda decided it was time to make her presence felt. "Albania isn't in the EU so he must be here illegally."

Karl's nod of confirmation was unnecessarily enthusiastic.

Craig was just about to move onto their second victim when the narco added something.

"I'm not sure how much use this is to you, but one of my lads heard something about an old friend of yours."

"Go on."

"Tommy Hill. He's been seen asking around about gangs."

Liam's eyes widened. "In Belfast?"

"Yep."

"The wee bugger. He's supposed to be in his rocking chair up in Templepatrick."

Rimmins shrugged. "Well, he was definitely seen in Belfast last night. Near the centre of town."

Craig frowned. That was all they needed; Tommy up to his old tricks.

"Thanks, Karl, and you, Geoff. You might want to

stay for the next bit, just out of interest."

He summarised the background to Colin McAllister's murder, adding the details of the rubber cement in his initialled air tank and the fact that they couldn't yet rule the wife and farm manager in or out, despite Annette's report of her second interview. Then he outlined Joe Rice's finding of the underground tanks and waited for the laughter to die down before he nodded Liam on to report.

"Well basically, if it turns out to be what it looks like, it seems McAllister was supplementing his farm income with a bit of fuel smuggling-"

Craig cut in. "A lot of fuel smuggling. That tank was the size of a large pond."

"Aye, it's like that IRA job all over again. Allegedly." He saw Ash's mouth open. "And don't you go saying 'what?' If you're too young to remember then use your internet search doodah to look it up. Anyway, we'll know more once Joe's finished digging. But it could account for the money the wife found in the house."

Craig nodded. "It could, but we still only have her word that she found it. She might have been in on the whole thing."

Annette was unconvinced. "I don't think so, sir. The Kennedys are worth millions. She definitely wouldn't have needed the cash. And why would she have bothered reporting it?"

"Could have been a diversion tactic. The rich stay rich by gaining more money, Annette, but we'll see. OK, that takes us onto our third murder."

A mixture of groans and shocked 'What?s' assaulted his ears. When they'd died down he summarised.

"Liam and I were asked to look at a case in Armagh today, again in a field just on the border. A man, named as Calum Fox, a well-known bookie, was found with his throat cut-"

"And his dick hanging out."

Craig dropped his head into his hands at the vulgarity, and waited for the next wall of noise. It came mostly from Nicky and Annette.

"Liam Cullen! You crude-"

Geoff Hamill shook his head despairingly, while Liam gazed around him, genuinely surprised.

"What? Would you have preferred me to call it his-"

Craig cut him off just in time. "I'd have preferred that you hadn't mentioned it at all! OK, everyone has the idea now, so move it along."

Liam shrugged. "Ach, you're all far too sensitive, that's your problem. Aye, well, anyway, it looks like Fox had been with a prostitute, or a killer pretending to be one. His throat was cut with a sharp blade and he bled out before he was found. We think the killer hopped the fence into the Republic, so, long story short, the Armagh police will be working with the Gardaí and we'll be supporting the lot."

Jake raised a finger to speak. "It's a bit of a coincidence that McAllister's pipe runs across the border and now, how many miles away, another man is killed by someone who nips across too."

Craig nodded. "Ash, how many miles is McAllister's tank from Calum Fox's murder scene?"

But Jake hadn't finished. "And D.C.I. Hamill has a transmission that mentions knackers, a term that's rarely used up here. Couldn't the new gang and McAllister's and Fox's deaths all be connected to each other, and to the Republic?"

Liam made a sucking sound. "That's a bit of a leap, son."

Craig wasn't so sure. "It *is* a leap, but not something I would dismiss entirely. OK, good, Jake. Let's work the three cases separately, but I'm tasking you to keep an eye out for any links that might emerge."

He glanced at his watch. It was almost six-thirty. Just then Ash spoke.

"One."

"What?"

"The two deaths happened one mile apart."

It was too close for comfort but he would think

about it tomorrow.

"OK, let's call it a day everyone. We'll reconvene in the morning at nine, but bear in mind that we're on call all weekend." He couldn't put off speaking to Jake any longer. "Jake, would you mind waiting behind for a moment."

Anticipating the conversation was already stressing him out, almost as much as that night's impending family dinner, which would be spent fending off his mother's questions about why Katy wasn't there. He was just thinking of an excuse to avoid it when Liam appeared at his side and gave his elbow a nudge.

"Look."

Craig scanned the room, not sure what he was supposed to be looking for.

"What?"

The D.C.I. nudged him again, even harder, almost earning himself a punch.

"There. Karl's lurking around Rhonda's desk. Imagine the kids if those two get together."

Craig really didn't care.

"Thanks for that, cupid, but I have better things to worry about. Come in for a minute, but *just* a minute. I have things to do." As he entered his office he gestured back at Sid Freeman. "SPAD."

Liam's eyes widened. "Here, that's a bit rough, boss. I know the lad's chubby but calling him a potato's going too far."

Craig burst out laughing. "I said SPAD not Spud. A SPAD's a special political advisor."

Liam tried to look like he understood.

"When I worked in London you'd see them all over Whitehall, wearing rucksacks over their suits, just like Freeman does. It was a style thing. Made them feel special."

"Oh, aye, aye. I see what you mean. Looks bloody stupid if you ask me."

"That's my point. It ruins your suits as well." He sat down. "OK, what did you want?"

"Me?"

"There's no-one else here."

"You asked me in!"

Craig realised that he had but didn't admit it, waving Liam out again with a request to send in Jake. Liam had guessed the meeting meant bad news even before Craig's expression shifted to grim.

Chapter Eight

The Cathedral Quarter, Belfast. Friday. 11 p.m.

Why were people so predictable? Correction. Why were young and immature people so predictable? The older members of society usually had a grip of their impulsive urges, or at least enough of a grip to do their misbehaving behind closed doors. But youth alone couldn't explain why Jake was in a dark alleyway with a complete stranger, so drunk that he could barely stand and wouldn't have done if he hadn't been supported by his crutch.

OK, so he was still young. Ish. But he wasn't a student or even on his first job, newly flush with money and determined to spend it on getting blocked. And perhaps someone who saw the full range of human nature at work *should* have had more maturity, except... it had been a hell of a six months. Twenty-fifteen would definitely go down as his annus horribilis, the one when he had almost died, and at the hand of his lover no less. Top that for trauma, TV soaps.

But he was a copper; he should be disapproving of his own semi-public PDA even as it happened. Except that he felt he deserved a reward tonight, just as he'd felt many times over the previous few months: the pampering in hospital post-attack, and again by his grandmother when he'd returned home; the odd blowout meal when he'd reached a milestone in his physio rehab; and of course there'd been his online gambling, secret sessions lit by the HEV light of his laptop when his granny had gone to bed. No major losses now, just the odd hundred pounds here and there; he couldn't even enjoy a good uncontrolled addiction without thinking through the outcomes like a good little cop.

So no disapproval tonight. Not in the club where he'd watched young men dance, writhing, their silhouettes projected against the ceiling like some modern shadow show. Not now either, here in a cold, wet alleyway, drunk and letting a stranger grope him, knowing exactly what came next. Leaning against a brick wall, his other crutch propped beside him like some reproving reminder of who he was. Still a victim, still dependent on props for support.

But that wasn't who he was, it was who he'd become because of Aaron. He shuddered suddenly, pulling his face away from his amorous companion's, barely able to think his ex-lover's name.

He'd been coping, sort of, or at least going through the motions at work and home, all the time psyching himself up for the trial and having to see his attacker again in court. The thought made him laugh suddenly, a harsh, angry sound that forced his companion to a wary distance. He repeated it, louder; making the distance between them grow and the light of flight narrow the younger man's eyes. He didn't blame him; he would run too if he was faced with him tonight. His laugh changed to a scowl and then a roar. It started in his chest and stomach and rumbled up until it spewed from his throat as a shout.

"LEAVE."

The youth stared at him, confusion clouding his dark good looks, until the sound of Jake's crutch smashing against a dumpster and an even louder "NOWWWWWW" decided his next move and left Jake alone in the alley, his head held up to a security light, awakened by his companion's sprint away. Tears began rolling down the detective's yellow-tinted face, strangely cold tears that tasted of salt as they ran past his nose and mouth. So many months' worth falling and flooding, choking him and soaking his shirt, yet he couldn't stop. He hated Craig for telling him the P.P.S. decision and he hated himself for barely being able to walk, but most of all he hated Aaron, the man that all this was about, safe in a psychiatric unit until he was miraculously ready to tell the doctors that he was sane.

The tears flowed on, slowly clearing Jake's mind like they were washing it, and as it cleared a calm resolve replaced his hate. He would bide his time, no matter how long it took, and when he was ready he would exact the just penalty that the state had failed to take.

****

High Street Station. 11 p.m.

Craig felt bad about lying to his mother, but the thought of answering twenty questions about Katy, especially twenty questions in Italian, with Mirella growing more emotional with his every monosyllabic reply, and the inevitable tears about how she'd hoped Katy would be her daughter-in-law, and how she would have to wait for years now to hold a bambino in her arms (not if Lucia and Ken get careless you won't, Mum) had been too much to think about after the two days he'd just had. So he'd lied.

As lies went it hadn't been a big one, or a black one as she'd taught him when he'd been young. White lies like 'yes, I really like that dress on you' had been viewed with some tolerance because they hadn't been for personal gain. You think not, Mum? He would have said that not having to deal with a sulk because he'd said he didn't like her dress was gain aplenty, but who was he to question Mirella's morality rules?

And by those rules, saying that he couldn't come to dinner because he was working to solve three murders had obviously ranked somewhere amongst the lighter shades of grey. It hadn't kept the disappointment from her voice, which had made him feel even guiltier, but the pale enough grey had tinged her disappointment with pride and somehow made things OK. Much as she hated the danger he encountered on the job, his mother took a grudging pride in saying that he was a detective; so, after an uncomfortable five minutes of lying, she'd handed him over to his father who'd known immediately why he wasn't coming to dinner and empathised, saying that they would hopefully see him next week.

But the call had left him feeling bad, so instead of

167

settling back to enjoy the football he'd recorded and cracking open a well-earned can of beer, he was sitting in High Street station opposite Mara Kennedy again, certain that she thought he was a sad git for having nothing better to do on a Friday night.

He scanned her face, only part of his scan being linked to the case. She was a beauty and he was a man, so he admired her for a moment before returning to the subject of her husband's death. Johnny Corbett sat half-dozing beside her so Craig made a fanfare of switching on the tape. He was rewarded by the elderly solicitor jerking forward in his seat. He cut immediately to the chase.

"Mrs McAllister-"

"Ms Kennedy."

He waved her objection away. For the purposes of the interview it suited him to emphasise her link to the man who had died.

"You said you found money at the farm that you were surprised at finding. Remembering that you're still under caution, please tell me the exact sequence of events leading up to the find."

She glanced quickly at Corbett and started speaking on his nod.

"It was a week ago-"

"Do you have an exact date?"

She frowned and then asked him for a calendar. Craig found one on his phone and after a moment she pointed to the twenty-second.

"It was a week ago exactly."

Craig slipped the mobile back in his pocket. "How can you be so sure?"

She gave a tight smile. "Because I'd just got back from Pilates and the class is only held on Fridays."

She'd leaned forward so he sat back, reinstating the distance that stopped this being just a chat.

"What time did you get back from your class?"

"I was early. The class starts at ten and normally lasts an hour, so with changing it's usually around ninety minutes overall before I get home. But the instructor was in a rush last week so she cut it short and I got home around eleven."

"Would your husband have been expecting you?"

She shook her thick hair and he wondered how it looked so groomed after the week she'd had.

"No. I'd told Colin I was taking Ben to the park afterwards, but it started to rain so I didn't."

"Your son went to Pilates with you?"

She smiled, broadly this time at the mention of her child. "He's only at school in the afternoons on Fridays so he always comes; lots of the girls bring their kids. They play in the courtyard outside. We can see them through the glass."

Nice as the image was it wasn't going to move them forward.

"So you and Ben arrived home, and then what?"

She shrugged. "We went upstairs and I sat Ben down with a DVD while I jumped into the shower."

He pushed swiftly past the image, urging her on.

"Then I went into our kitchen. It's above the workmen's area you'll have been in. I was just starting to prepare lunch when I noticed one of the drawers slightly open and an envelope poking out."

"Which contained?"

She frowned, remembering. "Money. Fifty pound notes. There were more envelopes in the drawer so I removed them all and started to count."

He raised a hand to halt her. "Can I ask why you counted it? Surely as your husband ran a business you would often have had cash in the house?"

She shook her head emphatically. "We did everything by bank transfer. That way we could keep track for the tax man. The only cash around would have been small amounts to pay the cleaner or a casual labourer." She gave him a sceptical look. "And it certainly wouldn't have been in fifty pound notes."

He asked his next question. "Didn't you worry that your husband might have come in while you were counting?"

"No. I knew Colin was working in the far fields that day, but anyway, why would I have worried? I wasn't frightened of my husband, Superintendent.

169

Colin would never have laid a hand on Ben or me."

"Yet you wanted Ben out of the house."

"Only when I'd finished. It was only when I realised how much money was there that I began to worry. That's when I contacted Johnny and he advised me to get Ben out."

Corbett nodded in confirmation.

"For the tape please, Mr Corbett."

The solicitor sighed. He was supposed to be playing bridge that evening, not sitting in a stuffy interview room.

"I confirm that Mrs McAllister contacted me on the twenty-second of January around twelve-thirty p.m. to tell me that she had found a substantial quantity of money that she couldn't account for in her home. Approximately fifty thousand pounds. I advised her to put the money back where she had found it and not confront her husband with the find. Later that day we decided that she should remove herself and her son from the house sometime over the next few days and together we would consult the fraud squad on what best to do next. Mrs McAllister brought Ben to Belfast on Monday the twenty-fifth of January and we contacted Inspector Dawson on the twenty-eighth."

"Just before we contacted you at The Merchant Hotel."

"Indeed."

Craig thought for a moment then turned back to his interviewee. "I want you to think carefully about my next question, Mrs McAllister."

She nodded.

"Exactly when was the last time you saw your husband and how did he seem?"

Without hesitation she said. "On the Monday we left. He was fine. I said I was going to Belfast for the day shopping then he went out to work on the farm."

His follow up question was swift. "When did you last see Mitchell Purvis?"

If he'd hoped to wrong-foot her he failed. She smiled and shook her head.

"We   weren't   having   an   affair   then,

170

Superintendent. We hadn't been together for months."

His voice was insistent. "When?"

She shrugged as if he was being stupid. "The day before. The Sunday. Mitchell was in the main hall when I brought Ben in from the swings at around three."

"Did you speak?"

She rolled her eyes. "Of course. We weren't teenagers who needed to ignore each other because things hadn't worked out. We discussed how the milking was going and then I took Ben upstairs."

"How would you describe Mr Purvis' mood?"

Her answer came snapping back. "Sulky." It made the night sergeant snigger in the viewing room. "He always acted as if I'd dumped him, when he knew exactly why the relationship had had to end."

"Which was?"

She stared at him as if he was an idiot. "Because I loved my husband, Mr Craig. Mitchell had never been anything but a distraction. Life on a farm can be lonely."

It made Johnny Corbett groan.

She rounded on him.

"What do you want me to say, Johnny? That I was madly in love with Mitchell? Would that make me seem like less of a tart? Well, I won't say that because it wasn't true. I liked Mitchell, but we got together out of boredom-"

Craig interrupted in a dry tone. "I'm not sure that Mr Purvis would say the same." Either way it was time to move on. "So you found the money, called Mr Corbett and put it back, biding your time until you could remove your son safely from the farm." He paused, watching her face carefully as he asked his next question. "Where did you think the money had come from, Mrs McAllister?"

Her expression didn't change. "I had no idea, but I knew it wasn't from the farm. If Colin had made fifty thousand he would have told me, or it would have shown up in our bank account. I did the accounts so I would have noticed immediately."

"Did you make any attempts to find out where it was from?"

She surprised him with a nod. "I drove around the land on the Saturday, when Colin was at the dairy market." She gave a weak laugh. "I don't know quite what I was looking for. Maybe a barn full of diamonds, or something, but I looked in every barn and stopped at every field and I couldn't find anything that looked out of place." She shook her head sadly. "I honestly have no idea where it came from, but it must have been what got Colin killed."

Craig's scrutiny didn't weaken. "Had you ever seen anything before that had made you suspect your husband of being dishonest?"

It made her smile. "Never. Colin couldn't lie to save his life."

Apparently not.

She stopped, realising how silly it had sounded. "Except that he must have been lying in some way, mustn't he, or why would he have been killed?"

Craig had almost finished.

"I just have two more questions, Mrs McAllister. In your opinion, could Mitchell Purvis have killed your husband? He was in love with you, after all."

It was her most empathic "Never" yet. She added "Mitchell couldn't kill a rat never mind a man. Colin had to do any killing there was to be done on the farm."

He withdrew a piece of paper from his pocket, watching her face carefully as he spread it out to reveal a map of the farm. He tapped the field where they'd found the underground tank.

"Can you tell me where that is, please?"

She leaned forward, turning her head this way and that to orient herself before placing a finger on the top of the map.

"That's north, isn't it? I'm not great with directions."

"Yes, that's north."

She ran her finger down and stopped at the farmhouse. "Well, if that's the house then where you tapped must be the southernmost field." As she moved her hand, Craig noticed that any mark there might have been from her wedding and engagement rings was invisible; an omen for how quickly she might forget her married life. Her finger halted and she nodded. "This is the border with the Republic so down here would be County Monaghan. The border is the boundary of our land so that's definitely our southernmost field."

"What's normally grown there?"

She shook her head. "Nothing. Colin said the earth wasn't good for crops. He used it for grazing the ponies occasionally. Mine and Ben's. Mitchell's mare as well." She gazed at him innocently. "What's so special about that field? There wasn't anything there when I checked."

The value in the field lay deep underground. The soil had looked fine for planting to him but he wasn't an agriculturalist; they'd need to take samples. If the land turned out to be OK for crops then the fact that Colin McAllister hadn't used the field for such would tell them that he'd known all about the tanks.

He stared at the new widow; still certain that she knew more than she was saying. How could McAllister have been running a racket on their land without her spotting something? Her good citizen's act over the cash could simply have been revenge because she'd thought her husband had been withholding money from her. OK, reporting it to the fraud squad was pushing the act a bit, but she wouldn't have been the first wife to think that getting her husband locked up would have left her free to keep all the profits herself.

He put the map back in his pocket and rested his hands on the table. It felt cool despite the overhead neon lights.

"You've outlined your whereabouts for the past week to Sergeant Harris?"

Corbett answered eagerly, sensing a slight thaw. "Mrs McAllister has accounted for every hour."

Craig's next words said that the thaw had been less than he'd thought. "We will be checking everything, and if we find even the slightest discrepancy-"

Mara McAllister shook her head desperately. "You won't. I promise."

He continued as if she hadn't spoken. "We *will* revoke your bail. In the interim I am bailing you to reside at The Merchant Hotel or your parents' home; we have both addresses. You must sign in at this station every day and if you attempt to leave Belfast you'll be arrested and held on remand."

Corbett pushed it. "Exactly what are you charging my client with? You can't-"

"I can under PACE and I will, and if you insist on a charge it will be obstructing a police investigation. Despite her protestations I don't believe your client has been entirely honest with us, so I suggest that you take the bail offer before I change my mind."

He stood up, pushing back his chair. "The night sergeant will make the arrangements." He stared at the widow. "Go and see your son, Mrs McAllister, and think very carefully about what I've said. If you've withheld anything from us we *will* find out, and then any chance you have to stay out of court will be lost."

He left the room, forgetting about her instantly, and drove home to spend a sleepless night thinking of the woman he loved.

****

Tates Avenue, Belfast. 4 a.m.

Tommy liked the night; the wee small hours north of midnight when houses were dark and roads could be crossed at a stroll. Or a strut, which was how he always walked. Cock of the walk, the King of Belfast, anointed by his own hand with his victims' blood. He smiled a closed mouthed smile, reminiscing about the good old days. He was still smiling and scanning the terraced street when he heard a slight rustling behind his back. He stood still and listened, knowing that any minute now a rat would appear; a skinny, lank-haired, human one.

As a shadow flashed at the edge of his vision

174

Tommy swung around fast enough to grab its cause, squeezing hard as the man in his grip attempted to peel his fingers from his arm. Finally he released his hand, casually lighting up a cigarette as the scrawny, leather jacketed man winced in pain.

"Long time no see, Coyler."

Ralph Coyle was still wincing; Tommy had a grip like steel. The wince was accompanied by a rattling cough, his condition worsened by the smoke the ex- paramilitary was blowing in his face. He'd run with Tommy for years, until twenty-thirteen when the whole gang except its boss had landed in prison, Tommy's ability to shrug off arrest almost as legendary as his past.

"Been out of Maghaberry since last year, I heered."

Coyle had recovered enough to nod, and as the cold air cleared his airways he retreated to a safe distance and spluttered out a reply.

"June. I gat extra time fer fightin'."

His voice was high and weak, a condition unchanged by the advancing years. It made Tommy laugh as it had always done.

"I see yer balls still haven't dropped. I bet that made ye popular in jail."

Coyle said nothing, knowing that any protest would mean more pain. Instead he watched as Tommy stubbed out his cigarette on a white stuccoed wall and then slipped his plastic lighter back into his jeans. Same old Tommy, hard as granite, but age *had* mellowed him a bit; ten years earlier the cig would've been stubbed out on his head.

Coyle gathered his courage, wondering how best to frame the question uppermost in his mind. Thirty seconds of mouth opening and closing later he blurted it out in a fractured squeak.

"Wat dee ye want from me, Tommy?"

It brought a swift answer in the form of a punch, followed by a glare as Coyle lay on the freezing ground.

"Ye meant to say, wat can I *dee* fer ye, Tommy, didn't ye?"

The follower nodded furiously, clambering slowly

175

to his feet again via a nearby car. "Aye, aye, that's wat I meaned, Tommy. Wat can I *dee* fer ye?"

Hill pulled out another cigarette, this time gifting a second to his old employee.

"Nye, I'm vary glad ye asked that, Coyler. Ye can pick up with yer mates in The Village, and find out who's takin' over west Belfast."

****

Stranmillis. Saturday 30th January. 7 a.m.

After a night spent tossing and turning, courtesy of all shades of angst, Craig staggered groggily into the shower, hoping that a blast of cold water would shock him to high alert. It succeeded for its duration, only to be replaced immediately by the walking coma that weeks of bad sleep had condemned him to. He had to speak to Katy and find out if they were really finished; he couldn't cope with living in limbo any more.

An hour later he was in the office, his mind leaping from one topic to the next. Katy and Miskimmon, the murders and Mara Kennedy, none of the thoughts deep enough to be useful but all amounting to a sore head. He heard Nicky arrive and place her handbag in her desk drawer so he yanked open his door and croaked "Paracetamol and coffee" in as pathetic a tone as he could produce.

Her response came from the Liam Cullen School of Man-management. She gasped and stared into his face.

"You looked like you died and they forgot to bury you."

She didn't even add a 'sir' to soften the blow.

Craig couldn't argue with the assessment; he'd seen his reflection in a mirror an hour before. He grunted "Uh" and returned to his cave. When he re-emerged thirty minutes later, following three espressos so strong he could have stood a pen upright in them, two paracetamol, one of Nicky's ginseng capsules and a sausage butty that she'd fetched him from the canteen, he resembled less a cadaver than a man with a very colourful past. It would have to do.

To the others who were filing yawning onto the floor he had to look like a man in control. That's what leadership was, wasn't it; acting like you knew which end was up even when you'd spent the night before with your head stuck up your ass.

He perched on a desk holding his fourth espresso of the day, and waved everyone to take their seats.

"Right. This will only take ten minutes. You already know what work you've got to do."

Craig saw Liam staring at him and then shooting Nicky a look that said it all. He was tempted to say something antsy to his deputy but he didn't have the energy.

"OK, Tommy Hill. Sergeant Rimmins said that he'd been seen in Belfast, so, Ash, I want you to check his GPS locator. Hill's on license and wearing an ankle bracelet, so he shouldn't be moving more than three miles from his house and even then only between certain hours." As he said it he noticed Davy sidling towards his desk. "Davy. Good to have you back. We'll catch up later today." He turned to see Kyle making a face. "After I see Inspector Spence that is. Annette, until I need Kyle, start to familiarise him with your work, please."

Annette's energy level was on a par with his own, so she yawned as she nodded and lounged back in her chair.

"OK, Liam, you and I will pay Tommy a visit today. Davy, while Ash is checking Tommy's locator I want you to check out ways ankle bracelets can be cheated. If there's a way to do it then we can be sure that Hill's found out."

As he sipped his coffee he noticed that Jake looked even worse than he did. It revived his guilt even though it wasn't his fault.

"OK, I re-interviewed Mara Kennedy McAllister last night."

Liam raised an eyebrow. Craig must hardly have rested at all. He confirmed his deputy's thoughts with a weak smile.

"I asked her about the fifty thousand she found and the field where we found the tank-"

Liam's words were out before he could stop himself. "You didn't tell-"

Craig's glance stopped him dead. "No, of course I didn't tell her we found the tanks! But thanks for teaching me how to suck eggs anyway." It earned him a laugh and perked everyone up. "To cut a long story short, I've bailed her to her parents' address or The Merchant, signing in at High Street every day." He turned to Davy again, before Liam could tell him he'd done something else wrong. "Davy, I want a trace on her mobile and the phone in her hotel room. I want to know everyone that she calls." He turned back to Liam with a sarcastic look. "That OK with you, boss?"

Liam thought about it and nodded, adding "Just as long as you don't do it again" ending with a guffaw.

Craig smiled and carried on. "OK, I'm not convinced that Kennedy wasn't going to shop her husband to Inspector Dawson just so she could take over the tank scam for herself." Just then he remembered something. "Ash, get onto Joe and tell him I want a sample of soil from that field analysed for crop planting suitability."

He answered Annette's questioning look. "Her husband said the field was only suitable for grazing because the soil wasn't good for growing things. If that turns out to be false then Colin McAllister knew all about those tanks."

Her questioning look deepened. "You think it could have been happening without him knowing, sir?"

Craig shook his head. "No, but I want to be sure. If he didn't know about the tanks and the fifty thousand wasn't his that removes a possible criminal motive for his murder, so we need to know ASAP."

Liam shook his head. "McAllister *must* have known about the money. Only he and the wife could have put it there. No-one else had a key to that part of the house."

Craig shook his head too. "We'd have to prove that

178

no-one had cut a copy and that would take too long."

Kyle perked up suddenly. "It might have been a domestic killing. A love triangle. If it was, that would remove any link between his death and Calum Fox's."

"I doubt it, but we need to be sure."

Craig scanned the faces in front of him; most of them looked well rested, or as well rested as you could look working a six day week. Only Jake and he were vying for the zombie of the month prize and he was more worried about what had given Jake his look. He stood up, more slowly than usual but still faster than most of them.

"OK, that's it for now. Nicky, time a briefing for four o'clock and if we don't need it we can cancel it." He turned to Kyle Spence. "Liam and I need five minutes, Kyle, then you and I need a quick chat."

As he turned towards his office Ash appeared at his side. "Hill's GPS says he's been only in Templepatrick and Davy says the bracelets are supposed to be fool proof, but they can be cut."

Craig nodded, resigned to the fact they would have to catch Tommy in the act.

As they were walking into his office Liam stopped suddenly by Nicky's desk.

"What the heck's that?"

Craig followed his gaze. There, in pride of place beside Nicky's framed photo of her son and husband, sat a cake the like of which few of them had seen before. Craig had.

"A croquembouche! My God, the last time I saw one of those was at a French wedding!"

As they gawped at the glossy tower of caramel and profiteroles Nicky preened herself. "I made it last night." Her gaze swept round the room proudly, until it alighted on Rhonda's astonished face. The smirk the P.A. gave announced "I win" more eloquently than any words. Liam was salivating.

"Is it edible?"

She slapped his inquisitive fingers away with a tut. "Of course it's edible. The profiteroles are full of fresh cream." She smiled smugly. "I made it in an hour."

Craig doubted that but said nothing, his mind made up. The bake-off contest had to be brought to an end or the team's impending obesity would be joined by blocked arteries. He raised Nicky's right arm.

"I hereby declare Nicola Morris champion baker of twenty-sixteen." It would give him a year to work out how to end the competition between her and Rhonda once and for all. "No more baked goods of any description are to be brought in for the rest of the year."

He dropped her arm again to a chorus of moans and hastily entered his office, dragging Liam after him. Once inside he slumped in his chair.

"Thank goodness that's over."

Liam looked less convinced but he was too busy staring at Craig to moan about buns.

"You look like crap, boss."

Craig laughed as he retorted. "Thank you, Miss Universe."

Liam continued. "But not as crap as Jake does. He was on the booze last night and no mistake."

Craig winced. "That was my fault." He outlined the P.P.S. decision, provoking a long whistle from the D.C.I.

"That must have been tough to hear. I'd have hit the bottle as well."

"The difference being that you would have got drunk, punched a wall and then shrugged it off. I'm not so sure that Jake can do the same."

Liam shook his head. "You're overestimating me, boss. I'm not sure I'd have been as calm at thirty, if someone had half killed me and left me in a wheelchair for months."

Craig was curious. "What would you have done?"

Liam stared past him at the river, thinking back to who he'd been twenty years before. After a moment he answered with a question. "You want the truth?"

"Yes. Warts and all."

Liam's pale eyes darkened and his lips tightened to a straight line. "You really wouldn't have liked me twenty years ago. I had far too much testosterone on board."

Craig raised an eyebrow. "More than now?"

"Ach, I'm a pussycat now. Must be the marriage and kids. But back then...well, let's just say, back then I'd have made Foster pay, no matter how long it took. And I'd have covered it so well that no-one would ever have known it was me."

It confirmed Craig's fears about Jake. He forgot what he'd wanted to talk to Liam about and waved him out again, spending the next ten minutes staring at the river, thinking. When he emerged from his office again he walked over to Jake's desk and beckoned Annette to join them.

"I've been thinking. Jake might be right about the deaths of McAllister and Fox being linked, so I want you two to head to Armagh. You're to link up with a Sergeant McDonnell and his Gardaí liaison."

He was rewarded by Jake's expression brightening, just as much as Annette's darkened. She pulled Craig to one side but he'd raised a hand to halt her before she'd even opened her mouth.

"I know what you're going to say, Annette. You've got enough to do and McDonnell can handle things well enough." He turned his back to Jake and dropped his voice. "Trust me on this, please. Jake needs to be so occupied with work that he doesn't have a chance to think."

She did trust him so she nodded.

"As soon as I can tell you what it's about, I will. Just best not to mention the court case to him for now."

He turned to see Jake readying to leave. Maybe if he got his teeth into two murders he would forget his own near miss with Foster, although even as he thought it Craig didn't hold out much hope.

He nodded them out and turned to find his two D.C.I.s in a huddle.

"You two had better not be talking about football."

Liam's snort said that he was very wide of the mark. "The Reys more like. Andy's just been explaining Matias' tattoo."

181

Craig perched on a desk. "Go on."

Andy pointed to a doodle he'd done of the tattoo during the briefing. "Apparently the castle is the symbol of Castile. That's where the Rey family originate from. Xavier has one too."

"And I assume the word Rock is because of the gang's name."

"Yes. Gang members have the word Rock and a symbol depending on where they come from: Castile, Antrim, Tyrone, wherever."

Craig shrugged. It was interesting but of no use to their investigation. "OK. The Reys are exactly who I want to talk about. Liam and I are going to re-interview Xavier-"

Liam looked at him askance. "Since when?"

"Since I just said so. Andy, I want you to chase up Matias' movements on Tuesday night and find out why his mates left him alone long enough to get killed. It might have been innocent or it could be something else."

"A setup?"

Craig nodded and motioned behind him. "Take Constable Freeman with you, please."

Andy didn't have to be asked twice. The youngster had grown on him. When the floor was clear apart from Kyle, Rhonda, Davy and Ash, Craig allowed himself a smile. He was good at tidying up. He really should do some of it at his flat.

"OK... Rhonda, now that Davy's back, I want you to shadow one of the analysts for the rest of the day; Davy can decide which one. It's time you found out how they support operations."

If he'd expected an argument from her he didn't get one; she quite fancied spending a day in the warm. He ignored Ash's finger pointing her firmly towards Davy's desk and Davy's immediate shake of the head. They could fight it out between them; he had better things to do.

He headed for the lift with Liam in hot pursuit. When they'd reached it Craig realised he'd forgotten about talking to Kyle and stuck his head back round the double doors.

"Get a move on, Inspector."

As Kyle had just found a comfortable spot in his chair and slung his long legs up on his desk, he was less than happy to be disturbed.

"Get a move on where?"

"High Street, with us. You're going to watch us extract the truth from the leader of the gang."

Spence tried for an innocent expression. "Certainly, sir, except..."

"What?"

"I thought I could be more use ringing around my intelligence contacts. To see what they might have heard about Belfast and Dublin gangs."

Craig thought for a moment. Kyle hated the street; he'd always been the same, so he could just be playing him to stay in the office. Or... he *could* be killing two birds with one stone; staying in the office but gathering Intel as he did. Pragmatism won out.

"OK, today you stay in the office and pump your sources, but tomorrow you're working with me all day and that means out in the big bad world."

Spence's smile had a definite hint of 'we'll see'.

****

Armagh Police Station. 11 a.m.

Magnus O'Shea pulled his people carrier into the carpark of Armagh's high-walled police station, marvelling at how official everything was in the north. He'd had his I.D. checked twice already; once at the outer gate and then by a spotty young carpark officer before he would let him in. He wasn't quite sure if everyone got checked so rigorously or whether his number plate from south of the border made him a special case. The plaque on the wall beside his parking space, commemorating officers killed during The Troubles, made him plump for everyone.

They might have their drug wars and burglaries to contend with in the Republic; even the odd 'normal'

183

murder now and then, but their counterparts in the north had done a far more dangerous job for thirty years so he'd forgive them a few I.D. checks here and there. He locked the car and turned towards the station's rear entrance, to be greeted halfway by a man whose voice he recognised from the phone.

Fred O'Donnell extended a hand. "Hello. You must be Inspector O'Shea."

"Sergeant O'Donnell, is it yourself?"

The expression made the sergeant smile. Delivered in O'Shea's southern accent it had a lyrical quality, far more musical than the usual "'Bout ye, O'Donnell" that he got from his own.

"It is indeed. And thank you for coming." O'Donnell swiped open the door and gestured to the left. "We're in a room down here. Two of our Belfast Murder Squad colleagues are joining us as well."

O'Shea laughed jovially. "The big guns, is it?" He meant it both ways; he hadn't seen so many cops carrying guns since an episode of Chicago PD.

When Annette and Jake had been introduced and the coffees and teas had been handed around, O'Donnell outlined the details of Calum Fox's death. Annette nodded Jake on to ask the questions. She'd resolved to do as little as possible on the trip because she'd worked out why Craig had wanted the sergeant involved. Something must have happened to hinder Aaron Foster's prosecution so Jake needed a distraction, and there was no better way to distract him than by making him do all the work.

"Inspector O'Shea, is Calum Fox known in the Republic?"

O'Shea crossed his arms over his thin frame, wondering again why he'd never developed a paunch like other men of his age. It wasn't for his lack of eating, that was for sure, but for some reason fat always settled on his arms and legs and nowhere else. It made him careful with his diet; a stick insect with balloon limbs would be a distinctly cartoonish look.

"Ah, well now..."

Jake sat forward eagerly. "You mean he is

184

known?"

O'Shea nodded his greying head. "He is. Nothing we could pin on him, you understand, or we'd have done it. But let's just say that Calum Fox wasn't a man who would've been given cream tea at the Taoiseach's house."

As a roundabout way of saying that Fox had been a bad 'un, it was pretty obscure. Annette cut in.

"Are you saying that Fox was unsavoury rather than criminal?"

O'Shea turned to her with a smile that said he liked the fairer sex. "You've got it in one, young lady."

At forty-seven even Annette knew young was pushing it. She decided to press the point; being patronised gave her the hump.

"So have you *never* had enough evidence to convict Fox or did you just not bother trying?"

The sharpness of the remark made O'Donnell jerk upright in his seat. "Now, I don't think-"

A raised hand from O'Shea halted him. His smile was still in place although Annette sensed that it was cooler than before.

"No, now, the Inspector here has a valid point. And very fiery ladies you have up north, if I may say." *You may not.* "Fox had a house in Donegal, so I never encountered him personally, policing in Dublin and Louth, but my information is that although he sailed close to the wind there was never anything concrete to pin on him."

Annette hadn't finished. "So his death came as a complete surprise to the Dublin Gardaí?"

O'Shea made a face. "Not a surprise but not entirely expected was what I was told."

She nodded. She still didn't like O'Shea but his answers made sense. They had quite a few of their own population whose deaths would leave them unsurprised, even though they would die without a conviction to their names. They were known as Teflon Targets. People who they knew were up to something but it could never be proved. She sat back, knowing that Jake was itching to ask more.

"Inspector, could Fox's sailing close to the wind have been linked with his bookmaker's businesses?"

"I believe it could."

"Syndicates, bribes or money-laundering?" Gambling was fertile ground for all three.

O'Shea shrugged. "I don't have the details but I would imagine all of those, plus Fox was heavily into the racetracks. Horseracing is big in the Republic, there's millions to be won and lost and he had men at every major fixture in the land, so doping might have been happening as well. I can get you more details on that if you'd like?"

Jake nodded eagerly. "That would be great. Anything that you can find."

As O'Donnell called a five minute comfort break O'Shea grabbed two cups of tea and carried one over to Jake.

"Sergeant O'Donnell said you might be linking Fox's death to another case. Can I ask you what that's about, Sergeant McLean?"

Annette intervened. "We'll be getting on to that in a moment, Inspector. As soon as Sergeant O'Donnell is back."

Jake glanced at her questioningly but he waited for O'Shea to leave for the bathroom before he voiced his thoughts.

"You really don't like him, do you, Ma'am?"

She shook her head. "No, I don't. He thinks he's God's gift."

Jake smiled knowingly. "That can't be the only reason or Liam would've been in your bad books for years."

She laughed at his astuteness. "Liam's delusional, not a patronising chauvinist like O'Shea. I just don't like the man. He's the sort that likes women tied to the stove."

She heard the others returning and made a show of sipping her tea daintily just as they opened the door.

O'Donnell settled in his seat and started again. "I've had some word on the forensics. The blonde hair found at the scene was synthetic."

186

The girl had been wearing a wig.

"And the print doesn't trace to anyone on our books." He turned to O'Shea. "But perhaps the Inspector here would run it through the Gardaí's as well?"

It earned him a smile and a nod.

"Right. Now perhaps one of our Belfast colleagues would like to update us on their possible linked case?"

Jake took the lead, outlining Colin McAllister's demise and that they had two possible suspects. He finished with.

"Of course, that may all alter now that the tank has been found."

O'Shea sat forward abruptly, the light of interest in his eyes. "Tank?"

"Yes. A tank containing laundered red diesel. It was found underground in McAllister's southernmost field with a pipe flowing from it to the border. Your colleagues in Monaghan are checking the adjoining field for anything it might be connected to."

O'Shea turned to his northern counterpart. "Fuel smuggling. We've seen it before."

O'Donnell nodded. "He probably thought we wouldn't expect anyone to try it again, so he'd be safe enough."

The Garda turned back to Jake.

"So what makes you think this is linked to Fox's death? He had his throat cut and you said your man McAllister died from a faulty air supply."

As Jake hesitated Annette noticed that his hair was hitting his collar. It had almost stopped growing after his accident so she was pleased, although if it hit it much harder Craig would be pointing him towards the nearest barbershop.

"I'm not sure. But two murders only a mile apart..." It sounded weaker than it had at the C.C.U.

"And you said you had two suspects for McAllister?"

"The wife and the farm manager. They had an affair last year."

Annette felt a sudden urge to make Jake stop

187

talking; to hold things back from O'Shea even though they were working together. She felt suddenly ashamed of her dislike of him, or at least that's what she hoped it was; if it was bias against him because he came from another force then she would feel even worse. Nonetheless she signalled to cut in.

"Our only real link is the deaths' geographic locations. One mile apart with both fields backing onto the border."

O'Shea stated matter-of-factly. "But McAllister didn't die in that field, did he."

She was caught off-guard by his logic. "Well no...he died at the slurry pit-"

"Which is where?"

An embarrassed blush lit her cheeks. "The north side of the farm."

Jake jumped in. "But the fact is that in two fields edging onto the border, one mile apart, a man has his throat cut and we find a tank that leads across. It's too close for coincidence."

O'Shea shrugged. "Sure the evidence will tell us. You might be right yet." He changed tack. "What about the girl Fox was with? Have you found anything on her yet?"

It was what they'd been planning to do that afternoon but Annette decided to bluff; it always worked for Liam.

"We're pursuing some leads. But I understood that part of your role was to help us find out where she went once she'd left the north?"

"Indeed it is." O'Shea reached into a briefcase that none of them had noticed him bringing and removed a DVD. He nodded towards a TV at the other end of the room. "May I?"

O'Donnell waved him on and a minute later they were staring at an image of a rain sodden country road.

"This is the main road that runs along the end of the track your killer would have been on, after she'd climbed the fence. There are no cameras on the track itself." He pressed pause and turned to Annette pointedly, indicating that their animosity was now running both ways. "That's if she *did* climb over. How do you know she didn't just run in the other direction on your side?"

Jake had the answer. "Because there was a clear blood trail from the car to the fence, and more blood on the other side."

O'Shea responded like someone had just invaded his country. "You were on our side?"

O'Donnell stepped in quickly to prevent the onset of war. "We have a common travel area, remember? The team just stepped across to have a look, that's how we knew we had to liaise with you. The girl definitely went into the south."

O'Shea continued, unappeased. "If she was smart she could have left the blood there deliberately to throw you off track. It doesn't mean that she didn't hop right back into the north."

He pressed the play button forcefully, and they watched for five more minutes as the rain pelted relentlessly on the road's tarmac at its junction with the rough farm track. Finally O'Shea stopped the tape and stared directly at Annette. She was his real audience. If he could win her over then all would be right with his world.

"There's hours of tape here, all of it like this; cars driving past on the road but none approaching it from the direction of the track. We had our lab look at it, but this is your copy if you'd like to do the same."

Annette thought for a moment. "What about the other end of the track? Are there any cameras there?"

O'Shea shook his head. "None. It's a mud track that leads to other mud tracks across the fields. The nearest CCTV is at a village shop ten miles away. It's a very rural part of the world."

Their killer had planned things perfectly. Not only had she chosen a remote field in which to kill Calum Fox, but she'd chosen one that backed onto a track accessible only by blind back roads. If they were going to find out their girl's name then it would have to be through legwork in the north.

Annette stood up. "Thank you, Inspector O'Shea.

Sergeant O'Donnell, could you furnish me with Mr Fox's phone logs before I leave, please? It's clear we have a lot more work to do on our side." She glanced at O'Shea and added "first", then pushed back her chair and turned towards the door, finishing with. "Once we have her name we'll let you know and the Gardaí can hopefully locate her in the south."

If Magnus O'Shea was taken aback by her abrupt exit he didn't show it and as Fred O'Donnell walked him to his car the Garda's mind was already on what Mary would be cooking him for lunch.

****

High Street Station. Viewing Room One. 12 p.m.

Craig had never believed in stereotypes, if he had done then he would have been a trench-coat wearing alcoholic living a sad, lonely life. Come to think of it... Nope. He shook his head as if the conversation was with someone else instead of in his mind. He didn't even own a trench-coat.

So anyway, he didn't believe in stereotypes; that brainy kids always wore glasses and that skinny people were neurotic. He stopped for a moment, thinking of Martin Grant. No, not neurotic, just a bit twitchy.

But not all Italians loved pasta and ice cream, just most of his cousins, and not all villains looked as if they were. He thought back to some of the people that they'd put away over the years: a property magnate, a judge, a senior cop; not one of them had dragged their knuckles along the ground or had 'thug' tattooed on their cheek.

But Xavier Rey had just blown his disdain for stereotypes right out of the water, and as if Liam could read his mind he nudged his elbow and pointed through the viewing room glass.

"Now that's a wrong un if ever I saw one."

Craig couldn't argue with him. Xavier Rey looked like every cartoon villain rolled into one, with his low-

190

browed, swarthy, folded face, set in a scowl that looked as if it had taken root years before, and his brawny, tattooed arms resting, fists clenched, on the table in front of him. Rey hadn't moved in the ten minutes they'd been watching him and Craig would have laid a bet that if they'd watched for ten more his position would have remained the same. Except that he didn't have the time to watch so instead he nodded Liam towards the door and psyched himself up for the interviewing fray. He was surprised when Liam didn't budge; instead he leaned in closer to the glass, tilting his head this way and that as if Rey would reveal a different side of himself if viewed in a different light.

Craig was curious. "What are you thinking?"

It wasn't a question he asked often of his deputy, or at least not in such a pointed tone. What are you thinking was a question for briefings, to be thrown out to the team in the hope that a gem or two might come back in return, or it was a question for quiet moments with someone you loved, hoping that their answer might reveal more of them or prompt an affirmation of their love. Suddenly an image of Katy filled his mind, making him catch his breath. He shook his head hard to erase it; it took all his energy to keep his feelings for her at bay and he didn't need them sneaking up on him at work. Thankfully Liam had missed his moment of introspection and was still staring through the glass. Finally he obliged with an answer.

"Two things. Why didn't Andy tell us Rey looked like a mass murderer?"

"Maybe he thought it was irrelevant. He *was* dealing with a bereaved relative, after all."

Liam continued as if he hadn't heard. "And how come Rey's never pinged our radar before? If looks mean anything that scrote has put his fair share of men in the ground."

Craig couldn't argue with his logic. Why hadn't they at least heard about Rey and his son, or The Rock for that matter? He covered his puzzlement with a shrug.

"Geoff seems adamant the gang isn't linked with

any deaths." He pulled out his phone. "But let's check again."

As Geoff Hamill answered he knocked the phone onto speaker.

"The Rock don't kill, at least that hasn't been our experience-"

Liam's scepticism was noisy. "Get away out of that. Rey looks like Bluto from a Popeye cartoon!"

Hamill's voice took on a huff. "He might well do but I'd have hoped the Murder Squad would have been beyond stereotypes." Craig had the good grace to blush. "People cooperate with The Rock because of their reputation, but they only deal in fraud and the like and any serious gang violence I've seen has always happened over drugs and girls."

Craig thanked him and ended the call quickly; just as Liam's "That you *know* of" emerged.

The D.C.I. added a derisive snort. "That just means they haven't found the bodies. Rey must have buried them bloody deep."

Craig shrugged. "Or it might actually be true, and if they don't kill it would certainly explain why another gang has risked encroaching on their turf." He opened the door and right on cue Jack Harris appeared. "Either way we'll find out. Hi, Jack."

The usually amiable sergeant looked decidedly pissed off. "Are you two going to be long? Only I'm getting no work done babysitting all these interviews."

Craig knew that something was up in Jack World.

"I can call someone down from Docklands to do it if you're busy, Jack."

Harris shook his head, irritated. "Ach no, sure by the time they got here you could be through."

Craig realised immediately what had happened. "Roger Litton's giving you grief about us, isn't he?"

The sergeant's silence said yes.

Superintendent Roger Litton was the force's undisputed number one pain in the ass. People like Gabe Ronson in Traffic were rule obsessed, anal idiots, and prats like Terry Harrison were the sort that you watched your back around, but for sheer vicious, climb over your granny to get to the top ambition, Litton was the one who took the prize.

Craig had known officers like him at The Met, where ambition had been like a smell that tinged the air; men so desperate to get to the top they probably brought a knife to work, just for the ease of stabbing their rivals in the back. It had been a competitive, toxic atmosphere, not least because it had made everyone second guess themselves and had got in the way of solving crimes. He'd hated it by the end but had only realised just how much when he'd returned home in two thousand and eight and had found a more easy going approach.

He'd never been ambitious, always driven more by his heart than his head and wallet, although people who knew of his friendship with the Chief Constable would probably disagree. But he would have liked Sean Flanagan whatever job he had done, and if they thought that Flanagan did him any favours then they would have been very wrong. But that didn't stop ambitious men like Litton disliking him because of it and as far as he was concerned he didn't give a damn, but if Litton was targeting Jack because of his squad's use of interview rooms, then they would be having words very soon.

He smiled at the veteran desk sergeant, who probably knew more about policing than ten Littons rolled into one.

"When did you start reporting to him, Jack?"

Harris's expression was glum. "Three weeks ago and it's been tote that barge and lift that bale ever since." He shrugged. "Ach, I'll just have to cope till retirement."

Liam's eyebrows shot up. He and the sergeant were the same age.

"Can you afford to retire, Jack? I'll have to work till I die."

Jack's retort was instant. "That's what you get for having sex."

"I don't have sex, I make luuvvv..."

The sergeant gave a scornful laugh. "I wonder if

193

your wife would say the same. Anyway, whatever you call it, you have two young kids. Mine are all grown up. But in answer to your question, no, I can't afford to retire, but I can't put up with Litton's carryon for another ten years."

Craig intervened. "You can't leave because of him either, so I'm going to have a word." He waved Jack's objections away. "Now, we've an interview to do, so grab yourself a ringside seat."

*****

West Belfast.

Andy trudged away from the small terraced house little better informed than when he'd arrived. Matias Rey and his two mates, Ryan Phelan and Niall Henderson, had met at eight o'clock Tuesday night on the Andersonstown Road, outside the Pyramid Burger Bar. He wondered what the link was between Egypt and hamburgers but googling their dubious historical associations would have to wait.

Davy's research that the three boys had attended school and church together had turned out to be correct. They'd been three little angels as well, if the photograph he'd just seen on Phelan's living room wall was any evidence. Along the line they'd swopped football cards, DVDs and girlfriends, and for ten years the three musketeers had remained a team, so when they'd left school it hadn't been a huge leap for them all to join The Rock and another generation of Belfast gangsters had been born.

Phelan had confirmed they'd had the burgers, lining their stomachs before a big night out on the town, then they'd grabbed a taxi from Rey's firm and headed to The Pit Club. By eleven the gig was over and Niall Henderson had left with some girl. Andy would get her name when he interviewed him next. It had left the other two boys to dander off in search of more drink.

They'd found it at one of Belfast's late night

shibeens, where the pure alcohol in the poteen had seen Ryan Phelan throwing up in a gutter after midnight, then being carted off in an ambulance to the emergency department of St Mary's Trust. Andy believed the story; the lad had lain on the settee during his entire interview, clutching his still sore stomach from being pumped out days before. It had left Matias Rey to find his way home alone at one o'clock on Wednesday morning. It was an eight mile walk so how better would the son of a taxi firm owner get home except to call a cab.

Except that if Matias Rey *had* made the call, he had never reached home. That left three possibilities: either he'd been followed and they'd lifted him before he'd called the taxi; or after he'd called but before the cab arrived; or whoever had collected him was working with his killers and had driven Matias to his death. The phone records would soon tell.

He took out his mobile and called the office, to be answered by a young man.

"Hello."

"Oh, hi, Davy."

"It's Ash actually, but all us analysts sound alike. Do you want Davy?"

"No. You'll do."

Ash answered with a grunt that told Andy just how flattered he was.

"Matias Rey's phone. Have you got the call log yet?"

Ash was still huffing. "Oh yes, in between chasing up on Miskimmon, and sticking a broom up my-"

"Very funny. Well, have you?"

The analyst made a show of rustling through some papers, deliberately making the D.C.I. wait. If Andy was stupid enough to believe that he kept information on anything more primitive than a smart-pad then he deserved to wait all day. When he got fed up rustling he read aloud in a bored voice.

"Rey's last call was on Wednesday the twenty-seventh, at one-ten a.m. It was made from the city centre and the receiving number was Rey's cab firm."

He signed off brightly with. "Have a nice day now".

Andy didn't waste time wondering why Ash was in a snit. Matias Rey's killers had abducted him just after that call. He thought of something and raced back up the path to knock on the front door. It was answered by a very wan looking Phelan.

"One last question. How would Matias usually have got home after a night out?"

The youth's expression said that the answer was obvious. "He'd have called one of his dad's drivers."

Andy was insistent. "He definitely wouldn't have walked?"

Phelan scoffed. "Are you kiddin'? It's miles and Matias'd had a skin full. He would have called a cab." He turned to go back in, his greying face saying that it was probably to throw up.

Andy waved his thanks and headed to the car and his next interview, wondering if Matias Rey's killers had been prepared to collect and kill all three youths, or if getting the other two out of the way beforehand had been part of their masterplan.

****

High Street Station. 12.05 p.m.

The previous five minutes of silence had been broken only by Xavier Rey's noisy tears of grief. After a few strained moments of implacability it had made his folded face redden and crease as he'd struggled for control, only to return to its original state until the grief overcame him again. Craig watched and waited, ignoring Liam's obvious impatience and resting calmly back in his chair; the man had lost his son and whatever he might have done in his past they had to respect that. Plus, Rey had agreed to talk to them without a lawyer or anything forcing him to.

The detective asked himself why. OK, he wanted to catch his son's killer, but most gangsters would have done that by putting the word out on the street. And Rey was obviously devastated, so the last place he

196

needed to be now was sitting in a cold, bright room. He was just about to ask why he was there when the gang boss fixed his gaze.

"You're wonderin' why I'm here."

His voice was low and surprisingly soft, with an accent that lay closer to Spain than Belfast. Forty odd years in Northern Ireland, just like Craig's own mother, and yet both still sounded more of their Mediterranean origins than the place they now called home.

Craig nodded, with a sympathetic look that earned him a silent 'huh' from Liam.

"Why *are* you here, Mr Rey? There must be a lot for you to do at home."

The gang master's eyes took on a faraway look and its message was clear. He wanted to be as far from his son's funeral arrangements as possible, as if the trappings of death would drive home a fact that he couldn't yet accept. Clear as it was to Craig, Rey's next words attempted to hide the truth behind a macho façade.

"I help you catch the man."

If it made the father feel better, Craig was happy to take any help that he could get. It was only then that he realised Liam was tapping the table. It continued irritatingly until he was about to tell him to stop then he realised he was tapping out a word in their shorthand. Guilt.

Of course. Rey felt guilty over his son's death and he'd missed it behind his grief. And guilt meant that he believed the death had something to do with the world that he'd involved his son in, which meant that to help them find Matias' killer he would have to tell them about The Rock. Craig glanced towards the glass, hoping that Geoff Hamill had joined Jack as he'd said he might. What Rey said next might crack more than just this case.

****

Stockmans Lane, Belfast. 12.30 p.m.

Maureen Stevens was surprised by the brisk knock on her front door and then her surprise changed into hope. Only the police knocked that briskly; Marc must have had enough of sending Katy flowers to no reply, so he'd turned up in person to sweep her reticence away. Her hope returned to surprise when she entered the hall and saw a small outline through the glass front door. Marc was tall, in fact she didn't know anyone that small except her friend Rose, and she was in Norway on her first cruise of the year.

When she'd decided that staring and guessing wasn't going to give her an answer, she walked down the hall and opened the door, drawing it back just as far as the security chain would stretch. Marc had fitted it for her, along with a smoke alarm, adding a lecture on how to stay safe in your own home. She missed seeing him but she couldn't interfere. Katy might be gentle but she had a huge stubborn streak, and the more that she advocated for her relationship with Marc the more she was likely to turn her back on him for good.

As the thoughts ran through her head she registered who her visitor was and slid off the chain, smiling and waving her in.

"Natalie. Katy will be so pleased to see you. Do you have the day off?"

Natalie Winter née Ingrams grinned up at her hostess, but not far. Maureen Stevens was one of the few people she'd met who was almost as short as her. Katy had an extra few inches on her mother but she wasn't exactly a giantess. All in all it made Natalie feel as if she was back with her own pint-sized family and she showed her ease by linking arms with her hostess and marching her firmly into the kitchen in search of a brew.

"I do, Mrs Stevens, and John's working this weekend."

As the kettle boiled, Maureen Stevens commiserated. "Poor John. They all work so hard,

198

don't they?"

It was answered by a snort and a rustling through the biscuit tin. "They wouldn't know hard work if it jumped up and bit them. Not compared to the hours Katy and I did when we trained." She glanced towards the hall. "Is she upstairs getting ready?"

"She's upstairs." She paused, realising she didn't know if Katy was getting ready or not, or what for. Still, it would be nice for her to get out of the house. Since her accident her only outings had been to the physiotherapist and the Trust. "Are you going somewhere nice?"

Natalie nodded, her mouth full of chocolate and crumbs. "Farachut."

"I'm sorry, what did you say?"

The surgeon gulped down her biscuit and reached for another one, repeating the word before she took a bite. "Parachute."

Maureen Stevens' eyes widened but her next question was cut short by her daughter appearing at the kitchen door.

"Hi, Natalie." Katy shot her a warning look as she walked past to give her mother a hug. "Natalie and I are going shopping, Mum. At The Outlet at Banbridge, so we might be away a few hours." With that she grabbed her chomping friend's elbow and moved her swiftly towards the front door. Her mother's voice carried after them.

"But Natalie said parachute."

Katy opened the door. "It's a new fashion range. See you."

As they raced to the car, Katy's mother was certain that she'd just missed something, but she couldn't for the life of her think what it was.

****

The C.C.U.

Davy stretched his long arms above his head and gave a noisy wide-mouthed yawn. It earned him a look of disapproval from Nicky and a hand pointedly covering her own mouth. His response was a shrug; he was too tired for good manners. Partly from moving all his stuff back from France and the travelling, and partly because his reunion with Maggie hadn't just been athletic, it had been ear numbing, courtesy of her mother putting pressure on her to set a date for the wedding and Maggie passing that pressure on to him.

He cracked his knuckles hard, earning an appreciative grin from Ash and a groan of revulsion from everyone else. He was unrepentant; if he had to suffer then so could everyone else.

He didn't understand all this wedding stuff. They'd only got engaged in December, so surely to goodness they could spend a few years enjoying that! He'd always thought of engagement as an experience rather than a finite event, an experience that should last as long as all six seasons of The Walking Dead, played in its annual slots, not five seconds congratulations and then onto the next thing, the way Maggie's mother seemed to think it was. It wasn't as if he was going to do a runner. He *wanted* to marry Maggie, so why was her mother acting like he was a wild horse that she'd finally got a bridle on, and if she didn't rope him down tight he was going to sprint out the gate?

His ruminations on the business of matrimony were ended abruptly by a yelp from the neighbouring desk. It was followed by the sight of Ash jumping up and circling his arms like he was stirring a pot, in a manically uncoordinated victory dance.

"I've found one!"

"One w...what?"

Nicky appeared suddenly beside his desk. "Yes, one what? Because it had better be one diamond for me, to make up for the way you two have just disturbed my afternoon."

Ash was unrepentant, jerking his way around the open plan floor, until even Nicky had to laugh. She beckoned him back and took a seat.

"OK." She moved her glitter-tipped forefinger

200

until it stopped at Davy. "You first. What's biting you?"

"Who s...said-"

"Save the excuses. Something's up. You never crack your knuckles like that. You know how much it annoys me."

Davy rolled his eyes. "I'm tired."

"And?"

He gave a heavy sigh. "Maggie's mum's on her case about setting a date."

"Ah, I see. So now Maggie's on *your* case."

He shook his head. "No, Maggie wants a long engagement as well, but she doesn't know how to s...stop her mum."

To everyone's surprise she laughed, annoying Davy with her lack of sympathy.

"That's an easy one. Just buy a place together. It will show you're committed and keep her mum so busy helping you choose the décor that she won't have time to wedding plan." She moved her finger along to Ash. "Next."

Ash was about to start dancing again when Davy dragged him back into his chair.

"Oh, OK then. You two are no fun." He jerked a thumb at his smart-pad. "The NSA's just found someone in Canada who spotted Miskimmon's hacks before I did. He's in Toronto so I'll have to wait a few hours before I contact him, but fingers crossed."

Nicky shrugged and stood up. "Can't help you with that one, I'm afraid. I don't have a clue about computers." As she walked to her desk she turned back. "But could you warn me if you're about to dance again. I want to film it for YouTube."

****

Niall Henderson's expression swerved between shocked sadness when Andy told him about his friend's death and leering victory when the D.C.I.'s questions turned to the girl that he'd left with on Tuesday night. It was clear that the only thing stopping Henderson from punching the air and shouting 'he shoots, he

201

scores' was a sense that Matias' death might render the gesture tasteless, although even in his restraint Andy could read the boy's belief that Matias would have been congratulating him on his romantic exploits had he still been there.

When Henderson's emotional vacillation had subsided and a sober expression had finally claimed his slim cheeked good looks, Andy began his questions again, this time focusing entirely on the girl.

"So you met her..." He shook his head in a mime of forgetfulness. "Sorry, remind me again of the name of the club, could you?"

Henderson gazed at his feet in a way that said he'd seen despondent people do it on television and he'd thought that it had looked good.

"The Pit. It's on May Street. We usually go there, or to the Limelight. Then we head on to a shibeen."

Andy nodded, smiling. "Of course. You said before. And the time you arrived?"

"Nine-ish. We had a burger at the Pyramid and then one of Matias' dad's cabbies dropped us off."

"Good. And..." Andy stopped abruptly, tossing up between walking the youth through his steps or cutting straight to when he'd met the girl. He plumped for a compromise. "Tell me what time you arrived and what you did before you met the young woman."

Henderson puffed out his cheeks, thinking; they expanded much further than Andy would have imagined and he wondered idly if the boy had played the trumpet at any stage of his life. He'd played the French Horn, courtesy of his mother's desire to have a musician in the family. He'd never got beyond Grade Two so eventually she'd given up, but not before he'd noted the cheek expanding qualities of frequently blowing out air. The youth's voice cut through his thoughts.

"Landed there around nine-twenty and got a few pints down us. I needed the head so I went to the one at the back of the bar and bumped into her on my way out."

The D.C.I. shook his head at the girl's perfect

technique. She could have spotted the group when they'd entered, waited until one had cut loose from the pack and then positioned herself strategically to bump into him. Although it didn't explain how she'd known exactly which club to wait at; Xavier Rey's cab office would be next for a tug.

He adopted a blokey tone. "Was she good looking then?"

The young man's eyes widened. "Hotter than hell. I couldn't believe my luck. Girls like that never even look at me."

But had he questioned it? Nope. Like most men he'd just thanked the gods and credited himself with far more charisma than he actually possessed. The detective leaned forward encouragingly.

"Tell me what she looked like, then."

Henderson grinned. "You know that one on the local News? Only younger."

Andy did indeed. Watching her back on replay had been one of his guilty treats for months.

"Blonde then."

"And the rest. Tan, short skirt. And what a smile. The perfect ten."

Andy nodded. If you were going to use bait it needed to be fool proof. Whoever had set Matias Rey up had left nothing to chance.

He relaxed back in his chair. "Go on."

The boys' grin could only mean one thing. In a competition between the girl and his mates, the mates hadn't stood a chance. It was the way of the world.

"I told the lads I was splitting and she took me back to her hotel."

Andy's ears pricked up. "Hotel? She wasn't a local?"

"Nah. Something foreign I think." The grin deepened. "To tell you the truth we didn't talk much." If he'd winked his implication couldn't have said 'I'm some man' louder.

"How did you get to the hotel?"

"Walked. It was The Majestic just down the road."

Chosen for convenience.

"How long were you with the young lady?"

It was a term the police used frequently in such situations although it very rarely applied.

"Dunno. When I woke up around eight on Wednesday morning she'd gone."

He had all he needed. With one move Andy was upright and authoritative. One hundred percent back in policeman mode.

"I'll need you to come to the station, Mr Henderson."

The youth looked confused, trying to keep up with Andy's swift change from all boys together to I'm in charge.

"We believe the young lady may have had something to do with Mr Rey's death, so we'll need you to work with a sketch artist. And I'll need the number of the hotel room."

As realisation dawned and guilt replaced his bravado, Niall Henderson raced for the bathroom to throw up. Meanwhile Andy phoned through the details to Davy, and the searches of The Majestic's registrations and local CCTV began.

****

High Street Station. 1 p.m.

If Xavier Rey had decided to write his memoirs he couldn't have told them more about his tribe. By one o'clock they had details of The Rock's structure, business areas and overall approach. Rey took a gulp of his cooling coffee and made a face, so Craig halted the interview and headed to the staff room to make more, less from domesticity than from a desire to stretch his legs. He was joined almost immediately by two D.C.I.s. Liam was first to speak as usual.

"Well, I'm buggered. Rey must have a death wish telling us all that."

Geoff Hamill shook his head. "He knows he'll be OK."

Liam raised an eyebrow. "How do you reckon

204

that?"

The question could have been worse. He could have added 'Shorty' at the end.

"Because in all the years The Rock has been operating there's never been a killing until Matias'. I told you before, they use intimidation not violence."

"Aye, but he's just given up his boss' whole organisation. If I was the top man I'd be rightly pissed off."

Craig shook his head. "He's given up nothing, Liam. He hasn't named any of his men and he doesn't have his boss' name to give up. All we've got are the gang's current business areas, which Geoff already knew, and hopefully when we go back in we'll get some of their trading and supply outlets across the north. Only some, mind you, and probably the least profitable ones. Plus, they can open new ones within a few weeks." As he finished, his mouth twisted into a smile. Geoff Hamill joined in, making Liam tut.

"Ach, now you're getting on my wick. What are you grinning about?"

A smile wasn't a grin but Craig couldn't be bothered to argue. Instead he nodded Hamill on.

"We're smiling, you big eejit, because Xavier Rey's about to commit sabotage."

"Aye, to himself!"

Hamill snorted. He was enjoying having the upper hand with Liam, even if it only lasted a minute more.

"No, *not* to himself. To whoever's been trying to take over The Rock's business."

Liam looked blank, prompting Craig to elaborate as he made the coffee and searched for five mugs.

"What is the rival gang after, Liam?"

Liam frowned. "That's obvious. To take over The Rock's patch and business."

Craig started to pour. "Correct. So, if Rey tells us where The Rock trades and gets its supplies, he'll effectively remove those options for the next bunch. Leaving them with...?"

"They'll still be top dog."

"Yes, maybe in that area but only for a while, and

being top dog won't feed them. Without the ability to trade they'll go under in a few weeks."

Liam's frown deepened. "No, but see, that's not right. The new crowd will be dealing in drugs and girls, not cigs and DVDs. That's more money."

Craig took a sip of his drink and searched around for a tray, waving Hamill to explain the rest. The diminutive D.C.I. was having fun. He began speaking in a deliberately slow voice, making Liam narrow his eyes.

"You see, Liam. By Rey giving us nice police officers some trade routes, he's ensuring that the whole of his patch will be flooded with cops from morning to night. It's a bit hard to trade in girls and drugs when the area's under the cosh."

Liam's but was immediate. "We won't be there forever."

Hamill nodded. "True, not in those numbers, but we will be looking at the area far more often than we did before. Up till now we've let bygones be bygones with The Rock because they haven't been violent. They also keep order in their community, so although we've rousted west Belfast occasionally we haven't been breathing down their necks. But we'll definitely be doing it if there are drugs and girls in play, and for a long time. Rey's about to ensure that."

Liam clutched at the nearest straw. "Ah but..." He thought for a moment. "Ah but, then the new boys will just move somewhere else. See."

"And meanwhile we'll be gathering intelligence on them and getting ready to bring them down."

As Craig handed round the drinks and got ready to take the other two out to Jack and his guest, he added. "There's just one caveat, Geoff. My guess is that Rey's men won't take Matias' death lying down. There could be trouble after the funeral."

Liam opened his mouth to say something but Craig shut it again with a glance.

"I know exactly what you're going to say. They're all criminals so why do we care if they kill each other."

Liam shrugged.

"I'll tell you why we care. Because there's a hell of a difference between criminals who defraud and those who kidnap and kill." He entered the corridor, leaving the others to follow his voice. "Come on. I want this new gang found before Rey and his men take the law into their own hands."

He handed Rey's coffee to Liam, waving him into the interview room, then he entered the viewing room to give the last mug to Jack. Five minutes later the desk sergeant was updated on a plan to flood south and west Belfast with uniforms as soon as Craig gave the word. When he re-entered the interview room, Liam was already scribbling down a list of The Rock's supply and trade routes that they knew would be out of date in a few weeks.

Chapter Nine

The C.C.U. 2 p.m.

Ash tapped hard on his static filled PC screen, earning him a laugh from the next desk.

"It's not a s...snowglobe, mate. It won't get clearer just because you give it a bash."

He ignored Davy's scepticism and tapped again, surreptitiously changing a cable connection beneath the desk as he did. The screen cleared instantly and the image of a dark-eyed young woman in her twenties wearing three nose studs appeared. As Davy gawped at the seemingly beaten into submission computer, Ash was gawping at the girl. Even from halfway across the world she was the cutest thing he'd ever seen.

He smoothed his green quiff down self-consciously, his smooth baritone cracking slightly as he said "Hi. I'm Ash Rahman. Are you the hacker in Toronto?"

The girl waved in reply, before answering in an accent that sounded strangely like she came from Belfast.

"Hi there. Yep, I'm Ashley."

Ashley and Ash; it sounded like a kid's cartoon. Davy sniggered and leaned in to watch his friend make small talk.

"So, you're from Canada."

The girl shook her spiked-up hair. "Nope. I'm from Antrim but my folks moved over here when I was two."

He'd almost been right about her accent but it hadn't been as random a guess as it had first seemed. A lot of Northern Irish people had emigrated to Canada during The Troubles and few had returned home again.

To deter Ash from turning the session into a cyber date, Davy moved his chair behind his friend's and gave a cheerful wave.

"Hi, Ashley. I'm Davy, the other analyst. Thanks for s...speaking to us today."

He could feel Ash glaring at him through the back

of his head.

"Ash has a lot of questions to ask you, about some hacking you did last year."

"Yep. Weather drones starting dropping randomly over here, so I thought I would see what was what."

Davy nodded his goodbye. "Great. I'll leave you with Ash then."

The intervention was the virtual equivalent of a cold shower and just as effective; Ash stopped drooling and started talking about the drones. Davy turned back to his smart-pad; he had plenty to do with the hotel registration list that had just come in. He was just setting up some searches when Andy strolled languidly over to his desk.

"Anything on that hotel room yet?"

Davy's expression said 'give me a break'. He reinforced the message with a pointed "Have you finished viewing those airport tapes yet?" which sent Andy scuttling back to his desk in search of chocolate.

The sight that greeted Craig and Liam when they entered the squad-room ten minutes later was of two analysts and a D.C.I. locked to their PC screens and Nicky smiling benevolently at the quietness of the room. She reminded Craig of his primary school teacher when the class was taking an afternoon nap.

Liam put paid to the peace by thumping down onto Nicky's desk and sending a pile of yellow stickies scattering to the wind. Before the P.A. could explode Craig asked her a question.

"Where are Annette, Jake, Rhonda, Kyle and Geoff Hamill's D.C.?"

The answer came from under the desk, where she was picking up yellow pads.

"Annette and Jake are on their way back from Armagh, Kyle went to meet someone in intelligence. Rhonda nipped out for a sandwich and whatshisname said he had to go home and walk his dog but he'd be back." She reappeared, adding. "It seems he wasn't expecting on call to mean working all weekend."

Craig helped her to her feet. "Liam, you should have picked those up, not Nicky."

The D.C.I.'s response was to raise an eyebrow and point to the tiny space beneath her desk. "You'd have needed a tub of grease and a shoe horn to get me out again." He added "Sorry, Nicky" and his best smile, earning him a loud "Huh".

Craig glanced at his watch. "OK, it's two o'clock. What time did Annette say they'd be back?"

"Around two-thirty."

"I don't suppose Kyle specified."

Nicky's reply surprised him. "He did actually. Three. He said his contact had to leave before then."

He considered for a moment and then headed back out the door. "Tell everyone we're briefing at three-thirty. Liam and I are going to Templepatrick but we'll be back."

Liam's groan accompanied him into the lift. "We haven't had lunch yet."

Craig's deliberately loud answer was to press for the seventh floor. "We'll buy sandwiches from the canteen and you can eat yours on the way."

Nicky heard the words and smiled. It was suitable revenge for her yellow notes.

****

Templepatrick. County Antrim.

Tommy Hill's home surprised both detectives. They'd always met him at Ella's other grandparents' before; a comfortable vicar's manse on the opposite side of town.

Before they'd arrived at the hard man's new abode Craig had pictured a duplicate of the sprawling Demesne in east Belfast, where Hill had been just one of the rats who'd turned its serviceable, if not particularly ornate buildings into a human sewer where no decent person was safe.

So they'd turned off the Antrim Road expecting graffiti to assault their eyes, and to see the baby rodents, the next generation of Tommys, scatter as they stepped from the car, their height, suits and three-sixty scans labelling them unmistakeably as police. But instead they gawped as Craig pulled past a sign heralding that they were 'Welcome to Rosetree Close', the greeting echoed in the well-trimmed bushes and hedges that had retained most of their foliage despite the time of year.

As the detective pulled up to a well brushed kerb, devoid of any flag's colours or acronyms naming the local gangs, he shook his head in surprise and voiced his thoughts.

"Do you think if Tommy had come from a place like this, he might not have turned out to be what he is?"

Liam's quick reply said that he was indulging in fantasy. "Get away with you. He'd still be the same murdering thug he's always been. There was sectarianism round here as well back then, and Tommy would always have found a Catholic to kill."

Craig conceded the point and locked up the car, following Liam up a short path to their target address. The door of the ground floor flat opened before they'd even reached it and a sarcastically grinning Tommy waved them in with an arm sweep and a bow.

"Wat tuk ye so long tee pay me a visit?" He jerked a thumb at Liam. "I'd have thought he'd hav been desperate to turn the place over before nye."

"Well, hello to you too, Tommy." Liam scanned the small home's modern décor as he talked. "Nice place you've got here." He threw himself down on a small sofa, making Craig wince as he waited for its springs to pop. "This is a step up from the ripped settee you had on the Demesne. Who did you rob to get it?"

Tommy bared his teeth in the closest they were ever going to see to a smile. "Nye, nye, Ghost." The old lag had given Liam the nickname years before because of his pallor. "If I wus a sensitive creater I'd be hurt by that remark. But, nat that it's ony af yer business, the council bought it fer me with a grant." He fell into a nearby chair with a mock sad expression. "Unferchinitly I've no tea ar caffee, ar I'd offer ye both a cup."

Craig answered before Liam could retort. "Thanks for the offer, Tommy, but we're not here on a social visit. We need to ask you about your movements this week."

The Loyalist's reply was to lift his leg to reveal an ankle tag. "Ask my electronic friend here." He smoothed down his tracksuit again. "'Cept that my guess is ye've already checked and it's tawl ye I wus here or in the village the whole time." It was a good thing a mate had nicked him a load of spare straps for his tag.

The teeth-baring smile returned. "Why de ye want tee know, officers? Is sumwun blaming me on sumthin' I huvn't dun?"

This time Craig's answer wasn't quick enough and Liam made himself heard. He leaned forward angrily in his seat.

"You're a lying git, Hill. You were spotted in Belfast this week and the only thing we need to work out is how you managed to fool your tag." He clenched his fists. "What were you doing there?"

Tommy did his best impersonation of an innocent man, which still looked guiltier than most. "I dun't know wat yer talkin' about. I've bin here awl the time."

Craig moved to stand over the aging killer. "You *were* in Belfast, Tommy, and we all know it. And when we've worked out how you fooled the tag I'll rescind your parole and put you back inside faster than you can blink. You're still on license for dealing in stolen goods, remember." He turned towards the door. "Although as whatever you've been up to this week will no doubt be linked to crime in some way, I expect you'll be back inside soon anyway for a few more years."

He signalled Liam to follow him out. He did, but only after leaning close to Tommy and giving a low growl.

"You're on notice, Hill. If you're seen anywhere near Belfast you'll be arrested and the next time you see your granddaughter it'll be to walk her up the aisle."

If Tommy was worried he didn't show it, but he *was* going to relocate the meeting he had planned for that afternoon.

****

Dundalk. The Republic of Ircland.

Dermot Faloon pushed the girl out of his bed to find alcohol while he made a call. It was answered quickly by an older man and his tone of voice said that anger had been the source of his speed.

"Where the hell were you?"

Faloon stared at his handset in mild surprise, then swopped its screen to 'missed calls' and made a face when he saw that there'd been five in the previous two hours. Sex had a habit of making him go deaf, not blind like his parish priest had warned.

"Sorry, boss." His contrition wasn't reflected in his tone. "I was otherwise occupied."

The undertone of lechery told his listener all he needed to know.

"Keep your dick in your pants until this is over, Faloon, or I'll have it chopped off. Understand?"

Faloon gulped out a hasty "yes."

The man moved onto other things. "Where's the girl?"

The youth glanced towards the door. "Making the tea." Gin flavoured tea of course. "Do you need her?"

"One last job should be enough."

"Like Fox?"

"Like I'll tell you when you need to know. Just get her ready and she'll be picked up at six. Tell her to look extra hot this time."

As the door reopened and the girl reappeared with a bottle and two glasses, Faloon signed off and glanced at the clock. They just had time for one more session then it was time for her to earn her keep.

****

The C.C.U. 4 p.m.

Craig was half-an-hour into the briefing when Nicky handed him a note that made his eyebrows rise. He slipped it into his pocket and then turned back to listen to what Annette had to say.

"So basically, we need to rule out that the girl isn't from here before the Gardaí will do anything."

Liam rubbed his chin. "Tricky when we have no matching prints and she was wearing a wig. O'Shea really said there was no sighting of her on CCTV in the south?"

She nodded. "The road behind the field was a dirt track leading to others that went on for miles. She could have disappeared off any one of them. But..." She turned to see Craig wearing a puzzled expression that she was pretty sure wasn't about the case. "There's just a chance we could find someone who saw her with Fox, sir, or we might get lucky and find the number he called her on. I suggest we pursue that end of things first before we get back to O'Shea."

The way she said the name made Liam laugh.

"I take it you weren't bowled over by our liaison officer?"

"Nope. A bit too much of the patronising charm going on for me. Jake can tell you."

Jake was frowning as well. Craig roused himself to ask why, praying the answer wasn't anything to do with Aaron Foster. It wasn't.

"I don't think O'Shea took the two deaths' proximity seriously enough. He seemed more interested in pointing out that McAllister died at the north side of his farm than acknowledging that Fox's murder and the tank were only a mile apart."

Annette was nodding. "I don't think O'Shea's taking anything seriously, sir."

Craig made a face. "There could be a reason for that. Liaison jobs are often given to people nearing retirement." He turned to Davy. "Is he, Davy?"

Davy lifted his smart-pad. "It'll be easy enough to find out."

Andy had been lounging in his chair as usual, now he sat bolt upright, spotting an opportunity to interject.

"I went to see the two youngsters who were out with Matias Rey that night, Niall Henderson and Ryan Phelan. Henderson left the others to go to a hotel with a girl. He said she was foreign, but he was vague about which country, and when he woke up in the morning she was gone."

"Decoy?"

"That was my thought. He's coming in to work up a sketch. It couldn't just be a coincidence, could it? Two girls involved in two of our deaths?"

Craig's reply was to pull the whiteboard across.

"OK, we have three murders with no connections between the victims." He glanced at Ash for confirmation.

"None that we can find so far, chief. Different ages, social circles, jobs, religions, modes of death..."

"OK, but keep searching." He scribbled up the three men's names, drawing a column under each. "So, Calum Fox dies in south Armagh, as does Colin McAllister, but Matias Rey dies in Belfast. Fox was killed by a woman, Rey by man or men but a girl distracted one of his companions, and anyone could have sabotaged McAllister's air tank. We're pretty sure Rey was killed because of his gang links, but McAllister was a farmer, albeit it looks like he was a crooked one, and Fox was a bookie."

Liam was nodding. "To me that's suspicious, boss. All three men were involved in or on the fringes of risky behaviour: gangs, gambling and maybe fuel smuggling."

Craig nodded slowly. "Maybe, but that still doesn't mean that their deaths were linked. Ash found no other connections."

Jake sat forward eagerly. "What about if they weren't linked to each other but all three were linked to someone else?"

Rhonda cut in quietly. "What about... to whoever is trying to take over Rey's gang?"

215

Kyle had been playing with a dummy cigarette, twirling it irritatingly in Craig's peripheral vision like a cheerleader's baton. Now he stuck it in his pocket and shook his head. "Doesn't make sense. If they were working for whoever's staging the takeover then they wouldn't have been killed, and Matias Rey definitely wouldn't have been trying to take over The Rock. He was already its boss." He lifted a sheaf of paper that had been lying on his desk. "I was going to come on to this."

Liam craned his neck to see. "What is it?"

"It's from one of my mates in Intelligence. He says there are definitely Albanians on the scene in Belfast and they're not the friendly sort." He held up a photograph. "This is Abaz Goga. He landed here in December and since then he's been flooding the province with dodgy gear. They know he's brought in girls as well, but so far they haven't been able to find where they're being held."

Craig took the photograph. "What makes you think this is linked to our case?"

"I don't yet. I just wanted to give you the heads up. But we've no proof that whoever's running the coup against The Rock was running our three dead men. However..." He paused, retrieving the photo and tucking it back into his papers. "What *might* make sense is if the dead men were killed because they were in the coup-master's way."

The room erupted with noise while Craig sat in the middle furrowing his brow. After he'd let everyone talk for a minute he raised a hand for quiet.

"OK. What Kyle said could make sense if, *if*, we could link Fox and McAllister to Rey's gang in some way. If they were all part of The Rock, that's providing the gang has branches outside Belfast which we haven't confirmed, then that *could* have made all three men obstacles in the way of a takeover, making sense of why they were killed."

He saw Liam about to interrupt and hurried on. "However, so far we have absolutely nothing to link them. Xavier Rey has just given us some of his trade and supply routes and, Liam can correct me if I'm wrong, but none of them had anything to do with bookies, petrol or Armagh. Liam?"

The D.C.I. shook his head. "Nope. As far as we know The Rock's trade is based in west and south Belfast and they don't deal in fuel, although the gambling's a weak link, maybe, with their numbers games. Rey didn't mention Fox or McAllister, but then he didn't give anyone's name."

"No, you're right, he didn't. So go back and run McAllister's and Fox's names past him and see if he blinks. But the operative words here could be *as far as we know*. It's very possible that Xavier Rey deliberately withheld information on the gang's operations outside Belfast."

Suddenly Davy gave a noisy "Yes!"

"Does that mean O'Shea is up for retirement?"

"End of the year."

Annette gave a defeated nod. "That explains why he was so unhelpful. He's probably just biding his time until he leaves."

Liam blustered indignantly. "That's no bloody excuse! He's getting paid until his last day so he should do the bloody work." He ended the sentence by glaring at Andy, who pointedly ignored him.

Craig sighed. "OK, so we have no direct connections between our victims, and a lethargic liaison officer." He wrote up the word 'girl' and tapped the board. "Two of our deaths have featured a young woman on the periphery. In Rey's case she was described as blonde, in Fox's they found a blonde hair, but we all know about disguises-"

Andy cut in. "Niall Henderson said she was blonde and foreign."

"Which country?"

"He didn't know."

"OK. The girl might be something or nothing, but as soon as you get that sketch send it over to Davy and Ash." He turned to the analysts. "I want it run through every security database here and overseas. Annette, get a copy of it to O'Shea to run through the Republic's database." He glanced at Kyle and Jake in turn. "I want you two to work with Ash on checking any connections between the three cases. Kyle, include the Albanians in that. Meanwhile, Annette, speak to Mara McAllister and Mitchell Purvis again, see if they knew any of the other victims."

He raked his hair. He was wrecked and if he was then the others must be too. It was time to wind up for the day.

"OK, Liam and I will follow up with Rey. Andy, I want you to check out the cab driver that dropped off the boys that night; he could have tipped off the girl where they'd be. Also, I want the cabbie Matias called after his friend went to the ED." He shot the D.C.I. a warning glance. "But absolutely do not let Xavier Rey know that you suspect any of his drivers or we could have another death on our hands."

He stopped for a moment, running through things in his head. Matias Rey: trade routes, cab drivers, sketch of the girl, Albanian links, hotel.

"Davy, anything on the hotel?"

Davy shook his head. "I've checked all registrations that day and the girl gave a false name."

Craig nodded and returned to his run through. Colin McAllister: follow up on Kennedy and Purvis, the forensics on the tank and farm, and the links with the south. Calum Fox... They still knew very little about Calum Fox.

"Liam and I will dig into Calum Fox tomorrow. One last thing, we visited Tommy Hill today and I'm convinced he's found a way to slip his tag. Put the word out that he's to be lifted if anyone sees him."

He stood up, pointing at Andy and Ash. "You two, join me in my office, please. I need an update on Miskimmon. And don't look so worried, it'll be quick."

Andy nodded, adopting his best man of the world expression. "Aye, 'cos some of us are heading out on the town tonight."

****

218

The update left Craig frustrated. Not at his men; they couldn't help it if Ronan Miskimmon had played hide and seek so effectively on the CCTV, or if their best lead so far might be from a hacker closeted in her bedroom halfway across the world, but the whole Miskimmon investigation gave him an unsatisfied feeling. The evidence felt shaky, as if at any moment the ground beneath them could collapse and the whole case would fall into an un-prosecutable black hole.

He slouched in his chair and gazed out at the rain swollen river, resigned to the situation yet not resigned, all at once. Any resignation was because whatever happened at their end, Miskimmon and Corneau would still languish in a Venezuelan jail for years, and it wouldn't be a pleasant stay. He felt a sudden pang and realised immediately where it was coming from. Eleanor Corneau; a young woman who had never known her father and been fed on her brother's hatred from the moment that she could breathe. Having met Miskimmon he somehow doubted that their late mother's gentleness could have combatted such vitriol. Corneau might have been redeemable if life had cut her a different break, but after years in a foreign jail he doubted that she would ever view the world favourably again.

The thought made him sit upright, defiance shunting his feelings of resignation forcibly out of the way. No, he couldn't let it happen; he couldn't let the visa fraud be all that they could prove. Not because of Corneau, or not wholly because of her, but because he was damned if Miskimmon was going to get off with a few years when he should spend the rest of his life in jail. He didn't know how but he was going to stop that happening. Feeling slightly better he lifted the phone to make the call he should have made an hour before.

****

Stockmans Lane. 6 p.m.

Maureen Stevens' eyes widened when she saw her

daughter; she looked more like she'd run a marathon than just had a gentle stroll around some fashion shops. She beckoned Natalie over and turned to fill the kettle, using the rush of water to cover her voice.

"Has Katy been running? She looks very flushed."

Natalie thought on her feet. "Ah, that'll be excitement. She saw quite a few things she liked in Banbridge and spent a lot of time trying them on." Adding for effect. "You know those changing rooms; some of them are so hot that you'd almost pass out."

It caused a concerned frown. "Please remember that Katy hasn't been well, Natalie. She needs to take things carefully."

Natalie nodded cheerfully, thanking goodness that Katy's mum couldn't read her thoughts. If she could she would have pointed her towards the front door immediately and Katy would never have been allowed out to play again. She carried the tray of tea things to the table where Katy was sitting, staring blankly into space. Natalie nudged her friend's foot beneath the table.

"Tomorrow should be fun."

Maureen Stevens brought over the teapot and sat down with a smile. "Out again tomorrow, pet? Where to this time?"

Natalie answered before Katy could. "The Ulster Museum. They've got a great exhibition on."

It opened a door that she hadn't meant to, so before her hostess could ask what the exhibition was about Natalie glanced at her watch hastily and stood up.

"I'm so sorry, Mrs Stevens, but I completely forgot the time. John will be expecting his dinner."

The sheer absurdity of the comment broke Katy's trance. If John Winter had been waiting for his wife to cook for him he would have starved to death a year before. But it gave her the impetus to steer her friend quickly towards the front door and she opened it wide, hissing under her breath.

"Shopping without buying anything? Now a museum exhibition I've no idea about? Mum's not stupid, Nat."

The tiny surgeon hissed back. "Well, what did you want me to say? Mrs Stevens, the reason your daughter's face is red and she looks shell-shocked is because she spent the day jumping out of aircraft from twelve thousand feet. Oh, and tomorrow she'll be doing the ton around a race track! She'd never let you out of the house again."

But Katy was on a roll. "And cooking for John? What was *that*? The last time you cooked for him he nearly had to have his stomach pumped."

Natalie shrugged. "Your mum bakes so I thought she'd trust me more if she thought I was the domestic sort."

"She'll think you've had a personality transplant!"

Natalie was halfway down the path with her fingers in her ears. "Nah, nah, nah. Not listening. I'll see you at eleven tomorrow. Bye bye."

While Katy spent an hour convincing her mother that yes, she really could window shop for six hours without buying anything, Natalie headed home via the Thai Takeaway, entering her own house thirty minutes later like Lady Bountiful, only to find her husband lying on the sofa watching an episode of C.S.I.

"Hi honey, I'm home." She held the soggy bags close to John's face. "Guess what I cooked."

He adjusted his position and kept watching. "You were coming from Katy's so you passed the Thai Pad on the way."

The words were out before she could stop them. "Who told you I was at Katy's? What has she said?"

"You told me last night that you were seeing Katy."

John turned to stare at her, in the penetrating way he did when he thought she was up to no good.

Natalie moved quickly towards the kitchen. "I'll just find some plates."

But he was standing in front of her before she could take a step. John leaned down so that his face was only inches from her own. "What have you been up to?"

Natalie ducked round her husband and pushed

221

through the kitchen door, a mumbled "nothing" floating back.

The pathologist was undeterred. He set off in pursuit and plopped down at the breakfast bar, scrutinising his wife in the same way he scrutinised the cases he was involved in every day. It mightn't have been his job to actually solve them but that didn't mean he didn't develop theories of his own, and more often than not they turned out to be right. After staring so hard that Natalie blushed John gave a satisfied nod.

"You've been up to something, my love, and as you've just come from Katy's my guess is that she's involved in it as well."

Natalie decided to brazen it out. She believed in the mantra; if in doubt attack, so she turned towards him with her small hands on her hips. "Well! It's coming to something when your own husband doesn't trust you."

She turned back to the bags and lifted a spoon, preparing to dish up the rice.

John rose and walked slowly towards her, making her back away until she'd reached the fridge. Natalie waved the utensil she was holding, menacingly.

"Don't you dare come near me, John Winter."

He kept walking until he was so close that she could feel his breath. His proximity made her feel strangely inclined to surrender but she brushed the distinctly anti-feminist urge aside.

"I'm warning you. I have a spoon and I'll use it!"

John smiled seductively. "And why would you want to hit your husband when all he wants to do is to give you a kiss?"

It caught her off balance. "Oh, is that-"

He pulled her to him, kissing her harder than he had all week. When he let go Natalie had to steady herself against the fridge. John pressed his advantage.

"Now, I know that you and Katy are up to something you don't want me to know about, so will you tell me now or do I have to kiss you until you do?"

He got his answer as the takeaway went cold.

Stranmillis. 10 p.m.

Craig didn't know whether to laugh or kick the waste basket when he arrived home, so he opted for a bit of both. What he'd thought would be a ten minute 'buck your ideas up' call with the Chief Constable had turned out to be a summons to his office, which had been a shock in itself. He'd always imagined rank and age prevented people having to work on a Saturday night.

Ninety minutes and two whiskies later he was in a taxi home with two decisions to make, to add to his already long list. One of them was clear but not simple; the other was simple but not clear. As he pulled off his clothes and climbed into the shower both faded into the background, his last remaining ten minutes of consciousness full of the woman that he loved.

****

Templepatrick. 11 p.m.

Rory McCrae's curiosity overcame his fear for a moment. The last time he'd visited somewhere Tommy had lived it had been a council flat whose nineteen-eighties' scruffiness had testified to that decade being the last time it had seen a lick of paint. His new place couldn't have been more different. Crisp white walls and beige carpet; apart from the kitchen which was a symphony in pine. He even had canisters marked Tea, Coffee and Sugar which prompted the UKUF boss to take his life in his hands and make a joke.

"Mine's black with two sugars, boss."

Boss. Years of different paths couldn't stop him regressing to subordinate mode whenever Tommy was around. No matter how tough he might act with UKUF Tommy had killed much harder men than him in his time, *and* been smart enough not to get caught. If the bus killing hadn't been so high profile that snouts of all denominations had come crawling out of their holes to

223

shop him, he doubted that Tommy would have spent a day in prison in his life. And if he found out even now who'd dobbed him into the cops, he would be adding yet another burial to his list.

Hill's reply was as predictable as the Ulster rain. "Get yer own bloody tea, McCrae. An' make me wan as well."

As McCrae scuttled off Tommy's voice followed with the words. "And dun't untidy my kitchen or ye'll be picking yer teeth out of the trash."

The niceties over McCrae sat down nervously on the low sofa, holding his mug carefully in both hands and over a copy of 'Guns and Ammo' that lay on the low coffee table. One drop of liquid on the carpet might see him flat on his back. Tommy squinted hard at his friend, because even though McCrae didn't realise it he was closer to receiving that appellation than anyone in Tommy's life. The friend gabbled nervously under the ex-paramilitary's scrutiny.

"Nice place ye huv here, boss. Nat like the council places out ar way."

Hill said nothing, letting him gabble. He wanted his old running mate nervous before he spoke; it was the only way he could guarantee McCrae would do exactly as he was told. McCrae shifted awkwardly in his seat, wondering whether to risk a sip of tea. His mouth had other ideas.

"The Demesne's still a shitheap. I wus dyne there earlier, seein' Gerdy Bonner like. He's out of The Mag." The ex-cons' nickname for HMP Maghaberry. "Nearly seven months nye. Says he wus aff tee the jab centre. Sumthin' about a job on a buildin' site."

After a minute's more gabbling, Tommy moved to the edge of his chair. The effect was like an electric shock, making McCrae rear back so sharply that he almost spilt his drink. Even Tommy's ensuing "tut" held menace.

"Fer fuck's sake put that cup dyne, before ye wreck my carpets."

McCrae obeyed so hastily he spilt some of the black, sticky liquid on the magazine. Tommy wanted to slap him but instead he rolled his eyes. A slap now might lose him the advantage and there was plenty of time before he left. He twisted his lips into a smile.

"I've a job fer ye, McCrae. But first I want everythin' ye know about gangs, like I asked ye to gather. I'll tell ye the rest when I'm satisfied with that."

There followed ten minutes of Rory McCrae mentally thanking his stars that Tommy hadn't exploded about the magazine, and giving him chapter and verse on the main gangs that ran Belfast north, south, east and west. Tommy pushed for more.

"Wat about the city centre? Who's working things dyne there?"

McCrae made a face and shrugged. "No-one's sure. Some say the Chinese have it, especially the bits round Bradbury Place. I asked Gerdy and he tawl me the east Europeans huv Smithfield, Royal Avenue and the Cathedral streets. They've stayed tight there, in case they foul someone else's turf, I guess."

Tommy considered for a moment; it made sense. Any further in any direction and they would encroach on the compass point gangs. Then he thought again, realising that someone already had and that was the very reason they were there. He decided to take his old lieutenant into his confidence, or as close in as anyone ever got. McCrae could be a lippy wee sod but he would never double cross him; he valued his scrawny neck too much.

"Sumwan's already dun it."

McCrae's eyes widened.

"Up west and south. The home gang up there's called The Rock, run by some Spaniard called Rey. His boy was just killed."

McCrae gawped. "The Rock? I've heered of them." He closed his eyes for a moment, recalling. "Counterfeits, launderin', gamblin' and cigs." They sprang open again and he added, fearful of one-upping Tommy's knowledge. "As far as I know, like, boss." He added a low whistle for effect. "Whoever dun them mustn't like their faces much. There's some heavyweight punchers in that bunch."

Tommy lounged back in his chair. "Well, sumwan tuk the risk. The Rocks might have the muscle but they're nat known for killin'." He shook his head disapprovingly. "Always a mistake, that. If word gets out ye dun't kill, sumwan will always fancy a crack."

He narrowed his eyes suddenly, making McCrae shift nervously in his chair. "That's why there's more fer ye to do. I reckon either the Chinese or European lot have been swimming outside their pond. I need ye to pit out yer feelers and find me which wan it is."

McCrae blustered out a reply. "But I'm busy with Garvan's. How the heck-"

Tommy lurched forward, his face turning a dark red. "I'm nat interested in how, ye wee shite. Just dee it. I've tried kneecappins and gat nathin' but ye've got ears everywhere. Git Coyler and Gerdy on the job. I'll bung them fifty when I get paid."

Realisation lit up McCrae's eyes. "Yer workin' fer The Rock! Are ye? Ye must be if yer getting' paid."

Tommy's growl was so loud and low it sounded as if it had come straight from hell. "DUN'T QUESTION ME, YE WEE BASTARD. JUST DO AS YER FRIGGIN' WELL TOLD!"

McCrae shrank like a slug dowsed in salt. "Sarry, Tommy. Honest ta Gawd, I didn't mean nathin'."

He was immediately angry at himself for the subservient display. He was the head of his own gang now yet saying sorry like a kid was the best that he could do. He rose to his feet, attempting to regain some control.

"I'll git the word out-"

"Nowan's to know who's asking."

"Nowan. Honest, boss. I'll get back to ye when I huv anythin'."

Tommy opened the living room door, casting a pointed look back at the wet magazine.

"Ye'll get back to me by tomara. Ony later and I'll cum lookin'."

He followed his subdued follower to the front door, yanking it open. But if McCrae had thought he was getting away unscathed it had been a fool's hope.

226

Just as he started walking through the door Tommy slammed it hard in his face, drawing blood.

"That's fer ruinin' my magazine."

The message was clear. Failure to deliver his information would exact a penalty far worse.

Chapter Ten

Stranmillis. Sunday, 5.50 a.m.

Craig's dreams didn't last long, his imaginary make-up conversation with Katy interrupted by a noise that wasn't inside his head. He grabbed his phone and checked the screen. It wasn't ringing and there were no missed calls. Nothing except a clock that was displaying five-fifty in a very inconsiderate way. It was then that he realised the noise was coming from the front door. Someone was hammering it and they'd better have a damn good reason why.

He stormed down the hall and yanked it open, shouting a hoarse "YES", only to be greeted by Liam's horrified face and then be pushed out of the way as the D.C.I. went in search of tea. It took Craig a moment to realise that he was naked and another to pull on his jeans and enter the kitchen in the same mood that he'd answered the door.

"You'd better have-"

Liam raised his eyes to heaven. "Thank God you've put on some trousers. I've just got to know you better than I'd never hoped." He reached into a cupboard. "Where're the teabags? They used to be here. I wish the hell you wouldn't keep moving things about."

Craig spotted his deputy's bustlings for the displacement activity that it was, so he took a seat, suddenly sober, and waved at the cupboard opposite.

"Bottom right. Coffee's in there too. Make mine strong."

As Liam boiled the kettle Craig grabbed a jumper from a nearby radiator and wrestled it on, then he waited until they both had hot drinks in their hands before asking the only question possible.

"Who's dead?"

Liam shook his head and took another sip of tea. Craig's tone turned insistent.

"Who's dead, Liam? NOW. Tell me it's not one of the team."

Liam's face was impassive but his pale eyes filled with fire. "None of our lot."

Craig released a breath that he hadn't even realised he'd held, then he inhaled again sharply. "Not Katy?"

The 'please God' was silent but definitely there.

Liam shook his head immediately. "Not Katy. Not anyone that we know or care about."

Craig could feel his anger building, aided and abetted by last night's two Bushmills. "Well, what the hell are you doing here then?"

Liam pushed away his cup. "Andy's been arrested for murder."

Craig gawped at him. "What? No. No way. Andy doesn't have the energy to stay upright, never mind kill someone!" He paused for a moment, marshalling his thoughts before asking the most important question. "Who's he accused of killing?"

Liam made a face. "Some woman. One of his neighbours heard screams so they dialled nine-nine-nine. Uniform broke in and found Andy in bed with a naked girl. She'd been killed by a single shot to the head."

Any residual grogginess Craig had dissipated with the sharp shaking of his head. "He didn't do it." He headed for the bedroom to get dressed, shouting out questions as he did. "Where is he now?"

"High Street. They called me soon as they realised he was ours and I got him moved down to Jack's."

"Good. Call John in to do the P.M. and I want Des on the forensics ASAP."

Liam made the calls and then wandered down the hallway to stand at Craig's bedroom door. His expression conveyed abject misery. "The inspector who called me said the bullet hole fitted a 19 millimetre parabellum just like a Glock holds, and Andy had gunshot residue on his hands. I know he's a dozy pillock but I wouldn't wish this on him."

Craig angled away from the mirror where he was fixing his tie and shook his head emphatically. "I don't care if Andy has 'I killed her' tattooed on his face in

229

blood, no way did he do this. Lots of guns use Parabellums: SIGs, M9s; it's a long list." He grabbed his keys and wallet and strode past his deputy to the door. "My car's at headquarters so I'll need a lift."

Liam was struggling to keep up. "Where are we going?"

"Andy's flat and then to collect my car. After that it's High Street then the lab."

He halted mid-step and turned to face the worried looking D.C.I.

"Don't look so concerned, Liam. This is good news."

Liam's jaw dropped. "GOOD NEWS! How the hell is it good news? Andy could be banged up for years and he'll definitely lose his job. Plus he has a kid to support and-"

Craig pulled the apartment door shut and raced down the three flights to the street. "When you've quite finished shroud waving I'll tell you why it's good." He strode over to Liam's Ford, feeling strangely energised. "It's good news because it's a blindingly obvious setup and we'll prove it, and hopefully gather evidence on the way. It also means that someone is getting so worried about us cracking the murders that they're desperate to try and throw us off-"

Liam cut in. "So why not target you then, or me?"

Craig shook his head. "I'm not sure yet. But whichever of us they'd chosen to set up, they're doing it because we're on the right path."

Liam's frown deepened as realisation dawned. "I'll tell you what else it means. Someone on our side has a bloody big mouth."

****

The Lab. 7 a.m.

By six-thirty the two detectives had left the murder scene and were heading to the lab, the order of play changed by Craig. Andy's city centre apartment had looked much as he'd expected, clean but untidy, with stacks of DVDs and Blu-rays dominating the living room. The man needed to get out more, although come to think of it, maybe not, given what had just occurred.

What he hadn't expected were the images on Andy's walls. In amongst the photographs of his two ex-wives and son, and a framed poster of a giant Toblerone that was an obvious pastiche on Warhol, there were several original works of Irish art that he recognised. A Harrington, a Scully and even a small Levine. It pointed to Andy being a serious collector. Craig paused for a moment to admire them, chiding himself yet again for not knowing or asking more about his officers' private lives.

His reproach was short-lived and after collecting his Audi both cars arrived at the labs. It was comforting to see the lights burning, not only because it meant that the kettle would soon be boiling but because knowing that John and Des had lost sleep as well gave the detectives a slightly sadistic but warm glow. Misery loves company.

Craig's greeting to his best friend continued in that vein. He thudded into a chair in John's office and nodded Liam to hit the kettle, while he prodded a finger at the tired doctor, who was curled sideways in his chair with his eyes closed attempting to sleep.

"Greetings, oh great one. What can you tell us about our girl?"

John didn't move so Liam's back-up plan kicked in. He flicked cold water in John's face, earning him a wild-eyed pathologist leaping to his feet.

"I was trying to sleep! I've been up all sodding night."

Craig waved him down unsympathetically. "Well, you're awake now, so what can you tell us?"

"I'm telling you nothing until I've had some tea. And I sincerely hope that you brought food."

Craig produced a bag of donuts and slid them across the desk. Two minutes later the colour had returned to even Liam's cheeks and John had begun to thaw.

"She died from a single bullet wound to the right

temple. Nineteen millimetre Parabellum, probably from a Glock or a SIG. Des is checking the markings at the moment."

"OK. Consistent with the story from the arresting officers. What can you tell us about the girl herself?"

John's expression was sad. "She'd had a tough life. Bruises all over her, some of them only a day old; someone had been very rough with her. I'd estimate her age at about twenty; I'm just waiting for the X-Rays to confirm. She'd made at least one attempt at suicide – cut her wrists—the scars say around two years ago. There are marks of self-harm as well, and she was definitely a user. I found injection sites on her arms and feet. Probably Heroin but I'll tell you for sure once the full tox-screen comes back."

Craig shook his head. "She sounds like she never stood a chance."

John nodded. "I'll tell you something else. She wasn't from here. From her teeth I'd say eastern European of some description. I can be more certain of where when we examine her bones. Her last meal was well over five hours before death, but there was alcohol ingested after that. A lot." He made a face. "How in hell did Andy meet her?"

Liam shook his head. "No idea, Doc. We're on our way to talk to him after this."

John took a gulp of tea and levered himself to his feet. "I'll take you to see her, then you can bugger off and let me get back to sleep." He shuffled into the dissection room, where the size of the sheet covered figure made both detectives gasp.

"My God! She's tiny."

"She is. Around five-two and seven stone."

He drew back the sheet, uncovering the girl's face. With her smooth, pale skin and dark brown hair she looked like a child, the only sign that she wasn't sleeping a small hole above one ear.

Craig motioned to cover her again and turned to leave the room, feeling nauseous. The girl must have been so vulnerable in life.

Liam followed, shaking his head. "Andy's twice her

232

age. What the hell was he thinking of picking her up?"

Craig couldn't answer he was so angry; right now his instinct was to kill his incarcerated D.C.I. John emerged from the room a moment later and immediately read their minds.

"I wouldn't jump to conclusions, gentlemen. One thing I failed to mention was the victim's time of death."

Craig turned quickly. "Which was?"

"Between two and three hours ago."

Craig glanced at his watch. That put TOD between four and five a.m., when she'd been with Andy, so why should that cheer him up?

John elaborated. "I rushed Andy's bloods. We don't have the full tox-screen yet, but I *can* say that your D.C.I. had so much Ketamine on board I'd be surprised if he could have walked never mind fired a gun."

Craig's urge to kill abated and he asked another question.

"Was she moved after death, John?"

"No. Or if she was it was soon after death, before lividity had set in. But from the sheets I saw I'd say that she was killed where she was found."

"You're saying she was shot while Andy slept."

John held up a hand. "That's your bit-"

Liam cut in. "So if Andy left the office at four-"

"Five-ish. I kept Ash and him behind."

"OK, say five-thirty then. We know he was heading out on the town last night, 'cos he said so. That means he went home, got ready and headed to a bar or club say around nine, and he managed to pick up a woman and convince her to come home with him within eight hours?" Liam shook his head. "Not a chance, boss. Have you ever see his chat up technique? It's woeful."

It made them all laugh, until John remembered the girl was lying only feet away and he moved them back to his room. He thought for a moment before speaking.

"Andy was examined by the F.M.E. at the station, who said he was completely out of it. They took samples-"

Craig cut in. "For?"

"Tox-screen and alcohol level, plus swabs to see if he'd had intercourse. I took similar swabs from the girl. But-"

"We'll have to wait till tomorrow for most of the results. So what are you thinking?"

"Well...one possible scenario is that Andy's a monster and we've all missed it, so he really did pick up a girl half his age, take drugs and have sex with her and then he shoot her in the head...but another is that he was drugged somehow, then taken unconscious to his own flat where the girl had already been killed. Or they went to his flat together, with Andy drugged, and someone else shot the girl to stage the scene."

Craig frowned. "What about the GSR on his hands?"

Liam jumped in. "And the neighbour who phoned in the fight?"

Craig shot him a sceptical look. "Anyone could have made that call. Odds on it came from a burn phone."

"They'll be able to pinpoint the location."

"So what? It could have been made from just outside Andy's place, before the caller disappeared. Actually, get Davy onto that, Liam. Andy lives in a city centre apartment, so there should be CCTV in the hallways or street outside."

John yawned loudly. "Do you want to know about the gunshot residue or not?"

Craig frown deepened. "It's hard to fake, John."

John shrugged. "Not really. Either she was still alive when they took Andy back unconscious and they put the gun in his hand and fired, or they wore gloves, fired the gun then turned the gloves inside out and slipped them on Andy long enough to transfer some superficial GSR, or-"

Craig gave a slow smile. Even half asleep John was on the ball.

"We get the idea. Basically you're saying to exonerate Andy we have to trace his movements between when he left the office and when she was killed."

John nodded and stood up. "Correct. Now, as you've woken me for so long that I'm unlikely to get back to sleep, I'm going home to wreck Natalie's sleep the way she wrecks mine every night she's on call." He stopped suddenly, glancing at Craig in a 'will I, won't I?' way. 'Will I' won.

"Before you go, Marc. Could I have a quick word?"

Liam took the hint, moving towards the door. "I'll see you outside."

He left one friend to tell another the information Natalie had given up on the tenth kiss.

****

The Republic of Ireland. 8 a.m.

The bedroom was dimly lit, all signs of morning hidden behind two serge curtains that hadn't yet been drawn. Offers had been made and refused but the man liked shade in his life, in more senses than one.

He listened carefully as details of the event emerged from his mobile in broken English, his only reply the occasional suck of disapproval and a far rarer "OK".

The caller paused, certain that he'd exhausted all there was to report, only to restart again, repeating himself, pressured by the silence on the line. When the silence failed to prompt him further the older man roused himself to speak.

"She's definitely dead?"

"Yes."

"The cop's been well framed?"

"Yes."

"You left the trail as we agreed?"

A final yes. Then more silence until neither had anything more to say and the call ended without a goodbye.

The man sat up in the half darkness, listening to the noises of the country until a light tap on the door broke his trance. He placed his phone inside his briefcase and then emerged to face the world.

****

Belfast. 8.30 a.m.

Craig had a lot on his mind. So much so that he'd left his car at the lab to retrieve later and become Liam's passenger for the second time that day. He wasn't looking forward to Andy's interview, albeit he was looking forward to it more now than two hours before. But until they could nail down the D.C.I.'s movements for the previous evening, which had better not show him even smiling at the dead girl, he would feel uncomfortable, something that he was demonstrating unconsciously now by shifting constantly in his seat.

Liam gave it five minutes and until they'd reached slow traffic on Victoria Street before he showed his displeasure, and it was in a way that on any other day would have made Craig laugh. The D.C.I. barked "sit still, Erin!" and then leaned over and grabbed Craig by the knee. It took only seconds for both men to realise what he'd done.

"Sorry, boss. I forgot you weren't-"

"A five-year-old girl? Nice of you to think I look so young. I won't even discuss the girl part."

Liam waved a hand vaguely around the car. "Ach, driving with two young kids is hell. If you put them both in the back they beat the life out of each other and if you put Erin in the front she jumps around on her booster seat. He gestured more pointedly at Craig. "Hence..."

Craig sighed. "I know. I'm all over the place, but-"

"You're worried about us not being able to alibi Andy."

Craig nodded. "Amongst other things."

Liam shot him a questioning glance but he ignored it.

"John's possible explanations for the evidence are just that. Possibilities. We still have to prove them."

Liam was more upbeat. "Never worry; we're

236

bound to find Andy on CCTV somewhere. Sure you can't move nowadays without someone taking a pic."

Craig shrugged a 'probably'. It was so half-hearted that Liam waited till he'd stopped at the lights again and then turned to face his boss.

"OK. Spill. Something else is rattling around that designer mind of yours."

It gave Craig his first good laugh of the day. He would have wondered what a designer mind looked like if he'd had the time, but he'd speculate on that another day.

"Lots of things." He paused, ordering his thoughts before restarting. "OK, they framed Andy because they think we're close, so if someone tipped the killers off about our cases then we need to find out who."

Liam shook his head. "We'll never do it. There are too many choices since we involved Drugs, Gangs and Armagh. Anyway, if we *have* been making any significant progress then it's news to me."

"Agreed, but the point is it's what our killers believe. So *something* we're doing now is going to lead us to them, and they can see it even if we can't."

"OK, so that means we need to re-look at everything, to try to see what they saw." He shifted into third gear and then tutted at the traffic up ahead. "It's not a bit of wonder my petrol bills are huge, when I'm stuck in traffic like this every day."

Craig had stopped listening at 'see what they saw' and started running through their cases again. Liam resigned himself to sitting still for five minutes so he slid on the handbrake and added more wisdom to the mix.

"Anyway, apart from working out why we're close to a breakthrough and working out who squealed, you've other stuff bubbling inside that bonce of yours." He glanced out the side window, wearing a grimace that conveyed extreme reluctance to ask his next question. "Are you thinking about Katy?"

There. It was out. He'd asked a personal question to which the answer was bound to include emotions. It was against everything that he stood for. As a rule he left emotions to his wife. Danni told him when he needed to be upset because he'd done something wrong, and other than that, as long as he was fed, watered and had enough money to pay the bills, he didn't experience any burning need to feel.

He'd only asked because Craig had been upset before the cases had started, although it had been shown only by him locking himself in his office and giving them all mindless crap to do, but still, he *was* half-Italian and you never knew what went on inside those hot blooded types.

Much to Liam's relief the only emotion Craig displayed in answer was astonishment, followed by a loud guffaw.

"My God! Did you just ask me how I was feeling?"

Liam blushed and grunted a vague "Yes".

"In all the years I've known you, I think that must be a first. OK, then, Liam. I'll tell you."

Liam's heart sank. Didn't Craig know the rules of male engagement? On the once-in-a-blue-moon occasion that they actually asked after each other's wellbeing, the polite thing to do was to shrug casually and say "I'm fine", not tweeze each emotion apart.

Thankfully Craig knew the rules very well and took great comfort from them. If he wanted to discuss his emotions he'd get drunk, sing a song and then cry into his beer. But it was a prime opportunity to wind Liam up so, as the D.C.I. braced himself for a discussion he'd rather eat hot coals than have, Craig deliberately drew things out.

"Well...Katy...she's...she's..." When Liam's eyes had widened to the size of a cartoon mouse running from a cat, he added casually "apparently she's taken up parachuting, and today she's racing round some track at one hundred miles per hour."

Liam heaved a sigh of relief, quickly replaced by a noisy "What?"

Craig nodded. "Yep. She made a list of risky activities from some actuarial table that she found, and she and Natalie are working their way through them. Having lessons to pilot a light aircraft, cliff diving and rock climbing are on there too, but apparently they're limited a bit by Katy's wrist still not being one hundred percent."

Liam was stunned into silence for a moment, then he nodded slowly and smiled. "Ah...I get it."

Craig didn't. "Well, explain it to me then because I've no idea what she's playing at."

Liam allowed himself a smug smile. It was his reward for asking the 'feelings' question a moment before. "She's trying to be brave."

"More like she's trying to scare herself to death."

The traffic finally moved and Liam slid the car into first gear. "Nope. Brave." He adopted the tone he'd heard experts use on TV. "I think...no, I *know* she was scared rigid by her car accident-"

Craig demurred. "It was no accident."

"Ach, we all know that, so would you stop interrupting." He ignored Craig's raised eyebrow and carried on. "She was scared rigid, quite rightly. She told Danni so and Danni told me. Anyway it's made her afraid of being with you. You know, in case one of our nutters tries the same thing again." He stared soulfully ahead. "It takes a brave woman to be married to a cop sometimes. It's not for every lassie. Never knowing if we're coming home at night and-"

Craig interrupted again despite his instructions. "That's a lot more common than a murderer actually targeting your spouse."

Liam jumped on his words. "Spouse it is now? Now that's a Freudian petticoat if I ever heard one."

Before Craig could query Freud's lingerie he had forged ahead.

"So she's trying to toughen herself up. She reckons if she can do dangerous things and not get killed then maybe she can cope with the odds of a nutter going after her again."

He gave a satisfied smirk and waited for Craig's response. None came but Craig did allow a small smile to twist his lips. Liam might be right. Katy could be trying to toughen up enough to cope with any future psychopath that he might encounter targeting her, which was incredibly unlikely; in fact he doubted that an actuary could actually give them the odds. But... if she *was* going to all this trouble then that meant she was thinking of giving their relationship another chance.

His smile was short-lived, in case getting too excited tempted fate, and instead of the response Liam had expected he responded with.

"The C.C. says I've got to make budget cuts. He called me in last night to discuss it." Amongst other things.

Liam struggled to keep up. "What's that got to do with Katy?"

"Nothing. I'd moved on."

"Without acknowledging that I'm right?" It was said in a 'not fair' voice.

"If that *ever* happens, I promise I'll say 'you were right, Liam'."

"In front of everyone?"

Craig noticed gratefully that they were approaching High Street, but Liam was still waiting for his reply.

"Oh, all right, then. If Katy and I get back together and she confirms that's why she was doing the parachuting and the rest, and they're both big ifs, then I'll state in front of everyone that you were right."

Liam pulled into the station car park. "Excellent. Although I think you should see her and confirm it." He sniffed knowingly. "Makes more sense than sending her half of Botanic Gardens every week. It must be like The Day of the Triffids at her house." He changed the subject before Craig could ask how he knew about the flowers. "The budget cut bit isn't so good. How much?"

Craig opened the door and muttered his reply, but Liam had ears like a bat.

"Fifteen percent! Where the hell are you going to chop that from?"

Craig jumped out and began walking towards the station's back door. This time his reply was crystal clear. "Your expenses, if you don't shut up."

Xavier Rey had acted as soon as he'd returned from the station the day before. He may have retired but everyone knew that he'd kept his finger on the pulse, so when his call came every lieutenant and captain in The Rock answered and the gathering was set for that night.

Halfway across Belfast another gang boss was doing the same thing, although Rory McCrae included a second name in his invitation; Tommy's reputation would guarantee that no-one ignored his summons, even though he couldn't be there in the flesh.

It was gearing up to be a busy night all round for Belfast's tribes.

The C.C.U. Sunday, 9 a.m.

Davy had tried twice to drag Ash away from his desk for coffee but it was only when he'd lifted his friend's smart-pad and walked towards the door saying, "Miss Canada can come through on this as w...well. The James has free Wi-Fi" that the junior analyst had shifted from the spot he'd been rooted to for the previous hour.

If Davy was hoping for a quiet breakfast dotted with jokes they'd both seen on the Net, he was about to be disappointed. Less than ten minutes after they'd ordered their coffees and Danish pastries, the familiar electronic bongs signalled that someone was coming through on Ash's screen. Davy sighed in defeat and went to the bar for some water, leaving Ash practically stroking his smart-pad as his new crush appeared.

"Hi Ash."

"Hi Ashley."

Davy stuck two fingers in his mouth, making the bar's landlord laugh.

"Love's young dream?"

241

The analyst rolled his eyes sceptically. "They've never even met. S...She's in Canada. Just helping us out with something."

Joe Higginson filled one glass to the top and dropped ice cubes into the other. "Just because she's across the Atlantic doesn't mean he can't fall in love." He gave a proud smile. "I met my wife at a line dancing competition in Texas and we've been married for twenty years."

Davy resisted a comment on country and western music and lifted the two drinks.

"I'll top up your coffee whenever you want it."

Davy nodded gratefully and turned to go back to the table, pausing just before he did. "Your w...wife. You met her in the flesh eventually, didn't you? Before you proposed?"

Higginson laughed. "Oh aye. But only three times. Once at the comp, once when I went to the US on holiday for two weeks, and the last time when she came over here for a month. I asked her the night before she went back." He pulled out his wallet, opening it at a photograph of a family group. "That's us. Happy as they come."

Davy nodded politely and glanced over at his friend, wondering if FaceTime on a smart-pad really counted as the same thing.

****

High Street Station. 9 a.m.

Craig slid a mug of hot tea across the table to Andy before taking a gulp of his own. Boiling hot drinks weren't normal practice for prisoners on suspicion of murder, but then there'd been virtually nothing normal about the past week, and he reckoned that Andy could be trusted not to throw it in his face.

Andy stared into the steaming liquid as if he was puzzled about what it was, understandable if it had come from a police canteen where the standard tea or coffee was a bit of both and tasted like neither, but was

242

usually welcomed anyway because it was wet and warm. But this tea had come straight from Jack's kitchen and been made by Liam's not so gentle hand; it was one hundred percent proof and strong enough to seal plugholes, so Andy's confusion couldn't have been coming from that.

It seemed to Craig more like the confusion of the newly bereaved. A mixture of how did this happen and it couldn't have done, mixed with, it must be happening to someone else. After a moment he nudged the mug closer to the D.C.I.'s hand.

"Drink it, Andy. It will make you feel better."

Illogical but familiar; everyone in Ireland knew there hadn't been a problem invented that couldn't be solved by a cup of tea.

As the D.C.I. stared at his two colleagues in turn Liam decided to try his patent brand of motivation.

He reached across and gave Andy's arm a thump.

"Ach, buck up, man. No-one believes you did it, so you'll be out of here in a few hours."

Craig's eyes widened in alarm and he knocked off the tape with a jab. "For God's sake, Liam, you can't say that in an interview. It shows bias!"

Liam turned to him, confused. "You mean you think he did it?"

Craig was caught on the back foot. "What? No. No. That's not what I meant. But we have to conduct this interview in an impartial, professional way."

It was too much for Jack. He broke his rule of a thousand interviews and pressed the viewing room microphone. "Bickering in front of my prisoner isn't professional. Come out of there now, both of you."

They didn't argue, appearing in the viewing room within seconds. Craig was shamefaced.

"Sorry, Jack."

Harris wasn't in the mood to be placated. "So you should be. Sir. D.C.I. Angel's confused enough without you two adding to it." He turned to face Liam. "And as for you! Thumping my prisoner on the arm-"

"Ach, it was only a tap-"

Jack's response was to punch Liam on the bicep,

243

making him yelp.

"How's that for a tap?"

He pulled open the door and beckoned Craig to follow him. Liam received a scowl. "You. Stay in here."

"But my tea's in-"

Jack's glare silenced him mid-word and within seconds a different pair of police officers appeared on the other side of the glass. Jack positioned himself beside the tape recorder and once Craig was seated he turned it on, adding his name for the record. Then he nodded Craig to ask what he needed to ask.

Ten minutes later they knew that Andy had left the squad-room the evening before at five-thirty and retrieved his car from Dockland's underground garage, following the route home that he always took, along Donegall Quay and Oxford Street, to arrive at his city centre apartment in Howard Street around six. He'd had an unhealthy dinner of hamburger and chocolate pudding, thankfully not on the same plate, and then showered and changed to go out for the night.

"Where did you go, Andy?"

"A bar called El Robo, sir. On the Lisburn Road."

"Did you drive?"

"No. I took a taxi."

"Were you alone in the bar?"

"I was meeting a mate from my old training station there. He's newly divorced like me."

Recycled wolves on the prowl. More Labrador than wolf nowadays but their intentions had been the same. Meet a woman, chat her up and see how far you can get. It was a typical boys' night out the world over, but this one had gone badly wrong.

"He called me about ten minutes after I got there to say he had to cancel. His ex-missus had come round wanting to talk."

"We'll need his name, Andy."

Andy obliged by leaning towards the tape. "Inspector Bob Lindsay. He's in the TSG."

The Tactical Support Group; riot police, aka the boys in green. It would be easy to check.

"OK, what did you do then?"

244

Andy exhaled with a loud whoosh. "Well, I was screwed, wasn't I? I couldn't hang about in a bar on my own without looking like a real saddo, but I'd just paid for a drink, so I waited for it. The plan was to chuck it down fast then head home via the takeaway."

The burger obviously hadn't been enough rubbish for one night. Jack motioned to cut in.

"OK, if that was the plan, D.C.I. Angel, what happened to it?"

Andy dropped his head into his hands, shaking it from side to side. "I don't know. I really don't know. " He lifted his eyes and gazed at Craig beseechingly. "You've got to believe me, boss. I was drinking and then the next thing I knew I came round at home with some uniformed lads standing over me, shouting at me to wake up, I had a dead girl in my bed."

"Who was she?"

Andy shook his head frantically. "I've no idea. I'd never seen her before."

"So we're not going to see you chatting her up on the bar's CCTV?"

"No way." He stopped suddenly, looking horrified as all the possibilities kicked in. "Unless my drink was spiked... The bar was crowded; it wouldn't have been hard." His face contorted with the effort of remembering. "I remember waiting for it and..." He shook his head desperately. "No...no, I can't remember anything after that, not until this morning when the police arrived-" He stopped again, his expression a mixture of shock and sorrow. "What if I *did* talk to her? What if I took her to my place? I don't remember. Honest to God, boss, I don't." His eyes grew wild. "I couldn't have killed someone and not remember, could I?" He seized Craig's arm. "Who was she? Why did someone want her dead?" When Craig said nothing tears filled the D.C.I.'s eyes. "Why can't I bloody well remember? How could I have killed an innocent girl? "

Craig sighed heavily. "I've one last question and then we'll leave you, Andy. Where do you keep your gun when you're off duty?"

Hope lit up the D.C.I.'s thin face. "The safe. I have

a safe and it's always locked. They *couldn't* have got my gun. She couldn't have been killed with my Glock. Ballistics will prove it."

Craig nodded, not convinced things would be that simple. "Where do you keep the key, Andy?"

Andy's hope died as quickly as it had been born. "On my keyring."

They could have accessed his key to open the safe. Craig tried for a reassuring tone.

"I have no idea how this happened, Andy, but we're going to find out. In the meantime I suggest you try to relax and let Jack here take care of you, while we see what the CCTV and bloods show."

He motioned Jack to turn off the tape and rose to leave the room. While the sergeant escorted a despairing Andy back to his cell with promises of better tea, Craig re-joined Liam in the viewing room.

"Tell Davy what's happened, but no-one else. We need him to chase the CCTV from Docklands' garage and traffic cams, and confirm the time that Andy says he got home. Then I want the taxi who took him to the bar. Check his mobile and landline for the number. And chase up this Bob Lindsay, he's not someone that I know, and get the CCTV from the bar, street and apartment hallways, plus the blood and gun analysis from Des."

Liam made a rude gesture. "What did your last slave die of?"

Craig's only response was "Fifteen percent."

****

The James Bar.

After twenty minutes of watching Ash grin at his smart-pad Davy grabbed him by the arm and the analysts began the short walk back to work. As soon as they got there Nicky beckoned them over to her desk. Davy jerked his head towards his friend.

"You'll have to make do with me. Romeo's busy."

Her ears perked up immediately, but she decided

246

that an update could wait for another day; there was too much work to be done. She waved a slip of paper at him.

"Liam's given me a web message address for you. It has a list of stuff he needs apparently."

Davy squinted at the note, shaking his head as he read.

"More s...stuff for our murders?"

Nicky shrugged. "Don't know. He was being mysterious, and I didn't have the time to drag it out of him. All I know is he said he needs answers on it ASAP. We'll be briefing at two."

Davy signed onto the web message quickly, trying to hide his shock as he read; he recovered quickly and started working on the list. He'd just logged onto the central traffic records when he remembered he didn't have that month's code.

"Ash, get onto Inspector Ronson and say the S...Super needs us to access his traffic cams."

Ash didn't turn or answer, still grinning fatuously at his screen. Suddenly Davy experienced an unfamiliar surge of anger and the urge to throw Ash and his smart-pad out the window. He was, as a rule, the embodiment of modern youth; a quasi-Emo-hipster who believed in peace and love. He'd never had a subordinate before but he'd always imagined that when it happened he would be an understanding, supportive chief, but his zen had been severely tested since Ash had acquired his gal pal, so he was about to experience the sharp side of having a boss.

In one stride Davy was across the floor, liberating Ash's smart-pad from his feverish hand. He turned it towards him and stared at the woman on the other end, giving her a tight smile and re-introducing himself.

"Thank you for assisting us with the hack information. I'll give you an email address to s...send any written info to, and Analyst Rahman will be in touch."

Then with a quick click the screen darkened and he slid Ash's smart-pad into his desk drawer and turned the key. Ash was on his feet immediately and Nicky turned her chair around to see what came next.

The green-haired analyst was furious.

"I was talking to her!"

"You weren't talking, you were drooling! And you can s...sodding well drool on your own time." Davy held up Liam's note. "We have to get answers to all this before the briefing at two, and I can't do it all by myself."

Ash's response was to storm off the floor, leaving Davy to slump in his chair and stare up at the roof. After what she considered a decent interval Nicky strolled across.

"Do you want to hear where you went wrong?"

"NO!"

She pulled over a chair. "I'll tell you anyway. Next time give him a warning that you're going to shut him down, instead of just doing it. Stand in front of his desk, say it and then count down from ten. If he doesn't budge, *then* lift his pad."

Davy objected. "But he did it all through breakfast! It w...was nauseating. We're not running a dating agency."

She nodded. "True...but I seem to remember that you met Maggie here at work-"

Davy jerked upright. "That was different! Maggie-"

She held up a hand. "And I told you off when you did. And I was wrong." She glanced towards the door. "Go and find him. He'll be in the canteen."

Davy frowned. "How do you know?"

"It's where he goes when he's annoyed. He fills himself full of e-additives like a kid."

Davy was about to fold his arms stubbornly when she shook her head.

"Don't cut off your nose to spite your face, Davy, no matter how much someone hacks you off. First rule of management. You might want to throttle Ash, but you need him to help you with this work." She glanced at the note meaningfully. "Because you're his boss so *you'll* be the one explaining to the Super if it isn't all done by two o'clock."

It was a persuasive argument, and as she returned to her desk Davy slid as surreptitiously as he could manage through the double doors.

****

High Street Station

Annette yawned loudly as she scribbled in Jack Harris' custody book, writing 'Reported as requested. January 31st' against Mara McAllister's and Mitchell Purvis' names. Jack appeared through the door from the cells and peered over her shoulder as she wrote.

"You're the only person I allow to write in my book except me."

He opened the door to the back office as she looked up.

"Why's that, Jack? Although I'm flattered, of course."

"Because you're the only copper I know whose handwriting doesn't look like a spider's on speed. You can't read a word from the rest of them. God knows how they decipher their notes in court."

She set down the pen and closed the heavy book. "They have brilliant P.A.s like Nicky who type things up for them."

The desk sergeant smiled. "What are you here for anyway?"

"I'd heard that Liam and chief were here doing something, but they've gone. I met our two bail-ees on the way in." She lifted her handbag and turned to leave. "See you soon, Jack. And get some rest; you look like you haven't slept all night." Something about the way he nodded made her stop in her tracks. "What?"

The sergeant tried to look innocent. "What do you mean what?"

There was definitely something up. Annette moved in closer and squinted at his face.

"You're hiding something."

As Jack opened his mouth to reply the front door opened, and Constable Sandi Masters clocked on for the day. In the flurry of greetings that followed Annette lost the advantage, and she left with only a nod from the desk sergeant to confirm her feeling that something was happening in their team.

Annette's curiosity was soon buried under the mound of work she was looking at that day. She pulled out her phone on the way to the car and called Jake.

"Jake. Meet me at this address, please." As she recited the detail Davy had found from a call on Calum Fox's phone she remembered something else. "And bring Rhonda. I want her to shadow us today. I'll meet you both there in ten."

Ten minutes later the three cops were staring at a shopfront that had seen better days. Annette knew she should have anticipated it when she'd heard the address; Belfast's Smithfield was an area that had, if not exactly a black reputation then one that was a murky shade of grey. She scanned the shop's peeling paintwork and half pink, half ebony façade. It really didn't need the sign that read 'Jenny's Services' to indicate that it was a knocking shop.

She took a deep breath and pushed open the door, dreading what she would find inside. She'd seen places like this before. Lino floors and a reception desk, usually with an overweight middle-aged man behind, and a group of tired, ill-kept girls dressed in lingerie whatever the hour or weather, seated along the walls on uncomfortable chairs. Most disturbing of all was the pile of thin, worn towels that they selected from once they'd acquired a punter; rarely washed well enough to conceal past stains. Perhaps it was her nursing past that drew her eyes to them, but she couldn't help wondering what diseases they might spread.

Jake noticed something else entirely; the man at the desk had a baseball bat by his feet. He signalled Annette quickly with his eyes then positioned himself by an inner door, ready to prevent the entry of more troops. As Annette showed her warrant card the girls scattered like nervous flamingos, leaving Rhonda to reassure them that it wasn't a raid. The man rose, to reveal a ten gallon gut that had been hidden beneath the desk. He was unlikely to try and outrun them at least.

"We'd like to speak to the owner."

The man shrugged then emitted a yell that could have been heard streets away.

"VERA. THE COPS WANT YOU."

It probably saved money on an intercom.

Two minutes later Jake felt a push at his back as the inner door opened, to reveal a tiny, seventy-something woman with candy floss hair and a cigarette hanging precariously from her lips. The rest of her was incongruously demure, clothed in an expensive tweed suit and a string of pearls that might have been worn by his gran.

The madam stepped past him and held out a hand to Annette, spotting her as the boss in a blink.

"Vera McAteer. How can I help you, officer?"

Annette let the hand hang in the air, her good manners beaten down by disgust.

"We're interested in a client who used your service yesterday."

The gaggle of girls made relieved noises and sat back down in their chairs, while the baseball player relaxed and wriggled further into his seat. Annette was tempted to bust him for something, even though that wasn't why they were there that day. The idea of walking away and leaving the girls to such a seedy existence really bothered her and she made up her mind to call Vice as soon as they left. She knew they would close the place down only for it to open again somewhere else, but she just couldn't leave it as it was.

Vera McAteer dropped her hand and stood quite still in front of her.

"Can I ask why?"

"You can, but we're not obliged to tell you."

Annette could hear her voice tremble as she spoke. She was furious with the elderly woman. In her book she should be motherly and protective of younger women, not living off their bodies in this dump. Vera McAteer knew when she was hitting a brick wall, so she nodded slightly and opened the door she'd entered by, leading them down a corridor towards a small back room. Rhonda gawped at the other doors leading off the corridor, knowing instantly what they concealed. She'd never been in a brothel although she'd seen them in the movies, but then she'd always thought that they were hyped up for effect. As Jake followed the three women he shuddered. He had a cousin the girls' age and it would kill him to see her in a cesspit like this.

The madam took a seat behind a small desk, waving the others vaguely to some seats. They declined and Annette got straight to business.

"Your number was found on the mobile phone of a crime victim." Amongst other dodgy numbers on Calum Fox's phone, but none of the rest had been houses of ill repute. "He called it three hours before the crime was committed against him."

Vera McAteer didn't react so Annette carried on.

"We believe that he hired the services of one of your young ladies and we need your help in finding her name."

McAteer swivelled her chair to face an old-fashioned computer, tapping on it at a snail's pace. After a moment she paused.

"Yesterday you say?"

"Yes."

"What time?"

Annette thought for a moment. Calum Fox had died between one and two p.m. the day before. She counted back, working out how long it would have taken him to drive to the brothel from his home in Armagh, collect the girl and then drive to the field where he'd died. She wondered why Fox had driven north for a prostitute when he could just have gone for a local girl but she parked the query for later and settled for eleven o'clock.

"He would have collected her around twelve."

"From where?"

The question underlined her doubts. The madam elaborated.

"Lots of our girls are home-based and work part-time. The ones out front are the permanent ones.

252

Others just work when it suits them."

Jake was curious about the logistics. "So how do you get paid?"

McAteer pursed her lips. "*If* we got paid, and I'm not saying we do, mind you, the girl might pay us in cash after the job. That's if we trusted her." She gestured towards the door. "You couldn't trust that lot as far as you could throw them, so they pay us a monthly rental up front." She added hastily. "That's if anyone paid us at all, and-"

Jake finished the sentence for her. "You're not saying that they do."

Annette wasn't interested in how the business worked. She just wanted to get out of the place.

"OK, so which girls were working yesterday morning? We'll need all their names and addresses, including the girls out front. Photographs too, if you have them."

She could sense the madam's reluctance but she didn't care. Fox could have met a free-lancer near Armagh or driven to Belfast and picked up a girl from the shop; they had to check them all. Thankfully Vera McAteer's records were as fastidious as her clothing, and in five minutes she'd collated a list and pressed print.

Annette issued a warning as she left. "This list had better be accurate, Ms McAteer. If it isn't then we'll be back."

But Vice would be there first.

Chapter Eleven

Garvan's Bookies.

Off you go, McCrae. Get out there, McCrae. Find out who's stamping on west Belfast's turf and let me know.

In other words, you stick your neck on the line asking awkward questions, while I sit on my ass in Pleasantville drinking a cup of tea. Except finding things out nowadays wasn't as easy as Tommy thought; they weren't living in his heyday during The Troubles any more. Back then the cops were too busy worrying about bombs and bullets to care about someone passing info in a bookies or a pub. Back then gangs had sorted out their grievances with a shooting or punch up and no-one had even blinked. What was one more dead paramilitary if it cleaned the streets? All it did was save the peelers a job. But not nowadays. Now the cops took a dim view of gang warfare, no matter which tatts you wore on your arms.

Rory McCrae stared at his cigarette ruefully, picturing its burning ash as a fuse counting down to the end of his life. If he asked the wrong question of the wrong man it might well be, then he'd either be dead or back inside The Mag for years.

His thoughts were interrupted by a knock so loud that it was either a raid or someone with more confidence than they deserved. McCrae's hand was on the handle before the third knock fell, his other around the neck of the teenager who'd generated the disturbing sounds. The UKUF boss leaned in, the cigarette in his mouth burning perilously close to the shocked youth's face. He wasn't normally so aggressive but Tommy's demands had done nothing to improve his mood.

The identity of his visitor added an extra edge to his annoyance. Zac Greer, once heir apparent to the UKUF crown, before his father Davy had been executed by rival paramilitaries and his mother,

254

Sharpy, had been killed by a bomb. Greer's ambition to rule still gave McCrae sleepless nights.

"What'd ye want, Greer?"

The darkening colour of the face above his hand said that if he wanted an answer then he had better loosen his grip. He did so, so abruptly that the shocked boy dropped at his feet. By the time he was upright again McCrae was back in his chair with his feet up on his desk.

Zac Greer coughed loud and long until finally a hoarse voice emerged. It had an unfortunately broken timbre that was less to do with youth and more to do with his father's legacy.

"McIlveen wants to know if ye want the money held in the safe till tomara?"

McCrae reminded himself again why he kept the boy around. It was partly because it was better to keep your enemies close, and partly because it amused him to humiliate the boy who had thought to be king by giving him menial tasks. He lit a fresh cig from the butt of his last one.

"What dee I normally dee?"

It had the sound of a trick question but Greer didn't hesitate.

"Keep it in the safe."

"So why wud I change this time?"

Greer's reply was a shrug and McCrae felt a grudging admiration for the lad's arrogance. It also gave him an idea. He scanned the youth's face for a moment and then unexpectedly gestured him to sit. The only chair except his sat against the far wall, so with a literal sense that might have been amusing on another day the young man sat down exactly where it was.

The gang leader was less amused than he was certain that Greer was taking the piss. His gesture was sharper this time.

"Bring it here. I'm nat yellin' fer miles."

A moment later the boy and the man were staring at each other, neither of them willing to blink. McCrae broke the silence.

"I've a jab fer ye."

Greer didn't move.

"Tap secret. I need ye to ask around and get me sum info."

The teenager angled his head and continued to stare. Combined with his narrowed gaze it said curiosity. It also said he was about to ask for cash.

"Hye much?"

McCrae lurched forward across his desk. "Wat did ye say?"

Greer held his ground. "Hye much? If this info's that important to ye, ye'll be prepared to pay."

The old lag was torn between giving Greer's throat another squeeze and giving him a pat on the back. Cheeky wee skitter Zac Greer might be, but he admired his nerve. After a full minute's silence, McCrae gave a slight nod. *OK, he would give him a reward, but one that lined his pockets as well when Greer lost it on a horse.*

"A ton behind the wire fer ye to bet with."

The monarch in waiting shook his head. "I don't bet. It's a mugs' game. It's cash or no way."

He had McCrae over a barrel and another, angrier nod finally gave him what he'd asked.

"OK. Shoot."

As McCrae laid out his desired end result, or rather Tommy's, two other themes were running through his mind. One was self-congratulation at getting the job done without risking his own skin, the other was schadenfreude, if he could have spelt it, because if Greer got killed or lifted doing the job then he'd be out of his hair at last. He would still hold that night's meeting on the off-chance of some information coming out, but his money was on the little prince to find out what he needed to know.

****

The C.C.U. 11.30 a.m.

When Craig and Liam arrived back at the squad-room

256

it was with a long list of things still to check. Davy rose immediately they entered and raced across to the men. "You're going to w...want to see this." He indicated the smart-pad beneath his arm. Craig led the way into his office and mimicked dying of thirst as he passed Nicky's desk. His pleas were answered and as Davy set up what he wanted to show them, she appeared with three cups and some biscuits on a tray. Liam glanced over her shoulder.

"Is that a doily?"

"It's the weekend. We always use doilies at the weekend at our house. Our Jonny's not growing up a savage."

How a lace paper circle could prevent her son's descent into anarchy was a question for another day.

As soon as she'd left Craig turned to the analyst. "Sorry to involve you in this, Davy"

Davy shook his head. "I just hope that I can help."

He tapped on his screen and they watched as Andy Angel clambered out of a cab on the Lisburn Road.

"I've checked with Inspector Lindsay and everything w...was just as Andy said. He cancelled Andy at the last minute."

Craig leaned in and pointed at the cab, making Davy press pause.

"OK, the cab came from a firm called Centre Cabs and I've checked with their office. They have a record of the driver collecting Andy at eight-thirty and dropping him at the bar at a quarter to nine."

"Have you spoken to him?"

"Yep. He s...sounded straight-up. Apparently Andy uses the firm all the time. Couldn't whoever planned this just have w...waited outside Andy's place and followed them?"

Craig nodded. It was the simplest explanation.

Liam lifted a biscuit and waved it over the analyst's head, prompting a shower of crumbs to fall into his lap.

"Andy doesn't look drunk there, boss."

Davy brushed the crumbs away in disgust as Craig nodded.

"I agree. So Andy had arranged to meet Lindsay as he said, he got the cab as he said, and he was sober when he entered the bar, just as he said." He glanced at Davy. "What about footage from inside?"

Davy made a face. "You're not going to like it."

Craig gave a resigned sigh and motioned him on. He'd already guessed what the cameras would show. Over the next five minutes they watched Andy walk to the bar, order a drink and take a call.

"Bob Lindsay?"

"Yes. I matched the time from his mobile. It lasted forty s...seconds."

Andy ended the call and slipped his phone back into his coat. They watched as his drink arrived and Craig signalled to press pause.

"I want that barman's I.D. He almost pushed the barmaid out of the way to serve Andy."

Davy nodded. "Already on it, chief. The bar manager is checking the rotas and he'll call me back once he has the name."

Just then Nicky knocked on the door and entered, giving Davy a note.

He read aloud. "The barman's called Jeremy S...Scott." He turned just as Nicky was exiting and handed the note back. "Ask Ash to run him through the computer, please. We need criminal records and his address and phone details. Thanks."

Craig smiled at his request being pre-empted and wished again that Davy would join the force. The analyst had already restarted the tape.

"OK, this is where Andy said he s...stopped remembering, but he also said he'd intended just to drink the beer he'd already ordered and then go home."

Liam nodded. "And?"

"Watch."

They were still watching ten minutes later as Andy had a second beer and then a third and a fourth. Davy paused the tape.

"Doctor Marsham phoned through with Andy's full tox-screen. It shows high levels of Ketamine and

Rohypnol-"

Liam gasped. "He was roofied!"

Davy nodded. "He was also s...slammed. His blood alcohol was still twice the legal limit this morning."

Craig was peering at the screen as they'd talked. "Davy, scroll back to Andy's first drink, please."

They watched as Scott handed him a glass.

"OK, now take us to the other drinks."

Liam frowned. "What are we looking for?"

"Watch...OK, stop there and zoom in on the server."

It wasn't a man this time but a girl.

"And the next drink."

Same barmaid.

"Davy, I want you to view any other tapes from the bar and see if you can find Jeremy Scott in the bar for the rest of the night."

"You think he was a plant, chief?"

Craig nodded. "He was put there to slip Andy the drugs. After that he left. Every subsequent drink Andy ordered was clean but added to the effect, and the roofie made him forget everything after the first."

As Davy's face fell Craig was reminded that everything might include what they all hoped Andy hadn't done. He motioned the analyst on and they watched Andy drink for another minute before Davy paused the tape again.

"The next ten minutes is just Andy drinking, but at fifty minutes in we s...see him talk to someone for the first time."

Liam stood up to have a better look, leaning his weight on Davy's shoulders and almost concertina-ing him into his chair. "On you go, lad."

Craig waved him back. "Get off him, Liam, or he'll end up five feet tall."

As Liam stepped back the analyst pressed several keys and a slim brunette appeared at the other end of El Robo's long bar. They watched as through a series of short movements and pauses, she eventually ended up by Andy's side.

"She was watching him from the moment she

appeared."

Liam grinned. "Maybe she fancied him."

Craig shook his head grimly. "I doubt it. She's lying in John's dissection room."

Liam gawped at the screen. "God, I didn't recognise her. She-"

"Looks so alive. Andy must have completely forgotten that he saw her."

Davy was the sole questioning voice. "Or he lied about it?"

The detectives shook their heads simultaneously. "No way. We interviewed him and he has no memory of any of this."

"S...She made a beeline for him then."

"Just like the barman. This was a setup from the off."

Liam made a face.

"What does that look mean?"

"Well...OK, so the girl chatted him up, and maybe she was put up to it, but who's to say she wasn't just supposed to get him in a compromising position-"

Davy finished the sentence. "So they could take photos and blackmail him, and s...scare us off the case."

Craig's "NO" was emphatic. "You really think they believed we'd be deterred by a few tabloid shots? Copper has sex with girl he's just met, shock horror. If that one worked then half the force would be on the front page." He shook his head. "We're dealing with *killers* here. So far they've killed three people-"

Liam couldn't let it pass. "You're linking Rey, Fox and McAllister now?"

Craig realised what he'd said and backtracked. "OK, one for sure. Rey. But they killed him, so do you honestly believe that they would bother to just frame Andy with photographs? No hope. They'd planned the girl's murder all along."

A worried look flashed across Liam's face. Craig knew what he was thinking.

"You're wondering if the drugs could have made Andy lose control and shoot her."

260

The veteran cop gave a reluctant shrug. "I don't think he's a killer, boss, but we all know what drugs and alcohol can make people do."

Craig's jaw set hard. "OK, I'm only going to say this once more. Andy didn't kill her, no matter how much crap he had on board. But...if they leave the bar together and John's time of death is right then we only have a short time in which to prove that somebody else did."

He motioned Davy to restart the tape and they watched as Andy and the woman grew increasingly amorous and then stepped outside into a cab. Before Craig could even ask, Davy told them he'd contacted the driver and a woman had called for the taxi. It had taken them straight to Andy's apartment block.

Craig motioned him to shut off the tape and Liam retook his seat. They sat in silence for a moment, just watching Craig steeple his fingers and have a conversation inside his own head. By the time it hit the air it made some sense.

"OK. The barman and the girl were definitely a setup. The plan was to slip Andy roofies and get him to take her back to his place. But there's no way from that girl's body language that she knew she was going to her death. Agreed?"

Liam nodded. "She wouldn't have volunteered for a suicide mission-"

Davy cut in. "If she was an Islamic terrorist she might."

Craig shook his head. "There's no sign of Islamic involvement in the case, Davy."

Davy shook his head. "I disagree, chief. S...Sixty percent of Albanians are Muslim."

Craig's face said he wasn't convinced. "First, we don't know that she *was* Albanian. Secondly, we're not even sure yet that Albanians are involved, and even if they are not all Muslims are terrorists. No, everything about that girl says basic honey trap and not even Andy would have fallen for that if he hadn't been drugged before she'd come along."

Liam gave a loud snort. "Are you joking? The

man's so desperate for a woman he'd get-"

Craig's scowl cut him off. "Whatever colourful metaphor you're about to use, don't, Liam. The fact is that Andy *was* drugged and the girl *was* a honey trap and I very much doubt she knew her death was part of the plan when she agreed. OK, we know they went to his place, so I need their exact time the taxi dropped them and I need every tape from the street outside Andy's block, the internal halls and corridors, and I want to hear the recording of whatever so-called neighbour phoned the cops."

Davy nodded briskly. "I have the requests out."

"Chase all the forensics as well, please. We're pretty sure they used Andy's Glock for the murder but I want Des to rule it in or out. And what happened to his safe? Was the gun still in there? Was it printed? Let me know."

Liam shook his head. "I can't believe he kept the safe key with his house keys! Anyone who mugged him could have got his gun."

"Forget that. We need to know if Andy *could* have opened the safe in the state he was in. Unless the girl was suicidal she wouldn't have opened it and handed a gun to a drunk. So that leaves us with a third party opening the safe, shooting the girl and leaving Andy to take the rap."

Davy stood up, eager to get on. Craig nodded him out but indicated Liam to stay. He kept on talking as if he hadn't been interrupted.

"That gives us three questions. Who shot the girl? Davy's on that. Who leaked information about our operation to the killers? We have to decide if that means someone we've interviewed put two and two together and told them accidentally or deliberately, or someone *on* our operation leaked deliberately."

Liam went to open his mouth but Craig pushed on.

"And three, we need to work out *why* they're trying to stop us, because if we're close to cracking this, which framing Andy to slow us down implies, then I *honestly* can't see how." As he stopped talking Liam seized his chance.

"OK, number one we're already on. Number three we need the team together to discuss and we've got that at two o'clock. Number two's the interesting one but I honestly don't think we have a hope in hell of finding out."

Craig went to argue but the D.C.I. shook his head.

"Hear me out, boss. Who leaked information on our investigation? The answer is it could have been any bugger we've talked to, or someone that *they* told about our chats. It's like one of those things you drew at school."

Craig wrinkled his forehead. "A graph?"

"Ach, no. Even I understood those. One of those ones where you tossed coins and wrote down heads or tails."

Craig nodded. "Probability trees. I see what you mean. Those can go on for miles."

"Exactly! And that's what we'd get if we tried to work out who told who what. I say we just accept there was a leak and instead of having a witch-hunt we keep things tight to the core team from now on."

It was a good suggestion but that wouldn't stop Craig searching for an answer. He glanced at the clock above Liam's head.

"What time did I say we were briefing again?"

"Two o'clock."

"OK, that leaves us two hours. Tell Ash I want to see him for a minute, and after you've done that, ask uniform what Xavier Rey's up to. Oh, and find Kyle, can you; he seems to have gone AWOL again."

Liam opened the door. "He'll be huddling in a cupboard with some of his spooky friends."

"Not on my time he'd better not be."

His last word was drowned out by Liam letting out a yell that almost perforated Nicky's ears.

"ASH! YOU'RE WANTED."

It was wrong on so many levels that Craig just rolled his eyes.

****

263

"I not sure what we'll do about viewing the airport tapes now, Ash."

Craig dragged a hand down his face in exhaustion. He felt absolutely wrecked. OK, he hadn't got much sleep the night before but that was nothing new, and he believed firmly in the adage 'you can sleep when you're dead'. Whether his sleep deprivation came from work or pleasure he was well used to it and it had never slowed him down, but today he felt like he was wading through treacle. For a man who believed emotional stress was a thing to be sucked up and glossed over, even he had to acknowledge that the situation with Katy was adding to his load.

He shook his head, banishing all trace of sentimentality, and focused back on the problem in hand. Andy was their super-recogniser and he was currently banged up in a cell.

Ash looked confused. "Where's Andy? He said he'd finish with the tapes ASAP."

Craig was startled; he'd forgotten that only he, Liam and Davy knew what had happened to Andy overnight. After a second's regrouping he decided to keep it that way. The last thing Andy would need once they'd exonerated him was his subordinates knowing that he'd picked up a woman when he'd been as high as a kite on drugs. What *was* certain was that if the D.C.I. viewed the tapes while under suspicion of murder, Ronan Miskimmon's legal team would jump all over his testimony in court.

He deflected quickly.

"Andy's been called away. Something to do with his flat." Namely, it being a murder scene.

The best lies always stick close to the truth and don't offer too much detail, so as the analyst opened his mouth to ask more Craig pushed on. Fabricating stories about Andy's malfunctioning plumbing or a gas leak would be above and beyond.

"While I think about that, tell me what else you've got."

Ash narrowed his eyes at Craig's obvious deflection; if the boss wanted to keep secrets that was

264

his prerogative, but all lies did was make people like him want to dig for dirt. He tapped his smart-pad into life and set it on the desk, facing the detective.

"OK. As you know the North American security services have their own databases of hackers that they keep an eye on. At our request they put out a general call asking if anyone had noticed anything strange happening with equipment, traffic signals and weather drones in the first half of last year-"

"That's before you started picking up anything?"

"Yep. I began spotting things in July. The logic is that if Miskimmon was just starting out then he might have made a mistake. Teething problems... immature processes... just... something."

Craig interrupted again. "Davy's got the EU people doing the same?"

Ash nodded, making his green quiff bob up and down. "Yes, but the Canadians were the first to come back to us. I've been talking to a hacker in Toronto and she's sent this through."

He tapped twice on the screen and the image of a woman in her early twenties appeared. Her multi-coloured hair and punky style couldn't disguise her prettiness, although to Craig she still looked like a kid. He admitted to being surprised that the hacker was female although he honestly couldn't have said why. It probably said something about his age and traditional view of the world, no matter how up to date he tried to be.

Ash's smooth voice cut across his thoughts.

"This is Ashley X."

Craig raised an eyebrow. "Is that her internet handle or doesn't she have a second name?" Another sign of age.

Ash smiled pityingly. "All hackers use a handle."

"What's yours?"

The analyst cheeks lit up in a blush. "Ash-Tag."

Craig smiled at the play on words and waved Ash-Tag on.

"OK. Ashley said she'd started noticing weather drones dropping or going off path last March."

Craig's ears twitched. Off path implied that she knew what their normal flight path was; confidential government information. He realised that the Canadian administration probably already knew their drones had been mapped and tuned back into Ash's words.

"So she and another hacker started paying attention. They hacked the software of a dozen weather drones and waited until three of them fell. Then they started digging."

Craig halted him again. "Just to be clear. The drones' operating system used the same algorithm as our malfunctioning systems?"

Ash realised he'd left something vital out. "Sorry, yes. I should have said that. All the government weather drones in the US and Canada use it. I knew that already from the ones that fell last year."

"OK. Go on."

"Well...like us, Ashley and her mate found the operating algorithm. They also found some extra code that had caused the malfunctions."

"The same as our piece of extra code?"

Ash smiled. "No, actually. Similar but not identical, so Ashley and I think it was an earlier version of Miskimmon's hack. Like theirs was Mark One and ours was Mark Two. Or maybe five. Who knows. But that's not the important thing. The important thing is that they isolated the hack and followed it back."

Craig's fatigue was suddenly replaced by excitement. He leaned forward and stared at the screen, hardly daring to ask the question. "To Miskimmon?"

Ash made a face that said no and yes. He tapped the screen and a series of numbers and dots appeared.

"This is the IP address of a computer they found in a hack. They managed to trace the code back to it and then found the IP was present in each hack that brought a drone down." He stroked the screen to scroll down. "These are the dates of the hacks. Davy's working on Miskimmon's locations when the hacks occurred."

Craig frowned. "Why? Surely he could have hacked in from anywhere in the world."

Ash looked pleased with himself. "Yep, he could, and when he did it here everything I found was bounced to Ukraine. But like I said, he was just starting out when he did the Canadian hacks and it looks as if he made mistakes." He pointed at the screen. "We managed geolocation through the IP address Ashley found. That means we have the locations of the computer when it performed each of her three hacks-"

Craig cut in. "I don't suppose any were in Northern Ireland?"

Ash's smile said maybe, but he wasn't ready to commit. "Anyway, so all we need to prove is that Miskimmon was nearby when they happened."

It wouldn't be definitive but it would move their case along. Something made Craig hesitate. It all seemed too easy and Ronan Miskimmon had already proved he was a crafty sod.

"Hang on. You're saying that someone hacked into the Canadian drones and brought them down and they didn't cover their trail? This has to be a trick."

Ash raised his eyes to heaven. "So cynical." Then he smiled. "Don't worry, we thought of that. Well, Ashley did. They've been working on this for months, tracing the signal to see where it bounced, and every time they've come back to the same three places." He shrugged. "All I can think of is that Miskimmon was just practicing then, and it was only when he was preparing to go for really important targets that he really began covering his ass." He made a face. "Like with ours."

Craig held his breath. He wanted to believe this was something, but by its very nature they were relying on the intangible; Wi-Fi signals and the Net. How could they ever prove things?

Ash read his mind. "I'm ahead of you there, chief. Every computer has a unique IP address generated by its operating system; it's what Vice use to trace paedophiles distributing online porn. I'm tracing this IP as we speak."

Craig exhaled. "If you find it what will that give us?"

"Well, if we're lucky it'll give us the purchaser's payment method and their name and address."

"And if we're unlucky?" He knew he was being a pessimist but better that than have things fall apart later on.

Ash thought for a moment before answering hesitantly. "Worst case scenario...well...I suppose-" He stopped abruptly and shook his head. "Honestly, chief, the worst I can think of is that he didn't buy the computer new, but even then we can find out who did and trace who they sold it on to."

Craig wasn't persuaded. "That's too optimistic, Ash, we've only got days before the P.P.S. proceeds on the visa fraud. And you've failed to mention the *really* bad case. What if Miskimmon didn't buy the computer anywhere? What if he stole it or built it from scratch? Don't underestimate this man. He's a slippery bastard."

Ash's expression had darkened as Craig spoke, but the swearword made him smile again. He liked it when Craig swore; it made him seem human like them.

The detective relented slightly. "Look, this is brilliant work, Ash, and I really hope you're right and we can nail him this time, but I just don't want cockiness to make you careless. This is the highest priority for both you and Davy over the next week."

"What about the cases?"

Craig stood up, making the analyst do the same.

"Those as well. Sorry, but it looks like no-one will be getting much sleep for the next few days." He opened the door. "Keep going with it and well done. We'll talk about it more later."

As the door closed behind the analyst Craig poured a fresh coffee from his percolator and sat back down behind his desk, his mind a maelstrom of Andy, budget cuts and weather drones, but front and foremost was the image of Katy whizzing round a racing track.

Chapter Twelve

The Police Intelligence Section. Malone Road, Belfast.

As Kyle Spence entered the building he'd called his professional home for fifteen years, the sting of homesickness made his eyes turn red. Not tears of course, he didn't do those, but a definite blurring and watering that if anyone queried he would say was an allergy.

He'd liked working in Intelligence, not least because being the holder of secrets had made him feel superior; an unattractive character trait but true. He'd enjoyed batting away requests for information with words like 'it's above your clearance level' and 'I couldn't possibly confirm'. It had given him the reassuring feeling that no matter how ordinary he was in the rest of life, here he was a king.

He'd also enjoyed Intelligence because he was good at it, and because, apart from the ground troops who did the tasks like tracing and following and all too often risked their lives, Intelligence was a carpeted, comfortable world where his greatest risk had been from a paper cut and the only thing red that ever got spilled was the red wine at the monthly staff buffet.

Now, courtesy of Craig, he was out in the big bad world, where cops got shot at and he had to mix with people whose accents were quite unlike his own. It was really too bad and if he hadn't liked Craig since university he would have made up his mind to obstruct all of the Murder Squad's investigations when he finally returned home.

His future return was one of two reasons he was there that day. He hoped it would be as soon as Annette's maternity leave ended; he also hoped that she didn't decide to take advantage of new regulations that allowed her to stay off for a whole year. By that time he would have gone totally native and Intelligence might not want him back. The other reason he would save for after he'd sorted the first with a trip to the unit's HR team. An hour later he was reassured that he'd be back home in his comfy office soon after the infant Eakin had appeared in the world, so he made his way two flights up to the office of D.C.I. Roy Barrett.

Barrett saw him approach through his glass walled office and greeted his protégé with a sympathetic look.

"How is it?"

The silent subtext being 'out there in the cold, hard world.'

Spence adopted a pained expression and gratefully accepted a chair and the offer of tea, before giving a sigh that would have done a Victorian matron proud.

"Let's just say I'll be glad to be back in the autumn."

Barrett sat forward eagerly. "Is that confirmed?"

Spence nodded. "Short of Inspector Eakin deciding to take the full year, HR have just said my secondment will be over in October."

The senior spook cheered up considerably. "Glad to hear it, Kyle, very glad... Now, it's always grand to see you, of course, but you could have just called HR so I imagine that this trip means you've something else on your mind."

Spence set down his cup, realising how much he preferred Intelligence's logoed porcelain to the Murder Squad's grab whatever you can find, six pounds for six, mugs. He sat back, taking a pen from his pocket and running it through his fingers like a card sharp as he talked.

"I'm here to pick your brains about something, sir. It relates to a case we're working on."

Barrett frowned slightly at the word *we*. Not 'Murder' is working on, *we* are working on. He hoped it didn't signal a defection to the dark side. Spence was still speaking.

"There have been three murders, one of which was the son of a local gangster. The others may or may not be related, we're still looking into that. You'll have heard of the gang. The Rock."

Barrett's eyebrows shot up. They'd been after The

Rock's general for years and never got a sniff. He nodded.

"We know the operational head or major was Xavier Rey, until he handed things off to his son, Matias. But we've never got a handle on the so-called general at the top. Was it Matias that was killed?"

"Yes. Drowned. Definitely murder. That's what I wanted to ask you about. The word is that another gang is trying to take over The Rock's operations and expand them to include drugs and girls-"

Barrett cut in. "Rey won't like that. They've always been resolute about not touching either."

Spence nodded. "They also never kill apparently, but this new bunch doesn't have the same scruples." He hesitated for a moment, knowing that his next words fell into a stereotype of 'foreigners bad and locals less so'. "Look, sir, it might be nothing, but I've heard a rumour that there might be Albanians involved. If there are I'm wondering how to find out more."

Barrett rested back in his chair and ran a hand through his thinning grey hair as he thought. Soon he would have nothing to run his hands through at all. He put his balding down to his job; holding all those secrets in your head was bound to have some sort of effect.

After a moment he scribbled something on a sticky.

"You didn't get this number from me. OK?"

Spence lifted the paper without looking at it. "Thank you, sir. But I'm curious. Why *didn't* it come from you?"

Barrett rose to his feet. "Let's just say that this is one of the Director's best kept secrets, and anyone who messes with those answers to her." He walked to the door. "When you make the call *don't* mention my name. And use plain English; you'll only get one question. Don't ask for a face-to-face or who you're speaking to; no-one but the Director knows that. But I do know that in cases of dire need this contact has always come through."

As he opened the door he added. "What you must never do, Kyle, is tell Craig or anyone how you got your information." He smiled slowly. "But your years here will have made you an expert at that."

Spence walked past him out the door but Barrett called him back. "That number will change immediately you get your answer, just in case you're tempted to use it again. Good luck."

Spence's only reply was a quick salute.

Chapter Thirteen

Zac Greer's walk could be described by a casual observer in one word; cocky. A more polite one might say jaunty, but the meaning was still the same; Greer was pumped up about his task. He'd been in line for the throne until McCrae had ousted him and through a process of obsequiousness and masking his true intentions, even extending as far as saying that his dead parents had been wrong in some ways, a lie that had cost him blood, he'd been brought back from the wilderness into McCrae's outer circle. If he did this job right he would move even closer, close enough to do what he needed to do.

He'd never paid much attention at school; every skill he'd needed in life had been played out in front of him since before he could talk. Secret deals and how to hide cash and play the poor man, so well that the government had given them benefits every week. He'd known what a gun cost by the time he could toddle, and how to smuggle dope and coke by the time he'd sat and failed his first exam. Formal schooling had been redundant, something to yawn through and avoid when possible, until he'd been old enough to quit without bringing the law down on his ma.

But he *had* paid attention in one class, Drama, and one particular play they'd performed had always stuck in his head. Mainly because there'd been blood, lots of it, squirting from fake daggers as Julius Caesar had met his sticky end. It had taught him two useful lessons: hide what you really feel till it can get you what you want, and don't kill the boss unless you're close enough to catch his crown as he falls.

Soon he would be close enough to kill McCrae and take back his inheritance. Zac didn't know he'd been given his new task in the belief that it would get *him* killed.

****

Docklands. 2 p.m.

As Liam gathered everyone together for the briefing Craig was still in his office. He still hadn't appeared five minutes later, so when Jake asked the question on everyone's lips "Where's Andy?" for the second time, despite him fobbing it off, the deputy decided it was time to give his boss a kick up the ass. He was just on his way to do so when Craig emerged, mug of coffee in hand. He grabbed the whiteboard on his way past Nicky's desk and dragged it unceremoniously into the centre of the floor.

"OK. We're busy, so I don't want a lot of discussion, just the facts." He set down his mug and grabbed a marker, writing up the number one. Just then Kyle wandered in, looking paler than Craig had ever seen him before. He motioned him sharply to a seat, in a way that said they'd be having words when the briefing was done.

"OK. Annette and Jake. I want up-to-date information on Colin McAllister's scene, our two bailed suspects and the forensics on the field and tanks. Shoot."

Annette saw Jake's mouth open and she shut it with a glance, knowing very well that he was about to ask the Andy question again. Liam had cut him off for a reason and if Craig wanted them to know where Andy was then they would.

"OK. Mara McAllister-"

Liam interrupted, deciding to lighten the mood. "Otherwise known as the merry widow."

Annette smiled. "Thanks for that characterisation, Liam. I'll never think of her again without the operetta ringing in my ears." She continued in a more serious tone. "She didn't look merry when I last saw her. She was on the way to tell her son that his father was dead."

Liam looked suitably chastened.

"Anyway, both she and Mitchell Purvis are out on bail and sticking to their stories. I saw them signing in this morning at High Street. Ms McAllister's staying at

274

The Merchant Hotel and Mr Purvis at a B and B."

Craig nodded. Nothing could have more starkly underlined their differing financial circumstances, and the end of their romance.

"As far as the forensics are concerned. Jake, could you cover those?"

Jake glanced at Liam as he opened his mouth to speak, deliberately saying nothing for a moment to make him uncertain what he might say. When he said "Doctor Marsham" Liam exhaled gratefully.

"Doctor Marsham has come back with information on the soil samples we sent up from the field. They were rich in the nutrients needed for growing crops-"

Craig cut in. "So McAllister lied to his wife."

Annette nodded. "And to Mitchell Purvis. I checked with him and he was convinced they hadn't planted in that field because the soil was poor."

Craig took a sip of coffee. "OK, so Colin McAllister didn't want anyone digging in that field, which says he knew about the tank all along." He'd just waved Jake on again when Liam noticed something.

"Here, Jake. Where're your crutches?"

Jake didn't look up as he answered and it made Craig's antennae twitch.

"I spoke to my physio and they said I can try with a stick now."

Craig's "well done" was tempered with concern. Not that Jake would fall; he would do fine with a stick. It was more that his sudden haste to return to full fitness could be being generated by a darker desire. The sergeant's next words confirmed it.

"I'm going to the gym as well."

Craig heard the unsaid words 'building myself up for revenge' loud and clear. But that was a worry for another day. He turned back to the case.

"Tell me about the tank."

Jake nodded. "It's steel with a hydraulic pump inside. The exit pipe connects with one in a field just over the border in County Monaghan."

Liam slapped a hand on his desk. "Bloody smugglers."

Craig shrugged. Shifting the evidence to fool the police was an old trick.

"OK, none of this gets us any closer to knowing whether the widow knew all about the tank and killed McAllister because she wanted the profits for herself."

Annette shook her head. "She must be innocent, otherwise why report the cash to the fraud squad?"

Craig was unpersuaded. "That's the obvious assumption, Annette. She tells Inspector Dawson-" He broke off suddenly and turned to Liam. "By the way, did you ever check up on that?"

Liam raised an eyebrow. "Well, not that you ever asked me to, but it just so happens that I did."

Craig laughed. "Sorry. I must just have thought it."

"And I did my resident psychic act. Anyway, Dozy says the widow *did* call the unit."

Craig balked at the nickname but he hadn't the energy to pull him up.

"OK, good. So Inspector Dawson confirms her story, but that still doesn't exclude her completely; she could have been trying to get her husband out of the picture. For all we know that fifty grand was the just the tip of the iceberg."

Liam couldn't resist a comeback. "Except that if she *was* planning on getting hubbie arrested then why would she have bothered to bump him off? She'd have got the tank money anyway. And if her's and Purvis' relationship is dead, that's another reason to bump hubbie off gone up in smoke. Her killing McAllister just doesn't make sense, boss."

Craig thought for a moment and then conceded. "OK, I grant it's unlikely that either of them killed him, but I still want them in Belfast until we find out who did." He turned back to Annette. "So, that leaves us with what else might have got Colin McAllister killed? Either he double crossed someone he was working with or for, or he was an obstacle that someone wanted out of the way. Any other suggestions?"

The silence that answered said no, so 'double cross or obstacle' went up on the board.

"Right, we'll come back to that. Annette, tell me

where you've got to with O'Shea."

She replied with a shrug. "Nothing more since the last time. I've sent him the sketch of the girl."

"OK, get back to him on that, and I want you and Jake in Monaghan, checking on the other end of that pipe. What about Calum Fox?"

As she answered he wrote up the number two.

"We have a lead there. Jake."

"OK, we paid a visit to a brothel in Smithfield. Fox called its number a few hours before he died."

Liam coughed grandly. "I think you'll find they're known as Personal Service Domiciles nowadays."

"You've just made that up!" Jake went on. "Whatever they're called they have some full-time girls who are based there, and some part-timers and free-lancers, most of whom are home-based. We've got a list of all the girls working when Fox died and we're working our way through it now."

Craig nodded. "Give a copy to Davy and let's see if we can narrow them down. Also-"

He turned to find the analyst tapping furiously on his smart-pad in a way he'd seen kids doing in arcades.

"You wouldn't be playing a computer game by any chance, Davy, would you?"

It resulted in another hasty tap then the pad was turned round to display Niall Henderson's sketch.

"Is that w...what you were about to mention, chief?"

The angelic look on his face fooled no-one but Craig decided to let it pass. Davy was one of the few people he knew who really *could* do several things efficiently at once.

"It is actually."

Liam shot him a look that said well-played.

"Compare that sketch to the passport and driving licence photos of the girls on Jake's list, please. Let's see if we can show a link between the deaths of Matias Rey and Calum Fox. Also, if any of the working girls comes from the south, ask O'Shea to check on them. I want this girl's name and who paid her to kill Fox. She didn't do it alone, I'm sure of that."

277

Suddenly something occurred to him. He stared at Liam and his wide-eyed gaze in return said that he'd just read his mind. The girl in the morgue looked remarkably like the sketch. Had she been used as a decoy to isolate Matias Rey and then sent in to kill Calum Fox, then finally killed herself to set Andy up? Her death would ensure that she could never give up her boss.

If it *was* the same girl then Annette's search for Calum Fox's escort would prove futile, but they couldn't reveal that without revealing that Andy was locked up and why.

Craig decided to discuss it with Liam after the briefing and moved on, writing up the number three. But Jake hadn't finished.

"Sorry, sir, but do you now definitely believe that not only McAllister's and Fox's deaths might be linked, because of their proximity, but Fox's and Rey's, because a girl was involved in both?"

Craig considered for a moment before answering. "Let's just say that I need every option explored before I rule anything in or out." He banged on the board firmly, indicating that the subject was closed. "OK, number three, Matias Rey. We know that two of Matias' friends on their night out were conveniently side-tracked, one in hospital and one by spending the night with the girl in Davy's sketch. That left Matias alone and vulnerable. I called Doctor Winter just before the briefing and we now have the final forensics. Matias Rey was killed by a combination of drugs and drowning. The injection he was given before he entered the river wouldn't have killed him without the inhalation of river water, but the drugs made him unable to clear his airways. Ash has more on his passage through the river, I believe?"

Ash lifted his eyes from his screen and nodded. "He went into the Lagan at Shaw's Bridge early Wednesday morning and was washed downstream. The current that night was slow which is probably why he got caught on the rubbish at Lagan Meadows. The algae shows us that he died around there. There was a lot of rain the next day so the current became much faster and that's when he must have been washed down to the weir."

Craig nodded. "OK, good. Keep going with that please. Let me know immediately you find something."

He turned back to Davy. He was leaning forward attentively, anticipating Craig's next request.

"We contacted Rey's cab firm and asked for all the records from the day before to the day after Matias' death. We didn't need that much but if we'd narrowed it any further Xavier Rey would have caught on that we s...suspected the cabbie who drove the boys that night."

Liam nodded. "We don't want another death."

Davy continued. "The cabbie who drove them to the club was called Gerry Delaney. Unfortunately he's dropped off the map. Joe Rice is looking."

"Is his car traceable? He might show up on a traffic cam."

Davy shook his long locks. "Nope. They always use pool cars so he would only have been using it for that night. We've an alert set up for his private motor, but nothing's s...shown up so far. Sergeant Rice went round to the house but there was no answer. He's chasing up Delaney's wife as well."

Craig sighed. Gerry Delaney was either out of the country by now or dead. This bunch covered their tracks well.

"OK, keep going on that, Davy, and on the cab Matias called to get home. Liam, did you find out what Xavier Rey's up to?"

Liam's expression said he was puzzled. "Well...by all accounts he hasn't left home since he saw us at High Street, but I checked with his phone provider and his mobile's been red hot. We don't have a warrant so we can't know who he's calling, but if I had to guess I'd say he's gathering his troops-"

Annette cut in. "He's calling a summit. That means they're going after someone."

Liam shook his head. "Nah. If Rey already had a name he'd just do them himself. If they're going after anything it'll be information. I'd say some street

279

scrotes are going to get a beating tonight to see what they cough up."

Craig raked his hair, thinking. Liam was right and they had no way of knowing whom Rey had called, or who they were likely to attack. He made a decision.

"Liam, get a warrant for Rey's phone logs and put Joe Rice on the house. I want Davy and Ash on finding out who Rey called, then we stop them attacking whoever they're going after. We don't need any more aggro on the streets."

Kyle had barely moved since he'd arrived but now he signalled to interrupt. "They'd be barking up the wrong tree anyway."

Craig raised an eyebrow. "You know something?"

The inspector glanced towards Craig's office in a way that said 'just you and me'. Craig added a third.

"Excuse us for a moment, everyone. Liam, you're with us."

No sooner had the office door closed than Craig turned on the untidy spook.

"Where the hell have you been all day, Kyle? If you've been playing stupid-"

Liam had been studying Spence's face intently and something he read there made him shake his head. "I think you should let him speak, boss."

Craig was taken aback. He was normally the one reining Liam in. He strode to the window and said nothing for a moment then he thudded into his chair and waved the inspector on. The reason for Kyle's pallor soon became clear.

"You know I'd heard a mention of Albanians. Well, I decided to have a word with my old boss."

Liam gave a snort that said what he thought of people hedging their bets, but Craig said nothing. Kyle was only on secondment so it made sense that he kept his foot in Intelligence's door. Spence swallowed hard before he continued.

"He gave me a number to call. An overseas number."

Craig's eyes narrowed, guessing what he would hear next. Liam didn't believe in guessing.

"Give me it and I'll call it now."

Kyle shook his blond head. "It'll already have been cut off." To prove it he re-dialled the number and set his mobile on speakerphone. The dead line sound was hard to miss.

Craig's guess was firming up. Kyle went on.

"I was told not to ask for the man's name. All I knew was that he was one of Director Richie's private sources. I was also warned not to tell you anything about him or the call, but..."

Craig finished the sentence. "But you're shocked that Susan Richie could let a bad man roam free, just for information? Come on now, Kyle, you're a big boy. This isn't the first time criminals have been protected informants, here or elsewhere."

He glanced at Liam, knowing they were both thinking of the case they'd had three months before, involving paramilitaries who'd acted as informants during The Troubles.

Spence hit back. "I'm not naïve, Marc, you know that. But this..."

Liam didn't have time for his angst. "What country did you call? Albania?"

Kyle answered in a tired voice. "Bosnia." It hinted at what was to come. "While we were talking a door opened and someone entered the room to speak to him. I heard them call him Jastreb."

Jastreb, the Hawk. One of the worse Bosnian Serb war criminals in the Bosnian War. There couldn't be two men who went by that name.

Craig swore beneath his breath. "You're certain?"

"Certain. A man International Courts has warrants out for, is acting as a source for the Director of Police Intelligence."

"Does Roy Barrett know?"

Spence shook his head immediately. "Not his name. There's no way he wouldn't report it if he knew."

"But now *we* know, and we need to decide what to do about it."

While the other men angsted, Liam opted for pragmatism. "So what did he give you?"

Kyle wasn't sure he'd heard right. "What?"

Liam rolled his eyes. "Well, we can all sit here whipping ourselves about what to do about the naughty Director, or we can use whatever info yer man gave you to solve our case first. So did he give you anything worth having?"

Craig almost laughed. Liam was right. Solve now, angst later. He waved Spence on.

"OK, Kyle, tell us what you got from him."

Spence shook his head in disbelief before answering. "I asked him about Goga, the Albanian who came here last year, and he said he was just the tip of the iceberg. He said Albanian gangs have been coming into the south for years and working with Irish criminals. At first it was just small, sporadic groups, but then they got pulled together under the leadership of one man. He's set up a network of independent cells across Ireland, all working in isolation but all reporting to him. None of them knows the others' details but Goga runs the one in Belfast."

Craig nodded. They'd organised themselves like terrorist cells. "Did he have the boss man's name?"

Kyle shook his head. "He said he changes his moniker every month and only the heads of the cells know who he really is."

Liam snorted. "He's not as smart as the general. *No-one* knows who he is, not even Xavier Rey."

"This guy's not afraid of disloyalty because he has a special hit team that kills anyone who steps out of line. Jastreb said he's completely ruthless, and that's bad coming from him."

Craig nodded. "That's obvious by the trail of dead bodies he's leaving in the north. Rey's general might be a crook but at least he isn't a killer."

Kyle nodded. "The last thing he said was that this gang will mow down anyone in their way." A look of disgust crossed his face. "He said it like he admired him."

Craig was unsurprised. "He probably does. Genocide was his way of life for years." He tapped a pen against the desk as he thought. After a minute he pocketed it and stood up. "OK, we'll give the team a sanitised update on this but the information on your source stays in this room until after the case. OK?"

Everyone nodded and Craig saw the colour return to Kyle's cheeks. A problem shared was a problem passed on by the looks of it.

They re-joined the group and updated them on the possible Albanian links, then Craig wrapped up and Liam went to harass the on call judge for his phone warrant. It left Craig alone in his office contemplating his next steps. Half-an-hour later his trance was broken by his mobile phone. He answered it without looking at the screen, surprised when John came on, shouting in a most un-John-like way.

"Get your ass down to St Mary's ED. You and I have something to discuss!"

****

Annette entered the lift to reception in silence and Jake took the hint not to talk, already occupied with thoughts of his own. He was calculating how long it would take him to bulk up through exercise, working on five sessions a week before or after work. The answer of six months was too long so he changed the number to seven and came back with four months. He gave a satisfied smile. Four months was about the length of time it would take him to appeal the P.P.S.'s decision on Foster's sanity, something he'd decided to do the night before in an alleyway, and tested in daylight until he was sure. If he could get it overturned then Aaron would get out on bail, pending his trial. That was all the access he needed to ensure justice of a different kind.

If Annette had been paying attention she would have read something in Jake's eyes, but she wasn't. She was too busy working out how much bigger she was likely to get before she threw in the towel and went on leave. At the rate she was eating she reckoned it would be about March so Kyle had better learn what he could about detecting in the next eight weeks.

When the bell dinged for the ground floor Jake suddenly noticed where they were.

"Why are we getting out here, Annette?"

She sighed and waited for the doors to open. "Because I was too tired to drive into the basement so my car's parked on Pilot Street."

As the basement entrance was only twenty feet further on it didn't make sense even to her. They'd reached the junction with Corporation Street before she spoke again.

"OK. We've got to see O'Shea, but I don't know about you, I'm too wrecked to go down tonight. Let's do it first thing tomorrow. I'll drop you to your car now and collect you in the morning."

It was an unexpected but welcome turn of events. If he was going to get fit he wanted to get started. Aaron was already four stone of muscle ahead.

****

St Mary's Trust. Emergency Department.

Craig wasn't quite sure what he'd expected to greet him when he entered the Emergency Department, but it wasn't the sight that he clapped eyes on as he walked through the sliding doors. Something in John's voice, irate as it had been, had suggested there was an element of, if not amusement about why he'd called him, certainly a vague subtext of 'I told you so'. Nowhere had he got the impression that someone might have died, and that much he'd got right, but as far as amusement went, by the expression on John's face he'd completely misread that part.

The scene in front of him had something of the theatrical farce about it. John was standing beside a very red-chinned Natalie, seated in a wheelchair with one leg elevated in plaster and her bandaged right hand grasping an elbow crutch, and not in a way that said she was about to use it to stand up and walk. She was wielding the prop like a weapon, with its end aimed at someone behind a curtained screen.

When John saw him enter, his frown, previously directed at the recipient of Natalie's ire, turned firmly towards his friend.

He strode across reception like a man possessed. "Here you are. Finally!"

Craig gawped at him. "You only called me ten minutes ago!"

But the irate pathologist wasn't in the mood for detail, instead he lifted a hand to indicate his bride.

"Look at her. Just look." He turned back to Craig, adding a triumphant. "You see!"

Craig didn't see at all. In fact he hadn't a clue what Natalie's obvious mishap had to do with him, but he liked her so he ignored her husband's performance and walked across to hunker beside her chair.

"How are you, Natalie? What happened?"

If he'd believed he would be answered any more sensibly by her than by John then he'd been sadly mistaken. Natalie's only response was an ominous silence and another jab of her crutch straight ahead. As Craig turned to find the enemy, Katy bolted from her hiding place and made off down the ward, leaving the stunned detective staring first at her and then back at Natalie and John. He finally found his voice.

"You're saying that Katy did this?"

Natalie's reply was dramatic.

"She tried to kill me!"

"Katy? *Katy* tried to kill you?"

In the second before she said yes he remembered a conversation he'd had with his mother when he'd been around ten. They'd been watching an old black and white movie where someone had murdered someone, and, in a sure sign of his future career, he'd asked Mirella what she would do if he ever told her that he'd killed someone. Her reply still lived with him. She had answered indignantly "I say no, you didn't"; such was her belief that her son could never do anything truly wrong. It had surprised him then but now he understood, because he was just as certain there was no way Katy could ever have hurt anyone, much less her own best friend.

As the word "yes" emerged from Natalie's mouth Craig started to laugh, not sure who was going to hit him first; Natalie with her crutch or John with his badly curled fist.

He raised his hands in peace before either one could. "I'm not laughing at you, Nat. I just can't believe Katy would deliberately hurt anyone. Tell me what happened."

As the sounds of indignation rose and fell he searched around for a chair, sitting down well out of crutch range. John was the first of the couple to make any sense.

"I warned you about this risk taking stuff, Marc."

Craig nodded. "You did."

"Well, today they went to the race track and Natalie went round first-"

"Do you mind?" Natalie reclaimed her war story with a glare at her husband. "It's my story to tell, not yours." The glare shifted to Craig. "I drove round the track without a problem. I reached a hundred and ten and the instructor said I was the best he'd ever seen on a first drive."

Craig made soothing sounds. "I don't doubt it."

He was struggling to keep a straight face, knowing exactly what was coming next. Katy wasn't a fast driver but it wasn't just conscientiousness that kept her driving slow. She hated speed. They'd visited a skid pan one day and her response to hitting a skid had been to take her hands off the wheel and cover her eyes and if he drove above eighty she practically blacked out in the passenger seat. So why she'd decided that doing the ton would be a good idea he would never know.

His thoughts were interrupted by Natalie's crutch waving perilously close to his nose.

"This is all your fault, Marc. If you didn't hang around with killers she would never have been attacked, and she wouldn't be trying to prove that she wasn't frightened now."

He ignored the comment. "I take it that it was Katy's turn to drive and she went a bit off course-"

Natalie's eyes almost popped out of her head. "A

BIT! A BIT! She aimed straight for where I was sitting with the cameraman."

They'd videoed it! That must be how all those calamities appeared on reality TV.

"You know she didn't mean it-"

Natalie wasn't persuaded. "Huh. She looked like she was aiming to me."

There was silence for a moment then, when he'd gauged that it was safe, Craig smiled at her chidingly.

"Aimed at you, Nat? Really? She couldn't have just lost control?"

"NO." Then. "Well... maybe." She gave a weak shake of her crutch. "But I'm still in a chair and I'll be out of the operating theatre for months."

A roll of John's eyes said that he would have to listen to her moaning all that time. Then, just in case Craig believed he'd nearly forgiven him, he shook his head solemnly.

"You really need to sort this out, Marc. Because Katy's trying to prove she can cope with being with you, Natalie almost got killed."

Craig didn't voice his thoughts that Natalie had probably encouraged Katy to pursue the most dangerous things on her risk list because she'd quite fancied the thrill herself. Instead he nodded diplomatically.

"Any idea where she might have gone to, Nat?"

She thought for a moment. "Her office maybe, or down to her apartment to change. She won't have gone back to her mum's yet, that's for sure. She's still covered in mud."

Craig decided to take a risk. "Why is your chin so red?"

John couldn't stifle his laughter. It earned him a dark scowl from his wife.

"Because when Katy drove *at* us, I threw myself off my chair and skidded along the tarmac into a steel barrier. That's how I broke my leg."

John added helpfully. "She skidded on her chin."

Natalie's scowl was bordering on the wild now. "I think he'd already worked that out!"

Craig leaned down to give her a kiss on the cheek. "Sorry, Natalie. I promise I'll talk to her."

She softened slightly. "If she'll let you... You could text her, but I'd leave trying to see her till tomorrow. She's feeling pretty bad about things."

He turned for the sliding doors, shaking his head. "If anyone should feel bad it's me."

Chapter Fourteen

West Belfast. 9 p.m.

Joe Rice watched as the men skulked into the Rey house and then as they left again two hours later, averting their faces from the neon street lights. It made the unassuming Belfast semi look like the headquarters of some secret society, which in a way he supposed that it was. Not one with special handshakes or rituals, but one where the men were bound by ties just as strong. The ties of criminality.

The Cork man had perused each face as the men arrived, videoing them for their I.D.s. Each one looked different, some small and some tall, some thin and some fat, but one thing was consistent, there was no mistaking the stench of corruption that they reeked. No avoiding the light of self interest in all of their eyes.

He amused himself by picturing the group wearing suits, instead of their motley selection of polo shirts and logoed T-shirts, stretched over huge guts or hanging off them, and paired with jeans so ill-fitting that they started halfway down each one's ass. Instead they were polished, groomed and Armani-ed, their stench masked by expensive eau de cologne. In the right light they could have been a group of crooked bankers or politicians, separated from the gangsters by an accident of birth more than by any moral code.

Joe chuckled quietly to himself and packed his camera away, then he dialled the number Liam had given him and started a train of events. At the other end of the line Davy and Ash were waiting for their download, ready to capture each face as the sergeant had sent it, run it through their database and match the men's mobile numbers to Xavier Rey's earlier calls. Thirty minutes later Craig, Liam and two teams of uniforms were escorting the men into police vans watched by their glowering major, with a warning ringing in Rey's ears that if he tried it again he would join his men in the cells, only his status as a grieving father saving him from that ignominy tonight.

As the vans drove down the Andersonstown Road Craig made up his mind. They'd leaned on Jack's hospitality too much recently so he directed the caravan towards Stranmillis Road Station where the saturnine Sergeant John Maguire met them at the door. He would have said welcomed, but he wasn't sure that a frown and a "Why me?" counted as a welcome in anyone's book.

"Sorry, John. Needs must and Jack Harris can't always catch it." Craig walked past him into reception. "How many cells have you got?"

"Eight. How many prisoners?"

"Seven, so we're in luck." He handed the station sergeant a list. "Just do the usual and then leave them to stew overnight. I don't want any phone calls made, so Liam's got their mobiles for your safe and your landline's mysteriously broken. OK?"

Maguire shook his head firmly. "Oh, no, you don't. I'm not lying so they get denied their calls."

Craig's response was to nod and then immediately walk outside. Five minutes later he returned with a pair of pliers and some wire in his hand. "Now you won't have to lie."

While Maguire grabbed his desk phone and gawped as he got a dead line, Craig searched round for his deputy.

"Liam, have you got those mobiles?"

"Aye."

Liam propped the man he'd been dragging against the reception desk and opened his suit jacket to reveal the phones. He wouldn't have looked out of place on a market stall.

Craig decided to give Maguire another chance, even though he already knew his answer.

"Would you rather not lock the mobiles in your safe, sergeant? By that I mean, will you feel the need to hand them back to the prisoners to make their phone calls as soon as we leave?"

John Maguire gave an emphatic nod. "I most certainly will." It was accompanied by a chastising stare that would have done a missionary proud. Craig was getting bored with the man's moralising so he decided to enlighten him on the dilemma that they faced that night.

"So you would allow them to phone their troops, who would then go and beat the crap out of the men that this bunch were on the way to do over themselves before we stopped them?"

The dark-eyed sergeant was taken aback but not quite gobsmacked so Craig pushed on.

"You have here seven senior members of The Rock, one of Belfast's most successful gangs. If you don't believe me check their tattoos. We believe that they held a summit this evening and left with instructions to beat information out of any unfortunate low-life they could find." He dropped a brass knuckle duster on the desk. "This and a selection of knives, bats and straps were found in their cars. So do you still intend to give them their phones?"

"I...but...the problem is..."

Craig voted with his feet, a big part of him knowing that what he'd asked the man to do wasn't fair. If anyone got heat for this it should be him.

"Let's go, Liam. We'll hold onto the mobiles. You can let this bunch go tomorrow, Sergeant. We'll leave Sergeant Rice and his lads with you to help keep them in line."

The detectives were at their cars before Maguire had recovered his voice. When he did he overcompensated for his correct but unsupportive behaviour by shouting loudly at his guests for the rest of the night.

Craig leaned on the roof of his car and yawned loudly. "Let's call it a night, Liam. If I don't get some sleep I'll be useless tomorrow." As he climbed into his Audi he already knew he wouldn't sleep a wink. They might have stopped some mischief but they couldn't police the whole of Belfast; the night provided too much cover.

Elsewhere in Belfast he was about to be proved right.

The Pit Nightclub. May Street, Belfast. 11 p.m.

All cities have two faces; one fit for the full glare of daylight and one that is only ever shown after dark, and they are as different as Red Riding Hood and the Big Bad Wolf. While daylight people might dip their toes into the dark occasionally, they never inhabit it with the ease of those for whom it is their natural habitat. Ditto with the people of the night. There is however one place where they meet in relative safety, and that is the world of casinos and nightclubs.

Zac Greer didn't gamble so casinos held no interest for him, but nightclubs were his natural milieu. Throbbing, strobing, pulsing; a shifting human river that he immersed himself in each weekend. Out of his head or off his face, whichever euphemism you prefer, he still listened to talk and made contacts, especially when he was buying his drugs. Tonight he would buy his weed with a different purpose in mind, and, as he worked his way around the edge of the throbbing dancefloor, he purchased information with each bag. But clubs are dark so the youth didn't see the man watching him, and as he left each dealer, variously frustrated, an angry signal removed them from the floor and into a small back room.

The watcher joined the small group, letting its members lie and beg and spit excuses, until after five minutes he held up a hand bearing a gun. It had a sobering effect. He motioned to his men, stationed behind each of the dealers, and they pushed them forward one by one.

"I want know what boy asked you, and your answer." The gun brushed each face in turn. "Don't waste my time with a lie."

The approach ensured obedience, and as the last but one dealer gabbled out his answer and was ejected the watcher knew that he finally had the truth. The boy had only got one truthful answer to his questions and both he and the squealing dealer would be dealt with later. Right now there was someone else who needed to know.

****

The C.C.U. Monday. 8.30 a.m.

Craig had surprised himself by sleeping through the night, although his aching muscles when he'd woken had confirmed it was more the slump of exhaustion than sleep of any depth. He would take whatever he could get; at least it had pushed the murders, budgets and Katy from his head for a few hours, although as soon as his eyes had opened he'd been hit by all of them again, plus a few additional things.

As the others filtered into the squad-room he poured a coffee and started to regret his baking ban. In the absence of breakfast he could do with a sugar hit. Nicky read his mind and ushered him into his office, nodding him to sit. She returned to her desk and reappeared a moment later with an old Scottish shortbread tin. As soon as he saw it Craig grinned.

"Nicky, you're a lifesaver. I'd love a biscuit, if you have one."

She pulled off the lid with a flourish. "Better than a biscuit; it's one of my coffee muffins. Fresh today."

He nodded ruefully; she'd ignored his ban. But at least she was keeping it on the down low and, as all he'd really wanted was an end to the debilitating competition between her and Rhonda, he decided that he couldn't really complain.

Just then Liam arrived. He spotted Craig's muffin and reached his fingers into the tin, only to almost have them amputated as Nicky slammed the lid.

"Ow! How come he gets a bun and I don't?"

She clasped the tin firmly to her chest. "He asked."

"OK, if I ask can I have one?"

"No. You're only being polite because I told you to."

Craig solved the dilemma like Solomon and tore

293

his cake in half, shrugging apologetically at his P.A. "Sorry, but it's the only way to stop him moaning."

She flounced out, disgusted, and he nodded his deputy to close the door, turning to business.

"OK, we may have stopped Rey last night but we can't afford the men to watch him constantly. Any suggestions?"

Liam pushed the cake into his mouth and began to talk. "Theff ffthing is-"

Craig held up a hand, halting him mid crumb-spray. "Don't say another word until you've swallowed that." He brushed the debris into the bin and waited for the gulp.

"Sorry, boss. I forgot it was in there."

It was probably true.

"OK...What I said was, the only way we can stop Rey organising them again is to lock him up, so I suggest we do that."

Craig shook his head. "We can't. The media would have a field day. Grieving father incarcerated, blah, blah, blah."

Liam thought for a moment and then gave a smile. "OK, then. Let's *threaten* him with being locked up if he tries it again, with a man tailing him very obviously so that he knows it's true."

Craig hemmed and hawed before nodding. "It'll have to do. Call Stranmillis and tell them they can let the others go this evening. Twenty-four hours lock-up should make them think, and get Joe to inform them it'll happen again if we see them up to anything. He can choose Rey's tail."

He took a sip of coffee and moved on to other things. "OK. Andy. Anything from the lab?"

Liam's response was to open the door but Craig shook his head instantly.

"They don't know about Andy."

"Davy does." He beckoned the analyst in.

"Sit down, Davy. What have you got for us?"

"Info from the lab, chief, and we've got some camera s...stuff as well. There's CCTV from where Matias Rey went into the river; a man leading him to

294

the w...water from an old fashioned car. Unfortunately it was too dark to see the make."

Craig's face fell but the analyst went on.

"The good news is that we got a blurry s...shot of its reg plate and Doctor Marsham's trying to clean that up now."

Liam grinned. "Well done, lad. If we get a reg we might get a name."

"The man got out of the left hand side, so it looks as if the car is from abroad."

Left hand drive; it went with the idea that Albanians might be involved. If they were they weren't trying very hard to hide it, and any optimism Craig felt was dampened by the thought that the plate was probably false.

"Anything more on I.D.ing the girl in the sketch? Or on the names Annette got from the brothel?"

Davy nodded. "I sent the sketch to Doctor W...Winter and he confirmed it's his dead girl." He frowned quizzically. "Does that mean that whoever killed her killed Matias Rey as well?"

Liam shook his head. "Organised them both. Andy didn't kill Rey."

Craig was indignant. "That makes it sound like he killed the girl!"

"Ach, that's not what I meant and you know it."

Davy pushed on. He had work to do and it wasn't getting done sitting there.

"OK, well, that means the girl who distracted Matias Rey's friend Niall is dead. S...She doesn't match any of Annette's escorts so far, but we've only got photos for the first three so I'll keep on it. The other thing is that I checked Matias' mobile. He called his dad's taxi office on Wednesday morning at one-o-five and someone answered, but there's no record of a cab being sent to pick him up."

The detectives frowned simultaneously but Liam was the first to speak. "What are the odds that the taxi driver that drove the three of them to the club might've pre-arranged to collect them, so when he answered the phone in the office hours later he just didn't bother logging the call?"

Craig shook his head. "Slim. No driver could deal with driving jobs *and* taking constant calls. And why would he have been in the office anyway? He'd have been out driving fares. Check it with the boys anyway, Davy, but I'm pretty sure the answer will be no."

Liam nodded. "Aye, you're right. They couldn't have known what time they were leaving and Matias would've just called the cabbie directly instead of ringing the office."

Craig went on. "There might be something else here. Davy, I want to know who was on the cab office phones that night. If our man *had* diverted the phones and was answering every call waiting for Matias to phone, it's unlikely any other cabs at all were dispatched that night-"

Davy frowned. "How do you make that out?"

Craig gestured at his desk phone. "OK, just say I divert this line to my mobile and you call asking for a cab. If I'm waiting for one particular call, am I really going to bother passing your request back to the office?"

"You might radio another cabbie with the job."

Craig shrugged. "I might, but it's unlikely."

Liam jumped in. "OK. So worst case scenario the other drivers were having jobs passed onto them by the driver waiting for Matias' call, or no calls were passed on that night at all. Wouldn't someone have queried the lack of work that night, or wondered why things weren't coming from the office?"

He glanced at Craig, waiting to be interrupted, but he nodded him on instead.

"So if the calls were diverted to our crooked driver, someone would've twigged, either from the lack of work or from his voice on the end of the line giving them jobs. We need to ask if that happened, and if it didn't then that means whoever was manning the office phones that night was in on Matias' abduction as well. When Matias called he was sent our Euro cab, driven by his killer, instead of one of the firm's own cars."

Davy thought about it for a moment.

"W...Why would Matias have got into a cab without a logo he recognised? His dad's cabs are all blue and white, not dark s...saloons."

"Forced in."

It was an untidy explanation and the analyst said as much.

"But then why didn't our European just get a job with Rey's firm? He could have driven the lads out for the night, then w...waited for the call, picked Matias up in one of the pool cars and then handed him off to the Euro car."

Craig shook his head. "It's a small, local firm. Why would Xavier Rey suddenly hire someone new? No, our best bet is some combination of what you and Liam just said. Check it out, please." He took a gulp of coffee before restarting. "OK. What have you got on Andy's situation?"

The analyst made a face. "There were no prints on the s...safe-"

Liam cut in. "They wore gloves."

"Maybe. Carry on, Davy."

"The murder weapon was definitely Andy's Glock-"

This time Craig interrupted. "Easily done if they got it from the safe."

"It was still in the safe when the police arrived."

Liam nodded triumphantly. "Well, there you go then. They took Andy's Glock from his safe, killed the girl and then put it back. There's no way he could have done all that if he was in the K-hole."

Craig's expression said perhaps but he waited for Davy to continue. "That's all we've got so far, boss. The splatter pattern says s...she was definitely killed at Andy's place and we're still waiting for all the CCTV." He looked embarrassed suddenly. "I don't know if this will be any comfort to Andy, but there was no s...sign that they'd had sex."

Craig glanced quickly at Liam, as much to stop an impending wisecrack as to say that the fact was significant.

"OK, thanks, Davy. Let me know as soon as you get anything more." When the analyst had left Liam spoke.

"You can stop looking so prim. I wasn't going to say anything rude about sex. Even I draw the line at jokes about a dead girl. What I *was* going to say was that it made sense. If Andy was in the K-Hole he couldn't have moved never mind had sex."

Craig sat back, steepling his fingers. "The question is... how much Ketamine was enough to put him there and can we prove it? What would put one man in the K-Hole mightn't touch another one."

Liam helped himself to coffee as he answered. "Very little in Andy's case, would be my bet. He's only ten stone dripping wet."

Craig's response was to walk out to Davy's desk. He scribbled down 'Ketamine, K-hole, dosage per stone and barman?' and handed him the note. He re-entered his office just in time to see Liam devouring the rest of his muffin so he begged a fresh one from Nicky and retook his seat.

"OK, we know Gerry Delaney has disappeared, but if there *was* someone else involved in Rey's cab firm hopefully we can get something from them, if they haven't skipped as well of course. And if Andy's dead girl turns out to be the escort hired by Fox, that links the Rey and Fox cases definitively, and gives us some evidence that Andy was framed."

Liam raised an eyebrow. "You're doubting it?"

Craig sighed. "I don't doubt Andy at all. But unless we find forensic proof that someone else shot the girl then proving he was framed to distract us might be our only hope of getting him off."

****

Gardaí Station. County Louth, Republic of Ireland. 12 p.m.

Annette could barely speak for anger. They'd driven two hours across the border to Monaghan to watch a

298

tank being excavated from a field that apparently belonged to no-one, and now they were in Magnus O'Shea's office asking questions that he was answering with a shrug, and "we've nothing on the girl in our systems, so she mustn't have come from here." They should have just saved themselves the trip.

The Garda added for good measure. "I did say that she'd probably doubled back into the north."

He did, but Annette thought he could have had the decency to look a bit sorrier about it. Jake saw her approaching apoplexy and interjected, trying to help.

"When you say the field doesn't belong to anyone, Inspector... What exactly does that mean?"

O'Shea looked bemused. He might be a native Irish speaker but even he was certain of the English he'd just used. He decided that a visual aid might assist the Belfast detectives and clambered out of his chair to lift a large binder down from a shelf. He set it in front of Jake and opened it at the relevant page.

"All the land in Ireland is registered, except for what's called common land. Like the field."

Annette summoned her last ounce of politeness. "Doesn't that belong to the Irish government?"

O'Shea wriggled his bottom back into his seat and thought for a moment before answering. "Do you know, I think you're right."

Jake stared at the page. "But there's nothing in the field's ownership column."

"That'll be to save some poor bugger writing Rialtas on every page." He saw Jake's quizzical look. "That means government." He gave a deep laugh. "Imagine that for a job, would you. All you do all day is write government against every piece of common land."

Annette had had enough of O'Shea's apparent amusement with everything in life. She nodded Jake to get ready to leave and muttered a farewell. By the time they'd reached the carpark her opinions were hitting the air with force.

"That bloody man would drive me to drink. His wife must be an angel."

Jake smiled, hoping that it would calm her down. "Well, I suppose-"

She yanked at the driver's door and climbed in. "If you're about to say it's not his fault that they don't know the girl, or that the field isn't owned by anyone, then don't. It's not what he says it's the way he says it, like he's so damned happy all the time."

"Maybe he is. He is retiring this year after all."

Annette's only response was a grunt and a very heavy right foot.

****

Garvan's Bookies. East Belfast.

Rory McCrae felt the commotion before he saw it, a thud of doors and vibration of footsteps that prompted him to break his rule of not fraternising with his employees and enter the shop. He was greeted by the sight of his men huddling and whispering, and as his gaze shifted beyond them he saw that the place was devoid of punters and someone had locked the front door.

"Who the fuck closed up?"

The group scattered like pigeons, leaving only one unfortunate who hadn't moved. The hapless man stood frozen and speechless, leaving McCrae to get his answer from a shadow by the door.

"We awl thought-"

McCrae's move was swift. He headed for the speaker and seized his shirt with a GPS like accuracy, hauling him out into the light.

"Ye thought? Ye thought? I dun't pay any of yeez to think." He pulled tighter for emphasis until the man's face was only an inch from his own, then he released the grip as quickly as he'd formed it and turned back to the man seated on the chair.

"I want to know why my shop's shut, McIlveen." He pointed at the man in a way that left no doubt that a blow would follow if he was displeased.

The man swallowed hard and found his voice.

300

"Becos of Zac."

McCrae's eyes widened. He hadn't heard from the youth since he'd sent him hunting.

"Wat about him?"

"Heez in the hospital. Sumwan beat him real bad."

McCrae frowned, several emotions coursing through him at once. The first was pleasure; the wee scrote had deserved a thumping years ago. The second was curiosity; if someone had taken the trouble to beat Greer then the boy must have found out what he'd asked. He turned back towards his office, grabbing the man on the way.

"Ye're driving me tee St Mary's."

No-one believed that the visit was out of concern.

****

The C.C.U. 2 p.m.

Craig was thinking thoughts that never reached the air in briefings when his desk phone began to ring. He ignored it for a moment thinking that Nicky would pick it up, but on the fourth ring she stuck her head around the door and he realised she'd transferred the call.

He lifted the handset hastily. "Marc Craig."

"I need an answer, Marc. By tomorrow afternoon."

The Chief Constable needed no introduction. Sean Flanagan continued in an unamused tone.

"And I'll need your draft budget for the fifteen percent reduction by next Friday at the latest. I've to go in front of the policing board the following Monday and it'll give me time to tidy things up."

Craig puffed out his cheeks, not at what he'd been asked to do, but at whether or not to mention what the Intelligence Director had done. He decided against it. He should give Susan Richie the chance to explain herself before he shopped her to the boss. His thoughts were interrupted by an atypical note of irritation in Flanagan's next words.

"You know, Marc, anyone would think I was offering you something unpleasant. I can tell you this much; if I offered D.C.S. Harrison the same opportunity he would bite off my hand."

Craig smiled at the image. He'd never pictured Harrison as a dog but the analogy seemed strangely appropriate. He kept his amusement firmly out of his voice.

"I'm sorry, sir. I'm grateful for the offer, honestly. I'm just preoccupied with this case, or rather cases."

Flanagan's tone softened slightly. "I don't suppose what's happening with D.C.I. Angel is helping either. Is there any word on that?"

Craig didn't hide his sigh. "We have him on tape leaving the bar with the dead girl and we have enough Ketamine in his blood to stop a truck-"

Flanagan cut in. "Well, that'll be it then. He was set up."

"Unfortunately it's not that simple, sir. The weapon used was his Glock and he has GSR on his hands. Doctor Winter says that can be explained forensically, but unless we can find CCTV of someone entering his apartment there'll still be room for doubt-"

Flanagan's response was definitive. "NO. We can't have that. It will taint the force's reputation, not to mention ruin his career."

Don't forget the rest of his life.

"Keep going, Craig. You'll find something. But I still need that other answer by tomorrow."

As the phone went down Craig felt even more pressured than before, so when his mobile began to vibrate he immediately knocked it off without a glance. He needed to think not talk and in order to think clearly he needed more information to work with. He walked out to Davy's desk just as Annette and Jake were walking in.

"Any joy in Monaghan?"

Jake answered quickly before Annette began to moan again; he'd already had hours of it in the car.

"Unfortunately the land is owned by the Irish government, so we've no name. And the Gardaí still have nothing on the girl."

Craig noticed Davy grinning.

"You look happy."

"I am. Interpol just came through on the girl's s...sketch. Her name is Kalyna Melnyk. She's also on our escort list, working from an address in Dundalk. Just over the border."

Annette slumped in her chair. "And O'Shea said she wasn't in their records!" She frowned. "Melnyk's not an Irish name."

"It's not. S...She was Ukrainian. In the south illegally."

Jake perched on his desk. "Trafficked?"

"Possibly. It's hard to know." Davy shot Craig a look that said he had something else, so the detective dismissed the others and pulled up a chair. The analyst dropped his voice.

"I've got the car reg from Des, chief. It was a nineteen-fifty-four Peugeot 203C Saloon. Classic car. Imported from France but never registered."

Craig sighed. "So we've no name."

"Yes, we have. W...We've had a stroke of luck. It was stopped for speeding a week ago. Guess where."

Craig crossed his fingers. "Armagh?"

"Better than that. On the main road that runs down the back of the McAllisters' farm."

Craig didn't dare get his hopes up. "Tell me they got the driver's details."

Davy allowed himself a small smile. "It was Colin McAllister."

McAllister! His frown was instant. The car was the link they needed between McAllister's death and Matias Rey's, and the girl had already linked Rey's and Fox's, so why wasn't he more pleased?

Davy was still speaking.

"The only reason they didn't fine him was because they knew McAllister as a local bigwig and he was only a hundred metres off his own land. They ticked him off and told him to keep the car off-road."

And didn't even check if it was registered or insured. Craig nodded his congratulations.

"Well done, Davy. OK, so that means the car

involved in Matias' killing was being driven by Colin McAllister in the week before. Any chance McAllister was the man on the river CCTV?"

Davy shook his head immediately. "Nope. W...Wrong height by a head."

"So what do *you* think? Someone stole McAllister's car to dispose of Rey?"

The analyst thought for a moment before answering. "What if w...when they were rigging McAllister's air tank they saw the Peugeot, s...stole it and then used it when they killed Rey to confuse us? In case we caught them on CCTV."

It made sense.

"OK, but Matias was killed in the early hours of Wednesday morning and McAllister not until the following day. How-"

The analyst cut in. "They rigged the air tank late Tuesday night and took the car then, banking that McAllister wouldn't check on it on the Wednesday."

"And even if he had done he would just have thought that it had been stolen. There'd have been no reason to check his air tank." He nodded as he continued. "So the same man killed McAllister and Rey, and we know the girl was a decoy in Rey's killing and killed number three, Calum Fox, personally, before she was then killed herself. She and the man were working together."

"And then he killed her."

Craig made a face. The girl felt more like a victim than a predator now. He stood up to go but Davy shook his head and tapped his computer screen.

"I don't want to get any hopes up, but..."

A video appeared and they watched as a shadowy figure walked down a city street.

"What am I looking at?"

"This is the CCTV from the traffic lights just up from Andy's building. It was taken at four a.m. on Saturday night. Look."

Craig watched as the man crossed the road on red, gambling on the lack of traffic. His head was down, as if he knew he might be photographed, and his clothes were ubiquitous. They watched as he approached Andy's building then the camera went out of range.

"Damn."

Davy ignored him and tapped on another screen. The man reappeared inside a building five minutes later and stood waiting for the lift.

"Tell me that's Andy's apartment building."

Davy nodded. Craig sat forward eagerly.

"Can you get the floor number he pressed from the lift camera?"

"Fourth. Andy's floor."

They watched as the man disembarked and walked down a dimly lit corridor, before turning sharp right at the end. Davy switched off the stream.

"Andy's apartment is in that direction, but there's no footage for that bit."

Craig chewed his pen, thinking before he spoke. "But it's reasonable doubt, especially if we interview the building's occupants and rule out if anyone of that description was due to visit an apartment that night. Well done, Davy." His expression said that he was about to ask for more. "Any chance you can find out how he got into the building? Did he have a code or key, or did he just keep buzzing until someone let him in? It took five minutes for him to appear inside. Also, before he reached the traffic lights. Which direction did he come from and is there any CCTV of the local roads? We might see his car. I doubt that he walked there."

Davy rolled his eyes. An analyst's work was never done. "Just one last thing, chief, and it might be coincidence, but his height matches the man's who killed Matias Rey exactly."

Craig jumped up, reenergised.

"Brilliant work, Davy. You might just save our bacon."

He turned to scan the room. Everyone was there but Kyle. Just at that moment he came running in, a lit cigarette in his hand. Nicky sniffed ostentatiously and he raced out again, leaving everyone wondering where he was going to dump it in a building whose windows didn't open and with paper in every bin. When the intelligence officer reappeared he had damp hands.

"Sorry about that, Nicky. I forgot. I flushed it down the bog."

Liam gave a disapproving tut. "That comes under the heading of too much info, mate."

Craig shot him a sceptical look. "And you're always such a gentleman, aren't you." He didn't wait for a response. "OK, as everyone's here we'll brief now. Gather round. I don't want this taking forever."

As the chairs scraped and crowded he got a coffee top-up.

"Right. Davy's just done some brilliant work that links the McAllister and Rey deaths. Davy."

As Davy brought everyone up to date, Nicky passed around some muffins, making Rhonda open her mouth to object. Craig got there first.

"OK, cakes only on Sunday, and Monday if there are leftovers." He closed off any debate. "Right, Davy's outlined the situation with the EU car. I want it found. Liam, get the men at the farm looking for it. If it's back in an outhouse or barn we need to find it. Annette, check with Purvis and Mara McAllister if they'd ever seen it around. It's important. Whoever killed Matias Rey was driving Colin McAllister's car, which means that the murders are linked."

Jake cut in. "Couldn't McAllister have been behind Rey's killing rather than them both being victims of the same man?"

Craig thought about it. "He couldn't have done it himself. As Davy's just said, Colin McAllister was the wrong height to be the man by the river. I grant you he could have organised Rey's death, in theory, but it's highly unlikely. What would have been his motive for a start?" He shook his head, dismissing the idea. "No. We'll stick to the theory of Colin McAllister as victim rather than perpetrator for now, so, Jake, I want you to alert traffic all across the province that we're looking for that car. Davy can give you the reg and make. OK, Davy's also managed to I.D. the escort Calum Fox phoned that day, and she's the girl in the sketch. Her name was Kalyna Melnyk and she's a Ukrainian national. She was based in Dundalk in the Republic, so her address needs investigating. Unfortunately we've discovered she's dead, but that doesn't negate her linking Fox's and Rey's deaths."

He could see Kyle preparing to ask how the girl had died so he turned quickly to Ash as distraction.

"Ash, Get onto intelligence in the south and find out what you can about her address and any possible trafficking operations. D.C.I. Hughes in Vice might know something as well."

Annette snorted. "I'm glad you're not putting O'Shea on the job. He's worse than useless. He couldn't find anything on her at all."

Craig frowned but didn't comment, turning back to Liam.

"What's happening with Xavier Rey's men?"

Liam shrugged. "Still in Stranmillis. Maguire's holding them until I give him the nod. I wanted to have a word with Rey first. Warn him off."

"OK, do that and then let them go. But keep a man on him. What about Tommy Hill?"

Liam sniffed loudly. "He had a visitor. Rory McCrae. But his tag says he hasn't left the house since we saw him."

Craig snorted sceptically. "And you really believe he didn't slip it again?" He shook his head. McCrae's visit wasn't good news. "I don't trust that tag so ask Templepatrick police to keep an eye out. I want to know if Hill even goes out to buy milk."

He turned back to the analysts.

"What can you tell us about Calum Fox's business interests?"

Ash replied. "He owned seven bookie's shops across the north, and kept stands at all the main race venues. There's no hard information on him being dodgy. Just the usual suspicions about people who make money off gambling."

"And the cab office?"

Davy nodded. "You were right. The office line w...was diverted to a mobile number, but they didn't pass any calls on, so none of the drivers got any work on Tuesday night. The number's dead now but it belonged to Gerry Delaney, the same cabbie who dropped off the boys that night."

"The pickup wasn't prearranged or he wouldn't have needed the divert-"

Davy cut in. "Meaning he was the murderer."

Craig shook his head. "Possible, but I doubt it. He would have been driving a cab not a private car. It's more likely that he was paid to ferry Matias to his killer who then put the boy in the Peugeot's boot. Annette, I want you and Jake to get down to that cab office and question everyone; if the calls were diverted for a whole evening someone inside that office must have played along. Take Geoff Hamill's man with you, please."

He stared at each of them in turn as he ran through a list in his head. He'd just decided to wrap up when Kyle gave a cough.

"Is that from the cigs or did you want to say something, Kyle?"

"Both. I've been asking around a bit on the Albanian question and I have a lead on a possible Belfast cell."

"Go on."

"There's a club called The Pit in the city centre that's got Intelligence's radar twitching. Mostly for drugs, but there's some word of trafficking as well. Girls are being brought into one of the smaller ports in the south and then distributed across the brothels there and up here. European girls mostly, and some Thai, but the word is the traffickers are Albanian, so I thought-"

Craig nodded. "OK. See what Karl Rimmins has heard about the club on the drugs side, and check the trafficking angle with Aidan Hughes in Vice. There might be something here, but let me know before you try to take it any further."

Spence nodded but Liam didn't trust spooks.

"Right, you all know what you're doing." Craig stood up. "Liam, with me." He turned to Ash. "I'll need an update on Miskimmon in five, please."

They entered Craig's office and he signalled Liam to close the door, bringing him up to date on what Davy had found. Liam gave a slow whistle.

"So there was another bloke at Andy's."

Craig couldn't believe his ears. "Now *you're* saying you thought Andy had killed her? You gave me an earful when you thought I did."

Liam shrugged. "I didn't really believe he did, but it's nice to see it disproved."

Craig fell into his chair. "Except it hasn't been yet. I need you to put someone you trust on door-to-door at that apartment block. We need to rule out that this man wasn't just visiting someone on the same floor that night. Davy can give you some photos to show around."

Liam snorted. "And who exactly do we trust with this information? Given that no-one's supposed to know that Andy's up shit creek."

It was a good point. Only a handful of them knew that Andy was in a cell. Craig thought for a moment and then smiled.

"Jack can do it. He needs to get out of the station more."

"Oh aye, and who's going to cover High Street while he's off swanning around?"

Another good point. Liam's score was mounting up.

"And before you say it, don't even think about me. I've got Rey to talk to."

He actually hadn't been thinking about Liam. There was another big man far better suited to the job.

****

St Mary's Trust. 3 p.m.

Where Rory McCrae had been raised they'd had a saying, and it was one that he had always held true. Sympathy comes between shit and syphilis in the dictionary, so if you're hoping for any then you know exactly where to look. He'd seen nothing in forty years to alter his opinion and Zac Greer's bruised and disfigured face didn't change it now, so instead of giving the youth sympathy he decided to try for a laugh.

He sucked in his teeth like a plumber giving an estimate.

"Ye've had the cowboys in there, son. I'd ask for a refund if I were ye."

Greer opened his mouth to speak, closing it again quickly as he tasted the pain that it would cause. McCrae cut to the chase.

"One nod fer yes, two fer no. Did ye find me anything?"

Mercifully it was a yes. Two nods would have made Greer's head hurt even more. McCrae was forming his next question when he realised it required more than the two options they had, so he searched around for a piece of paper and thrust a pen into the boy's swollen right hand.

"Write it dyne then. And make it readable, mind. None of yer usual scrawl."

As Greer struggled to form the letters with a fist like grip, McCrae turned his attention to a passing nurse, deciding that either he'd got older or they'd got younger over the years, but either way they were a damn sight better to look at than the balloon headed youth in the bed. He smiled to himself in a way that had nothing to do with women but everything to do with revenge. His plan had worked perfectly; he'd got the boy prince the thumping he should have had years before, and got him out of his hair for a while. Plus, depending on what ended up on the paper, he might get Tommy off his back.

When the pen went down he seized the paper and read the scrawled words with a smile, then, with a swoop that retrieved his pen and smacked Greer on the jaw on the way past, he was out of the ward and on his way to the carpark before the youth had finished his scream of pain.

****

Annette left the cab office with a lot of information, but how much of it would prove useful was anyone's guess. When she arrived back at the ranch she headed straight for Craig's office, only to be stopped by Nicky on the way.

"Jake's not with you."

A more sarcastic woman than Annette would have seized on the obvious comment as an opportunity, but she replied politely instead.

"He's taken thirty minutes personal time."

She wondered whether Nicky was just curious or if it was her way of barricading Craig's door. A wave on said that it had been the former so she knocked and entered, standing in front of the detective's desk while he finished a call. When he'd hung up Craig turned his chair away from the window and saw who'd been waiting, hurriedly offering Annette a seat. She abandoned her early pregnancy objections to chivalry and accepted it gratefully.

"You should have just sat down, Annette. I'm sorry, I didn't realise that it was you."

But her mind was already on other things. She was certain she'd heard Craig say "Fine, Reggie. I'll see you when you get here." But she was as un-nosey as she was un-sarcastic so instead of asking she simply began to report.

"Jake and I went to the cab office, sir. It turns out that the office was manned that night by a Declan Delaney, the younger brother of the man who'd dropped the three lads at the club earlier that night. They were working together and now they've both done a bunk. Davy's searching for them."

Craig rubbed his chin, thinking. "Had they worked there long?"

She nodded. "Years. The older one brought the younger one in once he'd learned to drive."

He shook his head. "Rey probably thought they were loyal to the gang. But they weren't at the end, which says that someone's making it worthwhile to

311

betray The Rock."

Annette shrugged. "Money talks. As long as you've no qualms about helping spread drugs and girls, which the Delaneys obviously didn't. I wouldn't be surprised if Ryan Phelan, the kid who ended up having his stomach pumped, hadn't had his drink spiked by them as well. The hospital wouldn't have bothered checking his tox-screen if they'd just thought he was drunk."

Craig sighed. "I suppose it could have been worse. They could have killed all three of them." He drummed his fingers on the desk thoughtfully. "What did Purvis and Kennedy say about the car?"

"It belonged to Colin McAllister. Apparently he'd fallen in love with one years ago on holiday, so Mara imported it as a gift for his last birthday."

Craig sat forward. "So how come it wasn't registered?"

"She said she'd never got round to it because he could only ever drive it off-road around the farm. He lost his license for drink-driving last summer and he wasn't due to get it back till twenty-seventeen."

Craig slumped back in his chair again.

"Did anyone else drive the car?"

"Never. It was Colin's baby."

"Where did he keep it?"

"Garaged in an empty barn."

He nodded. "That no-one but he visited. Whoever stole the Peugeot took the risk of its theft being noticed by McAllister the day before he died, unless..."

"They knew his routine. They checked the work rota at the farm when they did his air tank."

He shook his head. "They knew it before then. They'd read the kitchen calendar; it shows the work allocation months ahead. That's how they knew when McAllister would next be at the slurry pit, and that he'd be too busy on the Wednesday to miss his car." He stood up. "Where's Mitchell Purvis?"

Annette was struggling to keep up. "Why? He's-"

"We need to ask him how if they'd had any visitors they didn't know at the farm recently. Casual labour, deliveries, someone asking directions; anything.

Someone read the calendar and timed the killing of McAllister accordingly, then they stole the car and they or someone else used it in the killing of Matias Rey."

"We've already checked the farm workers, but..."

She pulled out her mobile and pressed dial. In seconds Mitchell Purvis' voice was rumbling down the line. Craig waited until she'd hung up before he spoke.

"Well?"

She sighed heavily. "They had a visitor a few days before the killing. He didn't think to mention it to us before because the man was barely there ten minutes."

"He left him in the staff kitchen, didn't he?"

She nodded. "The man was asking directions to Tassagh, a nearby townland, and Purvis went to the hall table to fetch a map. It would only have taken him seconds to check the calendar."

Craig nodded. "That was all he needed. He came back on the Tuesday, sabotaged the air tank and stole the Peugeot, using it in Rey's killing early Wednesday morning. By seven a.m. the next day McAllister was dead as well."

Annette gawped at him. "My God, they planned this perfectly."

He smiled at her. "Let's hope not. The day a killer plans the perfect murder we'll all be out of a job." He noticing how tired she looked suddenly and decided to give the job he'd been just about to allocate her to uniform. "Right, let's get Purvis in to do a sketch. It's a faint hope but you never know."

She made to rise but he waved her back down. "Jake can organise it when he's back. Where's he gone, anyway?

"To do something, that was all he said."

His curiosity was piqued. "OK, if you could just call Purvis and send a car to bring him here, then when Jake gets back they can work with the sketch artist." His voice softened. "Stay in the office for the rest of the day, Annette. You look tired."

She didn't argue so he went on.

"If you want to take your maternity leave early that's fine."

She nodded. "I'll have a think about it if that's OK? I'm more tired than I thought I would be by now."

"No problem. We have Kyle." He popped his head out the door and had a look around. Kyle was nowhere to be seen again. "Correction. We have Kyle when he deigns to appear. He still thinks he's in Intelligence, I'm afraid, with all that that entails."

She smiled and stood up to leave. "Don't worry, I'm sure he's doing something useful, and when I'm not here, he'll have to toe the line."

He wasn't convinced.

When Annette had gone he returned to what he'd been doing before she'd arrived. Reggie had agreed to break his holiday to do the door-to-door at Andy's apartment block and had been sworn to secrecy. He smiled to himself; the sergeant had jumped at the offer, but he wondered what Mrs Boyd had made of her husband's announcement that he had to go into work when she'd had an afternoon of odd jobs laid out for him. Her vengeance would probably see his dinner in the dog that night.

He had two other things to do. One was meeting with Ash; their earlier planned five minutes had got shunted by calls. The second thing on his list was at best a punt, but it was niggling at him and when something niggled at him there was only one way to sort it out.

He scribbled a few words on a sticky and went out to give it to Davy, stilling his coming questions with a look.

"Whatever you get is for my eyes only, Davy. Maybe some of your overseas contacts will come through."

The analyst nodded and Craig motioned Ash to come into his room, making them both coffees before sitting down.

"OK. What's happening on the search for Miskimmon's laptop?"

Ash rubbed his chin and for the first time Craig noticed a few stray hairs.

"Growing a beard?"

Ash nodded. "The hipster look is in. But I only need to shave once a week normally so I think it'll take me a while. I thought I might dye them green as encouragement."

Craig rolled his eyes and returned to the matter in hand. "So?"

Ash screwed up his face. "Maybe... Miskimmon's IP address isn't showing up on any traces."

Craig's stare said 'so?'

"He may have built the computer himself."

"How easy is that?"

Ash smiled pityingly. "If you mean could *you* do it, then no, it takes a lot of skill. But most IT people could."

Craig let the cheek pass. They were in geek land and he didn't have an A to Z. His next question was asked hoping to be contradicted.

"I suppose that means we'll never trace it?"

Ash took his life in his hands and grinned.

"Not so. There are two ways we might find it. One, a computer's IP address comes from its operating system, that's like Microsoft and Mac. He'll have to have purchased that from somewhere." He thought again. "Well, not necessarily I suppose. It could have been pirated-"

Craig made a hurry-up motion with his hand. "So what's the second way?"

Ash sniffed at being cut short. A genius was never recognised in his own land.

"The second way is for me to try to start the computer remotely. If the computer hasn't been destroyed and it's near a wireless hotspot then we might be able to trace its Wi-Fi signal, even if it's turned off. I can even turn on its webcam to see what sort of room it's in."

Craig gawped at him. "You can do that?"

"I'm a hacker. I can do lots of stuff."

Craig didn't know whether to be scared or not. "OK. Try both. We need to find this thing quickly."

He stood up, waiting for the analyst to do the same. But Ash didn't move, looking less confident suddenly.

"It might not be quite as easy as I just made it sound. I might need Davy's help for a while."

Craig motioned him to leave. "Whatever. Just don't hold him back on anything big."

As Ash left he smiled to himself. Partly at Craig being so obviously out of his depth - bosses needed to be flummoxed now and then - and partly at the fact that he got paid to do what other people got arrested for and what other job would allow that?

Chapter Fifteen

Monday. 3.30 p.m.

Liam drove into the C.C.U.'s garage wondering what to have for his belated lunch, as far as he was concerned his most important decision of the day. He'd just left Xavier Rey's house after giving the usual lecture about not interfering with police investigations, and warning him that he was being watched and any future attempts to beat information out of hapless low-lives, no matter how bad they were, would see him spending a night in jail.

As he pulled into a free parking space his mobile beeped with a message. He groaned as he read what it was about. As he pushed through the squad-room's double doors ten floors up he tannoyed the information to the world.

"One of McCrae's men's in St Mary's."

Annette shook her head tiredly. "Say it a bit louder. I think they missed it in the pub."

He ignored her and turned to see Craig hovering by Davy's desk, doing the senior officer's equivalent of hopping from foot to foot. It looked like a soft shoe shuffle, a fact that Liam didn't fail to point out.

"Danni wants me to learn that."

Craig turned round. "What?"

"Dancing. She wants me to do the ballroom classes at our church."

Craig was saved any further discussion by Davy handing him a note. The speed with which he seized it told his deputy that something was up. Liam sidled over.

"Fancy some grub?"

It was a timely reminder so Craig led the way across Pilot Street to The James. Thirty minutes later they were fed and watered and Liam began his intended interrogation by first offering up a few facts.

"OK. So Rey's warned off and under surveillance, Templepatrick Police said they'll keep an eye on

Tommy if they have time, but they're fairly stretched with a spate of burglaries. Oh, and one of McCrae's men's in St Mary's with a bad hiding."

Craig narrowed his eyes. "You can bet that Tommy's involved in that somehow."

Liam leaned in. "No doubt, but you've more important fish to fry, haven't you? I saw the way you grabbed that note from the lad."

Craig wondered at what point the engaged twenty-eight-year-old Davy would cease to be a lad in Liam's book and changed the subject. "I've put Reggie on Andy's door-to-door. I don't think his wife was pleased. She had a list of chores for him to do."

"Don't change the subject. What was Davy's note about?"

Craig's response was to set the piece of paper face down on the dark wood table. "Before I tell you, I need to tell you a few other things."

Liam sat back and rested his folded arms on his diminished paunch. "You've just been made a Chief Super."

Craig's jaw dropped. "How the hell-"

"Did I know that? Danni knows Donna, the C.C.'s P.A." He tapped the side of his nose and adopted a bad French accent. "I noze everyzing."

Craig laughed. "I see the holiday French classes failed."

But Liam was uninsultable. "Was that what Flanagan wanted to see you about the other night? And what does it mean for us?"

"Yes. And what do you mean by us? You and me us? In which case I promise I'll still love you."

Liam shoved his elbow off the table but Craig carried on without missing a beat.

"Or us, as in the Murder Squad?"

"The squad. Are you leaving for pastures new?"

Craig attempted a simper. "Would you miss me?"

"Don't *ever* do that again, unless you want a thump. So what's happening?"

Craig puffed out his cheeks. "What's happening is that I haven't accepted it."

"Yet. But you will. Anyway, why haven't you? It's more money."

"Strangely money's not everything in this world."

Liam gave a sceptical snort. "It is when you have kids to feed. My two would eat the dog if it didn't run away. I don't know where they get their appetites from."

Craig let the obvious jibe pass and continued. "Taking the promotion is conditional on me supervising another section and I've enough bloody work to do."

Liam was puzzled. Aidan Hughes ran Vice and Geoff Hamill ran Gangs, with Terry Harrison in oversight. And the Drugs and Fraud Squads were under D.C.S. Devon Murray. It didn't leave much to supervise. Then he realised.

"He wants you to run the spook squad!"

Craig nodded glumly. Intelligence was a poisoned chalice, with staff who coveted their roles as the keepers of secrets jealously, and a few who sailed far too close to the edge. He didn't have much time for Machiavellian practices, not even when they were on the side of the law.

"It's part of every Super's job to supervise and I've been lucky to get away with only the murder squads up to now. But both of our last big cases touched on Intelligence in some way, so the Chief thought it would be a good fit."

Liam chuckled. "That means you'll have the darling Director Richie and Roy Barrett to cope with, not to mention a hundred Kyles."

Craig rolled his eyes. "Don't remind me, especially after what Kyle told us. That's partly why I'm hesitating."

"What's the other reason?"

Craig stared into his cooling espresso, not answering.

"Don't tell me. It's the wumman."

The way he said it made them both laugh.

"Katy *has* to be a consideration. We see little enough of each other as it is, with my job and her on

319

call, and-"

"That'd all stop if you got married." The veteran cop adopted a martyred expression. "Then you couldn't *avoid* seeing her every night." It was punctuated with a sigh.

Craig reared back in his seat. "Now, hang on! No-one's talking about marriage. We're not even seeing each other at the-"

Liam dismissed his objections unsympathetically. "And whose fault is that? You need to talk some sense-"

Craig cut him off. "No. She's not ready."

"Oh, good God, man. Who ever is? If you're waiting for a romance to work by itself then you'll be in your grave before it does."

"Where did that bit of wisdom come from?"

"My mother, but she was right. You two are an omnishambles."

Craig arched an eyebrow at the trendy word. "Thanks for the relationship counselling but that's quite enough." His tone said that he meant it. He changed the subject. "If I took the D.C.S. post you might have to pick up the slack on some of our cases."

"Ach, away with you. How many intelligence emergencies do you think they get? And if you have the right director in place you'll only have to supervise."

Craig's face was grim. "That's the problem. I'm not sure Susan Richie is someone I can trust."

"OK, then. Get rid of her and put someone you *can* trust in the job."

Suddenly Craig had an idea; perhaps he could leverage a change in director as his deal breaker to take on the Intelligence role. He leapt to his feet, suddenly keen to leave. As he moved Liam grabbed the note out from under his hand, his eyes widening as he read.

"What the hell's this?"

"Information I was waiting for from Davy. I think we might just have caught a break."

****

Stranmillis Embankment, Belfast.

Natalie tutted loudly at the sound of her doorbell, partly because she was tired and sore and didn't relish any interruptions, and partly because John had set the tune to a noise generated by one of his equations and it sounded like a cat being killed. As she hobbled towards the half glass entrance her mood shifted from annoyance to astonishment at the sight of the huge bouquet filling her view. She opened the door, just about to forgive her errant husband when she recognised the deliverer's shoes.

"Katy?"

The bouquet bobbed up and down.

"Are those for me?"

Another bob. Natalie grabbed the flowers and hobbled away, still talking.

"Well, unless you intend to just stand there all day, I suppose that you'd better come in. I'm presuming these flowers are for me, as a grovel. Well, grovel accepted, as long as you make the tea."

Katy heaved a sigh of relief. "I'm so sorry, Nat. If you hadn't been trying to help me none of-"

Natalie waved her free hand. "Yes, yes, and if we'd never left the caves, blah, blah, blah. It's just life, so don't worry about it."

She entered the kitchen and plonked herself on a stool, stifling a laugh. "That was some exit from the ED, by the way. Ever thought of taking up sprinting?"

Katy boiled the kettle, wearing a rueful smile. "Did I look really stupid?"

Natalie placed her bandaged arm in full sight. "What I could see of it through my drug addled haze. John enjoyed it though."

Katy carried over a tray and made the tea, before summoning the nerve to ask. "Did Marc say anything?"

Natalie grabbed a biscuit. "Not much. I think he was just shocked that you could move so fast." After a gulp of tea she fixed her friend with a serious look. "Look. You two need to grow up. You're trying to prove that you can cope with an event that is less likely to happen again than me going to the moon, and Marc's intent on depleting the Dutch flower fields rather than force you to talk face-to-face." She swallowed the biscuit and took another, biting into it before reiterating. "Grow the hell up."

Katy could feel her temper rising, but it only manifested as flushed cheeks because she knew that her friend was right. Instead she turned her ire on the person who wasn't there.

"If Marc really wanted me to come back he would make me."

Natalie nearly choked. "Did you really just say that? How the hell could he *make* you?" She set down her mug, warming to her theme. "You'd actually chuck away a century of feminism in favour of him grabbing you by the hair and dragging you into his cave?"

Katy's flush turned dark red. "That wasn't what I meant-"

But Natalie wasn't letting her off the hook. "That's exactly what you meant, madam." She started laughing. "Just wait till I tell John."

Katy's blue eyes widened. "You wouldn't!"

"I certainly would, unless you tell me exactly what you expect Marc to do. The poor sod has sent you flowers and half a stationer's shop in the past month, and you've ignored all of it."

"I wasn't ignoring it. I was in rehab!"

Natalie scoffed. "And that stops you from picking up the phone?" Her voice softened, but only slightly. "Look, Katy, you're my friend, but I would be wrong if I didn't tell you this was getting ridiculous. The man loves you and you've punished him long enough for what some psycho did to you."

"I wasn't punishing-"

"You were. That's exactly what you've been doing and you know it. Well, enough's enough. Either take Marc back or cut him loose for good." She paused meaningfully. "But if you do, don't complain to me when he meets someone else."

Katy went from red to white in seconds. "Has he? Has he met someone? You have to tell me."

Natalie gave a knowing smile, knowing that jealousy often worked where pleading and logic failed.

"Well..."

When Katy's pallor had turned sufficiently grey she reckoned that she'd played her enough.

"Not that I know. *So far*. But you know fine well there are women who fancy him. Jacelyn in dermatology fluttered like a demented moth every time he came to visit you, and then there's-"

Katy shook her head. "That's enough, Nat. I get the message." She gripped her mug so tightly that Natalie thought that it would break. "I haven't been punishing Marc." She ignored the surgeon's raised eyebrow. "Or at least not consciously. I just honestly don't know if I'm brave enough to be with him." Her voice began to break. "It's not just what one of his criminals might do to me; it's what they could do to him too. I never know if he's going to be killed on a case-"

Natalie's eyes widened. "You think I don't know how that feels? John was shot. Remember?"

Katy gave her an apologetic look. "I'm sorry. You're right. It's anyone concerned with criminal justice that's vulnerable-"

Natalie cut in again. "How do you think *they* feel, Katy, about what *we* do? Lots of doctors get assaulted by patients, plus we're exposed to illness every day. We could be assaulted, or catch something, maybe even bring it home to them. But John's never asked me not to do my job. Has Marc asked you?"

The physician shook her head, chastened.

"OK, look. Nobody's denying that you had a bad scare. But it wasn't Marc's fault and the odds of it happening again are miniscule. You don't have to be brave enough to jump out of airplanes or race cars; you just have to decide if you love him enough to take the risks that come with him."

Katy nodded silently and rose to leave. She had a life changing decision to make and she had to make it alone.

****

The C.C.U. 4 p.m.

After an hour of frustrated tapping Ash rode his wheelie chair over to Davy's desk, hovering by his left elbow until the senior analyst stopped what he was doing with a sigh.

"What do you w...want?"

"How do you know I want something?"

"Because you never sit that close to anyone unless it's a blonde in a bar." He held his hand out for the paper he'd seen Ash scribble on a minute before.

Ash was tempted to deny that he wanted anything, just to maintain the macho image that no-one but he actually believed he had, but the P.P.S. had them on a deadline so he swallowed his pride and handed over the note. Davy scanned the paper, his earlier disinterest changing to curiosity.

"This might w...work."

Ash leaned forward eagerly. "Which one? Tracing the purchase or using the Wi-Fi?"

"The second." Davy lifted a pen and a sheet of A4, making some scribbles of his own before speaking again. "OK, let's assume Miskimmon would have had all his computers connected."

Ash's brown eyes widened. Why hadn't he thought of that? "You mean on a tailored LAN."

"Either a local area network or a w...wide one." As Davy said it he shook his head. "Nope, not wide, a WAN's normally used by organisations."

The police had had their own wide area network for years.

"OK, so say Miskimmon's got his own LAN and all his computers connect to it. LANs can stretch twenty metres indoors or further in the open air, but you need a Wi-Fi hotspot-" Just then something else occurred to him. "Have you traced the IP address yet?"

"Ashley did. To Belfast. She couldn't narrow it further than that and now we can't find it at all."

"W...When was that?"

324

"End of June. Miskimmon must have stopped using that computer then."

"Or found a way to mask it." Davy's face brightened. "Maybe it belongs to one of the three computers we found at his place near Moygashel."

Ash's face fell. "If it does then we're screwed. Des says the firewalls on those will wipe everything if they're even turned on; there's not even time to enter a password. They tried with one and it fried instantly."

Davy shrugged. "We need to rule them out at least. Des can use an external signal to check their IP addresses. Give him a call and get that moving."

Ash kicked himself for not thinking of it and did as he was asked. When he'd wheeled himself back to Davy's desk the discussion started again.

"OK, so until Des says different let's s...say the IP address Ashley found belongs to a fourth computer we haven't discovered yet."

Ash shot him a quizzical look. "Why didn't Miskimmon cover his tracks better? Letting Ashley spot the IP has to be a trick. Or this computer will turn out to be firewalled as well."

Davy shrugged. "He was just s...starting out then so maybe he got careless. Or maybe he's just so arrogant he didn't think we'd ever find out about that one. Let's face it, until Ashley came though w...we hadn't and Miskimmon could never have predicted a Canadian working with us."

He doubted himself immediately and started to mentally retrace his steps, tapping a pen against his teeth for so long that Ash wanted to rip it from his hand. Finally Davy shook his head.

"Nope. I think we're OK. If there's another computer it *can't* be firewalled, or if it is it'll be in a much weaker form. Miskimmon would never risk it."

Ash looked confused so he elaborated.

"Miskimmon was prepared to destroy the hard drives on the three computers we found, with the degaussing loop at his Moygashel place. Correct?"

"OK."

"And he also knew that even if we got the

325

computers out of there unscathed, as soon as we turned them on they would be fried by the high level protection he'd installed."

"OK. So?"

Davy gave an exasperated sigh and then tried another tack. "OK. Let's say that you're a super hacker."

"I am."

Davy rolled his eyes. "Modest, aren't we. Let's say you're Miskimmon and you're a super hacker then, and you've found a hack that can control an operating system algorithm that's used in drones, businesses and traffic s...systems all over the world."

Ash was beginning to see where he was going.

"Then you get caught, but you've made s...sure that any computers the police find are impregnable so that you go to prison for a much lesser crime, like visa fraud. So, how long do you get?"

Ash shrugged. "Five years, maybe? But it might be in a South American Jail-"

"It doesn't matter where it is. It's doable and in a few years you'll be out. But the police have all your files on the computers and even though they can't access it they'll never give them back. Files that you've probably spent years w...working on. Data that has a black market value of millions to the right person-"

Ash's jaw dropped. "I'd never lose it. I'd have a backup copy, maybe two."

Davy nodded. "Good. But on what? A memory stick or CD you've hidden somewhere?"

Ash shook his head. "The information could degrade and devices change so much that by the time you got out of prison it might be unreadable. I'd store it on another computer and hide it."

Davy smiled. "Now we're getting somewhere. So, OK, your data is on this other computer you've hidden but you want it back to s...sell. Right, next point. If all your computers are linked on a LAN then you can wake one computer up from any other quite s...safely-"

Ash interrupted. "That explains the firewalls on the three we found being so strong. I bet Miskimmon

326

never turned them on directly; he used a wake up LAN from the fourth computer that we haven't found."

Davy's smile became a grin. "Exactly. But if he'd put high level protection on the fourth, so high that he didn't even have time to put in a password, like with the computers Des has, then it would fry as s...soon as he tried to switch it on. So he must just have put lower level, password protection on the fourth computer, or even none at all. A LAN where one of the computers is accessible is the only thing that makes sense-"

Ash cut in. "And it has to be a computer, the phones they found in Moygashel wouldn't have enough memory to store all his stuff." He punched the air. "The labs can easily crack password protection so all we have to do is find the other laptop!"

"Yep!" After a moment of excitement Davy frowned. "Now, how to do it..."

Ash gave a smug smile. "I thought you'd have worked that out as well."

The senior analyst rolled his eyes. "Go on then. Amaze me."

Ash obliged eagerly. "You said it yourself. A LAN has a certain radius and needs a Wi-Fi signal." He stood up, heading for the door. "I'll tell you the rest when I get back from the lab."

****

McMorrow's Bar. 5 p.m.

Tommy turned his cut-glass whisky tumbler towards the only light in the dusty bar; admiring the prismed rainbow it cast on the wall as he waited for Michael Hanratty to appear. He'd positioned himself perfectly in the dark space. Facing the bar, back to the wall and between two doors; giving him a one eighty scan of everyone who came and left, and any man getting ready to shoot. It was a technique that he'd perfected in the bad old days when more than one bullet had had his name written on its tip.

As the clock struck five he glanced at Billy Ross.

He was leaning on the mahogany bar reading the paper, ringing his picks for the next day's racing with the pencil he kept wedged behind his ear. Tommy's throaty croak cut through the quiet.

"He's late. If he's nat here in ten minutes he can whistle fer his info."

Ross didn't look up. "He'll be here." He settled back to his odds without another word.

Five impatient minutes later the door to Tommy's right opened and the barman straightened up and poured a Jameson's, both the entrant and the alcohol appearing at Hill's table within seconds.

"Yer late, Hanratty. I wus leavin'."

The Rock's general shrugged. "So then you wouldn't have got paid and I wouldn't have my information, and why would we both want to lose?" He downed his whisky in one and tapped for another. "What have you got for me?"

Tommy normally expected to be wooed but he decided against dragging things out this time; there was only so long the cops would be fooled by a tag around a Templepatrick table leg that didn't move an inch.

"Money first."

Hanratty slid a slip of paper across and sipped at his second drink. Tommy peered at the note, eschewing his spectacles in a show of hard cool.

"What the fuck's this? We said cash."

"And my information is that the police are watching you like a hawk, so I opened an account down south for you and paid in the money in euros. You can draw it out anywhere in the world."

Tommy wasn't sure what to do. Punch Hanratty and walk. Punch him, take the paper and walk, or trust a paddy that the money was where he said it was. Ross decided to intervene.

"It's how I get paid, Tommy and I've never had an issue. The lads up here know nothing about it so you don't get asked questions and you don't pay tax." Just then he noticed the number on the paper. "Bloody hell! That's a tidy sum."

Tommy grabbed the slip and reared up in his face. "Mind yer own, bizness, Ross. I huvn't forgit that yer working for a Taig."

The Dubliner cut in. "I can assure you the money is there and safe, Mr Hill. Who knows, you may work for us again in the future and we can add to it." *That's if I don't sort you out first.* "Now. Can we get on with it, please? I have a driver outside waiting to take me home."

Tommy muttered under his breath for long enough to make his displeasure known then he straightened up and stared Hanratty in the eye.

"The Albanians have set up a network down yer way. They're bringing in girls and drugs through yer ports and spreading them all over the place." He shot him a look of disgust. "They're bringin' the filth up here as well nye. Ye Irish lat can kill yersel's if ye like but we dun't want none of that stuff."

The gang boss interrupted smoothly. "Your new found moral stance does you credit, Mr Hill, but as you know, I don't deal in either item. These men are taking over my patches and killing my men as they do. They're enemies to both of us-"

Tommy cut in. "Patches? Ye only told me about Belfast."

"Need to know. But yes, they've killed two of my other men in Armagh. But that's not what I came here to talk about. What more do you know about Belfast?"

"The leader's name. Abaz Goga or some crap like that. Came in last December and he knows we've been asking questions. Had one of my mate's men beat up."

Hanratty tutted. "Most unfortunate. It would seem to be in everyone's interest to get rid of this group."

Tommy looked sceptical. "Good luck with that. They've cells all over ar country and yers as well. The cells report straight to some big chief, but only they know who he is."

"Don't worry about that. We'll be paying Mr Goga a visit and I'm sure that he'll be happy to talk. Do you have anything on his whereabouts?"

Tommy shrugged. "I know he beat up ar lad in

329

some shithole called The Pit." He gave a croaky laugh. "Well named if it's anythin' like the clubs ye see on TV."

Hanratty nodded then he stood up abruptly and reached out his hand to shake. "It's been good doing business with you, Mr Hill." The hand was left hanging while Tommy kept sipping his drink. The gang leader was just about to drop his when Billy Ross shot the old paramilitary a warning look. It said you'd better not mess with this man, Tommy, or he'll squash you like a bug.

Tommy touched Hanratty's hand fleetingly and the southerner knew that as soon as he'd gone Tommy would be scrubbing his own hard. It meant nothing to him; he'd met bigotry before and he didn't judge men on their good manners. Hill had proved useful so, ignorant bigot or not, he would stay in one piece till he decided whether to use him again or not.

****

The C.C.U. 5 p.m.

Ash walked back onto the floor at the same time as Kyle, and just as Craig was exiting. The detective stopped for a moment.

"Nice of you to join us, Kyle. Ash, I'm going out for half-an-hour and I'll need an update when I get back."

The analyst smiled, knowing that what he had to report would be worth his time. As Craig continued on his way Jake appeared and followed him to the lift.

"Could I have a word, sir?"

"Can it wait an hour, Jake? I have a meeting. But as soon as I get back. I promise."

The sergeant nodded and as Craig finally entered the lift Ash rushed across to Davy, his bag still over his shoulder.

"That IP address doesn't belong to any of Miskimmon's devices. You were right; Des was able to suss it out."

Davy looked up from his searches on Abaz Goga,

330

glad of the respite. The Albanian's life before he'd entered Ireland illegally said that he wasn't someone they would ever have taken as a citizen.

"That means there's another computer out there. Now w...we just have to find it."

Ash opened his bag and brought out a laptop.

"Is that one of Miskimmon's-"

"Yep. Des said I could borrow it for a few hours."

Davy looked confused. "To do what w...with? You can't turn it on, you'll fry it!"

"Don't panic. I just need its Wi-Fi signal. Des lent me the reader they use to detect them."

Davy caught on. "You're going to use its signal to help find the missing one."

Ash grinned. "That's the plan. I'm banking that if they're close enough I can find the missing one with Bluetooth, then I can try a wake-up LAN from it to start this one up. Either way we should get a look at Miskimmon's files."

****

The Police Intelligence Section. Malone Road.

Susan Richie had eyes that had seen too much wine and skin that had felt more than enough heat. Both had aged her beyond her forty years, and contributed to her perpetually world-weary air, but the bulk of it came from the things she'd heard; things that Joe Public would find incredible even on the silver screen. Things that she and her team shielded them from.

She'd been puzzled when she'd seen Craig's name in her schedule and dismissed it as something to do with Kyle Spence's secondment, although why Craig couldn't have bothered Barrett with such trivia was beyond her. Still, he was easy on the eyes and ears, unlike some of the other men she'd met in the force. She was just picturing them together in a dark wine bar when her P.A. knocked on the door.

"Superintendent Craig is here, Ma'am."

She nodded him out, deciding to make Craig wait

331

for a while. He might be a Superintendent and her only a D.C.I. but she ruled this kingdom, something that he shouldn't forget. Her attempt at manipulation was short-circuited by the detective walking into the office and extending his hand.

"D.C.I. Richie. I hope it was OK to come in?"

Her eyes said 'well no, actually, it wasn't' and 'I'm going to kill that bloody P.A.', but her hand moved, first to shake his and then wave him to a seat. Craig cut straight to the chase.

"I'll tell you why I'm here, Chief Inspector. One, you've been in contact with a war criminal without reporting his whereabouts to the International Court at the Hague, and two, it looks like I'm your new boss."

The second was as big a surprise to him as it was to her, given that he'd only made up his mind to definitely take the promotion that moment, when he'd read the disdain in her eyes. He carried on.

"I'm now a D.C.S., and as such will be supervising both the Murder and Intelligence Sections, although of course the day to day work here will be led by the Director."

The Director; not *you*. It made her jerk upright as he went on.

"The appointment of that director will need to be discussed with the Chief Constable, but I can tell you now that it must be someone I can trust. So, can you tell me how long you've known of Jastreb's whereabouts and why he hasn't been reported to the Hague?"

Susan Richie's mouth opened and closed repeatedly as Craig sat back in his chair and waited patiently for her to speak. He would have had some sympathy with her shock if he hadn't read arrogance in every move since he'd walked in. When she finally found some words they sounded banal, even to her.

"I thought you were here about Inspector Spence."

"Clearly not."

He didn't embellish, hanging her out to dry instead. It went against his normal grain. He liked women, all women, and treating one harshly wasn't in his playbook. But war criminals changed all the rules. Richie tried again.

"We have many informants...that... sail close to the wind."

"I understand that, and using criminals as informants has been done before, but that doesn't apply to murderers in Jastreb's league."

She obfuscated defensively. "I can't report him because I never know where he is. He changes his number and location each time we speak."

"You've made absolutely no attempt to pin him down, have you? And if you have, then show me the evidence." He didn't wait for her to answer. "I'm putting you on notice, Chief Inspector. I expect Jastreb to be notified to the Hague and Interpol immediately, and I want all paperwork pertaining to him on my desk by the end of the day. I'll be informing the Chief Constable of this episode and next week we'll be sitting down to go through every case you're working on. Is that clear?"

Her only answer was a nod. Then he was gone, leaving her to contemplate just how much she would damage him if he attempted to move her aside.

****

Jake and Ash both rose the moment Craig walked back through the doors. He signalled Jake to join him in his office, leaving Ash with no option but to cover his suddenly vertical stance with a trip to the loo. Craig closed the office door behind them and waved Jake to a seat.

"What can I do for you?"

The sergeant stared at his feet. "I just wanted you to know that I'm appealing the P.P.S. decision about Aaron, sir."

Craig nodded, unsurprised. "Thank you for letting me know. To be honest I've been expecting you to say this for days." He sat down and leaned forward on the desk. "It's your right, of course, but do you mind me asking why?"

Jake's eyes widened indignantly. "Because he tried to kill me! And he drove all the way back from Derry to do it. In my mind that's premeditation."

"No doubt of that."

The younger man sat forward, warning to his theme angrily. "Now he's lied and convinced some bleeding heart psychiatrist that the balance of his mind was disturbed, just so he can get a lighter sentence. And I'm supposed to just take that lying down?" He sat back with a thud. "No way."

Craig kept his voice calm. "I totally understand your anger, Jake, but what's the end game here? Aaron gets sentenced to life for attempted murder? Will that make you feel better?"

Jake's fist slammed down on the desk. "YES. Yes. It'll make me feel a whole lot better. I hope he dies in prison. That would please me even more."

Craig nodded; knowing that now wasn't the time to try reason. "OK, Jake. Thank you for telling me. If Liam's outside could you send him in, please."

Liam's noisy appearance a minute later was almost a comfort. Craig poured two coffees as the D.C.I. made a frank observation.

"You look like someone's wrung you out too hard."

Craig pushed a mug across the desk. "Another one of your mother's?"

"Nah. That one I read in a book. Jake looked rough as well. What's happening?"

By the time Craig had brought him up to date on his visit to Intelligence and his conversation with Jake, Liam's eyes were like saucers.

"Bloody hell, boss. Not content with having Terry Harrison as an enemy, now you've got the ice queen! You must have a death wish. I wouldn't put it past her to have poison stashed somewhere."

Craig gave a very hollow laugh. "I don't suppose you fancy being the new Director of Intel, do you? I need someone in there that I can trust."

Liam shuddered noisily. "Not on your life. I'm a cop not a spook." He gestured towards the door. "Put Roy Barrett in charge. He's as sound as a pound and he's a D.C.I. as well, so you wouldn't have to pay him much more."

Craig thought for a moment. "That's not a bad idea. Roy's good, he knows the section, he..." He grabbed the phone suddenly. "Liam, you're a genius. I'll OK it with the C.C."

"Aye well, genius I may be, but before you dial the chief, what are we going to do about Jake?"

Craig was confused. "What about him?"

"Ach, don't tell me you haven't spotted what he's up to with this appeal."

"He wants Aaron to do more time."

Liam shook his head slowly. "Man, you might have brains to burn but you've less common sense than my kids this week. He's appealing it because he wants Aaron to get out on bail. Annette told me he nipped out to join a gym earlier."

"So? It's probably for his rehab."

Liam tutted. "Even Annette wouldn't believe that. My money's on him pumping himself up to take Aaron on, and only one of them is going to walk away from that fight."

If he was right they had a team member they needed to watch very closely.

****

When Craig's call to the C.C. was finished he spoke to Ash. Five minutes later Nicky was summoning everyone who wasn't already there for a snap briefing.

Craig cut to the chase.

"This is for information, not discussion, although I'll take some questions at the end."

A murmur went round the group but he stilled it with a hand.

"First. We now know for sure that the Rey, McAllister and Fox cases are linked, and the girl who was on the periphery of Rey's and Fox's murders has been found dead. Shot. Forensics are working on the bullet now."

Liam opened his mouth to speak but Craig shut it

again with a shake of his head.

"We're fairly certain that Mara McAllister and Mitchell Purvis had no involvement in her husband's killing, but we do know that the car used in Matias Rey's abduction was owned by Colin McAllister, so we think his killer stole it from the farm when he spiked his air tank. We're narrowing down the possible suspects." He turned to Liam. "Chase that please."

Just then Nicky placed a coffee in his hand. He took a quick sip and carried on.

"OK, we also know that two brothers, Gerry and Declan Delaney, who were employed by Xavier Rey at his cab firm, were involved in Matias' death; setting him up and later transporting him to his killer." He scanned the group with a warning stare. "On no account is that information to leave this room. The last thing we need is Xavier Rey on a witch hunt. We've already had to stop his men beating information out of half of Belfast." He turned to Jake. "Jake, Rey's men are at Stranmillis at the moment. Drop up and organise their release for around ten tonight."

Jake nodded, but it was plain he was confused. So were the others but Craig didn't have the time for explanations.

"OK. Kyle." He looked around until he spotted him sitting at the very edge of the group. "Our part-time attendee."

Liam mimicked cutting his throat as Craig carried on.

"OK, reluctant copper as Kyle is, he brought us a valuable piece of information that confirms something that Karl Rimmins first mentioned. An Albanian mobster, Abaz Goga has been in Ireland since last year. The EU savvy amongst you will know that Albania is not yet a member of the EU so Goga's illegal, and apparently he's not here alone. The word is that there are several-" He broke off and turned to the spook. "Cells was it, Kyle?"

Spence nodded.

"Several cells of Albanians dotted around Ireland, all being coordinated by a big boss. So far we have no idea who he is. So this is a second gang we're looking at, far more vicious than The Rock. They're smuggling in girls and drugs and distributing them everywhere." He suddenly realised he'd been standing and searched for somewhere to sit, perching on Nicky's desk. "This gang are killers, unlike Rey's lot. The Rock deals in fuel fraud, counterfeiting, gambling, smuggled cigarettes etcetera. Still crimes, but they don't kill. We believe that the Albanian gang sees them as a soft target and is trying to take over their patch and distribution routes. There's a lot of money to be made. That's why they killed Matias Rey, Calum Fox, who was probably involved in the gambling and counterfeiting side, and Colin McAllister, who we think was smuggling fuel on his farm. Having now taken out The Rock's main players they're going to try for its turf."

He paused and signalled Liam to summarise.

"Aye well, so the general of The Rock, whose name we don't know, is having his business taken over by the Albanian lot, headed up by another bloke we don't know, and that's what all the killing's been about."

Craig swallowed a mouthful of coffee and picked things up. "However, there's one big difference between the two gang leaders. The Rock's leader isn't known to anyone, not even Xavier Rey, whereas the Albanian's leader is known by the head of every cell, even though apparently he uses aliases. That knowledge makes him vulnerable and we're going to use it." He searched around for Annette. "Annette and Liam, I need to see you after this. First I want to cover one other thing."

He smiled over at Davy and Ash. "As most of you will know, Ronan Miskimmon and Eleanor Corneau will be charged with visa fraud unless we can prove they carried out the murders here using computer hacks. We have Miskimmon's computers but they're so well protected that even trying to turn them on will result in frying the hard drives and wipe all the files. Ash." The green haired analyst took a bow. "With Davy helping." Davy didn't even blink. "Has managed to locate information which might help us access those

337

files. If I try to explain how I'll only confuse everyone, but Jake, after you've dealt with Stranmillis I want you to accompany Ash to two locations that he'll give you after this."

It piqued everyone's curiosity.

"Take Rhonda with you, please. It'll be good experience."

He stopped talking and frowned, wondering if now was the time to mention his promotion. He decided that it wasn't and jumped off the desk, nodding at Kyle and beckoning him into his room. He deserved to know that he had a new boss before he heard it on the grapevine.

"Annette and Liam, I'll see you two next."

Once inside the detective turned to face his old roommate.

"Kyle, I think you should know that I've been given oversight of Intelligence."

Kyle's jaw dropped. "What about Susan?"

Craig's face was impassive. "She's being moved, but she doesn't know yet so I'd be grateful if you didn't say. Roy Barrett will be the new director and lead the unit day to day. I'll supervise in the same way I supervise the other murder teams." He swallowed, feeling boastful for even mentioning the next point. "I've been made up to D.C.S. and supervision is a compulsory part of the job."

Kyle grabbed the back of a chair and for a moment Craig thought he was going to pass out in shock. Then he murmured "Susan's going" and Craig realised that it wasn't shock he was seeing but relief. It made him curious.

"Was she that bad?"

"Could Pavarotti sing?"

Susan Richie obviously hadn't had the love of her troops.

Spence continued. "Roy's brilliant. He'll do the job well and he's as straight as they come." He paused before asking warily. "Where's she going to?"

Inside his head Craig answered 'jail, if I had my way' but outwardly his reply was. "No decision yet, as far as I know."

"She won't be happy without an empire to rule."

Craig shrugged. "It's not my job to make her happy." He turned to open the door. "Look, I just wanted you to know, but you must keep it to yourself until I've spoken to Susan and Roy. And only Liam knows about the D.C.S. post at the moment and I'd like it to stay that way."

Spence smiled. "You can trust me. I'm good at keeping secrets, remember." As he headed for the door he turned back. "About the Albanians. I've dug a bit further through my contacts and the word is that their big boss is based down south."

Craig sighed. "Damn. That could make him harder to find. OK, thanks for that. Call me directly with anything else you get."

As Kyle exited he beckoned in Liam and Annette and nodded them to take seats. He gazed at his inspector sympathetically.

"You look exhausted, Annette."

She went to demur then nodded instead. "I am."

Craig's reply was brisk. "OK, when this case is wrapped up I want you to take two weeks annual leave. You're owed far more than that."

She shook her head. "I was planning to take it all after the baby's born."

He smiled at her. "I'm not going to quibble if you take a couple of extra weeks then. God knows you're owed months for all the overtime you've put in."

She accepted gratefully.

"OK, this information can't leave the room." He sighed heavily and shook his head. "I think Magnus O'Shea is on the take."

Annette's eyes widened but Liam was unsurprised. He'd seen the note that Davy had handed Craig earlier that day. Annette opened her mouth to speak but Craig held up a hand.

"Let me tell you why, Annette. When you mentioned that O'Shea was unenthusiastic I initially put it down to his impending retirement, but when he was worse than useless over the girl and tank I began to wonder. We first suspected southern links when we heard the word knacker, then we had two deaths and a pipeline right on the border, so it wasn't a great surprise when Kyle told me just now that the Albanian gang boss is definitely based in the south. Yet O'Shea apparently knows nothing about anything."

He pulled Davy's note from his pocket and set it on the desk in front of her. "I suspected O'Shea might be on someone's payroll so I asked Davy to look into his accounts." She read as he went on. "His ordinary accounts show nothing extraordinary, but Davy dug deeper using his contacts abroad. This is what he's found so far and he hasn't even looked very hard."

Annette's jaw dropped. "There's a fortune there! He's been deliberately obstructing us. Trying to say he'd found nothing, when he'd probably I.D.ed the girl immediately."

Liam nodded wisely. "He's been on the take all right."

Craig shrugged. "We can only speculate how much O'Shea knows and doesn't know, but I want your assistance to find out."

Annette was furious. O'Shea had probably thought he could fool them because Jake was young and she was a woman. The patronising, arrogant... Craig interrupted her thoughts.

"Annette, as you've been dealing with O'Shea I want you to feed him a story. Tell him that you just thought you should give him an update, as he's the Gardaí liaison on the case. Say we've had a very important breakthrough but you can't say any more on the phone. When you meet say we've found that Albanians are involved in the killings. Name Goga and say we think he's the head of the Belfast cell and that there are more cells in the south. Say we're hoping to have the name of their overall boss very soon."

Liam looked at him quizzically. "*Is* he the head in Belfast?"

"Maybe. Anyway, Annette, tell O'Shea we're planning a sting on Goga tonight and once we have him he's bound to cough up the names of his boss, his contacts, anyone they've bought off-"

He was interrupted by a loud "Oooh" from Liam. "Nice one. When she mentions bought off she'll scare the shit out of O'Shea. We might get other bent copper's names as well."

Annette's face was glum. "If O'Shea has been paid off then it won't only have been to cover up the gang's activities and obstruct us. He'll have told them about everything we've done. They've been ahead of us all the way!"

Craig was pragmatic. "There's nothing we can do about that now. Feed O'Shea the information and say we're going to lift Goga from a Belfast club tonight."

Liam screwed up his face. "Why a club, boss?"

"Because clubs are where most drug dealing happens other than the street. We can use the club Kyle mentioned; The Pit, I think it's called. He says that's where the eastern European gangsters hang out. Check with Karl and Aidan on the chances of Goga being there. We'll get the information to O'Shea in person a couple of hours before the meet. If I'm right and he *is* dirty then he'll try to prevent us lifting Goga."

Liam was shaking his head. "If O'Shea's dirty, the first thing he'll do is call Goga and warn him we're on his tail."

Annette chipped in. "We could lift him?"

Craig's response was emphatic. "No. They have to meet face to face or we won't have anything."

Liam had a suggestion. "We could block O'Shea's phone so he can't warn Goga and has no option but to come to Belfast."

It was Annette who named the obstacles first. "He might have another line, or email. And there's no way the phone providers in the south will block O'Shea on our say so. It's a different country."

Craig was two steps ahead of her. "That's why I want you and Jake to meet O'Shea in Armagh. Once he's in the north we can get his mobiles and email locked down. We'll do Goga's phone and internet at the same time, in case O'Shea attempts contact."

Liam interjected. "What if he has another phone?"

Craig thought for a moment. "OK. O'Shea's the important one here. Annette, get Jake to slip a tracker and a signal blocker on his car. We'll just have to hope that even if he realises his mobiles aren't working and tries to call Goga from a payphone, the line he calls will be Goga's mobile and we'll have that blocked as well. It's the best we can do on short notice. Annette, liaise with Davy on whatever you need. Liam, check with Aidan and Karl on Goga's haunts before Annette meets O'Shea. Hopefully he uses The Pit like Kyle thinks, if not we'll name somewhere else to meet."

Liam's eyebrows shot up. "You don't want much, do you?"

Craig didn't answer. "Also, Kyle might have some useful thoughts if you get stuck."

Annette was still processing everything. Finally she nodded and stood up. "What time are you aiming for the meet?"

"Say eleven tonight?"

"OK. That means we need O'Shea in Armagh no later than nine-thirty, assuming he'll head straight there once we set the bait. Would you mind if I nipped home to check on the kids before we leave, sir?"

"Of course not. Go now. Jake will be busy for a while anyway."

He waved her out and signalled Liam to follow him off the floor.

"Where are we going?"

Craig stepped into the lift. "Reggie texted me to say he's finished his door-to-door and could we meet him at High Street."

"Fair enough." He thought for a moment. "Do *you* have any ideas how to get Goga to the club tonight?"

Craig shook his head cheerfully. "Not a one, but I believe in you implicitly."

Chapter Sixteen

The Lisburn Road, Belfast. 6 p.m.

"What exactly are we doing here, Ash?"

Jake reversed his Golf into a tiny space in the terraced street, making Rhonda smile. She was hopeless at parking and admired anyone who wasn't, but woe betide the person who insinuated it was because of her sex. Her feminist principles lay in very shallow repose, ready to jump up and bite any chauvinist on the ass.

Ash glanced out the window at where they were before he answered.

"We're here because that..." He pointed at a derelict shop. "...is one of two locations in Northern Ireland known to be used by Ronan Miskimmon. I don't think this will be the one we want but it's closest so we should rule it out first."

It didn't enlighten them much but Jake opened the door to get out, only to be summoned back.

"OK, briefly. An IP address was found last year by a Canadian Hacker, on some drone incidents very similar to ours. They happened before ours started and we think Miskimmon might have been rehearsing then and got careless, so he didn't hide his IP address as well. The geolocation on it said Belfast, Northern Ireland, and this is the only location we have for Miskimmon in Belfast."

Jake was following so far. "What if the computer's moved since then? Can't they check its location today?"

"We've tried but the signal's unreadable. This is all we have to go on."

"OK, so you want to search that shop for a computer?"

Rhonda blanched at the thought of her new jacket getting ruined in the dirt, but Ash's next words reassured her.

"Well...yes, but not in the way you mean search."

The analyst clambered out of the car with the

others following, preparing to be surprised. Jake gestured towards the shop.

"OK, shoot."

Ash warmed to his theme. "OK, Davy and I think Miskimmon's computers are all linked in what's called a LAN-"

Rhonda jumped in. "Local area network. We did those in computing A-level."

Ash nodded. "Exactly. We have the IP addresses of the three computers the boss retrieved from Miskimmon's place in Moygashel but none of them have the IP we're looking for. We can't even turn those on because Miskimmon's got them so protected, but we know they're still emitting signals so..." He pointed to his bag "We're hoping the signal from one of them will help us detect the fourth computer on the LAN when it's nearby."

Jake was sceptical. "How near?"

"Twenty metres indoors and more than that outdoors, providing there's a Wi-Fi hotspot."

The detective swept his hand in an arc. "We're in the Golden Mile, Ash. There'll be more Wi-Fi hotspots round here than you can shake a stick at."

The Lisburn and Malone Roads were known as Belfast's Golden Mile because of their conspicuous wealth.

"So go on. Do your stuff."

Ash knew a Doubting Thomas when he saw one and it made him determined to prove Jake wrong. When they reached the shop door he handed Rhonda the laptop bag and turned on the Bluetooth device Des had given him.

"Stand in the doorway please, Rhonda."

She did as she was asked, watching in fascination as the Bluetooth detected four Wi-Fi hotspots immediately.

Ash showed the detector to the sergeant. "These four are within a few feet of us." He walked back to the car and shouted across. "This is about twenty metres and I've got another three." He turned on his smart-pad and mined each of the signals in turn, but the only device he recognised was the laptop Rhonda was holding in the bag.

He tried closer to the shop's door, and one final time inside, Rhonda handing Jake the bag but declining to go in. Finally Ash shook his head in defeat and signalled their return to the car. Once inside again he explained.

"I detected the laptop we brought with us, but there's no other computer connected to its LAN around here. We need to go to Moygashel."

As Jake drove towards the M1, Ash knew it was their last chance to put Ronan Miskimmon away for life.

****

High Street Station. 6.30 p.m.

The interview room looked like a briefing room after a particularly long session, with cups of coffee and biscuits everywhere and five men in their shirt sleeves, four with their ties hanging loose. Craig noted with amusement that Reggie wore a tie even when on holiday. It was something that his father had always done but there were two decades between the men. A tieless Andy sat in the middle of the group; a hobbit in the land of giants, minus the hairy feet. A hobbit in a big fat mess.

Reggie took a gulp of his tea and made a face. "This is cold, Jack."

Harris' response was barely audible.

Liam perked up. "What did he say?"

Craig yawned before he answered; it had been a long day. "The bits without swearing sounded like 'who am I? Your wife?'"

Harris grunted in confirmation so Craig gestured Liam towards the door.

"Go and make some fresh tea, Liam. The pizzas will be here in a minute."

"Andy can make it. He needs to stretch his legs."

It made everyone but Andy laugh. When Liam had

grudgingly obliged and Jack had collected the pizzas from reception, Craig returned to the reason they were there.

"OK, we've spent an hour trying to figure how to get Andy out of this mess, and so far we haven't got enough. Reggie, do you have anything useful?"

Reggie seized two pieces of Hawaiian before Liam could get at them and then started to speak in his soft Donegall voice.

"So...I went to the block you live in, Andy, with a CCTV photo of the man that Davy supplied. I went door-to-door, trying to find anyone he might have been visiting, and the long and the short of it is he wasn't seeing anyone in your block that night."

Andy leaned forward eagerly. "He wouldn't have been if he was there to kill the girl."

Reggie nodded. "Indeed."

Craig gulped down a mouthful of crust and asked a question. "Did anyone remember buzzing him in?"

Reggie shook his head and Andy's heart sank.

"Not buzzing him in. No." He paused for what seemed like an eternity before starting again. "But a young couple remembered him following them in through the front door."

Andy jabbed a finger in the air. "You see! He didn't know anyone in the block and he didn't have a key, so he had to slip in. That's suspicious, especially late at night."

Craig looked at Liam to see if he had a comment, but he was submitting a pepperoni slice to a grim death.

"OK, so we're pretty sure this man shouldn't have been there, and we know he got off at Andy's floor and turned down the stretch of corridor Andy's flat is on. What we don't have is him entering or leaving the flat."

Reggie signalled to speak again. "We have him on CCTV entering at four a.m. and leaving again at four-thirty, and the girl's TOD was set as between four and five. It's pretty coincidental, sir."

Craig made a face. "Coincidence won't acquit someone, unfortunately..." He saw Andy's immediate

346

panic at the mention of prosecution, made worse by Liam placing a napkin on his head like a hanging judge. "Stop winding him up, Liam. What I was about to add was, although Andy's Glock was definitely the murder weapon forensics didn't find any prints on it or on the safe, which in itself is an anomaly. Andy says he put the gun in the safe before he went out that evening, so the lack of his prints on both of them is a flag. It suggests everything was wiped, and why would Andy have wiped things in his own house, even supposing he was fit enough to do it?" He stared at the weary looking D.C.I. "The prints had to have been wiped *after* the gun was used and we know you were barely upright when you left the bar. John says your blood level of Ketamine was so high that a horse would have been knocked out." He took a sip of tea. "We also have the fact that the victim was involved in two of our murder cases. So...all together, it looks like a setup." He paused before deciding to stick his neck out. "I'm hopeful we can introduce sufficient doubt."

Andy's eyes lit up. "I'm free?"

Craig shook his head. "Not until the P.P.S. formally declines to prosecute." He glanced at his watch and stood up. "Keep eating your pizza and I'll be back."

He left the room to the sound of Liam making choking noises and mimicking hanging by a rope, making Andy push away his still full plate. Jack followed Craig into the office.

"The P.P.S. charging team?"

"Please, Jack. I know it's late but see if you can get me through."

A ten minute conversation later where Craig outlined the evidence, and the decision they all wanted to hear came down the line. He hurried to tell Andy and then halted outside the interview room, thinking again. There was a reason Andy had ended up in this mess and he needed to be taught a lesson so that it didn't recur.

He re-entered the room wearing a glum expression.

"Stand please, D.C.I. Angel."

As Andy staggered to his feet even Liam looked shocked by Craig's demeanour. "Here, boss. They can't seriously be charging-"

Craig cut across him. "Detective Chief Inspector Angel, following my conversation with the Public Prosecution Service." Andy gripped the back of his chair with both hands and everyone in the room knew the image in his mind; a six feet by eight feet cell for the next twenty years. "It has been decided that you will be charged-"

Liam's noisy "Here now" and Reggie's "Dear God" added to the clamour inside Andy's head. His heart was thudding and his ears rang so loudly that he didn't hear Craig's next words.

"With gross stupidity."

Only the sudden grin on Liam's face made Andy look at the others, to see Reggie looking relieved and a stunned Jack gawping at their boss. Craig nodded Andy to sit before he fell and kept talking, louder so that he could hear every word.

"You're a complete bloody idiot, Andy, but the P.P.S. agreed with me that there was insufficient evidence to charge you. You were saved by your blood levels of Ketamine and John's statement that you couldn't have moved with it on board, never mind fired a gun. I want you to go home and rest for a few days-"

Andy shook his head immediately. "I can't go back there."

Craig didn't blame him. "OK, it's still a crime scene for now so we'll sort out a hotel." His voice dropped ominously, reminding Liam of his dad's when he'd done something wrong. "Sometime next week you and I are going to have a serious chat, D.C.I. Angel. There's a reason you were targeted by a honey trap and that reason could make you vulnerable again. OK?"

Andy nodded mutely, knowing that he was right. He needed to get his life in order and stop falling for any woman who threw him a smile.

Craig sat down. "OK, now. Finish your food and then Jack will get you a ride home to collect some clothes and book you into a hotel. Reggie, thanks for your help on this and please apologise to your wife for me."

Reggie smiled. "Never you worry. Her list of chores can wait one more day."

They finished their pizzas in relaxed silence then Craig nodded Liam to get ready to leave. As he walked past Jack he stopped for a moment.

"I haven't forgotten about D.S. Litton, Jack. I promise I'll sort him out next week."

Liam smiled as he realised Craig's added 'Chief' would give Litton no choice but to toe the line.

Then they were gone. To bring a crooked cop out into the open and maybe nick a drug dealer as they did.

****

Kyle knew that he'd got off lightly so far; he remembered Craig's temper from sharing a flat with him as students, and knew that the fact it hadn't reared at him yet had less to do with Craig's new found maturity and more with the fact that they'd been run off their feet. But Craig would get round to him when the case was over, that much was certain, so he intended to use whatever grace time he had to follow his own hunch.

As he drove towards the Intelligence Section he wondered what had happened to get Susan Richie canned, pushing away the feeling that it had been his revelation about Jastreb that had done the trick. He couldn't go there because that way led Armageddon; if Susan worked out that he'd made that call and by logic that Roy Barrett had helped him, then it wouldn't just be Craig on her future hit list, and Intelligence hit lists were often precisely that.

He swallowed hard and turned up Radio One, his thoughts shifting to Craig as Intelligence's new chief-of-staff. What would that be like? Day to day it would probably make no difference; Roy would steer the ship as calmly as he had when he'd just been its chief mate . But if the shit hit the fan, as it frequently did in

349

uncertain political times, Craig might step in and from his experience of him that would be something else.

As he pulled into the section's carpark he gave a heavy sigh. Either way, in Murder or Intelligence, there'd be no way of escaping Craig's supervision in future so he'd better just make the best of it, and what better way to do that than by impressing your new boss with a result.

****

Moygashel. County Tyrone.

Ronan Miskimmon's farmhouse wasn't as Ash had pictured it from the crime report. He'd expected something steel and shiny inside its rustic shell, as befitted the lair of a computer genius. Instead he was gazing at a stone floored, wooden furnitured house on the prairie, more suited to a real farmer than someone who'd been using the place to hide out. The only signs of its previous occupants were the sections of degaussing loop still hanging from the ceiling, something that if Craig hadn't stopped the C.S.I.s quickly would have fried Miskimmon's computers as they'd carried them past.

His ruminations were interrupted by Rhonda's quiet voice.

"Will this take long? It smells funny in here."

Jake nodded. "It's damp." He turned to the analyst. "Any idea of your time scale, Ash?"

"Not a clue."

He was too busy searching for a wireless router to be more accurate. On their third sweep he found it located behind a pine dresser, so small it could have passed as an adapter box. He didn't care how small it was as long as some C.S.I. hadn't broken it during their search. Thankfully whoever had printed it, evidenced by the grey dust still covering the surface, hadn't felt the need to dismantle it as well.

He hunkered down and nodded Jake to pass him his bag.

Jake leaned in, curious. "What's that thing?"

"Router." Ash took out the Bluetooth, Miskimmon's laptop and his own smart-pad.

"And?"

Ash would have tutted but he knew he'd have to explain after anyway, so he launched into a complex explanation hoping it would put the detective off asking any more. No such luck.

"OK, so you're searching for Miskimmon's LAN and then you're going to sync your smart-pad to it."

The analyst nodded. There might be hope for Jake's computer education yet.

"Then we're going walkabout in the hope of picking up another device."

Rhonda chipped in. "Which will be his fourth laptop."

Jake shook his head. "If it was anywhere in the house the search team would have found it. They know their jobs."

Ash ignored him and started wandering around the room, then out into the kitchen and utility room and up one flight of stairs, until he'd checked every room on the first two floors with no joy. In the middle of the bathroom ceiling he noticed a hatch.

"Jake."

Jake walked slowly up the stairs.

"There's a loft."

"Why do you need to go up there? Surely you would detect anything that's up there from here? It can't be more than twenty metres away."

Ash shook his head. "I need to be sure. Sometimes physical obstacles can-"

Jake cut him off with a shrug. He was already sure there would be nothing in the loft but he didn't want to listen to Ash whine. His next comment was designed to make the analyst do just that.

"You'll have to go up there yourself then. My legs aren't at full strength yet."

Subtext; if I fall while I'm still in rehab the boss will rip off your head.

Ash stared at the wooden hatch and gulped,

picturing an attic with only wooden beams and thin plaster board between him and perdition. Rhonda came to his rescue.

"Don't worry, little pom. I can be up and down again before you've made the tea."

He took the hint eagerly, never letting a misplaced sense of chivalry get in the way of logic; Rhonda was strong and fit, whereas he was a self-confessed weed who'd never met an exercise he didn't hate. Jake on the other hand looked uncomfortable at Rhonda's offer and decided to give it a try, but she glanced meaningfully at his legs and shook her head. She slipped off her new jacket, raring to go. Ash handed over his smart-pad, explained what she should look for and then wandered downstairs to make the tea. The kettle had barely boiled when he heard an excited yell.

"Get up here! The signal's jumped."

Ash surprised himself by sprinting up the stairs, only to find Jake clambering slowly up into the loft.

"You shouldn't be doing that." AKA 'get out of my way. I want to see.'

The detective slipped through the hatch and disappeared, his "YES" five seconds later saying it had been worth the trip.

When Ash joined them he was surprised to see the attic not only floored but carpeted, and furnished with filing cabinets and desks. It was more comfortable than the ground floor.

Jake scanned the long room. "This must have been their office." He pointed to more grey dust. "It's already been printed, but I didn't notice any reference to a loft in the report."

Rhonda's voice came from under a desk. "There wasn't."

One of Des' C.S.I.s was going to get a bollocking.

Ash walked over to a small Wi-Fi booster box and beckoned Rhonda to hand him his pad. There was no doubt; the signal was much stronger up here. Not only that but a new device had appeared on the Bluetooth and its name said that they might be getting close. ORIGIN. He crossed his fingers that Miskimmon had

352

named it that because it contained his earliest work.

"The C.S.I.s missed something. There's definitely a device up here." He grinned as he saw it was on Miskimmon's LAN.

Jake took charge. "OK. Rhonda, you start in that corner and work down the right hand side, and I'll start over here. Ash, what exactly are we looking for?"

"A laptop probably, or maybe a smart-pad. Some computing device anyway. You won't miss it. I'll start at this end."

They worked in silence for ten minutes, moving furniture and opening drawers. When they'd been through every cubby hole and cabinet twice over Jake finally admitted defeat.

"There's nothing here. It must be a rogue signal."

Ash waved his smart-pad defiantly. "There *is* something here. We're just missing it."

Just then Rhonda had a hunch and she held out her hand for the pad. "Just for a minute, Ash."

He handed it over reluctantly and waited to see what she did. For ten minutes she walked the room in silence, holding the smart-pad up as close to the attic's ceiling as she could, and staring at its screen the whole time. When she'd finished she walked to one end of the room and got on her hands and knees, moving the pad methodically across every inch of floor. Suddenly she let out a squeal.

"Here! Look."

Ash rushed over and grabbed the pad. There was no doubt about it, the signal was the strongest they'd seen it.

"It just jumped when I held it over this bit."

Jake threw his head back, laughing. "The clever bastard! He hid it under the floorboards."

In ten minutes they had the carpet lifted, to reveal a section of floor that had been cut out and replaced. Jake gloved up and reached down between the beams, withdrawing a dull metal box.

Ash gawped at the find. "That's why we had to get so close to pick up the signal. It's a Faraday Cage! It must have a breach in it somewhere or we wouldn't have got a signal at all."

He went to grab the box but Jake pushed him away. "It has to be printed first. Chain of evidence. Rhonda, get me an evidence bag from the car, please. And call the local station while you're there; they're taking you two back to Belfast with this. I've got to drive to Armagh. " He nodded Ash on. "Explain a Faraday Cage to me."

Ash was powerless to touch their treasure, so he used the time to explain grudgingly.

"Wi-Fi signals can be weakened by lots of things. Microwaves, cordless phones, even some baby monitors. Apparently garage door openers can-"

Jake interrupted, seeing him straying off point. "Faraday Cage."

The analyst nodded, his eyes fixed on the box so intently that if he'd said "my precious" the detective wouldn't have been surprised. He continued in a distracted tone.

"It's pretty much the only physical thing that can block a signal. Metal that's sealed and grounded." He gestured at the box. "Like that." He reached out a hand to touch it again only to have Jake bat him back.

"You'll get it once it's printed, then you and Des can do whatever it is you do and let's just hope that it works."

****

Armagh Police Station. 9 p.m.

By eight o'clock Annette had summoned Magnus O'Shea to Armagh and by nine he was sitting across from Jake and her, moaning about how they were ruining his week. She kept her tone deliberately meek. If O'Shea liked his ladies passive then that's exactly what he would get this time, much as it stuck in her throat.

She could be herself and make things harder, or play meek and mild and have him trotting after her like a dog; her energy levels made the path of least resistance the more attractive choice.

"I'm so sorry to make you come all this way, Inspector."

He melted into his chair as she spoke and the frown present since he'd entered morphed into a stupid grin.

"Ach now, don't you worry your wee self about that." All that was missing was the pat on the head. He continued pleasantly. "Happy to be any help I can."

And we're not even bribing you.

She continued. "It's just that this is too sensitive to discuss over the phone." She stopped suddenly, making a show of asking Jake to check that no-one was lurking outside. It was his signal to arrange the phone blocks and plant the devices beneath O'Shea's family estate. He returned a minute later, shaking his head.

"No-one there, Ma'am."

"Thank you, Jake." She folded her hands demurely in her lap, thinking it was the sort of thing that Mrs O'Shea would probably do, then she leaned forward confidingly. "You see, Inspector O'Shea."

There followed a tale of Albanian gangsters, drug runners and big bosses, and how they knew exactly where Abaz Goga, the Belfast cell leader, would be that evening and were preparing a raid for eleven o'clock.

O'Shea's expression changed from fatuous to serious. "Is that so? Well, my goodness you boys and girls up north certainly know how many beans make five."

It didn't require anything of her but a simper and she watched as the Garda edged his chair closer until she could feel his hot beer breath on her cheek. Drinking at work; that would be another nail in his box.

Her thoughts were interrupted by O'Shea's next question.

"I don't know Belfast well, so what sort of places would boyos like that frequent?"

Her mind said 'you know it better than you're saying' but she answered disingenuously. "Night clubs apparently." She smiled. "I never go to places like that, of course." *But I did when I was a student. Every night.*

He nodded approvingly, moving her up another length in the good woman stakes. Annette was really looking forward to nicking the man, it was just a pity there was no extended sentence for being a chauvinist. She was tiring of the game and they needed O'Shea on the road, so she added.

"Apparently it's called The Pit." Kyle's information had been confirmed by Drugs and Vice. Goga and his cronies used the club as their den. "A terrible place, as the name might suggest."

If they were right then O'Shea's next move would be to leave hurriedly, ostensibly for home but if the tracker didn't lead them to Belfast then she'd be very surprised. As the Garda walked swiftly to his car Annette took out her mobile and called Craig.

"That's him away now, sir. You can tell Davy to start tracking and we'll see you there ASAP."

At the other end of the line Craig alerted Davy. When he returned to his office Liam was relaxing in a chair.

"OK. I need suggestions. We know The Pit is Goga's usual hang out, but I've had plain clothes guys inside for hours and he hasn't turned up. How the hell do we get him there for eleven?"

Liam glanced at his watch and relaxed even further. "I'm expecting a call."

Craig sat down opposite. "From anyone in particular or do you expect me to guess?"

"I'll give you a hint. It's not Kyle. He's AWOL again."

Craig's face said that he wasn't amused by either of them. "Unless you have a death wish, Liam, tell me who's going to call."

Liam straightened up. "Ach, you're no fun nowadays, do you know that? Time was when you would have joined in a joke but not now. And don't go giving me 'I've three murders to solve' and 'I'm a D.C.S. now' because they've got bugger all to do with it. You're a misery because of that wee girl and I wish you'd just sort yourself out."

Craig's jaw dropped. "You *do* have a death wish."

The D.C.I. raised his eyes to heaven. "Oh, all right, I'll tell you. I'm waiting for Roller Brant to call. He owes me big time for my nose."

Craig started laughing.

"So you *do* still laugh, but only at my physical pain. You know what they call people like that."

"Friends?"

The exchange was cut short by Liam's phone ringing, so Craig listened for sixty seconds as he "yepped" and "noped". Finally he hung up and said. "Good man. I forgive him for my nose now."

Craig sat forward eagerly. "So?"

"So... Roller's passed word through The Pit that there's a German punter looking to buy a kilo of smack. But he'll only do business face-to-face and he's flying back home tomorrow, which means the buy has to be tonight."

Craig was sceptical. "Since when did Roller get so well connected?"

"Since his favourite sister got hitched to the lad who owns the club." He tapped his nose knowingly but very gently, in deference to its pain. "Keep your snouts close and you hear all sorts of useful stuff. Anyway, if that doesn't get Goga to the club tonight then nothing will."

Craig sat back, not bothering to hide that he was impressed. He thought for a moment before surprising Liam with his next question. "Does the sister look like Roller?"

"She does actually. Big ears and all. But as the man says, there's no accounting for taste."

****

The Lab. 9 p.m.

While Jake had handed Rhonda the metal box and then headed off to Armagh, Ash had kept their find well in his sights. By the time Des had docketed and printed the container the analyst had steam coming from his ears; this was their last chance to prove Ronan Miskimmon guilty and they weren't even sure they'd found the laptop yet.

He tried to focus on other things, but found himself peering at the box's rusted hinges wondering again if they'd provided the breach that had allowed the signal through. Something must have done, otherwise they would never have known the box was there.

Finally Des stepped back and nodded at his work. It was a fatal move; anything resembling approval was bound to be seized on by Ash as a sign that he could grab the box. Before the forensic scientist could say no or yes, the analyst had prised the iron box open, noting with satisfaction that not only was there a laptop inside but that one of the box's hinges had corroded enough to create a small gap. They had their breach.

He pumped the air triumphantly and then lifted the computer out reverently onto the laboratory bench. After a tense five minutes where he checked the signal again and confirmed the device was part of Miskimmon's LAN, he opened the laptop's lid and stared at its keyboard, muttering to himself.

"Faraday Cage. Smart move. Smart move."

Des recognised the nerves behind the words. "Brilliant actually. It's amazing you ever found it."

Ash didn't break his stare. "Rhonda's find. She crawled along the floor."

"I'm impressed." Ash's reluctance to take the next step and switch on the computer was palpable, so Des added logically. "What's the worst that can happen?"

The analyst turned towards him, his large eyes wild. "You *know* what! I could turn it on and the whole thing could fry."

Des shook his head. "That's not logical. At least one of the computers in the LAN has to be accessible; otherwise all of Miskimmon's work would disappear." He pulled up a stool. "Look, think it through. Miskimmon's been smug in interviews, Marc told me so. That means he's certain we can't access the computers that we took from the house. The three that he knows about."

Ash nodded him on.

"He wouldn't have posted his work on the Cloud, in case it was discovered. He wouldn't rely on a CD or a USB, in case they corrupted, so it's got to be on some sort of a computer. A computer that he has to be able to use to wake up the others safely, which means he can't have firewalls on it like the rest. It *must* be something he can access safely without frying it. *This* device. Origin. Unless you think there's a fifth computer somewhere?"

Ash's eyes widened. "Maybe there is." Then he shook his head. "No, no. This is it. He tried too hard to hide it. It must be."

Des nodded. "Well OK, then. Carry that thought through. If this is the key computer he's not going to firewall it so much that it can't even be turned on, so we're safe to go that far at least." He rummaged in a cupboard, producing a power lead. "It'll need charged after being in that cage for so long, but we can run it from the mains with this."

He slid in the jack and a light appeared instantly on the computer's side. After another minute he gestured to the on switch.

"Do the honours then."

But Ash was rooted to the spot. After a moment's last chance Des pressed the switch himself, eliciting a loud "NOOOO" from the analyst.

Too late. The screen lit up and started running through the welcome sequence as the two scientists gazed at it transfixed. Des held his breath, praying that Ronan Miskimmon had done what he thought he might have, and as the sequence ended and documents began populating the black screen he let out a cheer. He was right. Miskimmon hadn't even password protected it!

Ash couldn't believe his eyes. "He..."

Des grinned. "I thought he'd do that. Arrogant bastard. He thought we'd never find it."

"Have you seen-"

"Once before. A few years ago. Not as clever as Miskimmon and working in banking instead of killing people, but he thought he'd hidden his computer so well that he was flameproof. Didn't bother with a password, encryption, nothing."

Ash made a face. "He could have encrypted the individual documents."

"And if he has we'll crack them. The point is, you can show a court that this laptop has the IP address the Canadian hacks came from, and you can use a wake-up programme from it to start the other two." He glanced at his watch. "Now. I'm going home and so are you. You look wrecked and this will still be here in the morning." He brushed off the analyst's objections and shut down the laptop again. "We'll do it all tomorrow morning. Deal?"

Suddenly Ash felt exhausted from the stress of the previous few days so he gave up arguing. He watched as Des switched off the laboratory lights one by one, leaving only the light from their treasure blinking as it charged.

Chapter Seventeen

The Pit. May Street. 10.15 p.m.

Kyle had a plan. Arrive at the club, smoke two cigs in the car for courage, then join the early week clubbers in the darkness and blend in, preferably propping up the bar somewhere that he could spot Goga as soon as he appeared. It might have worked apart from two things: he was twenty years too old to be there, and he had a suit and haircut that made him stand out like a sore thumb. It was a particular pity that he'd failed to check the club's calendar; if he had done he'd have seen that Monday was always Punk tribute night.

Once through the door it was too late, although at least he now understood the bouncers' amused smiles. He made the best of it and hid in a booth, positioning himself where he could see both the front and bar doors. As he scrutinised each face in the small club a man was scrutinising his. He slipped into the bar's back room and interrupted his boss in the middle of a discussion, whispering something in his ear. Abaz Goga nodded.

"Keep him in sight until I say so. I waiting for someone."

He turned back to his companion as his lackey returned to his surveillance. Too late. When the acolyte emerged to look for Kyle, the policeman was nowhere to be found. He knew that he'd been spotted and had used the man's disappearance to hide in the gents and think through his plan. All he needed was to stay in the club long enough to find Goga. He'd watch until he did something illegal, then he would make the arrest and impress his new boss.

Unfortunately theory isn't reality and policing the streets is very different to policing a desk; any cop used to the real world would have told Kyle that his plan was likely to get him killed. OK, the Intelligence cases he'd managed had been high value smuggling rings and terrorists, but the closest he'd ever got to real live villains was positioning his agents on the ground and then watching their capture or kill on a satellite screen. Street policing carried risks he was ill equipped for, both in mind-set and in fact. He wasn't even wearing his gun.

But there was no reality check happening in Kyle Spence's head; all he was concerned about was making his arrest. It didn't seem to occur to him that off-screen criminals might fight back.

****

10.20 p.m.

In the club's carpark Craig and Liam were in the Audi waiting for Magnus O'Shea to arrive. Craig nodded to his deputy. "Get the mike, Liam. I want to hear everything they say."

Liam lifted the directional mike and put on the earphones, immediately wincing and yanking them off. "Bloody Hell! That noise is shocking."

Craig rolled his eyes. "You're pointing it at the club. Point it at the back room instead. Roller told you that's where Goga holds his meetings.

After a few more abortive attempts, Liam finally located the room, where the only noise was a man with a heavy European accent talking to someone else.

"Set it to record and then we wait."

They didn't have to wait for long. At ten-thirty Magnus O'Shea's estate car pulled up.

Liam gave a jaded shrug. "You were right. Another cop on the take. Still, at least it's not one of ours."

Craig answered without breaking his gaze. "We don't have any proof yet."

Liam snorted sceptically. "We have his bank accounts and as soon as Annette dropped the info he headed here. What more do you want?"

"Him in conversation with Goga, passing on Annette's information and preferably negotiating a price. Then we can nail him."

362

He could feel Liam's impatience to kick down doors, but he was more focused on the crooked cop. As they watched, Magnus O'Shea scanned three-sixty around him then he exited his car and walked briskly towards the club's rear door.

"He's been here before, boss."

Craig nodded and signalled to put the mike on speaker. He needed to hear every word the Garda said before they could make a move.

Inside the club Kyle had emerged from his hiding place in the bathroom. He scanned the dancefloor for the acolyte and when he didn't see him or anyone resembling the Intelligence photo of Goga, he decided that if the mountain wouldn't come to him he'd go to it and started walking towards the bar door. If he'd thought about it he would have realised just what a bad idea it was; entering your quarry's territory alone and unarmed without even evidence of a crime to arrest him on.

****

Five minutes of listening hadn't disappointed Craig and Liam. As soon as O'Shea had entered The Pit's back room he'd started talking, his tone saying that he was furious.

"What's wrong with your bloody phone? I've been calling you for over an hour! You need to get out of here."

The reply came in an accent they guessed was Abaz Goga's. "What you doing here, boss?"

Boss? Craig's jaw dropped. They'd thought O'Shea was just a cop on the take but it looked like they'd stumbled on more than that. If he was the gang's boss it explained why they'd setup Andy to deter them; they'd been far closer to solving the case than they'd realised.

The detective parked his surprise, listening intently as Goga went on.

"I waiting to do deal. Big punter from Germany."

O'Shea answered angrily. "There *is* no deal! It's a

363

setup. The cops are planning to catch you in the act. I tried to warn you but your phone's broken."

Goga pulled out his phone. "No signal."

Suddenly O'Shea realised what was happening and checked his own. "Both our lines-"

What happened next shocked them all.

****

Kyle had waited until the follower was at the other end of the dark club before slipping through the bar door into an almost equally dark back room. In the time it took for his eyes to adjust he realised there were two men already in there, one of whom he recognised from an Intelligence report. The recognition wasn't reciprocated but Abaz Goga instinctively sensed a threat. He moved at high speed, pinning Kyle face down on the floor.

"Who are you?"

O'Shea didn't need to ask.

"He's a cop, you moron. It's written all over his cheap suit." He pulled out Kyle's warrant card and then twisted his arm hard, making the D.I. yell. "Who's watching us? Where are the others?"

Outside the club Craig and Liam were staring at each other in shock. "Kyle?"

Craig added what they were both thinking. "What's that bloody idiot doing in there?"

Liam shook his head despairingly. "He's only gone and done a Lone Ranger." He banged his fist hard on the dashboard. "The stupid, irresponsible-"

Craig cut him off. "We can call him names later. Right now we need to stop him getting killed." As Liam set the mike down, still recording, they heard the unmistakeable sound of a pistol's slide. Craig was out of the car first and in thirty seconds both men were by the club's rear door, still listening through their ear pieces to what was happening inside.

Magnus O'Shea pulled up a chair as Goga pointed his gun at Kyle, still prostrate on the ground.

"How many men are outside?"

Kyle stared up at him blankly. "There's no-one. Only me."

As far as he knew it was true and his veracity showed in his voice. Goga stepped forward.

"Let me shoot him, boss. We make the deal at eleven then we go."

O'Shea's reply said what he thought of his man's intelligence. "There *is* no deal, you stupid prick. Whoever turns up now will be a cop." He grabbed Goga's gun and waved it close to Kyle's face. After a moment's more threat he nodded. "He's definitely alone."

The Garda glanced around for a clock. Ten-forty. They still had twenty minutes before the fake buy. He stood up decisively and threw Goga his keys. "Bring my car to the door while I get rid of him. We'll dump his body on the way south."

As the Albanian headed for the carpark door and threw it open, Liam and Craig pushed in. Liam clamped a hand over the gangster's mouth and an arm across his throat, squeezing hard enough to knock him out. As he dragged him to the Audi and radioed for backup, Craig was moving towards the interior door with his Glock in his hand. Once there he yanked out his ear piece and pressed his ear against the wood. He could hear Kyle pleading for his life, the effort and direction of his voice saying that he was lying on the floor.

"Please. You don't need to do this. If you kill a cop they'll never stop hunting you. Just leave me here and go." Kyle twisted his neck to look up at the clock. "You've still got time. You could be halfway to the border before our boys arrive."

O'Shea smiled coldly. "You heard too much. My guess is that if your boss knows anything he just thinks I'm on the take, and that's the way it has to stay. If he ever found out I was running the show, my life would go down the tubes."

Craig knew O'Shea was about to take his shot. He also knew that there was no time to kick down the door. He prayed that he was right about the two men's positions and held his Glock at chest height, unloading two shots straight through the wood. A hard kick and he was in the room, gun still extended, to find two bodies lying in a heap on the floor. He stopped in his tracks, his mouth dry.

Just then Liam entered, kicking O'Shea's gun away and saying something that Craig couldn't hear, still deafened by the shots.

The D.C.I. repeated himself louder. "Would you get up off that bloody floor, Spence! You can sleep when you get home."

A disjointed wriggling movement threw Magnus O'Shea's body to one side and Kyle Spence crawled out slowly on all fours, the only blood on him from the dead cop. Liam stared disdainfully at O'Shea's body and then hunkered down to take a closer look. There, in the Garda's chest and arm, were two holes still seeping blood. Craig's positioning had been spot on.

Liam gawped at the wounds and then at his boss. "How the hell did you manage that?"

Craig didn't answer so Liam gestured at his still raised Glock.

"Better holster that, in case someone else gets shot." He glanced back at O'Shea and then at the splintered door, shaking his head. "Forensics will have fun with this one. You must have hit him in the chest and spun him round, then the second shot caught him on the arm." He furrowed his brow, thinking. "Or maybe it was arm first then chest."

Craig finally found his voice. "It doesn't matter. It did the trick."

Liam narrowed his eyes. "You're not going to go all soulful about killing this one, are you? You know, the way you did with old Pitt."

It made Craig smile. "No. This one deserved everything that he got."

He turned to see Kyle frantically stripping off layers until he'd reached the only one not stained with blood, a T-shirt that he'd been wearing under his shirt.

"Forensics will want those, Inspector. And when you're feeling better we need to have a serious talk. I want to know what the hell you thought you were playing at."

When the cars had arrived bearing the C.S.I.s and pathologist, who just happened to be Mike, Annette's other half, the three detectives exited to the carpark where Abaz Goga was being loaded into a high-walled van. Liam leaned against the Audi's bonnet.

"Not a bad haul. A dirty cop and a gangster."

Craig shook his head. "Far more than a dirty cop. Goga called him boss, remember?"

Liam jerked upright. "You mean O'Shea was the head of the gang poaching Rey's turf!"

"It would make sense. Goga was a cell leader, so the only man he would have called boss was the one running the whole thing. O'Shea must have decided crime paid a better pension than the Gardaí." He pulled open the Audi's door. "We'll have to join the dots of course, but I'd be surprised if all of our killings don't trace back to him."

Liam climbed into the passenger side. "So Fox and McAllister were part of The Rock too? Minus the tattoos." He snorted. "Probably didn't fit their middle-class images."

Craig nodded. "It seems there's more than just the Belfast branch to that particular empire, but that can wait till tomorrow. We all deserve a good night's rest." He turned to see Kyle in the back seat looking subdued and still wearing the onesie forensics had given him when they'd taken his clothes. "Let's get him home first. If we're very lucky maybe he'll have some drink in the house."

The embarrassed spook cheered up instantly, recognising the comment for the olive branch that it was. He was still going to get a bollocking but not the huge one that he deserved, and he realised suddenly that he liked the camaraderie of being a street cop. Maybe his secondment wouldn't be so bad after all.

As the men prepared to leave they missed the green saloon waiting outside the carpark's gate. Michael Hanratty smiled to himself. On Tommy Hill's tip off he'd come to confront the Albanian but when he'd seen his old foe O'Shea arrive he'd decided to observe instead.

He'd been the bane of Magnus O'Shea's life since they'd both been young. Him a prize scammer and O'Shea a new Dublin cop, the Garda had arrested him more times than he could count but never made anything stick. The more it had happened the more O'Shea had hated him; he'd have hated him as well if he'd been struggling by on a copper's salary and had to watch criminals living in wealth. He whistled as he thought of the ambitious policeman he'd known as a youth. Back then O'Shea had been so self-righteous and moral he'd walked like he'd had a snooker cue up his ass.

Now what? Had he been working with the PSNI to arrest the Albanian? The two men watching from the Audi couldn't have been anything but cops. No, it didn't sound right. Last he'd heard O'Shea had been put out to pasture in the sticks, and if he *was* working with the northern police then why wouldn't he have joined them as soon as he'd driven up?

So he'd watched and waited as the scenario had played out. The PSNI with their directional mike, sprinting suddenly towards the club's rear entrance at something that they'd heard. A foreign looking man being dragged out and cuffed, then two shots followed by a C.S.I. team and a large corpse had emerged in a body bag. Three men had climbed back into the Audi instead of two, one of them in a white forensic suit and none of them Magnus O'Shea. It didn't take a genius to work out that O'Shea was the body in the bag; the once righteous Garda had been playing for the dark side and had met a nasty end.

As Craig's Audi drove past him Hanratty averted his face, starting his own engine a moment later and heading for the M1 south. He would confirm the facts through Xavier Rey but he had a hunch that the days of his men being killed were over and business as usual could resume. For how long was anyone's guess; O'Shea's death would create a vacancy that some ambitious young hound would soon fill.

Chapter Eighteen

The James Bar. Friday, February 5ᵗʰ.

All Xavier Rey had been authorised to confirm was that Fox and McAllister had both been members of The Rock. Beyond that he'd been ordered to shut his mouth. It tied up some loose ends in their cases and confirmed they'd been dealing with a feud between two tribes; any future action on the gangs' other activities would lie with Geoff Hamill and his merry men.

Andy and Kyle had both been spoken to severely, although how much it would change their behaviour was anyone's guess. Craig rolled his eyes as he saw Andy whisper something to his new sidekick Sid Freeman and then sidle down the bar towards some unsuspecting girl. At least he seemed to have got over Rhonda, which was just as well considering she and Karl Rimmins had been gazing into each other's black lidded eyes for the last half-an-hour.

Liam thudded down onto the bench beside Craig with two whiskies and an unceremonious "Shove up." He dropped his voice and added. "When are you announcing it to the troops?"

Craig glanced at him. "What?"

"Your chief super thing."

"Oh, that. Never, probably. My guess is that they all know already, seeing as you've got such a big mouth."

Liam was about to object then he conceded that Craig was right. "Aye, well. They needed some good news." He gestured at Kyle, who was leaning on the bar. "I see he's wearing his gun now."

Craig rolled his eyes. "I just wish he wouldn't wear it like he's Wyatt Earp."

The Glock was sitting very visibly on their new secondee's hip.

"Ach, he's just new-fangled with it, but I'll have a word. Still, you have to admit; he found Goga all on his lonesome. Not a bad man to have around."

Craig smiled; he'd already thought as much. He took a deep drink of whisky and changed the subject.

"Ash and Des have managed to access Miskimmon's computer. They used it to start up the others so we have all his files. Some of them are encrypted and they'll take a while to crack, but we've got enough to stop him being shipped off to South America so at least we'll have time to build our case."

"Will the P.P.S. prosecute Corneau on the same charge?"

Craig made a face that said he wasn't sure. "There's part of me thinks she was almost another one of Miskimmon's victims, but we'll re-interview them both then let the solicitors decide."

Liam nodded and gestured at his glass. "Top up?"

As he walked to the bar the side door opened and a plaster-casted Natalie entered with John. Craig rose to give her his seat while John headed for the bar. When the diminutive surgeon was settled she reached up and grabbed Craig by the tie, pulling his face down close to her own.

"Go outside."

"What?"

"Now. Go outside. There's someone who wants to see you."

Craig was out the door before the other men had returned. He stood in Barrow Square squinting into the darkness, until finally he made out a feminine shape fifty metres ahead. He followed as it moved towards the Lagan, until they were standing five metres apart, gazing down at the river's slow flow. He spoke first.

"Katy."

She raised a hand to cut him off. "Let me speak, Marc. If I don't say this now I never will."

His heart sank at the tremor in her voice; heralding as it might bad news. But he recognised how much it had taken for her to see him, so he waited for her to carry on.

Katy stared straight ahead as she spoke, the distant lights of Titanic Belfast flickering across her slim face.

"I love you, Marc, and I'll always love you. But what happened..." Her voice faded away for a moment before she gathered the strength to go on. "...it terrified me, and I'm still frightened...in case it happens again. I'm sorry if that makes me a coward-"

He went to speak but she raised her hand again, its curled fingers almost begging him to let her finish. "I know what you're going to say. God knows, Natalie's said it often enough, and I've said it to myself. It's not *going* to happen again, the chances are infinitesimally small." She turned to face him suddenly, taking a step back to underline that it wasn't an invitation to approach. "I *know* all that. I know it, but I'm still frightened." He could see a small smile twist her lips. "No matter how many reckless things I try to make myself brave."

She turned back to the water, staring into it in silence for what felt to him like minutes before she began to speak again. "I know we're all going to die, heaven knows I see enough of it every day at work. Strangely death doesn't frighten me. Not at all. But the hatred, the sheer evil that you deal with every day does. Killers, psychopaths, people who murder without a thought." She swung towards him again. "Does that make any sense?"

He nodded.

"And you're so *vulnerable*. They could kill you at any time. I'm frightened for you every day." Another small smile. "And I know that even if you became Chief Constable you would insist on being on the street sometimes, because you love it, you *love* the action. Don't you?"

Another nod.

"What's more, you need it."

He didn't reply. What could he say when he knew that she was right?

She sighed as if defeated. "And that's the man I fell in love with."

It sounded like something she would stop feeling if she could and her next words confirmed his fear.

"I've tried to stop loving you, Marc, over the past month. *Really* tried. I've tried to imagine dating other men, to picture what it would be like." His heart plummeted as she continued. "Another doctor maybe, or an accountant." She smiled suddenly, making him want to take her in his arms. "Can you imagine me with an accountant? He'd cut up my credit cards. Or a lawyer? No. Maybe an artist of some sort. Someone bohemian. That would be better. A gentle life."

She stopped abruptly, beginning to feel cruel. Her next words sounded resigned.

"But the problem is I can't. I can't even picture being with anyone but you."

His heart soared again.

"So what does that leave me? With you or on my own? Frightened or safe? Happy, or lonely and missing you."

Her shoulders slumped and Craig took it as his cue. He closed the distance between them slowly, waiting for an objection that never came. When he was within touching distance he stopped.

"I love you, Katy... and I can tell you all the things that Natalie has already told you about low risk, but I *know* that being with me will be frightening at times-"

She glanced up at him, tears in her eyes. "I don't care for myself anymore, but if someone ever hurt you-"

He reached out and took her in his arms, stroking her blonde waves gently. "I'll leave the job. I'll resign. I can't lose you."

She pulled away abruptly, shaking her head. "NO. No, you can't. It's your life. I can't ask that."

He gazed at her intently. "I'm *offering* to do it."

She shook her head again. "Even so. No. You would hate me for it one day." She dropped her eyes. "This is *my* problem and *I* need to get past it."

He reached out for her again and met with no resistance. As he held her close he whispered. "Let me help you, please."

She nodded against his chest, her tears soaking into his shirt. "You'll have to, Marc, because I can't seem to love anyone else."

THE END

Core Characters in the Craig Crime Novels

Superintendent Marc (Marco) Craig: Craig is a sophisticated, single, forty-five-year-old. Born in Northern Ireland, he is of Northern Irish/Italian extraction, from a mixed religious background but agnostic. An ex-grammar schoolboy and Queen's University Law graduate, he went to London to join The Met (The Metropolitan Police) at twenty-two, rising in rank through its High Potential Development Training Scheme. He returned to Belfast in two-thousand and eight after more than fifteen years away.

He is a driven, compassionate, workaholic, with an unfortunate temper that he struggles to control and a tendency to respond to situations with his fists, something that almost resulted in him going to prison when he was in his teens. He loves the sea, sails when he has the time and is generally very sporty. He plays the piano, loves music and sport. He lives alone in a modern apartment block in Stranmillis, near the university area of Belfast.

His parents, his extrovert mother Mirella (an Italian concert pianist) and his quiet father Tom (an ex-university lecturer in Physics) live in Holywood town, six miles away. His rebellious sister, Lucia, his junior by ten years, works as the manager of a local charity and also lives in Belfast.

Craig is now a Superintendent heading up Belfast's Murder Squad, based in the thirteen storey Co-ordinated Crime Unit (C.C.U.) in Pilot Street, in the Sailortown area of Belfast's Docklands. He loves the sea, sails when he has the time and is generally very sporty. He plays the piano, loves music by Snow Patrol and follows Manchester United and Northern Ireland football teams, and the Ulster Rugby team.

D.C.I. Liam Cullen: Craig's deputy. Liam is a fifty-year-old former RUC officer from Crossgar in Northern Ireland, who transferred into the PSNI in two thousand and one following the Patton Reforms. He has lived and worked in Northern Ireland all his life and has spent thirty years in the police force, twenty of them policing Belfast, including during The Troubles.

He is married to the forty-year-old, long suffering Danielle (Danni), a part-time nursery nurse, and they have a five-year-old daughter Erin and a three-year-old son called Rory. Liam is unsophisticated, indiscreet and hopelessly non-PC, but he's a hard worker with a great knowledge of the streets and has a sense of humour that makes everyone, even the Chief Constable, laugh.

D.I. Annette Eakin: Annette is Craig's Detective Inspector who has lived and worked in Northern Ireland all her life. She is a forty-seven-year-old ex-nurse who, after her nursing degree, worked as a nurse for thirteen years and then, after a career break, retrained and has now been in the police for an equal length of time. She divorced her husband Pete McElroy, a P.E teacher at a state secondary school, because of his infidelity and violence. They have two children, a boy and a girl (Jordan and Amy), both teenagers. Annette is kind and conscientious with an especially good eye for detail. She also has very good people skills but can be a bit of a goody-two-shoes. Since her marriage broke down, she has acquired a newly glamorous image and is now dating Mike Augustus, a pathologist who works with Dr John Winter. She recently discovered she was expecting their child.

Nicky Morris: Nicky Morris is Craig's thirty-nine-year-old personal assistant. She used to be PA to Detective Chief Superintendent (D.C.S.) Terence 'Teflon' Harrison. Nicky is a glamorous Belfast mum married to Gary, who owns a small garage, and is the mother of a teenage son, Jonny. She comes from a solidly working class area in East Belfast, just ten minutes' drive from Docklands.

She is bossy, motherly and street-wise and manages to organise a reluctantly-organised Craig very effectively. She has a very eclectic sense of style, and there is an ongoing innocent office flirtation between her and Liam.

Davy Walsh: The Murder Squad's twenty-eight-year-old computer analyst. A brilliant but shy EMO, Davy's confidence has grown during his time on the team, making his lifelong stutter on 's' and 'w' diminish, unless he's under stress.

His father is deceased and Davy lives at home in Belfast with his mother and grandmother. He has an older sister, Emmie, who studied English at university. His girlfriend of almost three years, Maggie Clarke, is a journalist and now News Editor at The Belfast Chronicle. They recently became engaged.

Dr John Winter: John is the forty-five-year-old Director of Pathology for Northern Ireland, one of the youngest ever appointed. He's brilliant, eccentric, gentlemanly and really likes the ladies, but he met his match in Natalie Winter, a surgeon at St Mary's Trust, and they have been happily married for over a year.

He was Craig's best friend at school and university and remained in Northern Ireland to build his medical career when Craig left. He is now internationally respected in his field. John persuaded Craig that the newly peaceful Northern Ireland was a good place to return to and assists Craig's team with cases whenever he can. He is obsessed with crime in general and US police shows in particular.

D.C.I. Andrew (Andy) Angel: A relatively new addition to Craig's team and its second D.C.I., Angel is a slight, forty-year-old, twice divorced, perpetually broke father of a five-year-old son, Bowie. A chocoholic with a tendency towards lethargy, he surprises the team at times with his abilities. His spare time is spent in the constant search for a new relationship and romantic subtlety isn't his strong point.

D.C.S. Terry (Teflon) Harrison: Craig's old boss. The fifty-seven-year-old Detective Chief Superintendent was based at the Headquarters building in Limavady in the northwest Irish countryside but has now returned to Docklands where he has an office on the thirteenth floor. He shared a converted farm house at Toomebridge with his homemaker wife Mandy and their thirty-year-old daughter Sian, a marketing consultant. Mandy is now divorcing him, partly because of his trail of mistresses, often younger than his daughter, so he has moved to an apartment in Belfast.

Harrison is tolerable as a boss as long as everything's going well, but he is acutely politically aware and a bit of a snob, and very quick to pass on any blame to his subordinates (hence the Teflon nickname). He sees Craig as a rival now and is out to destroy him. He particularly resents his friendship with John Winter, who wields a great deal of power in Northern Ireland.

Key Background Locations

The majority of locations referenced in the book are real, with some exceptions.

Northern Ireland (real): Set in the northeast of the island of Ireland, Northern Ireland was created in nineteen-twenty-one by an act of British parliament. It forms part of the United Kingdom of Great Britain and Northern Ireland and shares a border to the south and west with the Republic of Ireland. The Northern Ireland Assembly holds responsibility for a range of devolved policy matters. It was established by the Northern Ireland Act 1998 as part of the Good Friday Agreement.

Belfast (real): Belfast is the capital and largest city of Northern Ireland, set on the flood plain of the River Lagan. The seventeenth largest city in the United Kingdom and the second largest in Ireland, it is the seat of the Northern Ireland Assembly.

The Dockland's Co-ordinated Crime Unit (The C.C.U. - fictitious): The modern thirteen storey headquarters building is situated in Pilot Street in Sailortown, a section of Belfast between the M1 and M2 undergoing massive investment and re-development. The C.C.U. hosts the police: murder, gang crimes, vice and drug squad offices, amongst others.

Sailortown (real): An historic area of Belfast on the River Lagan that was a thriving area between the sixteenth and twentieth Centuries. Many large businesses developed in the area, ships docked for loading and unloading and their crews from far flung places such as China and Russia mixed with a local Belfast population of ship's captains, chandlers, seamen and their families.

Sailortown was a lively area where churches and bars fought for the souls and attendance of the residents and where many languages were spoken each day. The basement of the Rotterdam Bar, at the bottom of Clarendon Dock, acted as the overnight lock-up to prisoners being deported to the Antipodes on boats the next morning, and the stocks which held the prisoners could still be seen until the nineteen-nineties.

During the years of World War Two the area was the most bombed area of the UK outside Central London, as the Germans tried to destroy Belfast's ship building capacity. Sadly the area fell into disrepair in the nineteen-seventies and eighties when the motorway extension led to compulsory purchases of many homes and businesses, and decimated the Sailortown community. The rebuilding of the community has now begun, with new families moving into starter homes and professionals into expensive dockside flats.

The Pathology Labs (fictitious): The labs, set on Belfast's Saintfield Road as part of a large Science Park, are where Dr John Winter, Northern Ireland's Head of Pathology, and his co-worker, Dr Des Marsham, Head of Forensic Science, carry out the post-mortem and forensic examinations that help Craig's team solve their cases.

St Mary's Healthcare Trust (fictitious): St Mary's is one of the largest hospital trusts in the UK. It is spread over several hospital sites across Belfast, including the main Royal St Mary's Hospital site and the Maternity, Paediatric and Endocrine (M.P.E.) unit, a stand-alone site on Belfast's Lisburn Road, in the University sector of the city.

Printed in Great Britain
by Amazon

54808302R00215